GOD'S APOLOGY

'Friends,' said Hugh Kingsmill, 'are God's apology for relations.' This is an account of the friendship between three men: Kingsmill himself, Hesketh Pearson and Malcolm Muggeridge. Richard Ingrams never met either Kingsmill or Pearson, but through Muggeridge he came to consider himself part of a friendship centred on beliefs which he shares: a love of England and a deep feeling for English literature, a sense of humour, an unerring sense of the absurd and the pretentious, a fierce independence of opinion and a deep suspicion of political messiahs.

Kingsmill and Pearson were both admirable journeymen of letters; but Kingsmill never achieved popular success, and Pearson's success as a biographer came late and was intermittent. Both were outsiders in the fashionable literary world of the thirties, as was Muggeridge, and they all had a gift for friendship and conversation. In an elegant and witty narrative, Mr. Ingrams persuades the reader to share his admiration for the three men and enables us to feel their pleasure, and his, in their friendship.

Richard Ingrams has been editor of *Private Eye* since 1963. He has written a number of books including *Goldenballs*, *Romney Marsh* and *Piper's Places* (a study of John Piper).

God's Apology

A Chronicle of Three Friends

Richard Ingrams

'Friends are God's apology for relations'
HUGH KINGSMILL

A HAMISH HAMILTON PAPERBACK
London

First published in Great Britain in 1977
by André Deutsch Ltd
First published in this edition 1986
by Hamish Hamilton Ltd
Garden House 57–59 Long Acre London WC2E 9JZ

ISBN 0-241-11746-1

Printed and bound in Finland
by Werner Söderström Oy

ILLUSTRATIONS

Hugh Kingsmill: as a prisoner of war in 1916, about 1935 and shortly before his death.

Hesketh Pearson: during the Great War and with Bernard Shaw in 1945.

Kingsmill and Pearson in 1937.
Muggeridge and Pearson in 1950.

Malcolm Muggeridge: in about 1932 and today.

Introduction

'In friendship,' Malcolm Muggeridge wrote once, 'no standard applies except the standards of friendship. That is why it is the most delightful of all human relationships. Passion is not disinterested, but friendship is as nearly so as is possible in human beings. One wants nothing of a friend except the delight of his company. The satisfaction of appetite, the pursuit of power – these are, in the end, sombre activities which cannot but imprison the spirit. Friendship is their converse, and brings release.'

This book is about three friends – Malcolm Muggeridge, Hugh Kingsmill and Hesketh Pearson. But there is a fourth friend involved, too – myself. Favourite writers, though dead, can become close friends and the memories of the living will often help to illumine the writings of a dead man, who lacking that peculiar spark which a writer must have to survive, would otherwise be destined for obscurity. So it is here. Through being a friend of Malcolm Muggeridge, I have been able to enjoy a kind of posthumous friendship with Kingsmill and Pearson and from talking to him come to cherish certain books which, had I not known him, would perhaps have meant little to me.

I first met Malcolm in 1963 when we were introduced by Claud Cockburn who had come out of retirement to be guest editor of *Private Eye*. Since then we have become very close friends. Certainly I have learnt more from him than from anyone else I have met and can truly say of him what he said of the central character of this book, that he is the only person I know in whose company I have never experienced one moment of boredom. At the same time I owe to him several insights into the nature of power and ambition which have influenced my feelings about the political world in a profound way.

Visiting Malcolm at his house at Robertsbridge in Sussex and talking to him for hours at a stretch I was soon made aware of another figure in the background of whom I had never heard. This was Hugh Kingsmill, who died in 1949. In Malcolm's study there was a row of books more thumbed and battered than the rest and a rather blurred photograph showing a man striding through a park, his arm swung forward, his air confident and jaunty. Malcolm called him Hughie. In his conversation he referred to him constantly, with great affection and in a manner quite unlike his usual rather disparaging one when talking of his friends. He seemed to be almost the only man in Malcolm's life of whom he had not a harsh word to say. It struck me as extraordinary that in all the thousands of words which have been written about Malcolm, Kingsmill is hardly ever referred to; and yet he has obviously been the greatest single influence in his life.

I saw part of the explanation when I eventually began to read Kingsmill's books. The first, I think, was *The Poisoned Crown*. I found it heavy going and difficult to reconcile with the picture I had had from Malcolm of Kingsmill as a supremely funny man. The impression persisted even after reading Michael Holroyd's *Hugh Kingsmill: A Critical Biography* (1964).

It was more through another 'posthumous friendship' that I first began to get onto Kingsmill's wave-length. This was with Hesketh Pearson, who had been an intimate friend of Kingsmill, and also of Muggeridge, until his death in 1964. Of the three subjects of this book he is the one, I feel, with whom I have most in common. A prolific writer of biographies, whose tone of spirited and opinionated unorthodoxy I find greatly to my taste, he collaborated with Kingsmill in a number of books and, with Muggeridge, wrote a memoir of him.

Slowly, as I acquired these books over a period of years, I formed an impression of a group of three men, two of them – Kingsmill and Pearson – of the same generation, and the third, Muggeridge, the survivor, linked to Pearson by their mutual affection for Kingsmill; all three having in common a number of admirable and to me endearing characteristics – a love of England and English literature; a dislike of intellectuals; a deep suspicion of all institutions and any form of collective activity and a shared sense of humour with no traces in it of snobbery, nor any of the class consciousness which has vitiated so much modern writing.

At the centre of the group was Kingsmill himself. His books never sold, partly because he was out of sympathy with his time. (The prevailing tone of literary criticism and biography, the two fields in which he worked, has during the last fifty or so years been serious, pagan and 'progressive'. Kingsmill who was fundamentally a mystical and humorous man following, to some extent, in the tradition of Chesterton and Belloc, had virtually no success.) But there was another reason for his failure. He lacked the element of ruthlessness and egotism which a successful writer needs. He put all his energies and his genius into his talk. As another friend, Alec Waugh, said, 'I feel that a man who expresses himself with such abundance in the ordinary contacts of life does not need the substitute of writing. I feel that writing is for him what living is for most big writers, a side-show.' He was in short a teacher who found it easier to bring out the best in others than in himself, which is why to appreciate him, I think one has to approach him, as I have done, via his two favourite pupils.

My thanks are due to Dorothy Hopkinson (widow of Hugh Kingsmill) and to Michael Holroyd (executor of Hesketh Pearson) for permission to quote from copyright material and for all their help and encouragement. I am especially grateful to Dorothy Hopkinson for giving me access to hitherto unpublished material by Hugh Kingsmill. I would like to thank too the late Joyce Pearson; Sister Edmée SLG and the Rev. Brooke Lunn (Kingsmill's daughter and son); and Basil Harvey. But my greatest debt is to Malcolm Muggeridge for introducing me to his two friends and helping me in many hours of conversation to know three exceptional people and so attain something of their humour and their happiness.

Chapter 1

When Hesketh Pearson first met Hugh Kingsmill in
1921 the first thing that struck him was his laughter. He had a
natural exuberance about him which some people found overpowering and even offensive. But to others like Pearson it was
irresistible. A stocky, ruddy-faced man, casually dressed in a
brown tweed jacket and flannels, he had a high rather nasal
voice and an exceptionally loud laugh. 'I have never been so
stimulated by any company,' Alec Waugh wrote. 'He is like
the sun shining on you. You become happy. The present is
rich. The future radiant. You talk well. . . . He envelops you
with warmth and friendliness.' Another friend, William
Gerhardi, said the same of his first meeting with Kingsmill:
'There was about him, I noticed at once, a certain ebullient
naturalness, a glint about the eyes . . . which denotes a kind of
gaiety of spirit, the real name for which must be genius and
which intoxicates one.'

It was impossible to conclude that Kingsmill inherited his
warm and cheerful temperament from either of his parents.
His mother was the daughter of Thomas Moore, an Irish
Protestant clergyman and headmaster of Midleton College,
near Cork, where, Kingsmill wrote, he had done a great deal of
flogging: 'But he was unpretentious, and, did not, like most of
the Anglo-Irish middle class, consider himself an aristocrat
merely because he wore boots and did not live in a cabin.' His
daughter was a rather austere person, for whom Kingsmill
found it hard to feel any affection. 'Gloom was her usual mood,'
he recalled, attributing it to her harsh religious upbringing and
the disappointment of her early hopes of life as a missionary.

His father Sir Henry Lunn,* though a more endearing

* Hugh Kingsmill Lunn wrote under the name of Hugh Kingsmill to
distinguish himself from other writing members of his family and to, as it
were, disengage himself from his father whom he deplored but in a way loved.

figure, could scarcely be described as genial. The son of a Methodist grocer in Horncastle, Lincolnshire, whom Kingsmill described as a 'lovable old man in spite of a certain austerity nourished by a lifelong study of God's word,' he was throughout his life torn between God and Mammon. His instinct was entrepreneurial and he began making money when he was seventeen. He lost three pounds playing cards with some strangers on a train and in order to recoup the money began selling white mice through the columns of *The Exchange and Mart*. White mice led to sword sticks and then he invented a scoring dial which tennis players could fit on their rackets. Thereafter he concentrated on tennis. 'A certain Colonel Godfrey,' his third son Brian wrote, 'invented the metal pieces which are used to define the corners of a tennis court. These were not patented, and Father did a substantial business in "Colonel Godfrey's Marking Pins", which he expanded into a general lawn tennis business by circular letters.' The business was prospering when one night Henry Lunn had a dream. He was walking with a friend past a large house. 'That is my house,' the friend said, 'and those are my family and there is not a scrap of religion in the place.' This experience was apparently enough to make him abandon the life of commerce and study to become a missionary. He took a five-year course at Trinity College, Dublin, paid for by the sale of his tennis business, and then left with his wife for India. The missionary life however was not to their taste. Mrs Lunn was shocked by the comparatively luxurious conditions in which their colleagues lived, while her husband found that the climate did not agree with him. After an unhappy year they returned to London, where Henry Lunn fell out of favour with the Methodist hierarchy by publicly raising, at his wife's insistence, the issue of luxury in the Indian missions. As a result he was, according to his son, 'assigned to an obscure circuit'. Shortly afterwards he started a magazine called *Review of the Churches* and it was in this organ that he launched a crusade for uniting the Anglican and Methodist churches which occupied his energies for the rest of his life. Kingsmill attributed his father's ecumenism more to his social ambitions than his religious zeal. 'By the last quarter of the century', he explained, 'there were many Wesleyan ministers who felt a strong, if unconscious, nostalgia for a reunion with a church the ministers of which were, without more ado, gentlemen. Once, in his last years, I asked my father if he would not like to see Horncastle again, but he looked gloomy and replied that the associations of the place were disagreeable to him. When Napoleon said that the English were a nation of shopkeepers, he was, with his usual tastelessness, drawing attention to a fact which every Englishman who has risen in the social scale wishes to forget. To level the social barrier between the Anglican and Wesleyan ministers was, I think, one of the motives, however obscure to himself, of my father's reunion enterprise, and though it would have been simpler for him to be ordained in the Church of England after he left the Wesleyans, it was not in his nature to take so equivocal a step.'

Henry Lunn's first move was to organise in the summer of 1892 a conference at Grindelwald to discuss the reunion of the churches. The conference did not produce any dramatic results on the religious front. But Lunn discovered, having arranged the travel and accommodation of all concerned, that he was left with a considerable profit. So began what was to grow into a large and prosperous travel agency. The core of the business in its early years was winter sports. Henry Lunn was the pioneer of skiing holidays for the well-to-do. Noting that many large hotels in Switzerland were empty during the winter months he conceived the idea of the Public Schools Alpine Sports Club, with membership limited to Old Etonians and Harrovians who were offered exclusive access to a number of the hotels. (Membership was later extended to embrace lesser breeds, but foreigners were always debarred – 'Foreign ideas about women,' Lunn explained, 'are so different from ours.') The Public Schools Alpine Sports Club was the model of several successors. Lunn's technique was to establish a 'club', designed to appeal to some specific social or religious group – The Free Church Touring Guild, The Service Officers Club, The Church Travellers' Club, etc., to enrol a number of prominent people who agreed, in exchange for free travel facilities, to lend their names, and then to send out hundreds of circulars to suitable addresses culled from the relevant reference books. There was no mention of 'Lunn's Tours' and the effect was therefore to dispel any vulgar notion of a travel agency and to suggest instead a rather exclusive club, which the customer was being invited to join. This suggestion was reassuring not only to Henry Lunn and his clients but also to Mrs Lunn who disliked being reminded of the fact that her husband was a businessman and preferred to entertain a picture of him as a philanthropist.

The winter sports business flourished. It became 'the thing' to holiday in Switzerland. Parties of rich English people flocked to the new resorts where Lunn's young guides – including his sons and their university friends – were waiting to introduce them to the novelty of skiing. Races were instituted, somewhat to the annoyance of the local peasants, one of whom registered his protest at the invasion by depositing a heap of manure at the finishing post, which sent the competitors flying.

Tall, heavily built, with sad eyes and droopy moustache, Sir Henry (he had been knighted in 1910 for services to the Liberal Party) was always on the look-out for a profitable opening. After the First World War he was quick to realise the touristic possibilities of Belgium. Many civilians, he was sure, would wish to see for themselves the scenes of the recent carnage. There was in fact a ban on such visits as the War Graves Commission was still trying to tidy up the battlefields, but this did not stop Sir Henry announcing tours to Bruges, including a visit to Ypres – 'That'll be all right,' he told Brian, 'we don't say anything about battlefields.' By the time the tours began the ban had luckily been lifted and the resulting business was so successful that it made a profit of £3,000, thereby restoring Sir Henry's fortunes which had been, like Belgium, devastated by the war.

Though in the harsher economic climate of the thirties the business languished, Sir Henry was never short of imaginative new ideas. When in later life he was stricken by an enlarged prostate he discovered that Swiss doctors had perfected an operation which did not result in impotence. He decided to set up a clinic in England at which the operation could be carried out, and his first move was to circularise everyone in *Who's Who* over fifty. Muggeridge relates: 'A large number of circulars were prepared and addressed, purporting to come from a retired colonel of impeccable respectability living in Budleigh

Salterton. It was essential, for obvious reasons, that the circulars should bear a Budleigh Salterton postmark, and Hughie was despatched to this agreeable seaside resort to post them there. I saw him off at Waterloo Station carrying an enormous cloth bag full of the circulars. . . . At Budleigh Salterton, he told me afterwards, he went into the not very large post office and suddenly, overcome with confusion, remarked that he had a few letters to post. This grotesque understatement was soon exposed. Anyway, the colonel's communication to potential sufferers from prostate was duly dispatched from his native Budleigh Salterton. The next day Hughie felt the whole episode was rounded off when he discovered that he had sent one of the circulars to himself. It was waiting on the door mat for him on his return to Hastings, and was so persuasive that he almost decided to have the operation.'

'Life was very simple when I was a young man,' Sir Henry said rather wistfully in old age. 'It was wonderful to be a young Liberal in the sixties and seventies . . . I never doubted that we were moving rapidly towards a new world in which the problems of war and social justice would be solved.' The First World War did little to dampen his enthusiasm. He conceived the idea that if only the Christian churches were to unite they could somehow harness the League of Nations to bring about a lasting peace. He travelled round the world to promote this rather nebulous cause, addressing meetings, broadcasting, preaching in churches. But with the worsening economic conditions of the Depression Sir Henry's business began to decline and with it some of his confidence. Despite their different outlooks, Kingsmill maintained an affection for his father, which he never felt for his mother. As Muggeridge explained: 'Although he accepted the world's standards with zest and enthusiasm he was always aware that they were false.' There is no doubt that Sir Henry Lunn explains the importance his son attached to the figure of Don Quixote. The same image in serious form occurred to W. T. Stead, the popular journalist who, when his friend Sir Henry was knighted, wrote: 'He is one of those men for whom a knighthood is the most appropriate of all honours, for he is a knightly soul, constantly riding out on some perilous quest, from which he emerges time after time, bruised and battered and wounded sore, but never daunted or disheartened.'

Kingsmill was one of four children, three boys and a girl, Eileen, who died at the age of twenty-four. His elder brother Arnold was closest to him in his early years at school and university. Arnold was very much the dutiful son of his father, sharing with him a dogged rather admirable determination to play his part in the events of the day, organising committees, delivering lectures and producing an endless flow of books, never once wavering from the belief that he had something valuable to contribute. His two great loves were skiing and, after his conversion in 1933, Catholicism, and he devoted a large part of his life to promoting one or the other. Like his father, Arnold was not without humour. When he was received into the Catholic church by Ronald Knox, the latter said to him, 'I am not quite satisfied about your orthodoxy,' to which Arnold Lunn retorted: 'If you think in these hard times I have spent 15s 6d on a return fare to Oxford in order to go back a Protestant to London, you are very much mistaken.'

Arnold, being the eldest son, was groomed by his father for the succession as head of the family as well as of the business. Hugh, his junior, was spared such attentions and allowed a freer rein. He noted sadly that he was not deemed important enough for the lecture on the Facts of Life which Arnold in due course received, and he was even allowed by his father to develop his own religious opinions. To Sir Henry, Christianity was the be-all and end-all, but, Kingsmill remembered, 'he did not deliberately inflict this view on me. He seems to have despaired of me from the start.' Kingsmill both then and later was spoiled by his father and as a result never acquired the virtue of tact. His manners, particularly towards women, were often atrocious. A fellow officer in the war noted: 'He has a very sympathetic nature, but at times through thoughtlessness, gives the impression of being selfish. . . .'

When Kingsmill was eight the Lunn family moved to Harrow and he was sent to Orley Farm preparatory school for four years, a period which he always recalled in later life with pleasure. 'Everything,' he wrote, 'was novel. And there was mystery and fascination even in the lessons. I remember the smooth sliding ease of the second declension – *Bellum, bellum, bellum, belli, bello, bello*, the satisfying balance of the Severn's superior length against the greater historical interest of the

Thames, and the furious clash of little distant horsemen on the plains of Linden, where when the sun was low all bloodless lay the untrodden snow, and a theory I had that Greek was only English turned upside down, and all I would have to do when I came to it was to reverse the book.' In contrast, Harrow school to which he went as a day boy in 1903, was a brutal and dispiriting place. Day boys, of whom there were only thirty, were despised by the patrician boarders and Kingsmill was mocked for his inability to play games and for being the son of a travel agent. In addition the fact that Sir Henry was a Liberal and a pro-Boer, as well as a Nonconformist, brought on him and his family 'the odium of being *nouveaux riches* with the odium of not behaving like them'.

The atmosphere of the Harrow of those days is illustrated by an incident which Kingsmill recalled from his last year: 'A deputation of hunger marchers from Manchester asked the headmaster if they could address the school in the yard where roll call was held. The headmaster, a clergyman, told them that if they went into the yard he would have the hose turned on them, so they took their stand on some steps not far from the tablet which marks the place where the future Lord Shaftes-bury when a boy at Harrow saw a pauper's funeral, and resolved to devote his life to improving the condition of the poor. A crowd of over a hundred boys gathered round the six or seven hunger marchers, and raised a howl every time the leader tried to speak. He became confused, turned his eyes from side to side, and held out his hands with a helpless gesture which redoubled the hoots and cat-calls. One of his friends pulled at his sleeve, he looked round once more, and stepping down walked away with his companions, followed by yells of derision.'

Kingsmill felt sufficiently appalled to write a letter of protest to the school magazine:

Dear Sirs,

The aim of a public school, we are often told, is to produce not scholars but gentlemen. With a few exceptions the negative part of the work is well done. But no one who wit-nessed the scene outside the Bill Yard after Bill on Thursday Feb. 6 will feel equally sure about the positive part. . . .

Perhaps thirty years hence, when some of those whose cheap attempts at wit appeared to amuse a decidedly uncritical gathering, are being carted (or aeroplaned) to the 1938 equivalent for a guillotine, they will regret they contributed their mite to a consummation so little to be wished.

This letter shows Kingsmill as an independent young man standing apart from the collective emotion of the mass of boys. It also shows his sense of humour already fully developed and strong enough to control his indignation. He was by nature easy-going and genial. He responded eagerly to the beauty of nature and young girls. His parents' religion, a rather negative form of Christianity, had little hold over him and he abandoned it effortlessly at the age of seventeen. There followed a short period in which he felt overpowered by an oppressive sense of the vastness of the universe and his own confinement within it. 'No nightmare,' he wrote, 'was worse than this waking horror, which I experienced several times during my seventeenth year, with diminishing intensity towards the close of the year, as my imagination expanded and I began to be conscious of a reality beneath or beyond the reality of matter. This consciousness was stimulated by the poetry I was reading, and especially the poems by Wordsworth.' The strong mystical element in Kingsmill responded most naturally to the poetry of Wordsworth and it was only with difficulty that in later life he reconciled himself to the truth of Christianity which had been distorted for him in his early years by the unimaginative Puritanism of his upbringing.

He left Harrow without regret and after a few months in Germany went up to New College, Oxford, where he had won a history scholarship. In common with many others before and since, Kingsmill was disappointed by the academic life of Oxford. He had entertained a romantic vision of the university as the oldest seat of culture in the world, imagining culture vaguely as 'the key to a poetic impassioned enjoyment in life, and dons as the guardians of the key, lay priests dedicated to the task of interpreting and clarifying the philosophers, and only less glorious than the men they served. It did not take me long to discover my error – about as long as it would take a man who went into a hen house looking for birds of paradise.'

Kingsmill might have benefited more from Oxford if his subject had not been history. His only real interest was in English literature and in his final year, 1911, he read hardly any of his set books, immersing himself instead in Housman. 'The wonderful summer of that year,' he remembered, 'one of the finest in this century, is steeped for me in retrospect in the poetry of *A Shropshire Lad*, which fed my discontent with Oxford – a discontent most heartily reciprocated by my college authorities when the results of the finals came out in August. At evening in warm Cotswold lanes or by a poplar bordered pool in Herefordshire I seemed on the verge of Housman's world, where bliss and pain were mingled in a mortal but ecstatic draught, and whether a lad pined or was happy, slit another throat or his own, whether a girl was cruel or too trusting, at least no-one was bored, no-one sat for exams.'

Such sentiments did not endear him to his tutor, the historian H. A. L. Fisher, who described him as the most idle and useless pupil he ever had. Kingsmill failed to gain a degree of any kind and, at his father's insistence, went to Trinity College, Dublin, to see if he could do better there. He finally managed to gain a degree of some sort, and then, like his two brothers, he drifted into the family travel business. Sir Henry was immensely indulgent towards his sons, disbursing generous salaries and allowing them to add their university friends to the payroll. Kingsmill spent much of the period before the war escorting parties of tourists round Belgium in the congenial company of his friends. Of his charges in Brussels be noted: 'What really reconciled them to the Calvary of the morning (visit to the Musée d'Anvers) in Brussels was the visit to the Musée Wiertz in the afternoon, with its representations of mothers devouring their children and men prematurely buried trying to force open the lid of their coffins.' Kingsmill's pre-war life was jolly, sheltered and uncomplicated, and even during the war he somehow managed to maintain around him an atmosphere of masculine bonhomie. At the outbreak of hostilities he enlisted in a regiment of cyclists and having gained a commission in the Royal Naval Volunteer Reserve was sent to France in 1916. After only a few weeks at the front he was captured during a night attack on the German trenches. 'I was, at bottom, glad,' he wrote, 'that I had escaped to do the work I wished to do; but at the same time I was very sorry to be deprived of that chance of military distinction which everyone, however unmartial, aspired after. There were my men too. How they would fail to miss me!'

Kingsmill was sent to a prisoner of war camp for officers at Karlsruhe. Here he made the acquaintance of John Holms, whom he nicknamed Oxo on account of his chubbiness. Only nineteen, Holms greatly impressed Kingsmill with his knowledge of literature and they became close friends, spending hours together discussing poetry and quoting from their well stocked memories. Others who knew Holms shared Kingsmill's view that he was a genius who could have been a great writer. But even when he was young he suffered from depressions and alcoholism, which worsened as he grew older, with the result, as Kingsmill put it, that he 'mistook his aspirations for virtues and his emotions for masterpieces.' During and after the war Holms was supported by Kingsmill's high spirits, and also by his money, and it was therefore fitting that the only proof he ever gave of his ability as a writer was in the course of a long correspondence with Kingsmill which lasted all through the twenties but which was never published. Their friendship was a lopsided affair, Kingsmill, not for the only time in his life, allowing himself to be exploited by a strong and overpowering personality. 'I'm so tired,' he complained in a rare moment of exasperation, 'of giving out and getting nothing back!'

Pearson did not share Kingsmill's high opinion of Holms. 'He struck me,' he wrote, 'on the first occasion when I met him, as an inarticulate ass. But we all of us have a goose which we like to see as a swan.'

Another writer, also a prisoner at Karlsruhe, who agreed with Kingsmill about Holms, was Alec Waugh who, though only nineteen, enjoyed a certain prestige on account of his already having had two books published, including a notorious novel about public school life called *The Loom of Youth*. In April 1918, Holms, Kingsmill and Waugh were moved to another camp at Mainz, where they remained until the armistice. A special room called Alcove was set aside for them to write in and here they assembled punctually every morning with paper and pens. Kingsmill was at work on a novel called *The Will to Love*.

"LITTERATOOR"

A cartoon in the Karlsruhe camp magazine.
From left to right, Alec Waugh, Hugh Kingsmill
and Gerard Hopkins.

'He had been captured a year earlier than I', Waugh recalled, 'and by the time I arrived it was a third finished. In appearance he was an untidy man; loosely built, stocky rather than fat, with his short hair half brushed; he walked with a lurching gait. On his arrival at the Alcove he would take off his tie and collar and wrap round his neck a green velvet scarf. One needed to be physically at ease, he explained, if one's mind was to function freely. But though he was untidy in his personal appearance, he was punctilious in his habits. He would arrange neatly in front of him his pipe and tobacco pouch, his dictionary and *Thesaurus* and write his story in a clear open script. . . . He was then twenty-eight years old, and fourteen months captivity had not dampened his spirits. He had a basically sunny nature. He was warm hearted and affectionate, he had a great booming laugh.'

Life as a prisoner of war was passed in endless reading, talking and writing. Debates were organised, plays and revues written and performed. Kingsmill was not adversely affected by his confinement and in later life even looked back on it with traces of nostalgia. 'Taken at one stretch,' he wrote, 'the twenty-one months of my captivity were too many by quite half, but I have often thought since how satisfactory it would have been had I been able to bank them and draw them two or three weeks at a time whenever I wanted a respite from ordinary existence.'

It was typical of Kingsmill that he was left unscarred by the First World War, as he was by the Second. He had not, like others of his generation, been carried away by the jingoism of the early war period; nor was he at any stage disposed towards the pacifism which later became fashionable, especially among writers. Kingsmill saw for himself, albeit briefly, the horrors of the trenches and experienced the privations of imprisonment, but they did not alter his view of the world. What he wrote of a fellow prisoner at Karlsruhe, a French officer, Lieutenant Garray, could be applied as well to himself: 'He was too human and sociable, too fitted by nature to draw delight out of ordinary existence, to need the stimulant of any political agitation, however admirable its aims.' Throughout his life Kingsmill remained indifferent to 'public affairs' and politics, an attribute which later, at a time when the writer was expected to be committed and concerned, was to prove a great disadvantage to him.

When the war ended Kingsmill went back to work for his father, eventually taking charge of the Lucerne office. He was paid a lavish salary of £2,000 a year and had plenty of time to write. It was during this carefree post-war period that, in 1921, he first met Hesketh Pearson.

Chapter 2

Hesketh Pearson was, like Kingsmill, a naturally ebullient man. Tall and well-dressed, he had good looks and immense charm, which made him very attractive to women. He was born at Hawford, near Worcester, in 1887, the second son of well-to-do, respectable, Conservative, church-going parents. His ancestors he described as 'energetic and earnest' and many of them, including both his grandparents, his god-father and three of his uncles were in Holy Orders. His father, a large, unimaginative and intensely egotistic man, was interested solely in shooting and sport. His mother suppressed her artistic instincts for the sake of marital harmony.

When Pearson was nine his parents moved to Bedford, where he was sent, along with his elder brother Jack, to Orkney House School. The time spent there was the only unhappy period of his life. 'On the very rare occasion when I have a nightmare', he told Kingsmill many years later, 'I imagine myself back at my preparatory school.' The headmaster, a man named Blake, was a compulsive flogger. Pearson, for whatever reason, became one of his favourite victims.

Blake, 'a tall clean shaven man with lumbering gait, grey eyes, high forehead, thin lips and inflexible jaw,' seized every opportunity he could to thrash young Hesketh, who commented that he 'derived a single advantage from Blake's school: the worst things that have happened to me since leaving it have seemed relatively mild in comparison with those five years of helpless misery, and I would rather have died at any period of my existence than go through them again.'

At the age of twenty-one he met Blake, when his mother stopped to talk to him outside the Bedford church following Sunday morning service. Pearson pretended not to recognise him and, when Mrs Pearson said, 'Surely you remember Mr Blake?' replied, 'I remember him so well that if I saw him drowning in the river I would throw stones at him from the bank.'

When he was fourteen, Pearson went to Bedford School, where life was altogether easier. But, like Kingsmill and most other writers, he did not excel in his studies. He was remembered later for having scored 0 in an algebra examination, and all the efforts of the masters to interest him in his work were unsuccessful. From his earliest years Pearson evinced a bold and sometimes reckless attitude to life which, while it often landed him in trouble, helped equally to get him out of it. In his memoirs he recalled one of the Bedford School masters, 'a clergyman named Massey, called "Pot" on account of his belly. He lost his temper easily, his small reddish beard bristled with wrath, and, like all fat little men in that condition, he looked funny. An answer I gave to one of his questions annoyed him, and he trembled with rage, which made me laugh. Insensate with fury, he picked up an ink bottle and threw it at my head. I caught it neatly and threw it back, catching him on the belly, where it broke and deluged him with ink. He was so utterly confounded that he remained for several seconds with his mouth open, staring at me as if he could not believe his senses. Gradually he became conscious of what had happened, said nothing at the time, but at the end of the lesson took me down to report my behaviour to the headmaster. I simply explained that I had made a good catch, returned it, and could not be blamed for Mr Massey's failure in the field. This explanation appeared to satisfy the headmaster and nothing more ensued.'

It was customary in Pearson's family for boys who failed to shine at school to enter the church. His father was therefore keen that the young Hesketh should study classics with a view to taking Holy Orders. Pearson however firmly refused to do any such thing and was consigned to the next best thing – business. 'In those days,' he said, 'a fellow who was good for nothing went into commerce. I was good for nothing and I went into commerce.' He was given a job in the Royal Mail Steam Packet Company, whose managing director was the Pearsons' next door neighbour. Here he worked for two and a half years, failing in every way to advance himself. At some stage he decided that he would be better off working in a bank, preferably in the Far East, and applied for a job with one of the leading banks. The manager asked him whether he had any banking experience: 'I dealt with that question easily. Then he asked why I wanted to join his staff. The answer to that was easy too: I did not care for my present job. "But are you interested in banking?" he enquired. "Not in the least" I assured him. "Then, Mr Pearson, I do not think I shall require your services." That concluded the interview.'

Meanwhile Pearson had not endeared himself to the management of the RMSPC. A fellow clerk, a hard working man called Ray, the sole support of his widowed mother, was suddenly, through no fault of his own, given the sack by the company secretary. Pearson, enraged by the inhumanity of the affair, went straight to the manager and complained. The manager, after delivering himself at intervals of the ejaculations 'Ha!', 'Ho!' and 'Hum!', promised to look into the matter and eventually, though he refused to revoke Ray's dismissal, saw to it that he was given a fair redundancy payment.

From that moment Pearson was regarded as a dangerous subversive and shortly afterwards was asked to hand in his notice. Fortunately he had just inherited £1,000 from an aunt and was therefore more than willing to comply with the firm's request.

Having spent most of his legacy travelling round South America, Canada and the USA Pearson returned to England in 1908 and joined his brother Jack, who was running a car business in Brighton. Pearson, who knew nothing of motor cars, was put in charge of the showroom. From the workers' point of view he was an ideal employer, as he did not believe in exercising any form of authority over them, an attitude which at one point led his brother to point out that if the workers were allowed to come and go as they pleased none of the firm's orders would be completed. He added that drunkenness during working hours did nothing to promote efficiency. Pearson commented: 'I saw his point and passed it on, with apologies, to the men; but they had views of their own on the subject and did not let it affect their lives.'

The two years (1908–10) which followed were a happy period for Pearson. He fell in love, for the first time, with a

French girl he met on a trip to Brussels and she introduced him to sex, something she claimed could only be taught to an Englishman by a Frenchwoman. Pearson agreed. After parting with promises of undying devotion he returned to Brighton only to fall in love with a chorus girl. 'She was a brunette,' he recalled, 'with large dark eyes, a Grecian profile, and a perfectly proportioned figure. . . . Of course I thought myself in love with her, but later experience has taught me that my feeling was ninety per cent lust.'

The Downland country round Brighton was, in those days before the First World War, unspoilt. Pearson the victim of youthful love, or lust, explored it with intense pleasure. It was while walking on the Downs one afternoon that he experienced what was to him a revelation. He was at the time troubled by religious uncertainties. Brought up in an atmosphere of conventional bourgeois Christianity, Pearson rebelled against it but by the age of twenty-one was still a prey to worries about life after death and the meaning of existence. Walking along the Downs he saw below him the village of Poynings at the foot of the Devil's Dyke and decided to explore it. As he wandered round the churchyard reading the inscriptions on the tombstones he was overcome by morbid thoughts of death. He was about to leave when he saw a stone with a poem on it. It marked, he later discovered, the grave of a man who had been struck by lightning on the Downs, and on it were inscribed some lines from the dirge in Shakespeare's *Cymbeline*:

> Fear no more the heat o' the sun,
>   Nor the furious winter's rages;
> Thou thy worldly task hast done,
>   Home art gone, and ta'en thy wages:
> Golden lads and girls all must,
> As chimney-sweepers, come to dust.
>
> Fear no more the frown o' the great,
>   Thou art past the tyrant's stroke;
> Care no more to clothe and eat,
>   To thee the reed is as the oak:
> The sceptre, learning, physic, must
> All follow this, and come to dust.

> Fear no more the lightning flash,
>   Nor the all-dreaded thunder-stone;
> Fear not slander, censure rash;
>   Thou hast finish'd joy and moan;
> All lovers young, all lovers must
> Consign to thee, and come to dust.

Pearson wrote: 'In a moment my apprehension seemed to vanish. What I had previously regarded as merely a perfect lyric now appeared as a spiritual illumination, and I clearly perceived, what I must always have felt obscurely in my bones, that one's life could be a blessing or a curse without the least reference to what might or might not happen beyond the grave; that it was all-sufficient, an end in itself; that it would close either in the peace of cessation or in the peace beyond human understanding; and that it did not matter which, since both meant the annihilation of the human mind with its tribulations. A mood of extraordinary serenity followed by a phase of difficulty and doubt, and I have never since worried about the mystery of the universe, the ultimate truth, the nature of God, or any other insoluble problem.'

From the age of nineteen, when on a rainy day in a country house he first read *Hamlet*, Pearson had been a fanatical devotee of Shakespeare. During his brief period in the City, he went without meals, in order to have enough money to buy a ticket for one of Beerbohm Tree's productions at His Majesty's Theatre. He never missed an opportunity of seeing a performance of Shakespeare and could soon recite whole plays by heart, as well as reproduce the gestures and intonations of all the leading actors and actresses of that time.

The Shakespearean productions of Beerbohm Tree, with their splendid scenery, music and acting, were, literally, an eye-opener to Pearson. In spite of his hunger pangs the hours he spent at His Majesty's Theatre were the happiest he had known and Beerbohm Tree became his hero. Though no fool, Pearson had the habit of rushing in where angels feared to tread. In 1909 when he was living at Brighton he and a party of friends decided to come up to London to see Tree's production of *Hamlet*. Pearson recalled that the great actor-manager took his time with this part and that if he and his friends were to catch a train back to Brighton they would have to miss the last scene. This would not do. Pearson cabled Tree:

> Can you play Hamlet in a business-like manner next Thursday so as to enable me to catch midnight train from Victoria?

It was an extraordinary request for a young car salesman from Brighton to make of the greatest actor manager of the day, a man at the height of his fame. But Tree wired back:

> Cannot alter my conception of the part to fit midnight train but will cut a scene if you'll run to Victoria.

He kept his promise and Pearson caught his train.

In 1911, when his brother's car business seemed on the brink of bankruptcy, Pearson applied for a job in Tree's company. Though he had no acting experience, he could think of no better way of keeping constantly in touch with his beloved Shakespeare. It was also an act of defiance of his father. In those days to go on the stage was one way of demonstrating a rejection of conventional values.

Sir Herbert Beerbohm Tree, whose biography Pearson was to write many years later, was an exceptional person, in some ways a more remarkable and attractive figure than his now better known half-brother Sir Max Beerbohm. As creator and manager of His Majesty's Theatre he had enthralled the public with a series of sensational productions of plays ancient and modern, and dazzled everyone with his versatility as an actor. He was also the subject of anecdotes. He once went into a post office and asked to see a sheet of stamps. 'I'll take that one,' he said, pointing to a stamp in the middle of the sheet. On another occasion at Victoria Station he said to the man at the ticket office: 'Give me some tickets please.' 'What station do you want?' asked the man. 'What stations have you got?' Tree replied. Despite his fame Tree remained a genuinely humble man, kind and generous, and it was quite in character that he should have responded when the young Hesketh Pearson wrote to him in 1911 asking for work. 'Come and see me but don't be too optimistic,' Tree replied. 'You should have independent means or relations with court circles to be successful on the stage nowadays. If you have the former, why go on the stage?

If the latter, the kings and queens of real life should satisfy you, though I admit we can give you the romantic article better than they, because a cardboard crown is better than a top hat.'

Pearson was ushered into the great man's presence during a performance of *Henry VIII* in which Tree was playing Cardinal Wolsey. Tree told him to sit down and proceeded to stare at him for about two minutes. Then he said: 'Don't bite your nails. It's a sign of mental stagnation.' There was another silence. 'Don't suck your thumb,' said Tree, 'it signifies lack of stamina.' This irritated Pearson and he asked if Tree would like to write him a prescription. Tree immediately snatched up his pen and scribbled something down on a piece of paper. Handing it to Pearson he told him to come back after the next act. After he had gone Pearson looked at the paper. It said:

DISEASE: Want of philosophic calm, typically modern.
CURE: One performance of *Henry VIII*, to be taken weekly.
                                                              H.B.T.

Pearson returned to Tree's dressing-room during the following interval. 'Who are you?' Tree asked, 'what do you want?' The following dialogue, reminiscent of a Marx Brothers script, then ensued:

PEARSON: I want a job.
TREE: Can you speak German?
PEARSON: No; but does one have to speak German to go on the stage?
TREE: It would certainly be useful if you wanted to go on the German stage.
PEARSON: I don't.
TREE: Well, that settles it, doesn't it? Can you speak French?
PEARSON: Yes.
TREE: Fluently?
PEARSON: No.
TREE: What a pity.
PEARSON: Why?
TREE: Because one should always swear in a foreign language during rehearsals.
PEARSON: Is there any necessity to swear at all?

TREE: No necessity, but a great relief. Are you fond of your wife?

PEARSON: I haven't got one.

TREE: Yes, but are you fond of her?

PEARSON: How the dickens can I be fond of a wife I haven't got?

TREE: Ah, I hadn't thought of that. . . .

Tree was recalled for the next act. As Pearson left the dressing-room, Tree dragged him back and whispered in his ear, 'Have you ever been to Jerusalem?' 'No,' said Pearson. 'How interesting,' replied Tree.

Nothing was said about the possibilities of employment, but towards the end of the run of *Henry VIII* Pearson received a wire requesting him to report at His Majesty's. On the stage he found Sir Herbert seated at a table with two of his subordinates.

'Name?' bellowed one of these.

'Pearson.'

'Experience?'

'I beg your pardon?'

'I like his legs,' interposed Sir Herbert.

'But you can't see them through his trousers,' said his companion.

'That's why I like them.'

Pearson was given a walk-on part in *A Midsummer Night's Dream*. This production was followed by *Julius Caesar* in which Pearson was cast as Publius, an aged senator. He had only one line: 'Good morrow, Caesar'. In a frenzy of excitement at his first speaking role, Pearson practised for hours to reproduce the mannerisms of an old man. He acquired a long white beard and followed old men in the street to observe exactly how they moved. The great day came and Pearson was at the theatre two hours before the performance to cover his face with wrinkles. Standing in the wings, waiting to go on he practised his senile falsetto. At last the cue came. Unfortunately in his anxiety to get the old man's voice right, Pearson forgot the shuffle and marched on to the stage with youthful vigour. After three or four brisk strides he realised his mistake and was about to go back and make his entrance again when the actor playing

Caesar said, 'Welcome Publius', the line which in the text followed after Pearson's 'Good morrow, Caesar.' Pearson went completely limp and said, 'Hullo!'

'I expected the sack,' he wrote later, 'and was not in the least surprised when Tree came up to me at the conclusion of the scene and asked in that curious nasal voice of his:

' "What did you say to Caesar?" '

' "I'm afraid I said 'Hullo!', Sir Herbert," I replied, and was about to stutter some sort of excuse when he interrupted me:

' "Oh. I beg your pardon. My mistake. I thought you said 'What ho!' " '

It was while touring with a play by Alfred Sutro in the summer of 1911 that Pearson fell in love with an actress in the company, Gladys Gardner. He proposed to her by moonlight on the beach at Scarborough and she agreed to marry him when they had a little more money. They married in June 1912, after Gladys had informed Pearson that she was pregnant. To appease their respective families the marriage ceremony was antedated two months when the announcement of it was made, 'our caution being justified when Gladys gave birth to a son who weighed ten pounds, a trifle over-weight for a seven months baby.'

In his biography of Beerbohm Tree Pearson wrote: 'Like so many marriages, theirs was to consist of quarrels, reconciliations, infidelity, fidelity and tenderness, coldness, sympathy, hostility, the change of moods, the differing of outlooks, the inevitable clash of opposing wills. But through all their ups and downs she continued to love him and he never ceased to love her, if not exactly on the lines of the Church marriage service.' It is likely that he had his own marriage in mind as much as Tree's when he wrote this. Pearson was by no means the ideal husband, as he himself was the first to admit. A philanderer by nature, he ceased to make love to his wife after a few years of marriage and indulged in a series of affairs to which Gladys resigned herself. Despite this their relationship was a happy one, based on affection and common interests. Until Pearson's first real success in 1940 they were very hard up, but neither had any great concern with possessions. They lived modestly, in a succession of flats in the St John's Wood area. Gladys was plain and generally dressed in black. 'She was not much of a cook; but then she didn't have anything to cook,' a friend said. She was infinitely kind and generous and was devoted to her husband, helping him with the drudgery of research work for his books.

Pearson's attitude towards his wife was typical of him. Having defied convention by seducing her, he more than made up for it by 'doing the decent thing' and marrying her when she became pregnant. He then felt no subsequent qualms about his numerous infidelities. At the same time, such was his charm and good nature that his wife was prepared to tolerate his behaviour and remained devoted to him, as he did, in his way to her. 'I've had six great friends in my life,' Pearson once told his friend Basil Harvey. 'Gladys is one of them.'

They had been married for only two years when the war broke out. Pearson enlisted in August 1914, but after a few months was found to be suffering from tuberculosis and was invalided out of the army. He returned for a time to the stage but, becoming restless, volunteered for the Army Service Corps, which required only a perfunctory 'medical'. He was commissioned and sent out to Mesopotamia. The climate cured his tuberculosis, but in common with many others on that highly unpleasant campaign he succumbed to several other diseases, and in three instances came close to death. In every case he attributed his recovery to Shakespeare and particularly to Falstaff.

On the first occasion he was suffering from septic sores and for a month lay sweltering in a tent, the temperature varying during the day between 120 and 130 degrees. His legs were swathed in poultices the renewal of which was torture. At last the medical officer said his condition was worsening and that he might have to have one or even both his legs amputated. Operations in Mesopotamia at that time were nearly always fatal and Pearson was convinced he would have died, but for the fact that something comic about the doctor called to mind Falstaff's description of Shallow: 'A man made after supper of a cheese-paring: when he was naked he was for all the world like a forked radish, with a head fantastically carved upon it with a knife.' The lines set Pearson's brain to work, and he started trying to reconstruct as many as he could of the Falstaff scenes. In the process he became so invigorated that, ignoring the doctor's orders, he got out of bed and though in excruciating pain began to hobble about. The sores slowly dried up and within a fortnight he was convalescing.

Four months later, however, he succumbed to a combination of dysentery and malaria, the latter inducing 'moods of such black depression that no-one who has been lucky to escape it can have the least conception of the mental abyss into which the sufferer is plunged.'

During this despair Pearson started to read the first of the Shallow scenes in *Henry IV, Part 2* which a nurse managed to obtain for him. After three days he succeeded in reading the whole scene. His depression left him completely and he began to recover.

On a third occasion Falstaff came to his aid when he was suffering from a head wound. 'Again I was in hospital, dangerously ill. After feeling so sick that when I tried to ask a question of the nurse at my bedside I could not raise a whisper. My head throbbing painfully, I closed my eyes, and it may have been some minutes or some hours later that I heard the nurse say to the doctor, "He's got honour on the brain." That did not sound a bit like me and I mentally echoed the doctor's surprise. "Something about honour getting legs and arms," she went on. "Hm! that's strange," mused the doctor. "And he talked about surgical skill too," added the nurse. The words were wholly out of character, yet they were vaguely familiar. Suddenly it all became clear. In my delirium I had been quoting Falstaff's speech on Honour. The humour of the situation seized me, and in spite of the pain in my head the top of which seemed to be opening and shutting, I was convulsed with silent helpless laughter, in which condition I again passed out. The doctor told me later that my recovery had begun when for no apparent reason my body had been shaken by successive spasms, which were followed by several hours of peaceful sleep.'

Chapter 3

Pearson returned to England in November 1919. He was suffering from dysentery and malaria and weighed eight stone eleven pounds. He also had a head wound caused by shrapnel, which may have increased his natural irascibility. (In writing his memoirs he never explained the circumstances in which he was wounded, nor for that matter how he won the Military Cross.) At any rate he was cured of his dysentery and malaria by Bernard Shaw's homoeopathic doctor, Raphael Roche, and was soon able to resume his acting career. In 1921 he wrote his first book, a series of profiles called *Modern Men and Mummers*. The book contained an eulogistic portrait of Frank Harris and it was this that particularly appealed to Kingsmill when he read the book. He wrote to Pearson suggesting a meeting.

The two men met on November 21, 1921 at the Lunn offices in Endsleigh Gardens. Later they walked down New Oxford Street and Kingsmill bought a copy of his novel *The Will to Love*, which also included a picture of Harris, though of a rather different sort, and presented it to Pearson.

Kingsmill and Pearson took to one another at once. It was friendship at first sight. The two had a lot in common. Both came from conventional late Victorian homes, both rebelled against powerful and domineering fathers and both shared a strong sense of humour. At the same time there was something of Holmes and Watson in their mutual attraction. Kingsmill was unworldly, intuitive and essentially mystical in outlook. He was superstitious, interested in dreams, and given to periodic fasting. Pearson was practical and straightforward, a man who had 'roughed it' in military and civilian life. He had no interest whatever in theoretical matters. Their greatest bond was a love of literature and especially Shakespeare. Both knew his plays virtually by heart. Pearson could recite whole speeches, imitating all the great actors of the time, which reduced Kingsmill, and later Muggeridge, to hysterics. They began to meet regularly in pubs and tea shops, following a familiar routine of sitting up half the night endlessly talking about books and authors, improvising private scenes in the lives of great men. As Kingsmill was at this period working most of the time abroad, they wrote to one another, carrying on their discussions in letter form, and kept up the correspondence until Kingsmill's death in 1949.

It was through Shakespeare that Kingsmill and Pearson had both come into contact with the second great topic of their conversation and correspondence – Frank Harris. Harris, the son of an Irish merchant seaman had, as Kitty Muggeridge remarked of David Frost, '*risen without trace*' in the literary and political world of the nineties. He became editor of the *Evening News* at the age of twenty-seven, married a rich widow with a house in Park Lane and achieved his greatest success as editor of the *Saturday Review* (1894–8), numbering among his contributors Wells, Shaw, Beerbohm, Hardy and Kipling. But his personality was unstable and the effects of fame and the failure to distinguish between love and lust, politics and literature, or fact and fantasy, in the end parted him from reality. From about the turn of the century he became increasingly unhinged and subject to delusions of grandeur and persecution mania.

Young men like to have a hero to whom they can attach themselves in the process of rebellion against parental authority. To Kingsmill, brought up in a heavy rather puritanical atmosphere, Harris appeared as a liberator. His book *The Man Shakespeare* which treated Shakespeare as a human being, especially in relation to sex, made the strongest kind of appeal to a young man reacting against the scholastic and literary establishments of the time.

Earlier commentators on Shakespeare–Johnson or Coleridge, for example – attempted to reconcile the poet to their moralistic views, while the Victorians, Kingsmill observed, had pieced together an image of Shakespeare 'seated in a corner of the Mermaid : a wine glass of mild sack within easy reach, and a goose quill lightly poised, while kindling imagination slowly suffused his face with a seraphic if faintly imbecile smile'.

After this, Harris's picture of a passionate and fallible Shakespeare came as a welcome corrective. 'It may well be,' Harris wrote, 'for us to learn what infinite virtue lay in that frail sensuous singer.' In later years, when the process of dis-illusionment was complete, that sentence still had the power to recall the excitement which Harris inspired in someone suffering from the effects of 'three years of Oxford dons, pale, lustreless, vaguely agitated by the mysterious necessity which compelled them to go on breathing'.

Kingsmill wrote a fan letter to Harris in 1911 when he was still an undergraduate at Oxford. Harris replied affectionately, and after some further correspondence, the two arranged to have lunch at the Café Royal. From the start, Harris turned out to be not all that Kingsmill had expected. 'He was standing inside the entrance, a few yards from the street, peering short-sightedly at the persons coming in, a man below middle height, as I guessed from his work, but much broader and stronger than I had pictured him. He was wearing a bowler hat, and a braided overcoat. As he smiled hesitatingly at me he was so unlike my idea of a bitter impoverished genius and so near the conventional notion of a Jew financier, that I walked past him. But no one else seemed to be looking out for me, so I turned back and asked, "Mr Frank Harris?". His diffident air vanished. Shaking my hand, he said: "There is an excellent wine at the Savoy I want you to taste;" and a few minutes later we were seating ourselves at a table overlooking the Embankment, when he leaned forward and rumbled in a deep whisper: "Would you change places with me? There's a South African millionaire behind you whom I whipped once in one of my papers. I can't enjoy my lunch if I have to look at him."'

Adjusting himself to the incongruity of Harris's appearance, Kingsmill, like others before him, quickly fell under his spell. He was then fifty-six and although his great days as a 'figure' in London society were over and his grasp of reality was becoming steadily more weak, Harris still had the power to magnetize. He had glowing eyes and a deep bass voice, compared by Bernard Shaw to a trombone and by Max Beerbohm to the organ in Westminster Abbey. His technique with his male disciples was exactly the same as that which he employed with the young women he tried to seduce. In both cases he began by praising his listener's insight and discernment, before exciting his or her admiration and pity for an unrecognised genius. The world did not understand him. Still, he bore no grudge. Others before, Jesus or Shakespeare, for example, had suffered a similar fate. He enthused about literature, while at the same time implying that there was something called Life which was far more important than any book. The lack of logic in this argument was hidden beneath a flood of rhetoric.

All in all, to the young and impressionable it was a good line and Kingsmill succumbed. Harris escorted him round his various ports of call; he took him to Dan Rider's bookshop in St Martin's Lane, a popular meeting place for writers and artists of the day, and then to tea at Stewart's where they met Harris's wife, Nellie – 'a lovely woman', as Kingsmill noted in his diary. During the following months the two men met frequently. 'Lunn continued to write,' said Mrs Harris, 'and meetings took place between Frank and Lunn, and it was as though Lunn had fallen in love with Frank.' It was true. 'I had a sense of life opening up before me,' Kingsmill remembered, and his enthusiasm for Harris's work increased. 'Love is the very essence,' he wrote. 'Love of truth, love of beauty, and love of mankind struggling in its blind world of misery.' Harris glowed. 'Keep out in life as much as you can,' he urged Kingsmill. Books were a poor substitute for experience: 'I am not a man of letters particularly. I think I have done things far more astonishing than anything I have written. . . . Ah, Lunn, Lunn, 'tis a mad world but you will struggle through no doubt as I have done. . . .' Kingsmill did his best to 'keep out in life' by becoming friendly with a prostitute, confiding in Harris that if he had the money he thought he could 'save' her. Harris warned against such a course. 'A pretty girl in London,' he said, 'does not need to sell herself.'

Meanwhile Harris had introduced Kingsmill to the literary world. He met the poet Richard Middleton and Arnold Bennett, as well as Harris's other young admirers including John Middleton Murry: 'I have been telling him,' Harris confided, 'that I expect more considerable things from you than from any young man I have met for a long time.'

The following spring, 1912, Kingsmill stayed with Harris for three weeks at his villa in Nice. Together, in the evenings,

they strolled along the Promenades des Anglais, Harris
rumbling away inconsequentially. On their last walk prior to
Kingsmill's departure, Harris, after a long silence, vouchsafed:
'Christ goes deeper than I do, but I have had the wider
experience.'

Kingsmill was not in the best frame of mind to appreciate
this remark, having just experienced the first painful effects of
a visit with Harris to a Parisian brothel. Harris himself had not
indulged.

It was impossible for someone with as well developed a
sense of humour as Kingsmill's to be at close quarters with
Frank Harris for long and retain an attitude of uncritical
adoration. To begin with it must have dawned on Kingsmill
that in cultivating his friendship Harris had his eye for at least
part of the time on what he might get out of Sir Henry Lunn in
the way of money. Early in 1912 Harris was hoping to become
the editor of the *Daily Herald*, then about to be launched. When
his plans were thwarted, he set his sights on the *Athenaeum* and
asked Sir Henry if he would arrange to buy the paper on his
behalf. Sir Henry made the reasonable request that in exchange
for his negotiating the purchase, Harris should give his son,
Kingsmill, a small stake in the paper. But Harris refused and
the deal fell through. ('This incident,' Kingsmill noted,
'explains why Harris, in spite of a strong natural aptitude, was
a failure in affairs. With Caesar, Cromwell and Bismarck to
prove the contrary, Harris always believed that the two main
attributes of a man of action were a deep bass voice and a
ruthless disregard of everyone's feelings.')

Harris then made up to another young man with artistic
ambitions, Claud Lovat Fraser, whose father was a wealthy
solicitor. This time he was successful and Fraser senior bought
for Harris a respectable ladies' journal called *Hearth and Home*.
Lovat Fraser and Kingsmill were taken on the staff. Kingsmill's
attitude to Harris was gradually changing. He ceased to
worship him as a god and began to study him as an extraordinary human specimen.

Hearth and Home had hitherto been a fairly serious weekly for
middle class ladies and Kingsmill could not understand why
Harris had bought it. Harris, questioned about this, said
vaguely, 'It may help, lead to things'. The fact was that Harris

needed a paper, however incongruous, to keep him in funds. Editorship brought power and there was always something to be made from tipping shares and other questionable practices. Harris in 1906 had worked for some months on *John Bull* with Horatio Bottomley, one of the most successful confidence tricksters that Britain has known. Bottomley pioneered the skills of extracting money from firms in exchange for silence, running lotteries of which the results were faked, etc. There is no doubt that Harris picked up a trick or two from his association with the Master. Investment columns appeared incongruously among *Hearth and Home*'s regular features like 'Home Advice' and 'Health and Beauty', and what with these innovations and others, the regular staff was not immediately attracted to the new proprietor.

Kingsmill told the sad story of one stout lady who called to clarify her position with Harris:

'You must find this heat very trying, madam,' Harris said.

'Yes it is a little trying.' She dabbed her face nervously with a handkerchief. 'But, as I was saying, Mr Harris . . .'

'I wonder how much you weigh. Personally,' he looked at her with a scrutinising smile, 'I should put you at about fifteen stone.'

'Really, Mr Harris, I didn't come here to discuss my weight.'

'Are you a Jewess?'

After ten minutes of this she left, nearly in tears, but the paper had to pay her fifty pounds for breach of contract.

She was not the only lady to take offence. Harris was visited one day by another of his disciples, John Middleton Murry. 'Well,' said Harris, looking up from an advertisement for ladies' underwear which he was perusing at his desk, 'and what are you writing now?' Murry replied that he was thinking of writing about Matthew Arnold.

'Matthew Arnold!' Harris glared across at Kingsmill, who blushed. 'Matthew Arnold! You might as well write . . .'

The door opened and the young lady who wrote fashion notes over the pen name of 'Lady Betty' entered. Harris turned to her and flinging out his hands roared, 'He might as well write about dried excrement!'

In the meantime Harris seduced Kingsmill's fellow con-
tributor Enid Bagnold. She had met Harris in Dan Rider's
bookshop. 'Could it be Lord Kitchener cut off at the legs?'
she asked herself. Enid Bagnold was an exceptionally pretty
girl and Harris set his sights on her from the start. He took her
to lunch in the Savoy and spoke of Christ and Shakespeare
while she listened wide-eyed. 'Sex,' he told her, 'is the gateway
to life.' So, eventually, she confessed, she went 'through the
gateway in an upper room in the Café Royal.'

Back at *Hearth and Home*, Kingsmill was curious to know
what was going on. He questioned Enid Bagnold mischievously.
She tried not to give anything away. But Kingsmill must have
guessed, and it is difficult, given his temperament and her
beauty, not to conclude that he was a little jealous.

By now whatever illusions he may have had about Harris
had gone. On November 16, 1912 Harris went to America, his
ticket paid for by Sir Henry Lunn. In his absence Mrs Harris
invited Kingsmill to a dinner party, and during this a row
blew up between the two of them. Afterwards Kingsmill wrote
that he ventured to contradict Mrs Harris on a literary point
but, as Philippa Pullar points out in the most recent biography
of Harris,* this would not really explain what followed. Most
likely, Kingsmill made some jocular reference to Harris's
relationship with Enid Bagnold. Whatever he said, she reported it to Harris, who on his return angrily quoted Wordsworth, informing Kingsmill that he was 'moving about in
worlds not realised' and gave instructions that he was no
longer to be paid for his book reviews. This was followed by an
edict forbidding him to sell review copies of books. In 1913
Kingsmill resigned from *Hearth and Home* and the two did not
meet again for several years.

Luckily for Harris only four months later, a new disciple
offered himself in the shape of Hesketh Pearson, by now
established as a professional actor. Like Kingsmill, Pearson
had been bowled over by *The Man Shakespeare* and he too
wrote to Harris expressing his unqualified enthusiasm. Harris
replied at once: 'If as you say you are only in your twenties,
you have an astonishing mastery of words and rightness of
judgment.'

* *Frank Harris* by Philippa Pullar (Hamish Hamilton, 1975).

Eventually they met at Harris's flat in Lexham Gardens. 'I was deeply impressed,' Pearson recalled, 'and came away convinced that I had spent an evening with the only man who could put the world right. One remark of his hit a responsive note shortly after my arrival. Seeing a bust of Cecil Rhodes in the room, I asked what Harris thought of him. "Rhodes?" he queried. "Why worry about him? A second-rater. You have twenty times his brains." This created in me a receptive frame of mind.'

Pearson, however, was to be denied the close personal contact with Harris which might have shattered his illusions, as it had done Kingsmill's. Shortly after their meeting Harris became the editor of a scurrilous magazine called *Modern Society* and it was in this capacity that he was sent to prison in 1914 for contempt of court, after the paper had cast aspersions on the defendant in a divorce case which was *sub judice*. Harris spent a month in Brixton Prison and emerged filled with a vehement hatred for England, a country that rewarded its men of genius by putting them in prison. After a short period in France he went to America in 1915, where he blotted what little was left of his copy book by writing a series of articles in the *New York Sun* in which he appeared to take the German side in the war.

All this only endeared him to Pearson, who was happy to accept Harris's own estimation of himself as another Oscar Wilde, the helpless victim of British puritans and Philistines. In October 1915 Pearson wrote to Harris in terms which in after years would have made him blush a deep shade of purple: 'You seem to be gifted with something very like divine insight. Pray God you will some day be acknowledged for what you are. No one so human, no one so soulful, no intellect so noble and rare and beautiful, has been given to this country. Your whole personality, embracing as it does an unmatched loving kindness and complete understanding is beyond compare and to consummate everything you have been given the crown of thorns.'

Pearson, while not agreeing with Harris's views about the good intentions of Germany, remained his only faithful English friend and, risking the wrath of his military superiors, to whom Harris was a dangerous traitor, continued to correspond with

him during the war. Harris for his part poured out his woes:
'It is a harsh unfriendly climate for the soul – this one of New
York – and I have no roots here. I put out little tendrils now
and then, but they all get nipped.' He became an advertising
agent for the Chesapeake and Ohio Railway. Then in April
1916 he wrote to Pearson: 'I'm about to work desperately, for
I've given up being an advertising agent. Though the pay was
good, it brought me no nearer the mark of my high calling,
so I had to chuck it. Now I've got a small interest in some
Unpuncturable Pneumatic Tyres. If it comes off I'll make a
"pile". If it doesn't, I must just hugger-mugger along, keeping
eyes and ears and heart open for another chance.' As usual,
Harris was after a paper and at last in the summer of 1916 he
acquired one called, curiously enough, *Pearson's*, a literary
monthly which he proceeded to fill with the mixture as before.
For a time he perked up and felt able to tell Pearson the
following March: 'I've stopped the big leaks and the ship is
seaworthy. A last effort and I shall probably get the last few
years of my life free from money troubles and a chance to
write four or five terrible and beautiful volumes of autobiography, truer and more joyful than anything yet conceived.'

In the meantime he had completed in 1915 his life of *Oscar
Wilde*, a mixture of fact and fantasy, part plagiarised and part
original. Pearson was given the thankless task of trying to get
the book publicised in England. Harris sent him some copies
with instructions to solicit the opinion of a number of leading
writers. As both the author and his subject were in disgrace as
far as the British public were concerned, the response was, not
surprisingly, poor. Kipling said he disliked not only Harris but
Wilde. Arnold Bennett refused to discuss the book. H. G. Wells
said, with some justification, that Harris was a liar. Only
Bernard Shaw was helpful.

Still, nothing could dent Pearson's admiration and when he
published his first book, *Modern Men and Mummers* in 1921, he
included in it a glowing account of Harris, calling him 'the
most dynamic writer alive'. 'To Harris,' Pearson wrote, 'belongs the honour of transferring tense spiritual emotions to the
written page. His appeal is to the men and women who have
lived, not drifted through life.'

To the connoisseur of Harris, which Hugh Kingsmill now was, Pearson's profile was a delight. Since leaving Harris's employment in 1913 Kingsmill had, while a prisoner of war, written his first novel *The Will to Love*. The book contained a brilliant picture of Harris in the character of Ralph Parker. The story is that of a young public schoolmaster's daughter, with the body of Enid Bagnold and the soul of Hugh Kingsmill, a would-be writer, who falls under Harris's spell, and submits to his advances, losing her virginity in the process. Harris/Parker then blackmails her father for £2,500 to keep the affair quiet. The plot, like that of all Kingsmill's novels, is thin and at times unconvincing, but the portrait of Harris and the ambivalent feelings he evoked in others stands out:

> Those who had once loved him could save little from the wreck of their illusions. All seemed pretence: his work a prospectus advertising the non-existent riches of his nature, his friendship a craving for an audience, his love, lust in fancy dress. Yet, at least for a few, the conviction remained that mere vanity, however abnormal, cannot be the only incentive to produce great work. Somewhere, they felt, in the ruins of his nature, crushed but not extinct, something genuine and noble struggled to express itself. Memory recalled moments of eager enthusiasm, when his eyes shone with young unspoilt emotion, and other moments when the tragedy of his life pressed too heavily on him for bravado, and the simplicity of his speech seemed the prelude of a sudden realisation how far he had wandered from the way in which his genius should have travelled.

Kingsmill's portrait of Harris as a lascivious old roué forced Pearson rapidly to revise his view. After reading the copy of the novel which Kingsmill had given him on their first meeting he wrote a fortnight later, 'As a portrait of Frank, Parker is brutal but it's damned well done and probably true into the bargain.'

Kingsmill of course saw Harris in the last resort as a great comic figure, and once one saw this, everything fell into place. What could one do but laugh when Harris wrote solemnly to Pearson from his new and last home in Nice: 'Desire faileth and the voice of the grasshopper is loud in the land'?

Pearson began to look with new eyes on the man for whom he was running errands – sending him out buckskin braces and bundles of Old Etonian ties. Ironically the fulsome praise of Harris in *Modern Men and Mummers* backfired. At one of his lectures Harris was asked by an angry American why he had described New York as 'an old whore'. Harris denied having done so, whereupon the patriot read out a letter from Harris, quoted by Pearson in his book, which contained the offending phrase. A dozen people left the lecture hall in protest and Harris was furious. He wrote angrily to Pearson and Pearson replied in similar vein.

A lady was sent round to take the remaining copies of *Wilde* off Pearson's hands. 'Frank has now completely washed his hands of me and I have scrubbed mine of him,' he told Kingsmill. 'I had the last word and it was such a snorter that I expected a wire from Nellie at any moment saying that Frank had fallen in the Mediterranean.' Pearson now conceived a new plan: Kingsmill must write Harris's biography and he, Pearson, would assist in collecting the material. He made his peace with Harris and began to write to him again, though not in the same adulatory vein. Meanwhile, it was important that Harris should not get wind of the project. He had a nasty habit of revenging himself on his detractors by including in his writings fictitious and unflattering anecdotes about their sex-lives. 'If Frankie hears of my pious care for his fame,' Kingsmill wrote, 'I fancy I shall secure a footnote in the Life – a Vignette perhaps representing me as caught by Frankie in the act of trying to cure myself of the pox by intercourse with a goat, an antique cure – and how Frankie's attempt to win me to a more Christian frame of mind was rewarded with ill-conditioned abuse.'

Shortly afterwards copies of the first volume of Harris's

pornographic memoirs began to circulate. Kingsmill, working
for his father in Switzerland, couldn't wait to read one. 'I
would love to see his autobiography,' he wrote. 'Do give me
some idea of it. Surely it is not mere obscenity? Is it a catalogue
of all his affairs? Does he chant Swinburne while some flurried
damsel stammers "Not there! *There!*" '

Not even Kingsmill could have anticipated the nature of the
memoirs when they at last appeared. He was already familiar
with the semi-fictional accounts of Harris's meetings with great
men, of the type that had been collected in *Contemporary
Portraits*. Now, interspersed with these, were detailed descrip-
tions of his sexual experiences. 'They are chiefly remarkable,'
Kingsmill wrote later, 'for their mixture of obscenity – the
excitement of an old man trying to revive dead emotions – and
attempts at romanticism with sudden lapses into brutality'.
Nor was there any merit in the narrative technique. Kingsmill's
first reaction on reading the book was to lament to Pearson:
'I wish there was a little more perspective in his memories, not
quite so much of this fore-shortening effect. This sort of thing –

> I made some excuse to get her out of the room. The passage
> was empty. 'What is your name?' I gasped, stopping and
> touching her ankle.
> 'Miss Jakes,' she replied, drawing her foot away.
> 'Don't,' I cried. 'Don't draw it away! Your ankle is
> perfect – slender.' Before she could divine my intention, I
> had run my hand up her calf and touched warm flesh.
> 'How supple-soft!' I cried. 'Let me!' and I thrust my hand
> right up.
> 'Oh, how I reverence you,' I exclaimed gently stroking
> the slit. 'You are perfect woman, now at last I have found
> you . . .' etc., etc.

To my mind, this kind of narrative style would be all the better
for a dash of Henry James. For instance, the first sentence, "I
made some excuse to get her out of the room," might be given
in three Jamesian pages, after which the rest of the idyll in
Frankie's style would come as a pleasant change.'

When the second volume appeared in 1926 Kingsmill wrote
to Pearson: 'I was lent the second volume of Harris's *Life* in
Paris and am writing you my impressions of it. . . . In the first

place Harris has weakened in his ambition to purify mankind by incessant reiteration of the word "cunt". I imagine that he is being discouraged by the poor sales of the first volume and thinks if he uses the delicate synonym "sex" he will conciliate a larger circle, though of course his natural taste lies in the direction of small circles. In his introduction to the second volume he writes: "The inspiration of this second volume is the realisation of the virtue of chastity." However, he qualifies this with the admission, "I found out that chastity must not be continued too long". The first two chapters are devoted to student life. There is nothing much of interest in them, until he catches a severe dose of what he calls circumcision. I remember his telling me that he retired to Fluelen at the end of Lake Lucerne in order to recover from circumcision in four letters, but it doesn't suit his romantic spirit to put things so plainly in his autobiography. He therefore explains with much unconvincing detail the reasons which led to his being circumcised in his early twenties. The story serves the double purpose of accounting for the great pain he felt when endeavouring to undo a virgin and of demonstrating that he was not born a Jew.

'After leaving Germany he went to Athens. By this time he was recovered from his circumcision and at once put into practice his theory that chastity must not be continued too long: from Athens he went to Vienna and Ireland, all the time no doubt realising the virtue of chastity but not to any marked extent. He then takes us to London, and tells how he got the editorship of the *Evening News*. All this is quite interesting, but there is no attempt to admit to any methods that are not extremely gentlemanly. We then come to what he calls his first love, the heroine is Laura Clapton, and during the first year of his friendship with her, she had an affair with another man. Harris suspected this, and on the occasion of his first embrace with her the suspicion clouded his ecstasy. His actual words are: "When I returned I had only pyjamas on and as I went hastily to the bed I was conscious of absolute reverence: if only the dreadful doubt had not been there, it would have been adoration."

'We then have two pages to show what reverence can do. At the end Laura says to him, "We were one, weren't we?" Of course one doesn't know what she expected in the way of unification. Harris had certainly done what was humanly possible in that line.

'The best thing in the book is an account of the gluttony of the City Aldermen, but even here Harris has to romanticise himself. He went to dinner with a Sir William Marriott, and begins by saying Lady Marriott was a washed out prim little lady. However, the epic note is quickly struck. The villain is Sir Robert Fowler, Lord Mayor of London: the hero Harris; the heroine Lady Marriott. Harris has just taken a spoonful of clear soup, when his nostrils are assailed by a pungent odour. Presently farts are crackling all round the room. "I stole a glance at Lady Marriott: she was as white as a ghost, and her first helping of meat was still untouched. The quiet little lady had avoided my eyes and had made up her mind to endure to the end"; the barrage continues, another unmistakeable explosion – "and I could not but again look at my hostess; she was as pale as death and this time her eyes met mine in despairing appeal." "I am not very well," she said in a low tone, "I don't think I can see it through!" The scene ends with Perseus, hurrying a half swooning Andromeda out of earshot of the farting dragons . . .'

A few days later Kingsmill wrote again to Pearson:

'I think I ought to make some supplementary remarks about Volume II. . . .

'The sketch of Maupassant is really quite well done. Very characteristically, Harris, in the company of so potent a sexual performer, takes the line, when talking to Maupassant, that the pleasures of sense are ephemeral, and that the really great spirit cares for nothing but the immortality of literary fame. All the same, he shows a real appreciation of Maupassant's amorous frenzy and real sympathy with his madness. I think you will like the apostrophe with which he ends his story. I quote imperfectly from memory.

' "Ah Guy, dear, dear Guy, swallowed up in the vast womb of uncreated void." The imagery is very significant. It seems to imply that Maupassant had for once gone a little too far, and had been unable to find his way back. Harris does not tell us whether, with Maupassant's fate as a warning, he, in his future encounters, connected his left ankle to a bed post by a stout rope. . .'

'I started this letter with the full determination to say something really appreciative about the old ruffian, but as soon as one considers anything he writes at all closely, the fact that it is simply an advertisement for Frank Harris is so glaring, that it is very difficult to see such merits as it possesses. All the same there is one really well written page, on the melancholy mania of Chatham at the end of his life. There is also a certain amount of genuine emotion in Harris's account of Browning's funeral. Even here, however, he cannot refrain from picking out for special appreciation the great line –

He was ordained to call and I to come!

'In view of what he has just told us about Laura Clapton, and is about to tell us about a French courtesan, this quotation is rather overweighted with explanatory context. . . .

'I quite forgot the best touch of all in his account of his first embrace with Laura Clapton. He has just raised her night dress and continues, "Though a lover of plastic beauty, I could not at that moment spare more than a glance for her perfections. Separating her legs . . ." etc.

'It is typical of him to guard against the most unlikely criticisms while exposing himself to the most obvious. That, "though a lover of plastic beauty" is put in lest Edmund Gosse or Professor Mackail, reviewing the book should write, "We confess that we are a little dubious about the sense for plastic beauty with which Mr Harris credits himself. Take for instance the occasion on which he raises Miss Laura Clapton's night dress for the first time. We are disposed to question whether a genuine amateur of plastic beauty would have torn himself quite so speedily from the loving appraisement of a figure which if we are to believe Mr Harris . . . etc." '

Pearson continued to urge Kingsmill to embark on his Harris book. But Kingsmill always insisted that they would have to wait till Harris died before it could be published: 'Why doesn't Frankie pull down the curtain with his own hands and let me get to work,' he asked impatiently in 1923. 'The great difficulty will be not to be carried away by mirth. I want to pick out what is really good in the old boy's work and character – perhaps I might devote an appendix, two pages in large print to this part of my subject.' Pearson must have been insistent, for a week later Kingsmill was writing again: 'I'm taking the idea very seriously, but I can't be rushed . . . this is a big task. . . . Gestation must not be precipitated. . . . In fact I really am taking it seriously, old boy.'

'I wish to God you would get busy, old bean,' Pearson reiterated. 'Can't you have a month's holiday some time and settle down to the "bloody business"? I hope you are *collecting* data not mislaying it' – it was particularly important that the book should include the story of how Harris had written to Pearson from Nice asking him to send out six Old Etonian ties.

The world suddenly renewed its interest in Harris when in 1926 he was summoned before the magistrates in Nice and threatened with prosecution for publishing obscenity. This, he was convinced, was done at the instigation of the Foreign Office. Pearson sent Kingsmill a newspaper cutting about the case and he replied: 'I'm sorry for the poor old boy, as I would be for someone I surprised biting his way through a brick wall instead of going through the gate.' But he could not resist writing to Harris with advice on how he should conduct his defence; he should ask why Rabelais was allowed to circulate freely, while he was menaced with prosecution. Pearson however questioned the logic of this. 'Your Rabelaisian analogy is not quite sound. He dealt with fictitious characters. After all the ordinary objection to F.H.'s autobiography is that it deals too openly with living or actual people. One might say: "Gargantua's farts were elemental, and their stink was prodigious, a combination of excrement, armpits and unwashed feet." But if you substitute King Edward VII for Gargantua, your remarks are (as Asquith would say) liable to be misinterpreted as personal. Please do not think that I am over squeamish in the matter of reminiscential candour: I am simply looking at it from the point of view of King George V.'

Meanwhile a lady called Florence Smith had written agitatedly to Pearson asking what could be done to help Harris: 'I am deadly frightened about this trial business. If only one could smuggle him out of Nice.' Kingsmill, to whom Pearson forwarded the letter, observed: 'Florence Smith is developing into something really rather big. The idea of "smuggling him out of Nice" till the agitation has died down lifts her out of the ranks of the minor grotesques. I wonder how she visualises the law – apparently as a temperamental woman of uncertain age subject to outbreaks of fussy malice, but with little real staying power. And I should like her mental image of F.H. being smuggled out of Nice. Florence Smith in an enormous crinoline walking with stiff circumspection along the Promenade des Anglais – with F.H. under the crinoline trying not to disconcert his accomplice by following the sweet way of love according to routine.'

Eventually some distinguished French writers intervened on Harris's behalf and the prosecution was dropped. Harris was now over seventy. He was a man of great stamina and clung to life obstinately, refuting the rumours of his impending death. In March 1929 Kingsmill wrote to Pearson: 'By the way, my publisher writes to me that Frankie is dying. Do you know this? You might ring him up for information. A vein of tenderness was touched by the news, but one feels that the old boy has had a good run for everyone else's money, and old age is depressing him, and he would be better in his last and for the first time ótherwise untenanted bed. The world will go greyer for me, of course, but, as with Frankie, on the numerous occasions on which the death of some well known personage greyed the world, the effect will be very momentary.'

In fact it was to be over two years before Harris died on August 26, 1931. 'I miss him,' Pearson wrote when he heard the news, 'I mean his *being* – our laughter can never again have quite the old ring . . . I will not go so far as to echo Harris on Wilde: "The world went grey to me when Oscar died" but I did definitely feel that a bit of colour had left the universe and that we wouldn't be likely to spot that particular tint again.'

A biography of Harris, published the previous year, had included his only surviving poem:

> Here I lie dead at last at rest
> With a crucifix upon my breast
> And candles burning at head and feet,
> And I cannot see the flowers so sweet,
> And I cannot smell and I cannot weep
> And I cannot wake and I cannot sleep
> For I who laughed and loved am dead
> And laid out on my cold white bed
> With my jaw tied up lest it give offence
> And my eyelids closed with a couple of pence.

'All that trouble for twopence,' said Kingsmill.

In later life Pearson dismissed his enthusiasm for Frank Harris as the kind of folly of which any young man might be capable. It must be remembered however that Pearson was thirty-six when *Modern Men and Mummers* was published. The fact was that until he met Kingsmill, Pearson had no overall view of literature, no coherent philosophy by which to judge a figure like Harris. He was also at this period under the influence of Bernard Shaw, many of whose opinions, often idiotic, he adopted without question. When in 1916, Pearson dispatched the copies of Harris's life of Wilde to all the great literary men in England Shaw was the only one to respond. He invited Pearson round for a chat and in the course of the conversation did nothing to disillusion Pearson about Harris apart from making him realise that if there was anyone even greater than Harris it was Shaw.

Pearson proceeded to read all Shaw's plays and reached the conclusion that Shaw was possibly even more of a genius than he professed himself to be. 'For a time,' he admitted later, 'GBS even made me think he had a finer mind than Shakespeare's.' *Caesar and Cleopatra* in particular was a masterpiece 'the first and only time in English literature where a great statesman and a man is painted to the life'.

He was in this frame of mind when he first met Kingsmill. Kingsmill was not prepared to accept this view and wrote telling him why. Pearson replied, in the first surviving letter of their correspondence: 'Your criticism of Caesar is the only intelligent one I've ever heard or read. More than that. There isn't a professional critic in these islands, literary or dramatic, who could put the case against Shaw half as well as you have done. . . .' But, even so, Kingsmill was in error: 'You assert that neither irony nor poetry can ripen fully in a man preoccupied by action. This is grotesque. Next to Swift the most ironical person ever born in these islands was Wellington. As for poetry I could give you a dozen examples, ranging from the Greeks to Garibaldi, but will content myself with Napoleon, whose letters and speeches glow with real soul – stuff (forgive the Frankism) of poetry.' Shaw, he went on, 'the biggest clearest mind that ever graced this modern world of ours is now (as the prayer books say) "here on earth". The fact that he is not obsessed with sex helps his clarity. Passion of that kind clouds the mind, however richly it colours the experience and the purely creative faculty. . . . There is nothing in the language (the four gospels not excepted) that breathes so rare a spirit as Caesar's speech beginning "If one man in all the world . . ."

'I really must dry up. We'll never convince one another. It's a question of temperament I suppose. To feel or not to feel . . . I regard Shaw, who has put more of himself into Caesar than any other of his characters as *the* super-product of the universe *qua* man, and his *best* work the most useful matter extant.

'Let us meet again and often by all means: but I don't think we'd better discuss *Caesar and Cleopatra.*'

To Kingsmill these views were anathema. To begin with, he cordially disliked Bernard Shaw. 'No one,' he said once, 'has ever had so fine a sense of how near the stake a man may comfortably go in support of his opinions'. Shaw was a Utopian, or what he called a Dawnist, a Quixote looking for the kingdom of Heaven outside himself. Something in Shaw's nature, the element of charlatanism perhaps or his keenly developed materialist streak, jarred on Kingsmill and he found it always difficult to acknowledge Shaw's finer points. What Pearson, following Shaw, affirmed, namely that poetry and politics could in some way be reconciled was directly opposed to Kingsmill's philosophy. For him, the artist and the man of action were two quite separate people. At the heart of all Kingsmill's writings, though never explicitly defined, is the idea of conflict in man between the Will and the Imagination. The will is exercised in the life of action and the pursuit of power; the imagination in poetry, art, religion, humour and mysticism. The will draws a man towards the collective, the imagination towards himself. The pursuit of power was barren, the life of the man of action – Napoleon or Caesar – boring. It was an illusion that an eventful life was necessarily interesting.

Another of Kingsmill's most considered opinions emerged in their early exchanges about Harris. Talking with Kingsmill, Pearson soon acknowledged that Harris was at best a lovable rogue, lecherous, deceitful and a bit crazy. But did that prevent him from being a genius? Could you not consider his life and work separately? 'When you judge Frank as a literary artist,' he pleaded, 'please do your best to forget that he's a marvellous comic "turn".' Kingsmill would have replied that such a feat was impossible. To many it was, and still is, an attractive proposition that an artist can live a Jekyll and Hyde existence. Lytton Strachey for example, another of Pearson's heroes at this time, derived comfort from the example of Boswell: 'It would be difficult,' he wrote, 'to find a more shattering refutation of the lessons of cheap morality than the life of James Boswell. One of the most extraordinary successes in the history of civilisation was achieved by an idler, a lecher, a drunkard and a snob.' (Strachey conveniently ignored the important part played by Johnson in the enterprise.) Quite apart from its other attractions, a clear dichotomy between Life and Work makes the task of the critic or the biographer less arduous. Kingsmill, however, always insisted on the impossibility of maintaining a distinction of this kind, or of treating the imaginative faculty as 'a kind of conjuring trick blessedly unrelated to human experience'.

'To dismiss the poet,' he once said, 'and concern oneself only with the poetry has a specious air of dignity and superiority to personal gossip. But in practice this separation of poetry from the poet obscures the most important truth about literature, that no man can put more virtue into his words than he practises in his life.'

This was an uncomfortable truth that Pearson found it difficult to swallow. By temperament he was in sympathy with the Strachey view. Thus when Somerset Maugham in *Don Fernando* expressed the opinion that Cervantes had at one stage in his life lived happily off the immoral earnings of his female relatives, Pearson readily accepted his conclusions. But Kingsmill could not agree. 'To me,' he said, 'Cervantes and the *maquereau* type are exactly antithetical, and I may say that no efficient *maquereau* would thank Maugham for disparaging his profession by asserting that a feckless futile person like Cervantes had the qualifications necessary for the job. If Maugham had hazarded the guess that, having constituted himself guardian of *all* his female relatives, he occasionally thought it unnecessary to ask a sister or female cousin exactly how it came about that she was able to contribute quite such a sizeable sum to the household budget, I should not object, though I should not agree. But Maugham makes it clear that he thinks Cervantes approved and was mildly tickled by his daughter going to bed with all and sundry for his benefit. Now if Cervantes had been that kind of person, nothing is more certain than that he would have been, given his capacity for putting words together (1) a wealthy author, (2) a sentimental high flown author, (3) an author with the barest minimum of humour. If Maugham had set out to prove that the most popular playwright of Spain, Lope de Vega, who loathed Cervantes but could find nothing worse to say about him than that he was poor, was a pimp, I would have taken his word for it without asking for any evidence.'

Pearson found all this hard to take. Nor would he, to begin with, accept Kingsmill's view of Harris: 'I simply can't agree with you about Harris's "work",' he wrote. 'I really do think his "life of Wilde" unique. If you know anything better, anything as good in its line, please don't keep the secret to yourself. I think *The Bomb* is amazingly well done, and *Sonia* is to me incomparable – I haven't time to explain why. As to his critical work, his Shakespeare, it is enough that he influenced the whole trend of modern criticism.'

Kingsmill was taken aback by the surprising vehemence with which Pearson reacted to his suggestions, and found himself to his alarm trying to match it. 'The great thing is not to arouse my combativeness,' he counselled, 'as that will distort my judgement. I value your criticisms very much and you have already done me good, but I suggest (*b*) not (*a*) as the right method:

'e.g. (*a*) My God, Lunn, your puke about Shaw's Androcles makes me sick. Shaw as a religious teacher wipes the floor with your flat bottomed Buddhas, Assisis, and the rest of the addled goat-bearded rabbit-toothed bunch of mouldy rag-pickers whom for some inexplicable reason you are pleased to favour with your cock eyed approval.

'(*b*) I don't quite agree with your careful but in my opinion not quite complete estimate of Shaw as a religious teacher. It seems to me that you have, I won't say missed, but not altogether seized the full force of the second paragraph on p. 8702 of Shaw's introduction to that, in my view, supreme play "That remains to be Seen", etc.'

Kingsmill attributed Pearson's fierce partisanship to misplaced religious zeal: 'Your hatred of Christianity is a proof that your religious sense is still active, and you pour it into your literary affections. Now my great objection to the religious sense is that it tries to simplify life, thus impoverishing it.

"Thou, O Christ, art all I want"

'This is an obvious lie, for if it were true he wouldn't feel the necessity for proclaiming it. It should run: "Thou, O Christ, art all I want to want" and in that form is a weak and foolish sentiment.

'My view of literature is that a man appreciates what he can, and should keep his appreciation supple by not conceiving fanatical hates and loves, and also by not straining it where it doesn't arise naturally. Writers who don't appeal to me I don't bother about but I don't mind my friends liking them. . . .'

In his early exchanges with Kingsmill, Pearson reminds one of a horse being broken in. His nature was combative and he resented the air of conviction with which Kingsmill expressed himself. He was slowly being compelled to reconsider a number of his most cherished beliefs. His idols, Shaw and Harris, were tottering on their pedestals, and all because of an unknown and unsuccessful novelist. The fact that Pearson did in the end come round to Kingsmill's overall view is tribute enough to the influence which Kingsmill was able to exercise over him. This was in no sense a malign or dominating influence and looking back at his development Pearson was to a great extent unaware of the role Kingsmill had played in it. Like a good teacher, Kingsmill unobtrusively put him on the right track and although it was to be some years before Pearson found his vocation writing biographies it was largely thanks to Kingsmill that he did so.

In the meantime he had no clear idea what he wanted to do. He continued to act and to write for *John Bull*. In 1923 he wrote a book of sketches and stories based on his army experiences which was eventually published in 1928 under the title *Iron Rations*. Three years later he first mentioned to Kingsmill the possibility of writing biography, wavering between Oscar Wilde and Cecil Rhodes as possible subjects.

In his early biographical sketches Pearson was not only

influenced by Harris but also by Lytton Strachey, and allowed his fancy a free rein. Following Shaw and Strachey, he concluded that a biographer was a creative artist. 'No artist worth his salt,' he wrote at this time, 'is concerned with accuracy in detail if it doesn't suit his purpose. . . . In order to achieve essential truth one often has to sacrifice the essential facts.' As a demonstration of this kind of creative biography, intended as an answer to critics of his first book who had dismissed him as a mere reporter, Pearson wrote for the *Adelphi* magazine in 1923 an entirely imaginary account of a conversation which he claimed to have overheard between Bernard Shaw and G. K. Chesterton:

GBS: Have you any adequate excuse to make us for not being drunk?

GKC: I am desperately drunk. There is only one form of drunkenness that I acknowledge – the drunkenness of sobriety. As a consequence of not having tasted a drop of wine or ale today, I am suffering from *delirium tremens*.

GBS: In that case perhaps you will please tell us why you are sober?

GKC: That, I fear, is quite impossible. I can explain nothing when I am sober. Sobriety clouds the mind; drink clears it. I would explain anything, at any length, under the calm, clarifying influence of drink . . .

and so on.

This conversation was widely quoted at the time as if it was authentic. It appeared in a number of American journals and was reprinted in full in the leading Polish paper. It has since been published in *The Book of Great Conversations* by Louis Biancolli (New York, 1948) and was recently treated as a prime source in a scholarly work *Shaw and Chesterton: The Metaphysical Jesters* by William B. Furlong (Pennsylvania State University Press, 1970).

A second attempt by Pearson in this vein landed him in serious trouble. In 1925, for reasons which he afterwards found hard to define, he wrote a book entitled *The Whispering Gallery: Leaves from A Diplomat's Diary*. The book purported to be the memoirs of a British diplomat who had in the course of his career encountered almost all the great men of his day including Kitchener, Cecil Rhodes, Edward VII, Tsar Nicholas II, the Kaiser, Lenin, Mussolini, H. G. Wells, Bernard Shaw, Lloyd George, Asquith, Churchill, etc. This 'diplomat' had been privy to an extraordinary amount of top-secret discussions. He was present when Edward VII and his nephew Kaiser Wilhelm reviewed the balance of power; he had been at Downing Street during a debate between Asquith and Lloyd George about the conduct of the war. The Emperor Franz Joseph had told him dirty stories – 'His own affection for this species of entertainment was made audible at times by a number of sounds that reminded me of nothing so much as the distant whinnying of a horse.' The 'diplomat' had moved in literary circles too. He had bumped into Bernard Shaw once or twice, lunched with Henry James, and weekended with Thomas Hardy who told him: 'Fate stalks us with depressing monotony from womb to tomb, and, when we are least expecting it, deals us a series of crushing blows from behind. Though the rays of intermittent happiness are permitted to play upon us for our greater undoing, we are marked down for miserable ends.'

Pearson had for some time now been writing weekly profiles of prominent men and women in *John Bull* and he was therefore supplied with enough authentic material to make the book seem plausible to the casual reader. At the same time the publishers, John Lane The Bodley Head Ltd, were quick to see the commercial advantages of creating a stir by issuing the book anonymously and stoutly maintaining that it was a genuine memoir. Before doing so however they prudently resolved to protect themselves from the risk of any legal proceedings by making it part of their agreement that Pearson should divulge the name of the 'diplomat' to a director of the firm, on condition that it would not be disclosed. Accordingly Pearson, who was in Sussex at the time, arranged to meet a representative of John Lane in a hotel in Arundel. The man sent was Allen Lane (later Sir Allen), then twenty-four. Assuming that giving the author's name was just a formality Pearson with tongue in cheek named Sir Rennell Rodd, a former ambassador to Rome, now, at the age of sixty-eight, living in retirement. Sir Rennell (Haileybury and Oxford) was a cultured, rather pompous diplomat, who had in his youth embarked on a literary career and been a friend of Oscar Wilde, subsequently publishing a number of 'slim volumes' of poems. A man less likely to have written *The Whispering Gallery* it would have been hard to find.

Review copies were sent out in November 1926 with accompanying slips stating that *The Whispering Gallery* was in the publisher's view 'one of the most talked-of books of the season'. Lane's added: 'We can vouch for the authenticity of the volume as we know the diarist personally.'

Neither Lane nor Pearson could have reckoned with what followed. The *Daily Mail* of November 19 headlined dramatically:

A SCANDALOUS FAKE EXPOSED

—

MONSTROUS ATTACKS ON PUBLIC MEN

—

BOOK BY 'A DIPLOMAT'

—

REPUDIATIONS BY FIVE CABINET MINISTERS

There followed a lengthy denunciation of *The Whispering Gallery*: 'Reckless and impudent invention, distorting the personal reputations of British Public Men, reaches its climax in a book offered to the public today.

'The anonymous author claims in his preface to be a well-known diplomat of thirty years standing. The vulgarities of his style and matter would alone throw doubt on his membership of that distinguished service.'

In view of the fact that *The Whispering Gallery* not only slandered the dead but imputed 'conscienceless egotism and disgraceful levity to the British statesmen who held high office during the war,' the *Daily Mail* felt compelled to expose the numerous errors of fact which were proof that the book was a fake, e.g. the Kaiser's visit to London in 1907 was not his last; 'Bosphorus' was spelt 'Bosphorous', 'General Townshend' 'Townsend', etc. Not only was the author inaccurate, he was illiterate: 'He has not learnt even the elements of his own language', for he repeatedly misuses the auxiliaries 'will' and 'would', making Mr Joseph Chamberlain, for example, say 'I wouldn't be where I am if I had been a gentleman'. The *Daily Mail* commented: 'Those who know Mr Chamberlain and

have documents written by him in their possession know that
he spoke and wrote the King's English.'

It is unlikely however that the *Daily Mail* devoted so much
space to denouncing the book solely in order to defend Mr
Chamberlain's mastery of syntax. Pearson's opening chapter
entitled 'The Napoleon of Fleet Street' had consisted of an
account of how the late Lord Northcliffe, proprietor of the
Daily Mail, had tried, unsuccessfully, to hire the 'diplomat' as a
supplier of first-hand information from the chancelleries.
Northcliffe was portrayed as an emotional man subject to
violent changes of mood. The 'diplomat' described his behaviour when the two men met in Northcliffe's home:

> Suddenly I noticed that he began to get very fidgety. He left
> his armchair and paced several times up and down the room,
> throwing scraps of conversation at me as he did so in a
> nervous staccato way that made me feel quite uncomfortable:
> 'I can't get anything new nowadays. . . . Not one of my
> people has an ounce of imagination. . . . Damned fools! . . .
> Damned fools! . . . I've digested all the novelty possible in
> the newspaper world. . . . And spewed it out. . . . Nothing
> left to spew. . . . Idiots. . . . Not an ounce of brains between
> the lot of 'em. . . . Bloody fatheads! . . . What?'
>
> The 'diplomat' was quite taken aback: 'He shouted the
> last word at me with such force that I nearly ruined an
> admirable cigar by biting off half an inch.'

Northcliffe became more and more emotional, 'stamping the
floor, pounding on the various articles of furniture' and behaving like a lunatic, which, of course, he had been during the last
years of his life. It was an innuendo which would not have
endeared the 'diplomat' to Northcliffe's brother Lord Rothermere who had succeeded him as proprietor of the *Daily Mail*.
There was perhaps another reason why the *Mail* should have
reacted so strongly against *The Whispering Gallery*. The book
contained a comparatively sympathetic portrait of Lenin, and
a ferocious attack on Tzar Nicholas II. The latter in the
'diplomat's' view was 'an ill-meaning skunk . . . a cad, a
coward, a butcher and a blackguard' who had once ordered a
dissident student to be brought before him and 'thrashed with
a whip until he fainted'. All this came at a time when the *Daily*

Mail was running a hysterical anti-Communist campaign. Reds were discerned under every bed. It was not therefore altogether surprising that the *Mail* in its attack should give voice to the suspicion that the book might be 'a piece of insidious Bolshevist propaganda'.

The various living statesmen mentioned were quick to confirm the *Daily Mail*'s doubts about the book's *bona fides*. Lord Robert Cecil was quoted as saying: 'At no time in my life has Lord Balfour ever called me "Robert", nor have I ever smoked a cigar.' Winston Churchill called the 'diplomat's' account of his conversations with his colleagues 'puerile in their ignorance'. And Asquith stated 'I have never in my life called Mr Lloyd George "David" nor did he ever address me as "Asquith".' Pearson had told a story of how the proprietor of the *News of the World*, Lord Riddell, had as a young man pawned his waistcoat to buy a book for ninepence which he later sold to a collector for £100. Lord Riddell denied this, whilst admitting that he had once profited from the sale of some books: 'It is untrue that I sold my waistcoat to make the purchase,' he said. 'I have never pawned anything up to date.'

Naturally the publishers were delighted by publicity on this scale. The book was a sell out and orders poured in. As for the *Mail*'s criticisms, the publishers were unrepentant. 'The book seems to us to ring true,' they said. 'We still believe it is a perfectly genuine book. . . . There is no question of it being withdrawn. We should never have published it if we had intended to withdraw it.'

As a result of this statement, the *Daily Mail* now turned its guns away from the pseudo-diplomat and on to John Lane. In a leader headed, 'A Disreputable Publisher' the *Mail* reminded the public that only the day before it had shown conclusively, with the help of five cabinet ministers, that the book was a fake. 'After this,' stated the leader, 'it is amazing to find that the directors of the publishing firm . . . uttered not a word of regret – not a word of apology for the outrage committed by them in producing this book. They do not appear to realise the nature of the outrage they have committed. John Lane The Bodley Head Ltd is an old established firm of publishers who have previously been regarded as upholding the best traditions of their trade. But by their action in this matter they have lent themselves to a fraud on the public and have debased the name of their firm. It remains to be seen whether reputable authors will be willing to have their works published by a firm which is capable of such disgraceful conduct . . .' Meanwhile the *Daily Mail* had given orders that any advertisements placed by John Lane would in future be rejected: 'It is a pity that there is no law by which publishers can be prosecuted criminally for producing this kind of garbage.'

Though Northcliffe, its founder, had been dead four years, the *Daily Mail* still had the highest circulation of any paper at that time and was considered by many to be a powerful voice. Northcliffe had used it successfully, so it seemed, to campaign against Asquith and promote Lloyd George during the war and it was the *Mail* which, by publishing the famous Zinoviev letter in 1924, was widely credited with having destroyed the Labour Party's chances in the election of that year.

Faced by certain financial loss from the cancellation of advertising, the publishers prudently back-tracked and announced that they would withdraw the book. But the following day, Sunday, the press campaign against them showed no sign of abating. The *Observer* took up the cudgels. A leader headed 'Ghouls and Garbage' by J. L. Garvin referred to the book's author as 'an imposter and a cad'; the publication, he said, was an 'unscrupulous farago'; the conversation reported between Cecil Rhodes and Joseph Chamberlain was 'a reeking compost of falsehood'; all in all there was 'a limit to this kind of publication'.

The Directors of John Lane were by now rattled. They decided that if anyone was going to carry the can it would have to be Hesketh Pearson. He was therefore summoned to a meeting of the board and asked, in the first instance, to explain himself. 'Had I been in possession of my wits,' he wrote later, 'I would have told them squarely that I had written the book, and that they could no more have believed it to be the work of a real diplomat than the work of a dinosaur.' Instead of which, partly with the confused notion of protecting young Allen Lane, who, it appears, may genuinely have believed that Sir Rennell Rodd had written the book, he maintained the pretence of the existence of a 'diplomat' whose representative he was. In so doing he put his head into the noose.

The publishers went down to the *Daily Mail* and denounced Hesketh Pearson as the villain of the piece. 'The typescript of *The Whispering Gallery*,' they confessed, 'came to us from Mr Hesketh Pearson. His introductions to us were satisfactory, and he appeared to be a reputable literary man, whose books had been issued by other well-known publishing firms.' Alas, too late, Messrs John Lane now acknowledged that they had been the victims of 'a most ingenious hoax' and offered their 'deep regrets and sincere apologies' for any offence or pain they might have caused by publication. In order to make certain that Pearson's goose was well and truly cooked Mr Allen Lane was dispatched to Sir Rennell Rodd, who, in a state of shock and bewilderment, denied any knowledge of Pearson or the book.

The next day all Hell was let loose on the wretched Pearson. Under the heading, 'A case for the Public Prosecutor' the *Daily Mail* thundered: 'The fact is that an impudent literary forger, having invented a book of scandalous "diplomatic memoirs", took it to Messrs John Lane and by the trick of naming Sir Rennell Rodd as the secret author, induced them to believe that the book was the genuine work of a famous and highly-respected diplomat . . . Messrs John Lane have been victims of one of the most impudent literary forgeries on record. The fact that the book was believed to be by Sir Rennell Rodd doubtlessly affected the judgement of the firm in deciding to issue it to the public. From the first exposure of this tissue of lies and slanders to the final and complete revelation of the frauds practised by its author, only four days have passed. The next step in the sordid affair lies with the public prosecutor.' Lord Birkenhead, the former Lord Chancellor, now joined the chorus baying for blood: 'The *Daily Mail*,' he said, 'has performed a real and lasting service to the community by exposing and compelling the withdrawal of the rubbishy collection of lying slander called *The Whispering Gallery*. Anyone familiar with newspapers will understand the considerable legal risks that the *Daily Mail* took by its attitude, and this makes me as a lawyer appreciate the *Daily Mail*'s action the more. The fate of *The Whispering Gallery* will I hope warn garbage manufacturers and their publishers that they cannot with impunity slander the dead and insult the living.'

(It is interesting to note that only a few years later Lord Birkenhead was himself in trouble over a book. *The World in 2030*, which bore his name, was exposed by Professor J. B. S. Haldane as a flagrant plagiarism of one of his own books.)

Sir Rennell Rodd added: 'It appears to me that there should be some action taken for the protection of the public in this matter. . . . Perhaps the unkindest cut of all is that the author of the memoirs is said to have used such abominable English.'

Encouraged by this self-righteous uproar, and no doubt anxious on their own behalf to avoid prosecution, John Lane decided to institute proceedings against Pearson. On November 25 he was arrested and charged with attempting to obtain money by false pretences. Pearson was released on bail of £1,000 and the case was set down for hearing at London Sessions.

In the days that followed every pressure was put on him to plead guilty. His family suggested he should sue for mitigation on the grounds of insanity caused by the head wound he sustained in the Mesopotamian campaign. Kingsmill, like many men who are hopeless at arranging their own affairs, was very sure of himself when it came to advising someone else. Not only did he accompany Pearson to his solicitor's office, where he strongly urged the merits of pleading guilty, he also wrote to Bernard Shaw enlisting his support. Shaw replied: 'Poor Hesketh (damn his folly!) has to choose between the heaviest sentence the court can give him and a lenient one.' Pearson should throw himself on the court's mercy; 'Difficult though it may be for anyone to believe a man could be such a fool when it's easier to think him a knave; yet he had never imagined that the thing would be taken so seriously. Note (this is most important) that he must avoid the slightest reflection on Lane's, and withdraw all suggestion that they were not really duped . . . if his confession is not consistently *handsome*, it will be thrown away.'

Forwarding Shaw's letter to Colonel 'Dane' Hamlett, Pearson's brother-in-law, who had nobly undertaken to mobilise his defence, Kingsmill wrote: 'I should very much like you to read Shaw's letter. Whatever one may think of him as a writer, no one disputes that he is extremely worldly wise.' Another advocate of surrender was Sir Henry Lunn. 'I have had another talk with my father,' Kingsmill reported, 'and he again reiterated his conviction that Hesketh must not fight, and the opinion of my father, who has built a big business up out of nothing and who has had to decide dozens of important matters every year involving a working knowledge of law, is of some weight. . . .'

But Pearson's blood was up. He resolutely refused to give way and Kingsmill resigned himself to the worst: 'I am afraid poor old HP will get it in the neck,' he told John Holms. 'He is fighting the case instead of caving in. I am very sorry for the poor old boy. . . . He will probably get six months.'

The campaign for capitulation reached its climax on the eve of the trial when Pearson and his brother-in-law met their senior counsel, Sir Patrick Hastings, in his chambers. Sir Patrick painted a gloomy picture of the probable outcome and advised Pearson very strongly to plead guilty. If he did so, he would most likely be bound over, but if he fought and lost he might be sent to prison.

Pearson however was adamant. 'Pat gravely warned me to go home and talk matters over with my wife,' he told Kingsmill after the case was over, 'who next to myself would suffer most if I went to prison. I answered that if the prospect was from three to six years I would still refuse to confess I had wronged a pack of cads, cowards and humbugs like the Lanes.

'Gladys, I am glad to say, did the Roman-wife touch and backed me up. So together we faced the probabilities of Pentonville. It was all done in the finest classical-heroic style and I haven't yet regained my natural plasticity. I shall not pretend for a moment I didn't piss myself pretty frequently during the process of being classical, but that does not affect the sculptural superbness of the pose.'

The case opened at the London Sessions the next day, January 26. 'Considerable interest was shown,' the *Daily Mail* reported. 'Nearly a score of magistrates were on the bench and the well of the court and the gallery were filled, many of the public being women.' Once instructed to fight, Sir Patrick Hastings went on to the attack: 'He gave a magnificent performance,' Pearson told Kingsmill, 'I should imagine one of the finest of his life.' The defence had got hold of some lubricious books, Ovid's *Loves*, Balzac's *Contes Drolatiques*, and the *Golden Ass* of Apuleius, which John Lane had printed in limited editions with erotic illustrations. These were produced in court with the aim of showing that Lane's were unscrupulous profiteers.

Such a line of attack acutely embarrassed Allen Lane and his chairman, B. W. Willett. In the witness box, Lane first denied that the Ovid was, in Sir Patrick's words, 'a really disgusting book,' but when asked to read out a passage declined to do so. 'I hope no one will read it in open court,' said the chairman Sir Robert Wallace, KC, 'but the jury must see it.'

Hastings piled it on. There was not a single picture in any of the books, he thundered, which the witness 'would allow a decent woman to look at', and one particular illustration in the *Golden Ass* was 'the foulest thing that any judge in any court has looked at'. The judge, Pearson told Kingsmill, 'had to look at the drawings through the fingers of the hand that covered his face in horror. The jury (not the ladies) inspected these pictures with a care that leads me to believe their interest in them was not wholly legal. However, their faces showed a becoming sense of repugnance. . . .' Another of Lane's books, described by Sir Patrick Hastings as 'a modern anonymous novel' purporting to be 'letters from a lady to the captain of a ship,' was now produced. 'Can you find a single page in that which is not utterly foul?' Sir Patrick demanded.

Under this barrage the publishers began to wilt and Pearson's contempt for them increased. Had he been in their shoes, he noted, he would have read out all the controversial passages 'and emphasized with a horrible distinction all the most outrageous words'. He would then have quoted some of the spicier parts of *Pericles* and *Henry IV*, and flung the Bible in as make-weight: 'But that is where real cads and cowards always show themselves in their true colours. They could prosecute me, they could try to send me to gaol, they could do their utmost to ruin me, my wife and my child, but they daren't look their own publications in the face. The dirty little rats! Willett went greyer and greyer as he stood in that box; he aged ten years in as many minutes; and he spent the remainder of the day with his head buried in his hands.'

Once in the witness box himself Pearson did the only thing possible and admitted everything. Why had he mentioned Sir

Rennell Rodd's name? – 'I think it was because I could not think of anyone less likely to have written the book' (*Laughter*). Why had he kept up the pretence once the book was exposed? – 'Because I was mad.' He agreed that after the attack on the book he got frightened and told a whole series of lies. Prosecuting counsel, Sir Henry Curtis-Bennett, was amazed at such candour: 'Do you realise what you are saying?'

Pearson told Kingsmill: 'I simply replied that he would save himself an awful lot of breath if, for the sake of convenience, I admitted to double the number of lies he was going to tax me with. That took his breath away so completely that he had no more left to say, and he sat down.' After an absence of twenty-three minutes the jury returned a verdict of not guilty. 'Pearson was then discharged,' the *Daily Mail* ruefully reported, 'and on leaving the court was warmly embraced by his wife, who had been present throughout the trial, and congratulated by a number of friends.' When he congratulated Sir Patrick Hastings the latter said, 'Nonsense! You got yourself off by your evidence in the witness box'.

In spite of his acquittal Pearson did not emerge unscathed. For some years afterwards he was regarded in literary circles with extreme wariness. But, whatever his difficulties, he would have been cheered to know that the case had a lasting and traumatic effect on Allen Lane. Lane, a forceful and ruthless business man, went on to become, as the founder of Penguin Books, by far the most successful publishing tycoon of his time. Even so, he was sufficiently daunted by his experience in the dock to be very reluctant in 1960 to appear as a defence witness for one of his most famous and profitable publications, *Lady Chatterley's Lover*. *The Whispering Gallery*, his biographer narrates, was still fresh in his memory: 'Years afterwards he shuddered at the ordeal, and when the *Lady Chatterley* case came to court he was manifestly ill at ease and, indeed, declined to face the fast bowling as an opening bat and went in much lower down.'

Chapter 5

Throughout the early years of their friendship Pearson kept urging Kingsmill to give up writing novels and devote his time to criticism and biography. Pearson had been greatly impressed by the depth and humour of Kingsmill's insights and also his ability to select and relate revealing anecdotes.

A favourite was the story which Kingsmill told him about Asquith and General Corrigan, the flamboyant Irishman who had helped organise a revolution in Mexico and subsequently became the Mexican Foreign Minister. Kingsmill met Corrigan on a train when the General was visiting England. Corrigan had been to see most of the important politicians of the day, and Kingsmill asked his opinion of Asquith. 'Ah went to lunch wid Asquit, Ah did,' said General Corrigan, 'and he said to me, "Yes, young mon, you think politics is an easy game, eh? Everything nice and simple, eh? But you've got a lot of difficulties ahead of you, young mon, you have – ah yes!" And he went on like that until Ah got bloddy wild, Ah did, and Ah said to him "Mr. Asquit," Ah said "all you need is a bonnet on yer head and a petticoat round yer legs, and you'd make a bloddy fine old woman, you would".'

Kingsmill asked what Asquith had replied. At which the General looked a little uncomfortable and eventually revealed: 'Asquit said "General Corrigan, that remark might be misinterpreted as rudeness".'

This riposte, Pearson felt, contained the essence of Asquith, and Kingsmill's account of the story, like all the stories he told about Harris, convinced Pearson that he was a natural biographer with an unerring eye for the revealing incident. But Kingsmill, encouraged by Holms and later by another friend, William Gerhardi, who insisted on his pre-eminence as a writer of fiction, continued to toy with novels and short stories.

Since the war he had written only *The Dawn's Delay* (1925), which consisted of three stories, including one called *W.J.* Pearson did not like it: 'Your story, which seems to me very clever (horrible word – let me substitute "brilliant"), does not, for me, supply a long felt want . . . nor does it create a craving, which I suppose is the other aspect of literature one loves. Your letters on the contrary, sharpen my desire to see you busy with biography and criticism . . . I am perfectly convinced that you have it in you to produce a world shattering biographical masterpiece.' All in good time, Kingsmill replied. He intended in due course to give the world several masterpieces, both fiction and biography, but meanwhile he told Pearson, 'Life is so exciting and interesting that I mean to enjoy it while I am here, and my enjoyment is all the stronger for the sense of a perfect world beyond our reach and knowledge, but not beyond our own occasional perception while we are here. I hope to arrive in it some day in some form or another, but while here I mean to be here.'

To his friend Alec Waugh, Kingsmill, employed by his father to manage the Lunn's office in Lucerne at £2,000 a year, seemed to live the ideal life for a writer: 'He had warm and comfortable quarters. He was well fed. He could travel. He was in touch with human administrative problems. He was meeting new people, and different kinds of people. His routine offered him constant copy and he was not overworked.' In fact, as far as Kingsmill the writer was concerned, his affluence was a disadvantage. He always found the job of writing arduous and except while a prisoner of war, when there was nothing much else to do, and in later life when he was compelled to earn a living, would always choose an alternative way of passing the time if one presented itself. The lack of financial incentive meant too that he could afford to dabble with novels and short stories, a form of writing which, as Pearson rightly discerned, was not his *forte*.

Kingsmill was further hampered by the attitude of his wife, Eileen. They had been married in 1914 when Kingsmill was twenty-five. Eileen Turpin was a woman of simple, rather puritanical, tastes who disapproved strongly of her husband's literary activities. Such opposition a stronger man would easily have overcome. But in all his dealings with women Kingsmill displayed a fatal weakness. He was incapable of a natural relationship with a woman. If women didn't attract him, he ignored them. If they did, he fell hopelessly in love, becoming in the process as idolatrous and sentimental as a schoolboy, writing love letters which, he admitted to Pearson, 'for sentiment would make Barrie blush, and for imbecility would make the inmates of Colney Hatch sit up and take notice'.

In this state he allowed himself to be dominated. His wife was highly strung and her cloying possessiveness, as recorded by Kingsmill in his novel *The Fall*, recalls the character of Madeline Bassett in the Wooster stories by P. G. Wodehouse (Miss Bassett will be remembered for her description of the stars as 'God's daisy chain'.) It is difficult, too, not to see Kingsmill in the role of Bertie Wooster as a bumbling good-natured young man floundering out of his depth.

Kingsmill's youthful naiveté and the extent to which he was at the mercy of his wife are borne out by a ridiculous and very Wodehousean story he once told Pearson about the early days of his marriage, disguising himself in the person of a 'friend':

'It was in the early summer of 1915, and my friend, who had recently been commissioned, was training in the West Country. He had just married and he and his wife were living in rooms near the camp. They were both very young, and as the future was uncertain were apprehensive about children. So when once, in the early hours their fear was realised, the youthful bride begged her husband to rush to a neighbouring doctor whom, together with his unmarried sister, they had recently met socially. He seemed so kind, said the bride, and would be sure to help. Such sense as the husband possessed having been overborne by the entreaties of his wife, he dressed and set out, bewildered but resolute, his feet ringing sharply on the pavements of the silent sleeping town. No light shone in the doctor's house, a commodious residence standing in its own grounds. The youth, setting his jaw, pulled at the bell, but though it reverberated loudly no one stirred in the house until he had rung for the third time, when he heard a window go up and a voice asking sharply who was there. There was a portico over the front door and he therefore had to retire on to a grass plot in order to hear and be heard. From that grass plot, facing the doctor but glancing uneasily at the other windows for signs of the spinster sister, he began and sustained the following duologue.

' "I had the pleasure of meeting you the other day."

' "Speak up – I can't hear – "

' "My name is – "

' "I know – I know."

' "I'm most frightfully sorry to disturb you, but my wife is afraid she has – conceived."

' "What?"

' "Conceived. My wife's worried, upset. She thinks something may have happened."

' "I don't know what you are talking about."

' "It's my wife – she's very upset. We don't know what to do. I wondered if you would care to – "

' "I'll see you in the morning."

'The window went down with a bang.'

It was at Blandford during the first months of marriage that Kingsmill first experienced 'the strain of life'. When he was beginning a book, he wrote of himself in *The Fall*, 'he usually dreamt of Blandford: the downs where the camp had been turning into a steep mountain and the streets of the little town into a maze through which he hurried half as if he were pursued and half as if he were looking for something he had lost.'

The possibility of his being sent to the Front arose and his wife became hysterical, begging him to have an 'accident' which would keep him out of the action. When he was eventually posted to France he thought it best to keep from her the fact that he was in the trenches and pretended in his letters that he had a job at the base.

Eileen alternated between moods of hysteria and excessive affection. During the latter she would try to extract ludicrous promises from Kingsmill: 'If I die first you'll kill yourself at once, won't you?' Or indulge in romantic fantasies: 'We'll grow old . . . and when we're very old we'll live in a little hut and you'll be such a darling fat old man, and we'll just be there alone, and we'll die in each other's arms.' Kingsmill acquiesced wondering why he was so weak: 'All this ritual of reassurance, oaths of suicide, asseverations of fidelity. Supposing he made a firm stand, and told her – what? That he had occasionally been unfaithful and had no intention of committing suicide if she died first. He shook his head – not practical politics.'

What made life even more difficult was Eileen Lunn's disapproval of her husband's books. His novels, in her view, were immoral and his friends, Holms, Pearson, Gerhardi, etc, a thoroughly bad influence. 'Why should I like your friends?' she would ask. 'A horrible immoral lot, like your writings?' Things at last reached a crisis in 1927 when Eileen discovered the manuscript of his latest novel *Blondel*, and shocked by the account of a love affair it contained, extracted a promise from Kingsmill that he would destroy the book. He was now in a hopeless position, made more so by his falling in love shortly afterwards with a young woman called Gladys Ranicar, whom he met in Switzerland. In a sudden onrush of emotion combining elements of passion, remorse and self-pity he decided to leave his wife. She refused to give him a divorce and appealed to his father, Sir Henry, who threatened Kingsmill with dismissal if he left her. In the meantime, Gladys made it clear to Kingsmill that she could not see him again. There followed a last and well-meant attempt by Sir Henry and his eldest son Arnold to reconcile Kingsmill and Eileen, but it ended disastrously with Kingsmill, who was by this stage in an almost hysterical state, leaving his job and his wife and child for good.

Kingsmill was on the edge of breakdown. He felt guilty about abandoning his wife and child, though in calmer moments he realised that the marriage was a total failure. He was also at last breaking free from his dependence on Sir Henry. In Kingsmill's behaviour at this crisis there is evident an awareness, perhaps unconscious, on his part that his marriage, his continuing reliance on his father, and perhaps even his novel-writing, are all unsatisfactory and that he must make a fresh start.

But afterwards he constructed a different version of events in which he became the victim of his father's puritanical displeasure, thrown out of his job and forced to lead a life of penury because he sought a divorce from his wife. Years later he continued to nurse a grudge against Sir Henry which was quite illogical. His father, it was true, refused initially to give him back his job unless he rejoined his wife, adding that it would be inappropriate for a divorced man to be connected with The

Free Church Touring Guild. But in 1930, by which time it was clear that any reconciliation was out of the question, Kingsmill was once more working for his father; a year later, following the slump, the Lunn business virtually collapsed, which rendered any further grievances on Kingsmill's part irrelevant.

The upheaval had at least one beneficial result. Kingsmill, now deprived of his £2,000 a year, had to earn a living by writing. From a financial point of view his novels had been disastrous and *The Dawn's Delay* had sold only 106 copies. He was therefore forced to follow Pearson's advice and turn his talents to biography. 'There was nothing for it,' he noted sadly, 'except to include fiction, for the time being, among the things, persons and places from which I was parting.'

Informed by his agent that he could get an advance in England and America for a biography of Matthew Arnold, Kingsmill set to work at once and produced the book in a few months, helped as always by his encyclopaedic knowledge of English literature. But it was an unfortunate first choice, as Arnold did not appeal to him. Indeed, Kingsmill had little sympathy for any of the great Victorians. 'I have been reading Tennyson's life by his son,' he told Pearson in 1934. 'He is as self-centred as Dickens, but with much less feeling. I dislike him enormously. . . . Can you beat the following in any age outside the Victorian? Scene – the death of Tennyson. *Dramatis personae* – a few friends, household staff, son, daughter-in-law, and a clergyman, who addresses the defunct peer – "Lord Tennyson, God has taken you, who made you a prince of men! Farewell!" '

He added: 'I will say this for Tennyson – he wasn't Browning and that is a kind thing to say about any man. I really think Browning the most revolting person in what Harris, rightly, used to refer to as "recorded time". The grand Victorian quartet are, in my opinion – Browning, Tennyson, Ruskin and Dickens.

'This is the order of demerit, I think. Out of a possible 100 marks for loathsomeness, I would give Browning 85, Tennyson 70, Ruskin 65, and poor old Dickens 50. Of decent Victorians I would place Emily Bronte easily first (because she is no more Victorian than Hasdrubal or the Inca who Pissarro put on the spot), then Fitzgerald, and then Carlyle. In the intermediate class I should put Thackeray and Matthew Arnold – victims rather than exploiters – and such odd growths as Swinburne and Rossetti.'

'The Victorian writers,' he concluded in his life of Arnold, 'can be properly appreciated only if they are regarded as grotesques of genius.'

Matthew Arnold interested Kingsmill because he typified a common literary phenomenon, the poet turned prophet. Once again, in his book, Kingsmill insisted on the necessarily personal sphere of the poet: 'The poet,' he wrote, 'feels life not through the collective emotions of a nation or a party but through contact with individual souls.' Too often, though, men of instinctive poetic feeling had abandoned their calling in order to set the world to rights: 'Since the French revolution,' Kingsmill wrote in his introduction to the book, 'many poets in prose or verse, have left their proper work and become prophets; Coleridge, for example, and Tolstoy, Nietzsche, Carlyle, Ruskin and Arnold himself; and more recently H. G. Wells, Belloc and Chesterton.' 'Simply the thing I am shall make me live,' Shakespeare had said. But, regrettably, 'to be simply the thing one is, to remain in one's own sphere, filling it with one's actual self, satisfies a very small majority of mankind'.

The archetype of all such figures was Don Quixote, like Arnold, middle-aged when he first set forth on his crusade: 'Now, these dispositions being made, he would no longer defer putting his design in execution, being the more strongly excited thereto by the mischief he thought his delay occasioned in the world; such and so many were the grievances he proposed to redress, the wrongs he intended to rectify, the exorbitances to correct, the abuses to reform, and the debts to discharge.'

In exactly the same spirit Matthew Arnold addressed his mother in 1863: 'It is very gratifying to think that one has at last a chance of *getting at* the English public. Such a public as it is, and such a work as one wants to do with it.'

So Arnold by degrees became a lecturer, or, as Kingsmill put it, 'a general adviser to everyone on everything,' adumbrating reforms in the political, religious and cultural life of England. In this respect he resembled Bernard Shaw and it is perhaps interesting to find Shaw, speaking through the character of Don Juan in *Man and Superman* of 'the instinct in me that looked through my eyes at the world and saw that it could be improved' – another echo of Quixote.

In *Matthew Arnold* Kingsmill first introduced the expression Dawnism to describe the reforming zeal of Arnold and others: 'Dawnism, or heralding the dawn of a new world, or the millennium, the establishment of the kingdom of heaven on earth, the New Jerusalem, the dictatorship of the proletariat ... in short an excited anticipation that some form of collective action is about to solve all the troubles of the individual, is an intermittent but apparently incurable malady of mankind.' The word itself, though presumably owing something to Wordsworth's 'Bliss was it in that dawn to be alive', was derived from an observation Kingsmill made in his youth: 'In 1921 or 1922, emerging each morning from Euston Square underground on to the north side of Euston Road, I used to see across the way, a large poster displaying a crowing cock. The poster was an advertisement of the *Daily Herald* and the cock signified the *Daily Herald*'s conviction that the dawn about to rise in Russia under Lenin's supervision would shortly cross over to England. Years passed and then one day the cock was no longer in his accustomed place.'

Dawnism was embraced primarily by men of action – Lenin or Robespierre – but also intellectuals – Rousseau, Tolstoy, Nietzsche, Wells or Shaw – all of whom propounded a Dawnist philosophy in one form or another. But the phenomenon of Dawnism was as old as the hills. While working on the book Kingsmill had written to Pearson: 'I shall open with the major and minor prophets as a bunch of completely insane Dawnists. Have you ever read them? It's sheer lunacy. The imagery is that of a mad house. The earth shaking, heaven cracking, blood, whoredom, drunkenness, babes dashed to the ground, cattle running about in a state of distraction, dragons, God gnashing his teeth, famine, plague, roaring waters, etc. etc. – ending up with a new world – dragons expunged and God all smiles.'

Before embarking on his account of Arnold's life Kingsmill returned to the impossibility of separating the life of a writer from his work. Victorian biographers had worked on precisely the opposite principle with ludicrous results. For example, Kingsmill observed, 'A few years ago Dr Harper exposed the fact that Wordsworth in his youth had had a love affair with a

French girl, who had borne him a child and whom he had then deserted. In most of the comments I read on this incident the critics wrote as if Wordsworth had magnanimously suspended his celibacy as part of a general programme for the renovation for humanity; or had at worst committed a slight error of judgement in his anxiety to get into line with the finer spirits of the French revolution.' Matthew Arnold along with Thackeray and Carlyle had requested that their biographies should not be written; others had seen to it that dependable friends would do the job. They did so under the pressure to conform to Victorian respectability. Though Thackeray and Dickens had not so conformed, they went to great efforts to pretend otherwise. In the Victorian atmosphere, Kingsmill noted, 'Casanova himself would have become reticent, Benvenuto Cellini vague; while for any reasonably respectable person the fear that he might fall into the hands of a truthful biographer must have become, and indeed obviously did become, a continuous nightmare'.

Elsewhere he commented: 'If the Bible had been written in conformity with Victorian taste, the world would have known nothing of the circumstances that led up to the marriage of King David with the charming and popular wife of the late brevet-colonel Uriah; and the denial of Christ by Peter would have been dismissed in an obscurely worded footnote as a piece of scandal undeserving detailed refutation.'

All this came as a prelude to Kingsmill's assertion that 'Marguerite' lovingly referred to in some of Arnold's early poems was a real person – a young French girl with whom Arnold had fallen in love on a visit to Switzerland in 1846. Restrained by his upbringing and other considerations, however, Arnold did not allow the affair to develop. This revelation may seem rather anticlimactic after Kingsmill's introductory comments – a criticism he anticipated in a chapter called 'A Half Way Halt', when he imagined a reviewer objecting, 'Frankly I can't make out what all the fuss is about. Mr Kingsmill whips up our excitement by an elaborate defiance to the Victorian convention of reticence, and then, when the least we are entitled to expect is a picture of a little establishment on Lake Como, with a mysterious and bewhiskered Victorian gentleman crooning over the offspring of a secret passion for an Italian countess, all we get is a vague kiss or two

tentatively offered to a French governess, and apparently withdrawn before acceptance. Mr Kingsmill's right job is compiling
primers of literature for the use of the lower forms in girls'
schools. He would put the higher forms to sleep.'

Such criticism, as Kingsmill himself admitted, would have
had some justification. But it was surprising how much fuss was
caused at the time by his rather humdrum disclosure: 'Where,
I was asked, was my evidence that Marguerite had ever
existed? What was my authority for converting the gracious
creation of a poet's fancy into a disreputable Frenchwoman,
clandestinely enjoyed by the renegade son of an upright
father?' One critic wrote: 'Incredible as it may seem, Mr
Kingsmill suggested that there was an episode of disgrace, that
Arnold at Thun, in Switzerland, met a French girl, a governess-
companion, living in apartments, of a lower social order than
himself, and fell passionately in love with her. Arnold is said to
have seen her again in the second year, and then to have
parted from her finally. These suggestions are not supported by
a single scrap of evidence.'

In fact, Kingsmill's theories were proved to be correct when
some years later Matthew Arnold's letters to Arthur Clough
were published, and it was shown conclusively that Marguerite
did indeed exist. But Kingsmill's pioneering work was never
acknowledged. (This was the first of three occasions when
Kingsmill correctly inferred hitherto undisclosed love affairs
largely by intuitive methods. Later he was the first biographer
to accept the evidence of Dickens' affair with Ellen Ternan. He
also deduced the fact that John Middleton Murry had at one
stage been intimate with Frieda Lawrence – or, as he put it in
an apt and homely phrase, 'He did her a bit of good'. This too
was subsequently confirmed by published correspondence.)

Quite apart from Kingsmill's interest in Arnold's love life,
his rather boisterous comments did not endear him to the
critics. Some idea of his approach can be gleaned from his
remarks on Arnold's poem *Sohrab and Rustum*, familiar to many
generations of schoolboys.

'The story', Kingsmill reminds his readers, 'is of a single
combat in front of the Persian and Tartar armies, between a
father and a son, who discover their relationship only after the
son has been mortally wounded.'

He notes that *Sohrab and Rustum* may possibly carry under-
tones of Arnold's own relationship to his father Dr Arnold, of
Rugby but, apart from this, 'the poem is remarkable for nothing
but the elaborate laying on of local colour and the long-drawn-
out similes, smacking or intended to smack of the vital
simplicities of primitive life. When Sohrab and Rustum rush at
one another a din

> 'Rose, such as that the sinewy woodcutters
> Make often in the forest's heart at morn,
> Of hewing axes, crashing trees . . .'

'When Rustum, still ignorant that he has been fighting with his
son, stands over the dying Sohrab, Arnold compares him to a
hunter in the spring

> "who hath found
> A breeding eagle sitting on her nest,
> Upon the craggy isle of a hill-lake,
> And pierced her with an arrow as she rose,
> And followed her to find her where she fell
> Far off; anon her mate comes winging back
> From hunting, and a great way off descries
> His huddling young left sole, at that he checks
> His pinion, and with short uneasy sweeps
> Circles above his eyry, with loud scream."

and so on for eight more lines.

'On re-examining this simile, I find that it is to the breeding
eagle's mate, not to the hunter, that Rustum is compared; but
it really doesn't matter.

'As to local colour, we learn that the Tartars of Ferhana have
scanty beards and close-set skull-caps, that the Tartars of the
Oxus are large men on large steeds, and ferment the milk of
mares, a practice unknown to "the more temperate Toorkmons
of the south", that Peran-Wisa, the Tartar chieftain, carried a
ruler's staff in his right hand but no sword and wore a sheep-
skin cap, black, glossy, curl'd, the fleece of Kara-Kul; and
so on.

' "What then", Arnold asks in the preface of 1853, "are the
situations, from the representation of which, though accurate,
no poetical enjoyment can be derived?"

'Were Arnold alive, I should lead him discreetly apart and tell him that the answer would probably occur to him after a re-reading of *Sohrab and Rustum*.'

It was perhaps not surprising in view of such passages that Kingsmill's book did not go down well in academic and literary quarters. Arnold, melancholy, 'liberal', with a romantic attachment to Oxford and a generalised interest in 'culture' and the improvement of society, made a special appeal, as he still does, to 'men of letters'. Typical was the *New Stateman*'s critic, who evinced a tone of suitably controlled outrage and indignation at the way Kingsmill had treated one of the greatest Victorians: 'Mr Kingsmill continually calls him Matt, which plainly he is not entitled to do. . . . Mr Kingsmill's digressions throughout the book are ludicrous. . . .' Mr Kingsmill was quite wrong in classifying Arnold as a Dawnist – 'He was an eagerly interested European; his mind was occupied with public affairs,' and so on. It was the voice of the cultured literary man, appalled at Kingsmill's lack of tact and good manners. Matthew Arnold, the writer concluded, if confronted by Kingsmill, 'would have asked, as he asked of Adolescens Leo, the bright young journalist, "Now would you call that young man a man of delicacy?"'

This review with its air of cultured condescension was an indication of what lay in store for Kingsmill in the way of criticism, and there is no doubt that he was upset by it. 'I think I was unwise,' he said in a letter to the *New Statesman*, 'to refer to Arnold as "Matt", but I did not bear in mind, while I was writing the book that certain of my reviewers would be more anxious to display their breeding than try to understand that I called Arnold "Matt" only in what seemed to me the appropriate context.'

'The *New Statesman* as a Dawnist paper,' he wrote to Pearson, 'attacked me very sourly last week. I thought it advisable to answer.' Pearson replied, 'I saw the *New Statesman* review, which was sheer unadulterated piffle of the most ball-aching nature, and your answer, which wasn't half ruthless enough. Your method of de-balling people is far too gentle. The scalpel is useless; you should use a spade. Don't cut – CRUSH!' But Pearson himself did not care for the book. 'The obvious criticism,' he said, 'is that as an exposition of Kingsmill it contains too much Matt and as an exposition of Matt contains too much Kingsmill. . . . You have not made me in the least interested in Matt, but you make me extremely interested in Kingsmill: I should really like to meet the latter. Please phone me and fix up a meeting.'

This verdict was sound. *Matthew Arnold*, viewed simply as a book about Matthew Arnold, was not a success, but seen as a rambling discussion on a variety of themes, with Arnold as the starting point, it was. Taken as a whole, like most of Kingsmill's books, it was unsatisfactory. But it made up for its formlessness by occasional sentences and paragraphs which revealed a highly original thinker. This was the thought behind a letter which Pearson wrote to Kingsmill on December 4, 1928.

My dear Hughie,

Matt arrived the other day. Many thanks. Its arrival gave rise to the following duologue between myself and my wife:

H: Here is Hughie's book, darling! I'll start reading it to you this evening.

G: But I read it in proof.

H: How much?

G: Oh, quite a lot!

H: Yes, but how much?

G: Well, all the chapters you said were so good.

H: How many?

G: Three, I think.

H: That's absurd! You can't get any idea of a book from three chapters. We will read the lot.

G: Why?

H: Well, dash it all! Why not?

G: Because you said all the poetry stuff was boring.

H: Yes, but that is only part of the book.

G: You said it was the larger part.

H: Did I? I'll have another squint. (*A long pause while H. refers to book.*) Yes, there does seem rather a lot of poetry. Pretty second-rate too, by the look of it.

G: Then why read it?

H: All right; we'll cut the poetry and just read what Hughie says about it.

G: Do you want to read about second-rate poetry?

H: Well . . .

G: You always say you don't care to read *about* even first rate poetry.

H: That's true, but . . .

G: Yes?

H: Oh, very well! We'll cut all the stuff about poetry and read about the man.

G: But you said there wasn't much about the man.

H: Not an awful lot, I admit.

G: And that, anyhow, he was a first-class fathead.

H: So he was!

G: Well, do you like reading about first-class fatheads?

H: Some of the best biographies are about mediocrities.

G: Name a few.

H: Oh, I can't remember them off hand!

G: But you said Hughie's book was more critical than biographical.

H: Yes, it is – and he's a damn'd fine critic too!

G: Well, if you are going to cut his criticism, as you said, what's left?

H: I said we'd cut the criticism of Matt's poetry, but there is a lot of the man.

G: The first-class fathead, you mean?

H: It isn't so much the things he says about Matt that are interesting, but the things he says about life in general – his criticism of life is always excellent.

G: How many chapters contain his criticism of life?

H: Well, there's the one on Dawnism – a masterpiece!

G: Go on.

H: And there is the marvellous chapter on the Sanctity of Married Life.

G: Yes?

H: And there's the Half-way Halt chapter.

G: Yes, those are the three you told me not to miss. What others?

H: Oh, there are chunks of rattling good stuff, all the way through.

G: Very well; pick out the chunks and read them to me.

H: I'm damn'd if I will! We'll read the lot or nothing!

G: Except the poetry stuff.

H: Quite so.

G: Well, first let me finish this crossword puzzle. Do you know a word of six letters meaning a marine mammal of the Indian Seas – it's got an O and a G in it?

Kingsmill had previously discussed his work with Holms. But from now on he came to rely more and more on Pearson, to whom he submitted almost all his subsequent books chapter by chapter before sending them to the publisher. Pearson was rarely, as in the case of Arnold, critical of his friend's work and his usual response was unqualified and extravagant praise. If he did offer advice, Kingsmill seldom took it. But his unwavering support sustained Kingsmill's morale, as did his genuine indifference to the opinions of others. Taxed by his second wife to explain the attraction of Pearson, Kingsmill said that he was the only person he knew who lacked vanity. To Kingsmill, who was easily rattled by the unfavourable verdicts of critics, Pearson, with an invincible faith in his own judgement, remained a tower of strength.

In March 1928 Kingsmill had settled at Thonon on Lake Geneva where he lived for a year and a half in virtual solitude. Here he completed *Matthew Arnold* and started without delay his second biographical book. 'A friend of mine,' he told Pearson in July, 'was here recently and suggested that I should write on four Victorians, to illustrate the abnormal extremes produced by the Victorian atmosphere. I think that this is an excellent idea, and my four (say 25,000 words each) are in couples – Dean Farrar, Samuel Butler, W. T. Stead and Frank Harris.

'Dean Farrar. I want to deal with the curious Victorian discovery that pubescent boys are a fit theme for the novelist. *Eric* is the type of this singular preoccupation, complete with hero, villain and heroine who dies, of course, and is of the male sex. In a word, Dean Farrar as a suppressed homosexualist. Butler as a kind of inverted Farrar, with ten times the brains, also homosexually inclined and a kind of would-be repectable pariah. W. T. Stead lustful Puritan journalist. Frank Harris lustful journalist.'

The result, which was eventually published under the title *After Puritanism*, was a more successful if less boisterous book than *Matthew Arnold*. 'My own favourite,' Muggeridge wrote, 'is Stead, a really fascinating figure. As a subject Stead suited Hughie perfectly. He was sufficiently absurd to bring into play his humour at the very top of his form, and sufficiently near in time and spirit for Hughie to get him to the life.'

W. T. Stead, whose editorship of the *Pall Mall Gazette* had changed the face of Victorian journalism and whose exposé of child prostitution, published under the lurid heading 'The Maiden Tribute of Modern Babylon', had caused a major sensation, had, before his death in the *Titanic* disaster, been a close friend of Sir Henry Lunn. It was Stead, after Sir Henry fell out with the Methodist authorities, who had given him his chance in journalism and encouraged his early efforts in the travel agency business; impressing on him the need to advance up the social ladder. 'Now you've got onto bishops, Lunn,' he once said, 'don't ever go back to curates.' Stead, like Sir Henry, was a Nonconformist, puritanical and prurient, but he too had an engaging side to him. 'To the nation as a whole,' Kingsmill wrote in his unfinished autobiography, 'Stead, with his campaigns for raising the age of consent and for expelling from public life such politicians as were detected in adultery, seemed the chief voice of the Nonconformist conscience. But the Nonconformists themselves regarded him with some uneasiness. He was a free-lance who thought himself of more importance than all the Dissenting churches rolled into one, and though he kept within the Puritan code, it nearly gave way under the strain. A champion of all distressed women, he could not resist trying to fascinate them, and the friendly services he did them often ended in a tight-rope performance over the abyss of sin. Long practice had made this balancing feat second nature to Stead, but the women enjoyed it less.'

During this first period at Thonon Kingsmill completed another book, *The Return of William Shakespeare*. This was a book he had been working on for some years. It incorporated, within a farcical framework about the Bard being brought back to life, his views on Shakespeare, the man and the writer. Tracing the biography of Shakespeare in his plays is a hazardous task, as there are quite enough different texts to support any theory and most commentators, like Frank Harris, for example, tell us more about themselves than about Shakespeare. That

Kingsmill was sensitive to the difficulties involved is borne out by the fact that he put his ideas into a fictional context.

Kingsmill's central theme was the struggle of Shakespeare to rise above worldly ambitions and the love of fame which pre-occupied him especially in his youth. Breaking away from the conventional view of Shakespeare as a serene and detached observer of life, Kingsmill pictured him, on the contrary, as someone who was only too easily embroiled in private and public passions. 'I think his interest in the personal side of politics almost as strong an influence as sex in his plays', he wrote to Holms. A turning point in Shakespeare's attitude to politics was the ineffective rebellion of the Earl of Essex. From that time Shakespeare, who had glamourised kings and princes, developed a detestation of Queen Elizabeth which he put into the character of Julius Caesar. The identification of Caesar with Elizabeth was perhaps Kingsmill's most original contribution.

All these ideas were discussed endlessly in conversation and correspondence with Pearson. There was not always agreement. Pearson declined at that stage to accept the Caesar–Elizabeth theory, as he still cherished a romantic image of the Virgin Queen as a 'lady of astonishing versatility and the most Shakespearean creation in the kingdom'. By the time, however, that he came to write on Shakespeare himself he was converted to Kingsmill's view, equating Elizabeth with the dictators of the twentieth century.

On one matter, however, he refused to give way, maintaining adamantly that Falstaff was the summit of Shakespeare's achievement. Kingsmill always gave pride of place to *Lear*. It was therefore in a spirit of mock trepidation that he sent the proofs of his Shakespeare book to Pearson:

I hope to be back in under four weeks and will get part two to you before my return, so that the physical violence stage will be over. None the less I shall stand back a bit after I have rung the bell, so as to give myself every chance.

Mr Birdly, a retired accountant testified as follows: I was returning home from Marlborough Road Station on foot, according to my usual practice, at about 7.15 pm, when I observed, without giving him special attention, a man walking a few paces ahead of me. He appeared to be of solid build and was dressed like a gentleman. As I passed number 88 the door was opened to this person, whom I had observed ringing the bell. The person opening the door used the following words (*consultation in court with words written down*) – 'You bloody swine! Would you! Lear! You fucking shit! Take that!'

The person addressed grappled with his interlocutor and a desperate struggle ensued. On returning with a policeman, I was distressed to find the assailant and his victim at the bottom of the steps. Both were in a dying condition, and profusely covered with blood. Their speech was somewhat indistinct, but I caught the following words from the assailant – 'Hope teach lesson' to which the victim responded, expiring immediately afterwards 'Can only repeat'.

In July 1929 Kingsmill met Dorothy Vernon who was later to become his second wife, when Eileen finally agreed to a divorce. They lived for a time together in London before returning to Thonon in 1930. Here their eldest daughter Edmée was born. Eventually they settled in a house called *Rien et Tout* overlooking Lake Geneva. 'I was curious,' Kingsmill remembered, 'to hear how the agent would explain this somewhat Barriesque name. My question greatly embarrassed him, for I put it to him before signing the contract, and he was naturally reluctant to explain that the '*Rien*' was the material value of the place, and the '*Tout*' its spiritual value. '*Ça veut dire* . . .' he contorted his hands. '*C'est difficile à expliquer* . . .' he twisted his eyebrows. '*Rien – ça exprime* . . .' I patted him on the shoulder and he smiled wanly back.'

Kingsmill's second marriage was altogether more successful and long lasting than his first. But from neither partner's point of view was it satisfactory. To his friends Kingsmill seemed somehow trapped and at the mercy of his wife; while Dorothy, a beautiful and perceptive woman, resented her exclusion from her husband's literary life. Kingsmill, who was decidedly old fashioned in his attitude towards women, tried to keep his work, his friends and his family in separate compartments. 'Keep things in their frame, old man, keep things in their frame,' he said to Alec Waugh when the latter expressed a desire to meet his wife. This attempt to live a number of separate lives only led to tension with Dorothy who considered that some of the time and energy he lavished on his friends could have been more constructively applied to work which would enhance his own reputation. Despite all this, they lived together for twenty years until Kingsmill's death, bringing up three children in a strong family atmosphere that flowed, when conditions were favourable, with much good humour and affection.

At Thonon, Kingsmill completed a short book about his experiences in the war called *Behind Both Lines*, as well as his biography of Frank Harris and a collection of parodies, *The Table of Truth*. The latter are on the whole disappointing, with the exception of a parody of Housman which the poet himself declared was the best ever written:

> What still alive at twenty-two
> A clean, upstanding chap like you?
> Sure, if your throat 'tis hard to slit,
> Slit your girl's and swing for it.
>
> Like enough, you won't be glad,
> When they come to hang you, lad:
> But bacon's not the only thing
> That's cured by hanging from a string.
>
> So, when the spilt ink of the night
> Spreads o'er the blotting pad of light,
> Lads whose job is still to do
> Shall whet their knives, and think of you.

Chapter 6

Looking back on his life, Hesketh Pearson saw the age of forty as a turning point. 'I suppose,' he said once, 'that until one finishes the painful process of mental growth and character formation somewhere in the region of forty, nearly every year shifts the angle of one's outlook.' Then change was partly a matter of coming to terms with humanity. On another occasion he wrote, 'The youth of twenty who does not think the world can be improved is a cad; the man of forty who still thinks it can is a fool'.

The long period of development was due in some measure to Pearson's temperament. He was by nature a man of strong impulses and enthusiasms. Even in middle age he retained many of the characteristics of a younger man. He experienced difficulty in reconciling the opposing strains in his character, being what is popularly known as 'a mass of contradictions'. Thus he proclaimed himself an atheist, but at the same time had a passionate devotion to the Church of England; he hated homosexuality, but his hero was Oscar Wilde; he told his friends he was a pacifist, despite the fact he won the Military Cross in the First World War and threw himself with gusto into Civil Defence work in the Second.

He was possessed of unusual vitality. Writing about his friendship with Pearson, Muggeridge remembered in particular 'a special gusto which characterised everything he said and did'. The force of his personality could be disconcerting, especially to anyone who threatened to cross his path.

He related to Kingsmill an incident which occurred shortly after the publication in 1934 of his book on Gilbert and Sullivan; 'As my future biographer you will be interested in the following duologue which took place between myself and a total stranger at the Highgate Ponds today:

STRANGER (sitting by me on a seat): Excuse me, sir, but haven't we met before? I seem to know your face.

SELF: Indeed?

STRANGER: Yes, would it – would you think it impertinent of me to ask your name?

SELF: In the ordinary way I should think it most impertinent of you, as I prefer to take my recreation incognito. But circumstances alter cases, and as I want to sell you a book, I look upon your request as not only reasonable but polite. My name is Hesketh Pearson. I am the author of a biography of Gilbert and Sullivan, just published. And advertisements for it appear in today's *Observer* and *Sunday Times*.

STRANGER (after embarrassed laugh): Then I don't think we have met before (A pause. Then with a rush): Of course I know your name.

SELF: The book is published by Hamish Hamilton. The price is ten shillings and sixpence net, and it is very reasonable at the price. Having met me in the flesh, I'm sure you will want to meet me in the spirit. Buy it. Good day.

Sometimes his reaction in such circumstances was more extreme. Up until the age of sixty he suffered from a strong temper, which resulted in sudden outbursts of hysterical rage – 'I seemed to see red shutters going up and down before my eyes and I felt as if something inside me were about to burst. In that condition I exploded, saying outrageous things in a virulent manner, quite unconscious of what I was saying and how I was saying it'. These rages lasted only five minutes, but their effect could be devastating.

In addition to temperamental difficulties, Pearson, like many others who survived the First World War, went through a period of reaction afterwards which gave rise to wild and rather unpredictable behaviour during the twenties. The campaign in Mesopotamia had been particularly unpleasant. 'You asked me whether Mespot affected my health seriously,' he wrote to Kingsmill in 1928. 'It did. It cleared me of consumption – I was given three years to live when I sailed for Basra – and gave me Malaria and dysentery – septic sores and a nasty wound on the top of my skull. I have since been cured by a quack (introduced to me by GBS) of the first two – have never had a return of the third, and may have to be operated on for the third time in respect of the fourth. My family strongly advised me to plead lunacy, as a result of shrapnel on the brain in *The Whispering Gallery* case.'

Pearson was forty-two when he wrote his first biography, a life of Erasmus Darwin. Appropriately, he was enabled to do so by Kingsmill. 'By the way,' Kingsmill had written to him on November 21, 1928, 'being entirely broke, and seeing that GBS had recently advised people to sell his letters, while at the same time threatening proceedings if they were published, I thought I could without prejudice to anyone concerned sell GBS's inaccurate forecast of your trial which he sent me. I got four pounds ten at Sotheran's. Why don't you sell some of yours?'

Pearson, who had a large collection of letters and first editions took the tip and raised £200, enough for him to give up acting for the time being and write his book. The subject was dictated by the fact that Erasmus Darwin was a mate al ancestor and through his mother and other relations Pearson was able to obtain much unpublished material.

Once he started writing he realised that he had at last found his vocation. Everything fell into place. All traces of the influence of Harris, Strachey and Shaw, any tendency to indulge in fancy at the expense of fact was discarded. 'I was wholly of Johnson's opinion,' he said, 'that truth alone is valuable and interesting, as far as a human being is able to apprehend it.' Pearson's first book has all the good qualities of his last. He chose his subjects wisely, writing about men with whom he himself was in sympathy – wits, rebels and iconoclasts. 'I love people,' he told Kingsmill, 'who blow respectability and the Establishment to bits. Hence my portrait gallery: Erasmus Darwin, Sydney Smith, Hazlitt, W. S. Gilbert, Labouchere and Tom Paine.'

Pearson stated his *raison d'être* in the introduction to his first book. 'The majority of reliable biographies,' he wrote, 'are unreadable, and the majority of readable biographies are unreliable.' Even Lytton Strachey was suspect on this score. Though Kingsmill and Pearson, like all their generation, admired Lytton Strachey when *Eminent Victorians* was published, .they both subsequently became more critical of his technique. 'I don't myself care for the Strachey habit of soliloquy,' Kingsmill noted in 1926, and went on to picture Mahomet as Strachey might have done – 'as his camel jogs through the desert murmuring "Two wives, not enough variety to balance the discords. Three wives? Well, perhaps, but one of 'em will always be odd wife out, while the other two are sitting in each other's laps, and so she'll come whining along to her husband and make the poor fellow's life a burden. No! Four – that's the number. . . ." ' Other popular biographers of the day included Emil Ludwig and Philip Guedalla, both exponents of what Pearson called 'Panoramic biography' in which disparate incidents and characters were put together in a historical jigsaw for the sake of dramatic effect – 'That month a loaded cab rolled across Belgrave Square, plunged into Chelsea, and set down a wide-eyed couple with a canary and a multitude of baggage before a newly-painted door in Cheyne Row. Lord Grey, a trifle weary, repaired the gaps in his cabinet. . . .' It was the kind of narrative, Pearson observed, in which everything seemed to take place 'in the failing light' of an October, November, or December evening.

His own style was simple and straightforward. There were no 'tricks'. He wrote so unassumingly that many critics thought him superficial. Edmund Wilson and George Orwell, for example, used respectively the word 'journalism' and 'hack' in relation to his *Oscar Wilde*. All that they meant perhaps was that Pearson did not, when writing of a literary figure, devote page after page to criticisms of his subject's works. His aim was always to tell the story and he had the ability to select what was of interest from a mass of material and weld it all together into a readable narrative. Story-tellers and stylists were quick to recognise his gifts. Graham Greene commended 'his admirable forthrightness. Mr Pearson as a biographer,' he said, 'has some of the qualities of Dr Johnson – a plainness, an honesty, a sense of ordinary life going on all the time.' Max Beerbohm referred to his 'shining skill in narration'. At the same time, what gave his books their flavour was his own personality. As the *Punch* critic, R. G. G. Price, wrote: 'Mr Pearson has a sturdy Cobbett-like opinionatedness that is often enfuriating but at least gives his books character.'

By the end of 1929, the year in which *Doctor Darwin* was published, Pearson was once again back on the breadline and forced to resume his acting career. He found appearing on the stage less and less congenial, especially as so many of the plays in which he performed were, inevitably, second-rate. During February 1932 he was given a part in a film, which he found even more depressing than the stage. 'I am writing this in a film studio at Islington,' he told Kingsmill. 'The incompetence of these people is incredible. I have been here an hour and a half already, and beyond being made up, nothing has happened to me. I am about to do my first talkie, but I don't think that the job will last more than a day, or two at the outside. I am playing the small part of a sergeant of police. Can you imagine anyone less suited to a Bobby? One gets well paid for cooling one's heels, which is the only decent thing about it. £6 a day, less 10% agent's fee. But it is a frightful waste of time and a dreadful bore. Also, to quote Frankie, it brings me no nearer to the mark of my high calling, wherever or whatever that may be. It is in short, a sod's life, without the moral satisfaction of sodomy – at least I presume it must be moral, for I cannot conceive it to be physical.'

A year previously, during the first night of Noël Coward's *The Young Idea* at the Empire in Edinburgh, Pearson forgot all his lines and had to 'conduct the opening scene within hearing of the prompter'. The experience made him more than ever determined to give up acting. But there was still the necessity to support his family and he was back on the stage the following May in a play which included the following dialogue:

SHE: I ought to tell you, Adrian, that I am a virgin.
HE: I wouldn't have asked you that.
SHE: But you are glad to know?
HE: Yes.
SHE: And you? I am not the first?
HE: No. Do you mind?
SHE: I am glad. You give your skill for my virginity.
HE: You are pleased that I am fledged, etc, etc.

Pearson was saved any further humiliation of this sort when, two months later, his friend Colin Hurry offered him a job. Hurry was an example of a type of literary patron more common in the thirties than today – the cultured Advertising Man. Pearson first met him in 1918, when they were both serving in Mesopotamia. After the war Hurry, who in his spare time wrote poems which Pearson much admired, went into the advertising business, eventually becoming managing director of Carlton Studios, a large and flourishing concern. In 1932 he took Pearson on the payroll. In exchange for a retainer of £5 a week Pearson was expected to be on tap to attend the occasional function given to entertain a client. The pay was just enough to enable him to write biographies. Kingsmill noted enviously: 'You are now in the position I was in in the old days at Lucerne – a capitalist with cultural interests, and you ought to write me a long letter three times a week.'

Hurry's gesture was the disinterested one of a friend, as it is unlikely that Pearson did much to further the success of Carlton Studios. Hurry had already experienced his unpredictable behaviour some time in the early twenties, when he took him to the Cecil Hotel to meet an important American Rotarian. Hurry began the interview by asking him why he had come to England. 'We come over here . . .' the American replied 'to be loved.' The remark for reasons which he could not quite define sent Pearson into a fit of hysterical laughter and Hurry had to escort him from the room, returning to explain to the Rotarian that his friend was still suffering from the effects of shellshock.

All the same, when looking back over his years as an employee of Hurry's, Pearson concluded that he had kept himself in check remarkably well. Though easily bored, he was adept at registering polite interest, something that Kingsmill never bothered to do, and sat through innumerable lunches listening to opinionated businessmen with equanimity. Only once did he allow his feelings to get the better of him, when seated next to the publicity manager of Lord Rothermere's Associated Newspapers. This man had recently returned from Nazi Germany and began to describe in great detail his highly favourable impressions of the Hitler Youth movement. Though suitably appalled, Pearson kept quiet until the Rothermere man, after saying that something like the Hitler Youth was needed in England, embarked on a second narration of his German visit.

'Makes yer think, eh?' he concluded, turning to Pearson.

'Nothing could make you think,' Pearson replied.

Thereafter, he noted with some degree of understatement, the businessman's attitude towards him 'cooled'.

Thanks to Hurry's retainer, Pearson now began to write in earnest. His next subject after Erasmus Darwin was Sydney Smith and the resulting book, *The Smith of Smiths*, was one of his most successful.

But to begin with he found himself dogged by the consequences of *The Whispering Gallery* affair. Hamish Hamilton had shown interest but stipulated, in view of the widespread ignorance about Sydney Smith, that the book should have an introduction by a well-known literary figure. It so happened that the historian G. M. Trevelyan had written to Pearson to congratulate him on *Doctor Darwin* and Pearson therefore approached him to do the foreword. Trevelyan agreed, but after writing an enthusiastic piece in which he said that 'one of the world's most singular and gifted men is here allowed to stand and unfold himself,' he learned that Pearson was the author of *The Whispering Gallery*. As he was a friend of Sir Rennell Rodd's he felt obliged to withhold his introduction.

Gladys Pearson burst into tears when she heard the news and Pearson in a rage despatched an angry note to Trevelyan. Subsequently Kingsmill wrote to Trevelyan pointing out the financial loss that Pearson would sustain, whereupon Trevelyan with exceptional generosity agreed to pay Pearson £300 by way of compensation, three times the amount of his advance. 'He is a dear old boy,' Kingsmill wrote to Pearson, 'barring his astonishing attachment to Rodd, which I see he himself calls a misfortune in his letter. There is no doubt Garibaldi would have shot GMT out of hand, but to a humane spirit there is something touching about the old lad.' Pearson now approached G. K. Chesterton, who agreed to do the introduction. 'G.K.'s introduction is very good,' Kingsmill said, 'though it undoubtedly deals more with Smith than you. But it does really show a genuine appreciation of ss and the praise of his humour shows that GK is not yet quite lost. It is terrible to think of what he must suffer as a Catholic, especially when he wakes up in the night, with all his defences down. Good cartoon – GK at 2 a.m. realising that he is a Catholic.'

Pearson's next book, *The Fool of Love*, was a biography of Hazlitt, which had a poor critical press owing to the emphasis that Pearson put on Hazlitt's disastrous love affair with Sara Walker, his landlady's daughter. The book sold only 700 copies. 'It is sickening about Hazlitt,' Kingsmill wrote, 'but the work you have done will necessitate a new and proper view of wн henceforth. It seems to have rasped all these people at the moment.'

Unlike Kingsmill, Pearson was not unduly rattled when his books were attacked: 'Has any writer,' he once asked Kingsmill at a time when his friend was fuming over a hostile review, 'gone through life to the accompaniment of universal praise? How on earth can you expect it? You are as touchy as a lady with a club foot. Seriously now, do you honestly, deep down in your heart and soul, care two farts what anyone thinks of your work so long as you yourself are pleased with it? If you do, I am sorry because you are in for some sticky half-hours during the next twenty or thirty years. . . . Cultivate indifference, apathy, sluggishness, all true British qualities.'

Pearson regained the good will of critics with his following book, *Gilbert and Sullivan*, in which he successfully interwove the biographies of two very different personalities. It was followed by *Labby*, a life of the Victorian journalist and politician Henry Labouchere. Of the two books. Kingsmill preferred the first: 'There is something depressing about Labby, whereas Gilbert and Sullivan are such admirable foils that the story of their linked destinies spins me along without a hitch.'

The publication of *Labby* had one curious consequence. Lord Beaverbrook wrote to Pearson to congratulate him on the book and to ask if he considered that Lawson, at one time editor and part-owner of the *Daily Telegraph*, and Labby's arch-enemy, was 'a good man'. Pearson told Kingsmill: 'Now I confess myself unable to deal with this adequately. What on earth is he getting at? Shall I reply: "In answer to your last question, Lawson was a newspaper proprietor?" Or shall I let him down lightly? – thus: "Lawson was as good as a Fleet Street magnate can be; that is to say, he was fouler than Satan; no one certainly not Dante, etc, etc".' 'Beaver's letter,' Kingsmill wrote, 'is incredibly funny but pathetic too. Don't bump him off. Why not reply – "many thanks for your letter. I think it is stretching the meaning of the word to call Lawson good, but let's hope he was, for in that case most of us will be on velvet in the next world. Thanking you again for your pleasant remarks, yours sincerely. . . ." PS. Beaver, like Cromwell, is, I understand, much exercised as to his reception on the other side, so I think that my suggested reply just about meets the case, for while playful it strikes a much needed note of optimism.'

The last of Pearson's pre-war biographies was that of another famous rebel, Tom Paine, published in 1937. It was written at the suggestion of Muggeridge and dedicated to him. The book was a favourite of Kingsmill's, who constantly re-read all of Pearson's books: 'It is the best portrait of an historical Don Quixote extant,' he wrote. 'I am not sure that I didn't like it second to Hazlitt, though Sydney Smith is naturally much richer. Where it gains on ss is in the universal significance of TP as a perfect example of an individual trying to benefit the world at large and therefore necessarily getting into ever-increasing trouble. He is a really tragic figure. What is so interesting is the preference of the world for politicians on the make to persons genuinely interested in their welfare.'

Chapter 7

In May 1930 Kingsmill, suffering from the effects of a boil on his backside, went to Birmingham to have it lanced. From Miss Dora's Private Hospital in Newall Street he wrote to Pearson:

The chain of circumstances is instructive. You may remember I was suffering from a boil. My father recommended a five-day fast and a pot of marmite, on Friday. On Saturday, I met a friend called Ibby James at the club, with an elderly Birmingham dentist (Wellings), whose daughter he wishes to marry as soon as his present wife sees her way to blessing the banns. Old Wellings was much affected by my state and persuaded me to come down to Bournville, where he lives, so that he might ferment my backside.

I was rather shy of appearing as a Mysterious Stranger, whose only charm was an inflamed bottom, and whose only requirement was solitude and the best room in the house.

Well, my backside got simply frightful. I went through bloody hell on Tuesday, and all that night, and the blasted thing swelled all over. Finally a surgeon came in, and said it was a bad abscess and must be cut at once – apparently they burst internally and then one is finished.

So they brought me here and cut the damn thing. I'll never forget the pleasure of going down to the operating room with my hell-fire rump and knowing I'd be unconscious in a minute. The anaesthetist advanced tactfully to allay my fears and said, 'I am the man who puts you to sleep', to which I answered, rather readily I think, 'I've been looking for you for days'. Most of my chloroform and post-chloroform talk I hear was round Shakespeare, Chamberlain and Stanley Baldwin – obviously what FH would call the formative forces in my intellectual life. Since writing the above, my nurse tells me that I told her that I had passed through all my life again under the anaesthetic, and had been much saddened by it. I wonder if there is any truth in this.

He added by the next post:

I quite forgot the funniest incident of my backside epic. I wrote to my father to tell him I could not take up work this week, etc, etc, and he advised himself of the general situation over the phone to my doctor, etc.

This morning a telegram arrived. I assumed it was from him and would convey paternal relief after my operation.

It ran, 'Your doctor knows my Birmingham cousins. If they call speak carefully about Eileen'.

It took me about two hours to recollect the septuagenarian ruins referred to. I have seen them once in my life. My father has probably seen them oftener.

Apart from its humour (and I can imagine nothing funnier than a Max cartoon of HK referring in non-committal terms to his wife during the course of a visit from two Birmingham Nonconformist kinsmen) this telegram gets my father and all the careful complicated chaos of his morality as well, I think, as Asquith's *bon mot* got him.

Shortly after leaving hospital Kingsmill travelled to Manchester to spend a weekend with Malcolm Muggeridge and his wife Kitty. Kitty's father George Dobbs had worked for Sir Henry Lunn since 1907 and Kitty had known all the Lunns from an early age. She had first come across Kingsmill in his days as a Lunn employee, remembering him as a rather incongruous figure in a brown track suit laughing and falling over as he escorted parties of young lady skiers up the nursery slopes. It was Brian Lunn, Kingsmill's younger brother, who suggested that Muggeridge, then working on the *Manchester Guardian*, might be able to arrange some book reviewing work for Kingsmill.

Muggeridge was twenty-seven. He was born in Croydon and was one of five brothers. His parents were of the lower middle class and his father H. T. Muggeridge, a self-educated man who left school at thirteen, earned his living as a clerk in the city of London. His mother came from a working-class Sheffield family. H. T. Muggeridge was a crusading socialist, who became a Labour councillor in Croydon and later an MP, and the young Muggeridge, brought up on the works of Wells and Tawney, Shaw and William Morris, identified himself very closely with his father's crusade to bring about a new and just society based on Fabian principles. Because of their political beliefs the Muggeridges were set apart from their neighbours in Croydon and Malcolm grew up with a strong sense of being an outsider, which he never wholly lost.

At Cambridge, as a former secondary schoolboy, his contemporaries being almost all from public schools, his feeling of isolation, of being the odd man out, was enhanced. He read chemistry, physics and zoology, subjects which held no interest for him, and managed to scrape by with a pass degree. On leaving Cambridge he went to teach in a Christian college in South India, returning to England in 1927 to work in elementary schools in Birmingham. In the same year he married Kitty Dobbs, whom he had met first through her brother Leonard, a friend at Cambridge. Kitty's father was not content with a son-in-law who was an elementary schoolmaster in Birmingham and it was as a result of his prompting that Muggeridge applied for a job at a government school in Egypt. When transferred to Cairo University he began to submit reports on Egyptian affairs to the *Manchester Guardian* and these were so well received by the paper's special correspondent, Arthur Ransome, and by the editor, C. P. Scott, that he was offered a job on the editorial staff in Manchester and at last had the sense of discovering his vocation in journalism.

The first meeting with Kingsmill always remained a vivid memory. 'You know that curious feeling,' he later told Pearson, 'one has of meeting someone with whom one is going to be intimate. You feel as though you know them already. Features, tone of voice, gestures all are at once familiar. Thus I remember in the dark cavernous Manchester station with people streaming through the barrier, picking out Hughie without the slightest difficulty and greeting him as though we were old friends instead of strangers.' They went back to the Muggeridges' flat in Wilmslow Road, talking to each other with the easy fluency which some children evince on first acquaintance. Kingsmill told Muggeridge of his experiences in the nursing home, of how happy he had been, for a short time cut off from all his worries. On Sunday they set off for Stockport Station. Kingsmill had the idea that Pearson would be passing through, on his way back from an acting engagement in Newcastle. But this was a misconception and Pearson did not show up. Muggeridge and Kingsmill walked up and down the deserted platform for about half an hour and then abandoned the rendezvous. 'We went off however, feeling quite satisfied,' Muggeridge told Pearson. 'If we had not met you, we had gone to meet you; and anyway in his company I discovered for the first time that Stockport Station was full of interest.'

In the evening Muggeridge took Kingsmill along to the *Manchester Guardian* office in Cross Street with the hope of getting him some reviewing work. This project, like the meeting with Pearson, was unsuccessful. The paper's literary editor, Allan Monkhouse, described by Muggeridge as 'sensitive, talented but somehow forlorn', was rather intimidated by Kingsmill's jovial presence. Kingsmill was almost always at a disadvantage in literary circles on account of his unfailing cheerfulness. 'I have noticed,' said Muggeridge, 'a strong pre-disposition to believe that writers should, like Don Quixote, wear woeful countenances – the more woeful the higher their earnings. There was little trace of woe in Kingsmill's countenance, and his earnings were correspondingly meagre.' He lacked, too, any ability or willingness to ingratiate himself with other people. More often than not, for no very clear reason, he actively antagonised them in a way that he could not understand. 'How not to tread on corns in a world of bunioned centipedes?' he once asked himself despairingly in a notebook. He never found a formula, and the result was that the many attempts his friends made to secure him employment almost always ended in failure.

Leaving Allan Monkhouse, they adjourned to Muggeridge's room where he tapped out an editorial for the next day's paper. Just as Kingsmill had opened Pearson's eyes by making him laugh at Harris, so with Muggeridge, he began by bringing home to him the essentially ludicrous nature of leaders. Like Harris, they were filled with self-importance, propounding panaceas and setting the world to rights. 'At that time I was still very young,' Muggeridge said, 'and inclined to over-seriousness. For instance, I was very serious about politics and even about the *Manchester Guardian*.' In Kingsmill's presence the stock-in-trade clichés of the leader writer immediately became hilarious jokes – 'the people of this country', 'it is greatly to be hoped', 'surely wiser counsels will prevail'. That night one leader began: 'One is sometimes tempted to believe that the Greeks do not want a stable government,' and the writer went on to express the hope that 'moderate men of all shades of opinion' would rally together. Kingsmill was perhaps reminded of another old Liberal Party hack, Sir Henry. He, too, had entertained the belief that moderate men would somehow rise to the occasion.

Muggeridge, however, was not yet ready to accept Kingsmill's detached view of the political world, or to see the rival ideologies as manifestations of Dawnism. He still retained sufficient faith in his father's socialist views to be appalled by Ramsay Macdonald's agreement to head the National Government of 1931. Everything in which he had been brought up to believe had been betrayed. The hopes of a New Dawn were shattered. Liberalism, socialism, Fabianism seemed to be utterly discredited. But Marxism remained. The moderate men had plainly failed, but was it not possible that the revolutionary immoderates in Russia had found the answer? 'I resolved,' he said, 'to go where I thought a new age was coming to pass: to Moscow and the future of mankind.' He became the *Manchester Guardian*'s Moscow correspondent and sailed with Kitty for Russia in 1932. Their intention was, once they had established themselves, to sever the connection with the *Manchester Guardian* and live the rest of their lives in Russia.

Muggeridge returned to England some nine months later in a mood of utter disillusionment. Russia had been like a nightmare. Nothing he had seen corresponded in any way with what was being written and believed in progressive circles. A New Jerusalem had been hailed: but he saw only tyranny and famine. It was all a hoax. What frustrated him was the refusal on the part of the socialists and fellow travellers to accept the truth, about which he, as an eye-witness, had no possible doubts. Even the *Manchester Guardian* had cut some of his reports, a fact which angered him intensely. 'You don't want to know what's going on in Russia or let your readers know,' he told the editor in a letter of resignation.

It was only when he was much older that he wrote: 'People believe lies not because they are plausibly presented but because they want to believe them.'

The Russian experience left Muggeridge in a spiritual vacuum. Now everything in which he had ever believed had turned to dust. In the autumn of 1933 he took a job at the League of Nations in Geneva, where he and Kitty stayed for eight months before returning to London. The publication of his book *Winter in Moscow*, in which he described the scenes he had witnessed in Russia, increased his sense of isolation as its tone was directly opposed to the progressive orthodoxy of the day. To add to his disappointments, a novel, satirising the *Guardian*, which he wrote in Moscow, was withdrawn when the paper threatened legal action. Angry and desperately short of money, he took a job as assistant editor of the *Calcutta Statesman*. Leaving his family in London, he spent a year in Calcutta, which he described later as 'easily the most melancholy of my life'.

On September 18, 1935 R. H. Bruce Lockhart, then editing the *Evening Standard*'s gossip column, wrote in his diary: 'Malcolm Muggeridge, the author of an anti-Bolshevist book on Russia and of a suppressed novel on the *Manchester Guardian*, joined us today. Clever, nervous and rather "freakish" in appearance. Holds strong views.' The offer of a job on the *Standard* had come to Muggeridge out of the blue in the shape of a telegram from the paper's editor, Percy Cudlipp. He accepted with alacrity and hurried home to rejoin his family in Grove Terrace, Highgate. Here in his spare time from the *Standard*, he finished a life of Samuel Butler commissioned from him by Jonathan Cape before he left for India.

The commission came about as the result of the sort of misconception of which publishers are so often capable. Cape had assumed that Muggeridge, who, judging by his Moscow book, was a rebellious young man, would naturally warm to Butler and therefore prove the ideal person to undertake a new biography to be published in the centenary year of his birth. The executors agreed and gave him access to all the Butler papers. In fact, if the idea was to promote Butler, they could not have made a more disastrous choice.

Butler, whose reputation has slumped dramatically since 1934, was at the time a literary sacred cow of considerable proportions. Each generation has its rebels with whom it identifies and, in the case of Butler, as Hesketh Pearson said, 'The pre-war generation regarded him as their symbol of revolt against the family, just as the post-war generation regarded D. H. Lawrence as the symbol of their revolt against – whatever it was he revolted against.' The author of a rather lukewarm satire, *Erewhon*, Butler would have remained deservedly obscure had it not been for the publication after his death of *The Way of All Flesh*.

This partly autobiographical novel tells the story of Ernest Pontifex (Butler), son of the Reverend Theobald Pontifex and his wife Christina. Theobald is a country parson of a conventional Victorian type, who brings his son up strictly, instilling in him a knowledge of scripture and the classics from the start. When he is older he is sent to Roughborough School (Shrewsbury), then on to Cambridge, where he falls in with an Evangelical group called the Simeonites and is later ordained in the Church of England. As a curate in a poor London parish he lives in lodgings and in a fit of untypical passion assaults a girl living in the same house, for which he is sent to prison for six months. On emerging from prison he renounces the church and becomes a tailor. He meets a young girl, Ellen, once a servant of his father's, and they get married. For a time all goes well. Ellen has a baby, but then to his horror Ernest discovers she is an alcoholic. Things look bad; then one day, Ernest meets his father's old coachman, who tells him that *he* is married to Ellen and that his marriage must therefore be invalid. Ernest experiences a 'shock of pleasure', as it releases him from any further responsibility for Ellen, who after admitting that 'Ernest is too good for her', goes off to America, and their children are left in the care of a bargee's wife at Gravesend. Ernest comes into a fortune left him by an aunt, and lives affluently ever after.

It would be difficult to find a more unlikely story, or a more unsympathetic fictional hero than Ernest. His hatred of his parents, disagreeable though they are, is obsessive and unpleasant and extends even to making fun of his mother on her death bed; he is a raging snob, believing that 'the most perfect saint is the most perfect gentleman', and is obsessed by money: 'A man can stand being told that he must submit to a severe surgical operation, or that he has some disease which will shortly kill him, or that he will be a cripple or blind for the rest of his life; dreadful as such tidings must be, we do not find that they unnerve the greater number of mankind; most men, indeed, go coolly enough even to be hanged, but the strongest quail before financial ruin.' Such is the view of the book's narrator, who is supposed to be Pontifex's godfather, but is in fact Butler, who believes strongly that boys should be taught while still at school how to speculate on the stock market and that professorships of speculation should be established at Oxford and Cambridge. Butler himself had learned book-keeping by double entry when a young man and believed it to be 'the most necessary branch of any young man's learning after reading and writing'. Naturally this godfather is delighted by the final outcome, observing of his protegé: 'He is richer than ever, for he has never married and his London and North-Western Shares have nearly doubled themselves.'

Following the publication of this lamentable book, Butler ceased to be thought of as a minor Victorian eccentric and was hailed in the best critical circles as a liberator. Father-hatred became fashionable. Bernard Shaw, who referred to Butler as 'a great man' and 'a man of genius', wrote in his preface to *Major Barbara*: 'It drives one almost to despair of English literature when one sees so extraordinary a study of English life as Butler's posthumous *The Way of All Flesh* making so little impression.' As a result of Shaw's enthusiasm, a second edition was published in 1908, an annual dinner of Butlerites was inaugurated and thereafter his works enjoyed a steady sale in elegantly produced volumes.

Although the initial enthusiasm for Butler died down in later years, he continued to be regarded with admiration. He was the sort of person who appealed to the literary Establishment of the period. In many ways he corresponded to the fantasy of what a writer should be like – a man of independent means living quietly in bachelor lodgings writing his books, putting down interesting thoughts and carefully worded aphorisms in notebooks.

Butler had rebelled against religious orthodoxy – but not too much. 'We should be Churchmen,' he said, 'but somewhat lukewarm Churchmen.' He gave his view that Christianity was true, 'in so far as it had fostered beauty, and it had fostered much beauty'. And he was homosexual without having the lack of taste to indulge in Oscar Wilde-like practices. All these facets endeared him to a certain sort of literary type, who relished disrespect for authority and convention, provided it did nothing to upset the *status quo*. A typical Butlerite was E. M. Forster. Liberal, well-mannered, donnish, and like Butler, homosexual, Forster named *Erewhon* as the one book that had influenced him more than any other. Butler he said 'although a rebel . . . was not a reformer. He believed in conventions, provided they are observed humanely. Grace and graciousness, good temper, good looks, good health and good sense; tolerance, intelligence, and willingness to abandon any moral standards at a pinch. That is what he admired.' Ironically, Butler, lyrical champion of the capitalist system, was taken up by a number of left-wing dons who found the rather spurious account of working class life in *The Way of All Flesh* appealing. G. D. H. Cole was an admirer and, more recently, Professor Richard Hoggart has enthusiastically commended the book.

It was against such a formidable orthodoxy as this that Muggeridge directed his attack. Nor was his book simply written for the fun of demolishing a cult. Butler's rejection of his father and his family, his obsession with money, his cautious homosexuality, all these were anathema to Muggeridge. There was a deadness, a lack of humanity in his life and in his writing which was repellent. He showed that despite appearances, Butler was a deeply timid and conventional man. His attitude to his father, described vividly in *The Way of All Flesh* and hailed as a noble act of rebellion against Victorian humbug, was exposed as mere adolescent silliness which had little to justify its vehemence. The importance he attached to money, and especially to money earned by the manipulation of stocks and shares, was as unattractive as his romantic and, again, adolescent snobbishness. Muggeridge gave a vivid account of Butler's homosexual attachments: to Charles Pauli, the good-looking dominating con-man whom he supported financially throughout his life, to Hans Faesch, a Swiss student, and to Henry Festing Jones the ponderous artist who lived with him in Clifford's Inn and afterwards wrote a turgid two-volume biography of his friend.

It was while finishing his book in 1935 that Muggeridge resumed his acquaintanceship with Kingsmill, who in turn introduced him to Pearson. Muggeridge had a very possessive feeling about Kingsmill and knowing of the great friendship that existed between him and Pearson he felt a bias against him until they met. Then, like everyone else, he succumbed to Pearson's charm, his warm generous nature and his perpetual high spirits. The three took to meeting regularly in the Horseshoe Tavern, at the bottom of Tottenham Court Road, conveniently situated near the British Museum, where one or other of them was bound to be researching. Kingsmill's book on Dickens had just been published and he was about to start on a life of D. H. Lawrence; Pearson was working on his biography of Labouchere.

The conversation at these meetings invariably revolved round books and authors. Pearson and Kingsmill talked of the great writers and poets as though they were their friends, or enemies, giving them points for good and bad qualities. They would often fantasize, imagining G. K. Chesterton or Abraham Lincoln on his wedding night, or Disraeli announcing to the House of Commons that he was going to marry Queen Victoria. Kingsmill was also fond of literary quizzes: 'Which author would you most like to be with on a desert island?' 'Who are the men you most admire?' 'Who would you most like to have been?' In response to the last question, Muggeridge on one occasion opted for Chaucer, Johnson, Cromwell and St Augustine:

PEARSON: On what principle have you arrived at this odd collection?

MUGGERIDGE: Well, Chaucer as poet, Johnson as a human being, Cromwell as a man of action, and Augustine as a saint.

KINGSMILL: Augustine's not my idea of a saint.

MUGGERIDGE: Don't forget we're discussing who we *want* to be, not who we *ought* to be. I hope to become a saint, and Augustine wasn't in any hurry either.

The figure of Wordsworth was a constant cause of badinage between Pearson on one side and Kingsmill and Muggeridge on the other. For Kingsmill, Wordsworth had expressed better than anyone his own feelings about the nature of reality. 'The ecstasy of his finest work', he once wrote, 'is always mystical – is never, that is, explicable in terms addressed purely to the intellect.' Pearson, a humanist, with little interest in any poetry apart from Shakespeare's, regarded Wordsworth with intense dislike – especially when he discovered, while writing *The Fool of Love*, that Wordsworth had slandered and disowned his one-time friend Hazlitt. 'By the way,' he told Kingsmill while working on the book, 'I was reading a section of Hazlitt to Gladys last night and she questioned the advisability of one passage which I think unexceptionable. However, I promised I would submit it to you, though I do not promise to abide by your verdict. I cannot think what there is to object to in it. Pray speak frankly on the point. Here is the passage:

Wordsworth was clearly two men. One of them expressed himself in poetry that is much liked by half-dead dons, half-alive eunuchs, half-witted pederasts and Mr Hugh Kingsmill. For the other Wordsworth there is no name in the ordinary vocabulary of polite invective, while the finer shades of irony would have been lost on the man himself and would make little impression on his enthusiastic disciples. There is, nevertheless, a short sharp word which so admirably describes the type of man he was that, however unwillingly on the part of the present writer and however unpleasant to the eye of the reader it must be used. It is a word that is seldom seen in dictionaries, though it is frequently heard on the streets. It is neither a Saxon word nor a Norman word; it is late-British and it is thoroughly British. It is a word that has but a single universally recognised meaning. It is direct, expressive, and final; and it fits Wordsworth exactly. He was a shit.

'Get Dorothy to throw some light on what I must suppose to be Gladys' essentially feminine objection to this passage.'

Muggeridge, though he admired Pearson's book on Hazlitt, sided with Kingsmill on the Wordsworth question. But Pearson held his ground. 'Dear Mugg,' he wrote, following a disagreement on this point. 'We'll never agree about Words-worth . . . I don't see why you should assume that because a man feels nobly in solitude he cannot be a shit in society. I am devoted to Bozzy, whose nobility is proved by his admiration and affection for the Doctor, but I should be the last to deny that he was contemptible in his everyday behaviour. You appear to want a man *all White* and apart from the fact that no man is all white, he would be utterly uninteresting if he was. . . .

'Now about the difference between Hazlitt and Wordsworth over the French Revolution. Hazlitt's later view was a *felt* loyalty to his youth's idealism, Wordsworth's was a *considered* disloyalty: the one stuck to his guns, the other deserted his and went over to the enemy. You and I would have deserted our guns; we would not have turned them on the side for which we had been fighting. And that, my lad, is the whole point. Hazlitt, we would agree, was stupid but he was also chivalrous. Wordsworth was sane – oh, so very sane! – and treacherous. You must remember that more than a century of revolutions have taken place since the French one, and you and I have learnt wisdom in that time. But the French Revolution was novelty and anyone might be excused for believing that it heralded a dawn. I did not personally hope much from the Russian revolution: but had I felt sufficiently idealistic to think it wonderful at the time, I think I should still, though disillusioned, pay tribute to the ideas that fostered it. Certainly I should not turn completely round and praise the Tzardom. Wordsworth would have done so if he had seen a sinecure or the Sacred Order of the Ruddy Romanoff in the offing. I think he was essentially a dishonest man. And now let's talk of something else.'

Pearson's literary and historical likes were as vehement as his dislikes. 'The truth is,' Muggeridge recalled in later life, 'that the subjects of Hesketh's biographies became a circle of absent friends whom he felt bound to champion in all circumstances and on all counts.' One of the few occasions on which they seriously fell out was when Muggeridge referred in a book review to Tom Paine, one of Pearson's heroes, as 'poor besotted Tom Paine'. This may have been a case of Muggeridge giving a friend what Kingsmill called 'an unexpected jab', but whatever the motive it caused a Pearsonian explosion. Angry words were exchanged when they met.

But as always Pearson's anger soon subsided and when Muggeridge wrote regretting their disaffection he replied:

I hasten to tell you that there is not a grain of grit in our friendship so far as I'm concerned. . . . All of us admire people we don't like and like people we don't admire. When I read your 'poor besotted Tom Paine' I realised at once that you and I admire quite different things, but it did not alter my feeling of personal affection for you by a gram (whatever a gram may be). I have written a book to prove that Tom was neither poor (except in possessions, and I knew you didn't mean that) nor besotted, but on the contrary that he was rich in spirit, brave beyond anyone in history, noble minded if anyone ever was, the most honest man in the annals of public life, and so generous that he was willing to give his life for a man whom he had never met: further, that he was the clearest-headed thinker of his time, the most humane man of action of whom we have record, pleading as he did among a pack of wolves and cowards for the life of a monarch he disliked on principle (at the peril of his own life), that he was as selfless as Christ, to whom he bears a close resemblance, and that his only serious weakness was an unconquerable idealism, which drove him to drink as it drove Christ to Calvary. Though I have given concrete evidence for all this in my book, all that you are really saying is that the evidence is a lie and my conclusions bullshit. All that I can say in reply is that my opinion of your intelligence is lowered and that I am sorry you should think me a deluded ass, but I remain as fond of you as ever I was. . . . You are one of my very few friends. Please remain so in spite of Tom Paine.

Whatever their differences – and they were many – Pearson and Muggeridge were both bound by their admiration and love for Kingsmill. 'It became,' Muggeridge said, 'a firm and steady triple friendship with Kingsmill in the centre, and Hesketh and myself on the two flanks, and in a certain sense communicating through him.' Both men were jealous of any outsider who tried to get in on the act and resented Kingsmill's rather half-hearted attempts to bring other people into the circle.

The artist Joe Maiden, who illustrated the Kingsmill–Muggeridge collaborations, made a drawing of two incidents of a day in the life of the 'Horseshoe group' which showed what Muggeridge called the 'rotarian side' of Kingsmill's character: 'This might involve my being unwillingly introduced to some Swami from Bengal, or refugee poet from Central Europe, or Viennese psycho-analytical witch-doctor, or levitating esoteric Slav in the faint expectation that the repugnance Hughie knew me to feel for such characters might be overcome by actual contact with them.' In the drawing, Maiden portrayed an occasion on which Pearson and Kingsmill were lunching together in the Horseshoe when a poet sat himself down at their table uninvited and began to talk to Kingsmill. Pearson was very annoyed and turned his back on the two of them, pointedly ignoring Kingsmill's attempts to bring him into the conversation. Afterwards, when they walked to the Museum, Kingsmill reproached Pearson for being rude. Outside the Reading Room they met Muggeridge, and Kingsmill, welcoming the opportunity to knock off work, went into the library to collect his books. There he became involved with an Indian student who expressed a keen desire to be introduced to Muggeridge. Muggeridge, however, was as unenthusiastic about the Indian as Pearson had been about the poet. When asked by the student what he thought of India, he replied succinctly, 'Quite interesting'. He then left the building with Pearson, Kingsmill following dejectedly behind.

While working on his life of Butler, Muggeridge had been to see Albert Cathie, who had acted as manservant for Butler at his rooms in Clifford's Inn, where he lived with his devoted companion Henry Festing Jones. In his monumental two-volume life of Butler, Jones described how Butler had been in the habit of visiting a French prostitute in Handel Street once a week. What Jones omitted to say, Cathie told Muggeridge, was that he himself, at Butler's instigation, had also made regular weekly visits to the same lady, Madame Dumas.

One day when the three friends were seated in the Horseshoe Muggeridge told Kingsmill and Pearson what Cathie had said. Kingsmill's eyes at once lit up and he began to develop the theme. Butler and Jones would not have gone on the same day. That would have been too much for Madame. Butler went on Tuesday, say, and Jones on Thursday. 'A day

Hugh Kingsmill as a prisoner of war at Karlsruhe in 1916 with Lieutenant Garray and John Holms, Kingsmill is on the left. Below, Kingsmill about 1935, and shortly before his death

Hesketh Pearson, in
uniform during the Great
War, and with Bernard
Shaw in 1945

Kingsmill and Pearson, Aberdeen June 1937 (above)

Muggeridge and Pearson in 1950, photograph by Margaret Ryder (below)

Malcolm Muggeridge in about 1932
and (below) in 1977, photograph by
Eric Hands

of recoupment' – Kingsmill was beginning to laugh – 'being adjudged advisable'. Madame did not know the names of her clients. Would she refer to '*Monsieur Mardi*' and '*Monsieur Jeudi*'? She must have been hurt when Butler asked him to oblige his young friend in addition to himself. 'Why should she be?' Muggeridge asked. 'Well, old man, Butler has been visiting her for years – presumably she has come to have a sort of wifely feeling for him – and then one day he suddenly

Trials of a Rotarian ....

or Hugh's Dark Day

A Deep Depression, centred over Tottenham Court Rd., is moving Eastward to Bloomsbury.

FURTHER OUTLOOK : FRIGID

READING ROOM

– Joe Maiden.

dumps young Jones on her – tells her that Thursday suits
Jones best and that he'll stick to Tuesday as hitherto.' (All
three were now laughing.) 'I picture her,' Kingsmill continued, 'sitting in a darkening room, after Butler has told
her about Jones and perhaps sighing – *"Encore un rêve disparu!"*

The three men, still laughing, got up and paid for their
lunch. Kingsmill now suggested that they should visit Handel
Street and see for themselves the scene of Madame's 'erotic
calvary'. As he strode along with rolling gait his arms swinging
like a sailor's, Kingsmill envisaged the two earnest and bowler-
hatted homosexuals each mournfully plodding towards Handel
Street on his weekly errand. Butler, he proposed, took with
him a little sponge-bag containing his toilet requisites.

The three reached the house and Kingsmill now began
to speculate on whether Madame ever discussed the relative
performances of Butler or Jones with the other: '*Votre Monsieur
Mardi n'est pas très fort*' or '*Monsieur Jeudi reste toujours jeune,
n'est-ce-pas?*' By now Pearson and Muggeridge were helpless
with laughter and with tears streaming down their faces
were reduced to hanging onto a lamppost to control themselves.
Kingsmill, himself hysterical, paused. 'Poor old man!' he
gasped. There was a sympathetic silence and then the laughing
resumed, to the astonishment of the passers by.

After the treatment of his Matthew Arnold book by the
critics, Kingsmill had a shrewd idea of the sort of reception
Muggeridge's *Butler* would get. At the same time he himself
found it difficult to judge his friends' books objectively.
Almost always he showered them with praise and, whenever
possible, included passages from them in his anthologies.
So it was probably at the instigation of his friend Douglas
Jerrold, whose firm Eyre and Spottiswoode were publishing
the *Butler* after its rejection by Cape's, that he wrote to
Muggeridge urging him to tone it down: 'It is very good
indeed,' he wrote, 'in the most important respect of all,
namely that it is absolutely sincere and very penetrating
about the chief persons concerned – and how concerned they
would be! But I think you ought to give it the most drastic
revision for two reasons. First, from the practical standpoint
you will be flayed alive by every single critic, and secondly,
from the artistic standpoint, the nausea at life in general

leaves one with the feeling that even Jones is not much inferior to anyone else. You may say that is how you feel. In fact, you do say that there is no such thing as objective truth. But if this is so, you are not entitled to your moral disgust, which fills the book. You are only entitled to the disgust which a bad egg would evoke, and that does not make writing or anything else worthwhile. Take Swift – his indictment of humanity gets its force from his own sense of values, as expressed in the Houyhnhnms – a bleak sense of values but definite. . . . The great fault of the book is over emphasis, and the intrusion of nausea. If I were you I would cut out every single physical image in the book which your own fancy supplies. . . . The gist of this letter is that you have a standard of values which you allow your nausea to submerge and that you ought to revise the book acc. to this standard and expunge all the nausea. I think a calm detachment about Jones would be much more effective and that you should allow him some interest in and affection for Butler. I should put it at 50% at first, dwindling to 15%.'

Muggeridge, wisely, did not rewrite the book according to his friend's instructions. It was his view of Butler and he could not hope to share Kingsmill's more sympathetic attitude.

Pearson wrote: 'The book is splendid but, my God! you are asking for trouble. You'll be excommunicated, black-balled by the Athenaeum and probably assassinated by Erewhonians.' These prophecies were accurate. The leading critic of the day, Desmond MacCarthy, who was a founder member of the Butler cult, was rumoured to be so disgusted by the book that he threw it into the Adriatic. He devoted two successive articles in the *Sunday Times* to a defence of Butler. E. M. Forster later called the book 'an attack so disgruntled and so persistent that it may well be the result of a guilt complex'.

It is true that *The Earnest Atheist* is an unbalanced book, in the same way that Kingsmill's book on Dickens is un-balanced. But like so many of Muggeridge's attacks, for all its lack of sympathy, its minor inaccuracies and exaggerations, it is fundamentally right and true. Again, despite the scorn that was poured on it at the time, it altered for ever the general view of the victim. It was impossible thereafter to regard Butler in a sentimental way either as a liberator or as just a kind, gentle person who wrote books. It was the realisation that this was the case and that earlier estimates of Butler had been hopelessly romantic and exaggerated that made the critics so angry.

'Nothing,' Muggeridge once said, 'enrages people more than to feel they have engaged in unprofitable adulation.'

Chapter 8

By early 1936 Muggeridge was becoming increasingly discontented with his life on the *Evening Standard*. 'He is not happy and wants to get out,' Bruce Lockhart wrote in his diary on February 8, 1936. 'Thinks it is ridiculous that people like himself and me should not be consulted about anything and should have our stuff "subbed" by some half-educated nitwit.'

Kingsmill, who called Beaverbrook 'Robin Badfellow', encouraged Muggeridge to make the break with journalism and devote his time to writing books. He urged him to come and live near him in Sussex. Muggeridge did not need much persuading. After first looking over a house in Hastings, he and Kitty, with their four small children, moved eventually into the Old Mill at Whatlington, near Battle, a large eighteenth-century house, formerly an inn, which they bought for £800. Here he settled down to write. 'It was a fairly austere existence,' he recalled. 'Water came from a well which had to be pumped by hand, and drinking water from a spring some little distance away. Each day I fetched two bucketfuls. Bathing was done in a small bath in front of the kitchen stove . . . and, of course, we had no car. The nearest shopping centre was Battle some two miles away: and we would usually walk or cycle in and out.'

The Kingsmills, who had returned to England in 1933, were living in Hastings. It was a town to which Kingsmill was greatly attached. He had lived there for some time with his first wife at the Albany Hotel, which had been acquired by Lunn. The hotel, situated on the sea front, had a clientele consisting of the elderly and affluent whom Kingsmill once described as 'excrement living on increment'. Now he and his family installed themselves at 24 Laton Road, a large solid house which gave Kingsmill an illogical feeling of security. He liked it best of all his many homes and never afterwards referred to it without what Muggeridge called 'a nostalgic groan'.

During the years before the war, Muggeridge and Kingsmill met two or three times a week. Sometimes Muggeridge cycled into Hastings and they went walking on the cliffs or in the huge park-like cemetery overlooking the town. Alternatively, Kingsmill would catch a bus out to Battle, walking the remaining mile or so to Whatlington. 'Usually I would meet him along the road,' Muggeridge wrote, 'delighted when his solid figure loomed up and he began to wave and shout his cheerful greeting – "Hullo, old man, hullo. . . ." Never have I seen him without a warm rush of happiness. He created this feeling – a delight in the prospect of his physical presence, more strongly than anyone I have ever known.' On the days they did not meet, they engaged in marathon telephone conversations, two or three hours long, to the annoyance of their wives and also, in Kingsmill's case, those members of the public who were queuing up to use the post office telephone. Dorothy Kingsmill noted how after these talks with Muggeridge, her husband was utterly exhausted.

If Kingsmill and Pearson were like Holmes and Watson, the Kingsmill–Muggeridge relationship had perhaps more in common with that of Johnson and Boswell. Kingsmill and Pearson were nearly exact contemporaries, while Muggeridge was fourteen years younger than Kingsmill; again, something of the change that was evident in Boswell's mood when he was with Johnson can be seen in Muggeridge's response to Kingsmill. Boswell, as his diaries show, was by nature moody and sensuous when left to himself, but became transformed when in Johnson's company. So too Muggeridge, unsatisfied and restless, was exhilarated and refreshed by being with Kingsmill. As he himself acknowledged: 'He made one feel mentally alive as no one else I have ever met did. He raised one up to his own level.'

'It is a favourite proposition of mine,' Muggeridge wrote to Pearson, 'which I often discussed with Hughie and with which he largely agreed, that highly imaginative people are invariably miserable when they are young, and on the whole grow progressively happier. . . . It seems to me that the general rule is that the imagination makes for unhappiness when young and can produce serenity when old. Its first struggles with appetite are painful and leave many bruises, and its first realisation that the world of time is irretrievably imperfect, whereas delight is only in perfection, cannot but create much anguish. Once this period is passed, the imagination becomes an even greater solace, until now, in middle age, I feel that it alone makes life worth living, and that to be deprived of it, whatever compensations there might be, would drain life of its delight.'

Reading Muggeridge's own account of his life and the scattered references of his contemporaries makes it clear that he suffered deeply in his early years from a sense of dissatisfaction and an inner restlessness which only left him at the onset of old age. He fought against everything that threatened to tie him down. He stayed in no job for more than a few years and he had a habit of rounding on those who thought they were his friends that was always disconcerting. He was easily bored and made little attempt to disguise the fact. Pearson used to talk of his 'N.A. (standing for "Next Appointment") look.'

In these circumstances his friendship with Kingsmill was all the more remarkable. Pearson remembered that though he had heard Muggeridge criticise most people and things he had never heard him speak of Kingsmill without affection and admiration. Even so, in the early period of their friendship there were some moments of strain, resulting from the intensity with which Muggeridge treated their relationship. He was, much more than Pearson, emotionally involved with Kingsmill and even developed telepathic links with him. Initially he was jealous of Kingsmill's other friends, a fact that caused occasional ructions: 'What has upset me,' Kingsmill remonstrated during one such episode, 'is the amount of will you put into your friendships. There is bound to be will in every relationship, but there oughtn't to be much in friendship. Realising that you felt possessive about your friends, and noticing some examples of it, I have been uncomfortable, being certain that when the occasion occurred you would attribute the same feeling to me . . . I suppose I have some possessiveness over my friends, but as I have always cared for them because they have been a refuge from the will, I don't think I have much, nor do I think

I would have any if it was not provoked by someone else feeling in that way.

'There is one other thing which often crops up between us, and that is your view that there is not much difference between any one person and any other, and that a man who has any money to spare is as ruthless an egotist as a multi-millionaire or Ghengis Khan. Really this view is simply a means of excusing oneself from trying to improve oneself, and it is also a way of getting rid of the superiority to oneself of people who are trying to master the will. I think that the difference between Buddha in his best moments and Stalin in his worst (or best) is as near being immeasurable as anything in the world of time can be, and that it is only if one believes this that one can begin any improvement in oneself. To see that the will is bad, without trying to rise above it is like looking at Mont Blanc and feeling that one has climbed it.'

'I do wish,' Kingsmill said on another occasion, 'that you wouldn't keep me in a state of uncertainty about yourself. You know how much I enjoy our talks, but I never know when you will give me an unexpected jab.'

In these traces of forgotten rows one can see Muggeridge, like Pearson before him, kicking against the influence which he knows Kingsmill is exercising over him. He too was being given a belated education. No schoolmaster or don had inspired Muggeridge during his time at school and university. Now Kingsmill appeared, late in the day, as a teacher of genius, to introduce him to literature and to show how it was not a means of escaping from life but was in itself one of the most important things in life. The notion of Dawnism and Kingsmill's concept of the struggle between Will and Imagination was another crucial lesson. All this Muggeridge absorbed to such an extent that afterwards he could never be sure when he was quoting Kingsmill and when speaking for himself.

Like Pearson, he was introduced to Don Quixote and Dr Johnson, and there is hardly an article written by him thereafter which does not contain some reference to one or the other. Through his friendship with Kingsmill his latent religious sense began to develop and he came to love the mystical writings of Blake and Wordsworth. 'To see all heaven in a grain of sand' expressed the ability that Kingsmill had of finding some general message in the most trivial things and people in life. 'Either everything is interesting or nothing is,' Muggeridge wrote later. Wordsworth expressed the love of nature and also the 'sense sublime of something far more deeply interfused' which could be achieved from the contemplation of natural phenomena. As a result, he says, of his companionship with Kingsmill, Muggeridge began to experience for himself moments of mystical awareness: 'On the first occasion I was standing with Kingsmill on the cliffs just outside Hastings, and looking down on the old town. It was an autumn evening, slightly misty and very still, with a sharp chill in the air. From the chimneys below, pale smoke, briefly separate, then becoming indistinct, and, finally lost to view; merging into the grey gathering evening. I was suddenly spellbound, as though this was a vision of the Last Day, and the wreaths of smoke, souls, leaving their bodies to rise heavenwards and become part of eternity.'

Kingsmill had an ability, shared by all great humorists, not just to amuse people but to make them happier in the process. His younger brother Brian, who was also living at Hastings at this time, always turned to him at the many periods of crisis in his life and was, momentarily at least, cured of his depression. What was said on these occasions cannot now be recalled, even if it could have been at the time. Kingsmill once said, 'People who can repeat what you are saying are not listening', and it is a common experience for those who have really enjoyed a conversation to remember afterwards nothing of what was said. Brian Lunn was no exception. But they did not discuss his misfortunes. 'Most of the talk,' he wrote in his autobiography, *Switchback*, 'was concerned with personalities, as in my experience most talk of literary men is, although their knowledge of literature and of the personalities of past writers may be drawn upon to illuminate their gossip. Nor is this strange, since human nature is the raw material of writers. Amongst practical men the retailing of personal anecdote is usually considered subversive, not only because they feel it an infringement of their pact of collective security, but because the sort of gossip I have in mind is often concerned with matter which, having little practical importance, is of interest only in its relation to character. Much of our talk was doubtless about

Father, an inexhaustible subject, owing to his ingenuity in adjusting his conduct to harmonise with his own view of himself as a meek idealist somewhat hampered in his devotion to great causes by the burdens of a business which he had altruistically brought into being in the interests of his staff.' (Kingsmill took the keenest interest in his brother's autobiography and gave him a great deal of assistance. This last passage bears all the marks of his style.)

Brian Lunn (known in the family as Bee) had had an unfortunate life ever since he suffered a breakdown during the First War. Sent out to Mesopotamia as an officer in the Black Watch, he had not been there long before he began to suffer from delusions. At one time he imagined his Company Commander was his brother Hugh, then later that he himself was in Heaven: 'I thought I had entered upon immortality because I felt content to prolong indefinitely my morning shave or any other part of the day's routine.' He was sent back to England and Netley Hospital. On his first day there his companions at breakfast were two German naval officers whom he mistook for Nietzsche and Wagner. Resenting this misapprehension as well as their fellow patient's loud Lunn voice, they asked to be transferred and Brian was left to pace round the room trying to settle the quarrel between an imaginary Dostoievsky and an equally non-existent Turgenev. Gradually he recovered and after a few weeks was well enough to go home to his parents. But he was never the same again, if he had ever been, in Kitty Muggeridge's phrase, the same before. He was subject to epileptic fits as well as attacks of depression, during which he made a habit of attempting suicide. Luckily he was never successful. (Thus, when he tried to gas himself, the meter ran out.)

In 1921 Sir Henry Lunn, at Kingsmill's instigation, took into the firm a friend of Alec Waugh, the writer Douglas Goldring, and Brian fell in love with his wife Betty. After asking his wife, 'Are you in love with the fellow?' and receiving the answer 'Yes', Goldring ruefully retired from the scene and Brian moved into his Battersea flat. Sir Henry and Lady Lunn were then in Switzerland and Kingsmill was given the task of delivering to them a letter from Brian in which he tried to put the best complexion on the affair. The attempt was a failure and

Kingsmill had to report that his picture of Brian 'with revolver in one hand and gin bottle in the other, saved by Betty, had failed to transform the situation into one acceptable to his parents.' Sir Henry, who had recently decided to take advantage of the devalued currency by posting all his circulars from Austria, sent Brian off to Vienna to take charge of the operation. There he was joined, secretly, by Betty and the couple enjoyed some weeks of bliss before their idyll was interrupted by the arrival of Sir Henry Lunn, who made them promise not to see each other again until the divorce of Mr and Mrs Goldring had been settled. When they agreed and Brian, as was his wont at times of stress, began to cry, Sir Henry asked them to kneel down while he said a prayer. He then went off to Oberammergau to see the Passion Play.

Brian and Betty were married for six years and after some initial unhappiness, as a result of which he nearly jumped out of a bedroom window, their liaison was for a time satisfactory. They had two children, Bridget and Michael, and lived on Haverstock Hill. Brian continued to work for his father, having returned to London when the government passed a bill banning the postage of circulars from abroad. Then in 1929 he and his wife met a Polish painter called Popovitch in a pub near the British Museum. When Brian and Betty started to quarrel, Popovitch challenged Brian to a duel. Brian explained that you could not challenge a man to a duel for being rude to his own wife. In the ensuing months Popovitch and Betty Lunn became increasingly enamoured of one another and when she invited him to stay in their Hampstead house, he eagerly accepted. This arrangement resulted inevitably in friction and after some unhappy scenes Betty and 'Pops' went off together to Paris.

Their departure led to another suicide attempt, later recounted by Michael Holroyd: 'Being by the sea at the time, the most ready and convenient means was obvious. The only objection which he could see was the unpleasantness of getting wet, and this he partly offset by borrowing a mackintosh from a passing stranger. Fully equipped, he set out across the beach and entered the sea. Fortunately, knowing nothing of the peculiar behaviour of the tides, he had not realised that the shallow water extended for over a mile off land. A lonely but resolute figure, growing smaller in the distance, he continued paddling out, while the level of the water still obstinately refused to rise above his ankles, until at last, weary and dispirited, he was forced to abandon the attempt and turn back.'

In the meantime, he had instituted divorce proceedings against his wife, which involved hiring a French private detective to observe the movements of 'Pops' and his companion in Paris. This zealous officer sent back such delightful data about 'Madame L.' ('She is about 1·68 metres tall and well-formed') and 'Monsieur P.' ('He is about 1·70 metres tall, bronzed, clean shaven and wears a chestnut suit') that Brian Lunn resolved, in the event of his ever becoming rich, to hire the detective to report on his own movements.

His divorce made final, Brian settled down at Hastings, lodging with a Mrs Pitcher, whose daughter had been looking after the children since their mother went off with 'Pops'. Early in 1935 Pitchers and Lunns moved to Baldslow, a suburb of Hastings, to Rowton House, built by a monumental mason, with stained glass windows and a marble staircase. Lunn wrote: 'The gravestone business was still carried on in the yard, where tombstones, awaiting a purchaser, leaned against the walls, bearing the words "In loving memory of—".' All his life Lunn had been a heavy drinker, but now at Hastings under the benign influence of Mrs Pitcher he became more abstemious. The nature of his relationship with the widow is difficult to determine. Lunn did once launch into a rhapsodic account of how he had embraced his landlady on the cliffs at Fairlight, describing in highly coloured terms the sea, the wind, the elemental forces. Kingsmill however would have none of it, allowing only that there had been 'a convenient copse'.

Like all the Lunns, including Kingsmill, Brian was keen on exercises and cold baths. It was his custom to go for an early morning run and swim, and he became a familiar figure in Hastings, running through the streets on his way to the beach, dressed only in shorts, formerly the property of the late Mr Pitcher, a petty officer in the Navy. 'Hullo, Gandhi!' a group of children shouted after him one day, and once, he wrote, 'on the cliff between Fairlight and Eastbourne a man laden with faggots said thoughtfully "Does the summer affect you?"'

Despite his difficulties Brian Lunn wrote three or four books, one in collaboration with William Gerhardi, but in another ambition, to become a barrister, he was not successful. He suffered a further setback when in 1939 he fell off the top of a bus and fractured his skull. As a result of this he had, thereafter, to wear on his head a plaster contraption, which he normally concealed beneath a hat. But occasionally he would disconcert strangers by taking the hat off in pubs, with sensational results. Another of his rather disconcerting habits, when out drinking, was to take someone else's drink. When the person remonstrated, Brian would stare fixedly at him and say: 'You're dreaming'.

Kingsmill was particularly fond of his brother, finding in his chaotic attempts to adjust himself to the world an exaggerated version of his own. By now, Kingsmill was beginning to suffer, at any rate financially, from the continuing failure of his books. He had written at least ten, and not one of them had sold enough copies to earn its advance. His *Frank Harris*, which was expected by everyone to be a best-seller, had enjoyed only a moderate success. Even *The Casanova Fable*, written in collaboration with William Gerhardi and decorated with mildly erotic illustrations, had failed to put him on the map.

Nothing had done more to obstruct Kingsmill's writing career than his book on Dickens, *The Sentimental Journey*, published in 1934. Dickens was still an English institution and those who set out to criticise him, as Kingsmill did, were asking for trouble. The book was widely misinterpreted and its hostile reception sowed the seeds of a growing resentment on Kingsmill's part against all critics and publishers, and a corresponding suspicion and wariness towards Kingsmill on the part of the latter. Looked at calmly, *The Sentimental Journey* has only one fault – a lack of balance. 'It is a brilliant book,' George Orwell wrote, 'but it is the case for the prosecution.'

Kingsmill had a habit of judging all writers by the highest standards, which meant comparing them to Shakespeare, Cervantes and Johnson. Dickens not having the imaginative detachment of any of these three had failed to reach the same level in his humour. Kingsmill set out to correct the picture painted by Chesterton and others of Dickens as a 'simple and robust genius', a laughing democrat brimming over with jollity. Dickens's comic figures were, for Kingsmill, grotesques inhabiting what he called 'a Cockney fairyland' and lacking the emotional richness of Falstaff and Quixote.

Dickens himself, so far from being the uncomplicated extrovert that Chesterton portrayed, was immature to a degree that prevented his genius from fully flowering. In youth he had pursued success as ruthlessly as any man of action but, once he obtained his goal, he continued to nourish a sense of grievance against his parents and an overwhelming feeling of self-pity which, together with the 'ideal longing of adolescence', remained his strongest emotion. Dickens, in other words, never grew up; a fact which is attested by the evocation in all his books of the nightmare world of childhood with all its horrors. 'As Dickens could not get out of himself,' Kingsmill wrote, 'could not lose himself in nature or anything else, he communicated his fever to whatever he described and there is therefore no pure beauty in his writings, or outlet into infinity. His world seems to be roofed in by the ceiling of an enormous theatre, and its atmosphere is either oppressive or crackling with electricity.'

If Kingsmill had gone on to stress the virtues of Dickens, which managed to flourish in spite of these flaws, he would have written a better book. As it is, one has to read between the lines to discern his appreciation of Dickens's good points. He himself later acknowledged this fault, admitting that 'the egotism of Dickens aroused mine, I put too much energy into pursuing him from chapter to chapter, with no pause in which to renew my sympathy for him'.

But what really upset the Dickensians, as well as the critics, was the use Kingsmill made of Dickens's love affair with the actress Ellen Ternan. The details of this story had been published in the *Daily Express* in April 1934, when Kingsmill was working on his book. He immediately saw the importance of it and in a brilliant analysis showed how Dickens had embodied the character of Ellen Ternan in all his later heroines – Estella in *Great Expectations*, Bella Wilfer in *Our Mutual Friend*, and Helena Landless in *The Mystery of Edwin Drood*. In each case the woman's name echoed that of Dickens's mistress – Ellen Lawless Ternan. These revelations called forth a storm of obloquy against Kingsmill: 'I was, I learnt with pained surprise from my reviews, a peerer through keyholes, a Freudian dabbling in garbage and a grave-desecrating ghoul.'

Dickens, whose books hymned the joys of family life, had carefully built up an image of himself designed to conform with his fantasies and the public had readily accepted him as the patron saint of domesticity. It was admittedly true that he had in the end decided to live apart from his wife, but their separation, it was believed, was due to a regrettable incompatibility, whose true nature could not be comprehended by lesser mortals. Moreover Mrs Dickens, not Dickens, was the instigator. This extraordinary piece of humbug survived long after Dickens's death and was carefully fostered by Chesterton and other enthusiasts. The idea therefore of the God-like Dickens falling in love with a commonplace actress who eventually became his mistress was something that the Dickensians could not stomach.

Later, of course, the story was accepted, Kingsmill's ideas were absorbed, and the public's view of Dickens underwent a suitable modification. But no redress was ever made to Kingsmill and he continued to be belittled. Typical was the famous American critic Edmund Wilson who, in his long essay 'Dickens: The Two Scrooges' published in *The Wound and the Bow*, dismissed Kingsmill as a poor imitator of Lytton Strachey and an amateur Freudian, and then went on to trot out his conclusions about Ellen Ternan as though they were his own.

It was not surprising in view of such treatment, that Kingsmill began to nourish a grudge against critics, which at times grew to such proportions that he fancied himself the victim of a conspiracy. In this state of mind he read deliberate slights and insults into innocuous articles and reviews. In March 1936 he suspected that an article by Desmond MacCarthy was directed at himself. He wrote to MacCarthy: 'Your remarks on adolescence in your article this week interested me very much, but I do not think you altogether appreciate the standpoint from which Dickens, for example, lays himself open to criticism in his treatment of his early years. He pictures David Copperfield from the outside as a small and rather pathetic figure. Children, I think, do not look on themselves as small, but on grown ups as large. In other words, they take themselves as the measure. If the soul is full grown at birth, as I believe, a child is like a stranger in a foreign country, who has to learn the language before he is at home, and can deal with his surroundings. Blake reproduced his early feelings from the inside, but did not dramatise himself as a child in a world of grown-ups, as Dickens did. . . . I do not know whether you had me in mind in your remarks on the modern attitude to adolescence, but I hope that this letter will convince you that my criticism of Dickens in his treatment of childhood was not based on any contempt for the emotions of early years.'

MacCarthy, as ever courteous and discreet, replied at once: 'Dear Mr Hugh Kingsmill, I'm a great admirer of your book on Puritans and if all those to whom I've praised it, bought it, I have added, I should think thirty copies to its sales. With reservations I admired too your Johnson yr Matthew Arnold *no*. Yr. Dickens I haven't read. I anticipated exasperation and didn't try it. I expected you would be too analytical . . .'

Kingsmill let the matter rest for a time. Then in February 1937 he wrote again to MacCarthy: 'When I wrote to you last spring you were ill, and so when you told me you had not read my Dickens, thinking it would exasperate you, I said nothing. I hope you are now well again, and will be able to give your calm consideration to this letter. I think the first of my books to appear after you began to review for the *Sunday Times* was Matthew Arnold. You say you did not like Matthew Arnold, and I understand your dislike. A year later my *After Puritanism* appeared, and you tell me that you recommended it to many of your friends. What surprises me about you is that having read a book of mine which you greatly enjoyed, you have allowed your original bias against me to persist through all these years. In spite of your enjoyment of *After Puritanism*, the most you could say of it in a broadcast, was that it was, "decidedly clever". After this you fell silent about my books. You knew Harris's work, and wrote to Shaw and to Harris himself in praise of it, yet when my Harris appeared you not only did not review it, but you referred obliquely to Harris in such a way as to damp interest in my book. From this time on I saw that you were determined to ignore me, if not to damage me. . . .'

Such claims, which MacCarthy had little difficulty in

countering, show clearly the depth of Kingsmill's resentment. The specific charges he made were of course wholly unfounded and irrational. But behind them lay a justifiable antagonism against MacCarthy as a symbol of the literary Establishment which had ignored him. MacCarthy was the leading critical arbiter of his day whose tastes, cultivated in Eton, Cambridge and Bloomsbury, were wholly opposed to those of Kingsmill. It was MacCarthy who, as literary editor of the *New Statesman*, printed the review questioning the propriety of his referring to Matthew Arnold as 'Matt'. At the same time, Kingsmill subconsciously felt that in a just world he would occupy MacCarthy's position of power, while MacCarthy would be a struggling writer.

The outburst against MacCarthy was not an isolated one. Kingsmill engaged in an angry correspondence at about the same time with the *Observer*, accusing the paper of deliberately ignoring his books. But the effect in both cases was counter-productive and Kingsmill, already looked on with suspicion as a Stracheyan debunker of great men, now acquired the reputation in some circles of an embittered 'outsider' with a chip on his shoulder.

Kingsmill suffered, too, from a failure to conform with the spirit of the age. During the thirties in particular, when most English writers were obsessed by politics and topicality, Kingsmill was almost bound to be ignored. Authors had to be up to date. There was an unspoken assumption, too, that they should take sides in the ideological struggle between Communism and Fascism, preferably siding with the former. It was also important to be *au fait* with the latest literary departures on the Continent and in the United States. A figure like Cyril Connolly, who started his career as a protegé of Desmond MacCarthy, was typical of the successful young 'man of letters' of the period, well up in Eliot, Sartre, Hemingway and Scott Fitzgerald, friendly with Auden and Spender, sympathetic towards Marxism. (It was Connolly who coined the phrase 'the Modern Movement'.) Kingsmill was by no means ignorant of contemporary writing – as a lifelong book reviewer he could not avoid it – but he never thought it more important or interesting than that of the past. As for politics, Muggeridge liked to tell the story of how he had been walking down the Strand with Kingsmill at the time of the Spanish Civil War when they met a fellow writer who announced with pride and excitement that he was 'off to Spain'. Kingsmill said: 'I suppose the cost of living is cheap there.'

It was not surprising that as the years went by Kingsmill became increasingly hard up. 'In their financial aspect,' he once wrote, 'the lives of writers, painters and musicians suggest a man leaping from ice floe to ice floe across a wide and rapid river.' Muggeridge commented, 'For Hughie, alas, the distance between the ice floes did not grow any less with the years, and the jumping from one to the other made him increasingly breathless.'

Muggeridge himself was during this pre-war period very short of money. He too was out of step with the times, notably in so far as his attitude to Communism was concerned. Kingsmill had no regular income, while Muggeridge received only five guineas a week for reviewing novels for the *Daily Telegraph*. Kingsmill had some support from his family, but in the main he relied on publishers to supply him with funds. To make money quickly he compiled a number of anthologies, having achieved his only real success with *Invective and Abuse* published in 1929. ('Invective,' he once said, 'is what you say about other people, and abuse is what other people say about you.') It was followed by *More Invective* (1930), *The Worst of Love* (1931), *What They Said at The Time* (1935), and *Parents and Children* (1936). The last was put together in two weeks, a sign of Kingsmill's urgent need of funds, as well as his encyclopaedic knowledge of literature. 'I have not yet seen the anthology,' he wrote to Pearson, 'and shall look at it with interest, for I have only the faintest idea what it is about, to say nothing of the contents. That is one advantage of working under pressure. I imagine Balzac and Scott were frequently to be observed reading their respective works with eyes starting out of their heads with excitement.'

Kingsmill developed the art of securing advances from publishers with the dedication of a military strategist. A trip to London was entailed, which meant securing, if possible, the Free Pass which had been presented to Sir Henry Lunn by the railways in gratitude for all the business he had put in their way. This talisman, passed from hand to hand, was in continual use on the London–Hastings line. Once in town, Kingsmill did the rounds of publishers and other possible sources of money. 'Just passing a publisher's office,' Muggeridge recalled, 'stirred up in Hughie thoughts of contracts and advances. We were walking along a street once, and noticed the name of a particularly obscure publisher. "Do you think," Hughie asked eagerly, "if I went in now he'd give me an advance?" I said I thought it was highly doubtful and his enthusiasm cooled and we passed on to other matters.'

The sale of review copies of books could always be relied on to bring in what Kingsmill valued most – 'Something liquid'. New books were to him simply merchandise which could be exchanged for cash at Thomas Gaston's bookshop in the Strand. Kingsmill never had more than a score or so of books in his possession. When reviewing a book he had the knack of absorbing its contents very quickly. It could then be 'Gastonised'. If short of cash he would even give his children review copies in lieu of pocket money. Gaston only once refused to buy a book. It was called *A Study of Co-operative Movements in the Punjab*.

Both Muggeridge and Pearson gave Kingsmill money when they could. Strictly speaking, such money was loaned, but in practice it was seldom repaid. Neither of them minded this, both being exceptionally generous by nature, but also aware of the great and unrepayable debt they owed to Kingsmill. Muggeridge in particular was anxious to do something in return and even offered, when Kingsmill was more than usually hard up, to get a second mortgage on his house and give him the proceeds. Meanwhile they both did whatever they could to help get Kingsmill work, but their efforts seldom bore fruit. Pearson once tried to obtain for him, through a friend, the assistant Librarianship of the House of Commons, sending him detailed instructions before the crucial interview:

Dear Hughie,
A few hints for your forthcoming appearance at the House of Commons:
Hair cut
Shave
Hat

> Respectable lounge suit
> Socks to match ditto
> Shirt to match ditto
> Tie to match ditto
> Collar fastened to stud
> Shining shoes with laces to match
> Soft speaking voice
> False teeth in position
> No satchel or book encumbrances
> Remember you once held His Majesty's commission
> Clean vocabulary.
> Yrs. H.P.

Kingsmill may have done his best to comply, but he did not get the job.

Like his father, Kingsmill was never short of ideas for making money, the only difference being that his did not have the desired result. In 1936 he conceived, with the encouragement of Muggeridge, the notion of starting a new humorous magazine, and they inserted an advertisement in *The Times*:

> A GROUP OF WRITERS who believe that there is room for a weekly which would deal wittily and honestly with the modern world, would be glad to hear from anyone interested in financing such a venture.

Kingsmill, in the meantime, drew up a manifesto:

> The critical press of England is in a poor state today. *Punch* is losing in its sales because its ultra-respectable prosperous atmosphere no longer corresponds to the temper of the age. There is no critically humorous paper in England today. Nor is there any serious paper which has much, or any individuality. We live in an age which has kept the conventions without the convictions of the Victorians.
> The paper we propose to start would have the independence of outlook and treatment which characterised *Punch* in the forties of the last century. It would cover the whole ground of modern life, politics, books, the theatre, cinema, the City. . . . We should try to write from the commonsense standpoint of the eighteenth century, the

century of Swift and Johnson, before the world was laid waste by Rousseau, the French Revolution, and all the doctrinaires of the nineteenth century, ending in Marx, the inspirer of Lenin and Nietzsche, the inspirer of Hitler.

The response to this bold prospectus was poor. A well-wisher in a Home for Indigents expressed the hope that they would 'get the money (I having none, by the way)', but still more, that they would put 'honesty before wit'. Another man wrote from Zurich to suggest that they should 'form a company the way the people do who make potato chips, or soap, or substitute butter, and ask the public to subscribe'. 'The only other communication we received,' Muggeridge wrote, 'was from the publisher of a magazine for badminton players. With some difficulty, on a grey January day, we found the office of the publication and had a brief conversation with its editor and publisher. In selling a magazine dealing with badminton, he said, the first step was to locate circles interested in the game. If, by the same token, we could indicate to him where circles interested in humour were to be found, he felt sure that he would be able to meet with a corresponding success with a humorous publication. We agreed that this was the nub of the matter, and said that if we could think of a formula for tracking down humour addicts with the same certainty that he had been able to track down badminton enthusiasts, we would communicate further with him.'

That was the end of the project.

A more successful attempt at a new humorous magazine was made the following year when Graham Greene and a number of associates launched *Night and Day*, another would-be usurper of *Punch*, with strong similarities to the *New Yorker*. In spite of its impressive list of contributors – Greene himself, Evelyn Waugh, John Betjeman and others – the magazine floundered and a libel writ from Shirley Temple finished it off after a year. Muggeridge and Kingsmill wrote regularly for *Night and Day*, their most memorable contributions being a series of 'Literary Pilgrimages by HK & MM', written in a dialogue form, which Kingsmill and Pearson later developed in their books. Kingsmill loved to visit places with literary associations from which he always gained some valuable insights. The most ambitious of their expeditions was to Paris and the great-great-grand-daughter of Wordsworth, a Madame Blanchet, direct descendant of Annette Vallon, with whom the poet had had a brief love affair in his youth, abandoning her to bring up their child, Caroline, alone. 'We often used to wonder why he left her,' Madame Blanchet told her two visitors, 'when she loved him so devotedly; especially as it seems he had *un sens moral très développé*'. She showed them a copy of the *Lyrical Ballads* sent by the poet to Annette. 'I've never read it myself,' Madame Blanchet confessed. 'I don't know any English. Some of his poems have been translated into French, but . . .' She shrugged her shoulders – and we hurriedly imagined a translation – *Il y avait un temps quand les prés, les plantations, les ruisseaux, le terre et chaque spectacle vulgaire* . . .

The last of the Literary Pilgrimages was published in *Night and Day* in December 1937, under the title 'Dawn in Wimpole Street'. Kingsmill and Muggeridge had decided to visit the house of Arthur Hallam, Tennyson's great friend, whose death in 1833 had inspired *In Memoriam*. Subsequently the poet had been in the habit of going to Hallam's old house in Wimpole Street at dawn and the two resolved to do the same:

> Preparatory to seeing Wimpole Street at dawn, we spent the night at a Turkish bath.
>
> As an attendant took off our shoes MM said: 'What was Hallam like to look at? Is there any portrait?'
>
> HK: The portrait is rather disappointing, I believe. Chubby. One would have said a good life.
>
> We walked to our couches across a dim hall, water gurgling in the distance, a faded red carpet, here and there tables and red plush chairs, a marble swimming pool at the far end – the total effect rather West of Suez . . .
>
> As we walked in our loin cloths towards the hot rooms, through an ante-chamber where one or two lolled reading evening papers, MM said: 'Why did Tennyson love him so?'
>
> HK: He was everything Tennyson wasn't – bubbling, knew everyone, marked out for a triumphant career, popular and of course brilliant.
>
> In great heat we sat upon a stone slab. On another slab

close by an enormous body was spread out like a derelict
whale, occasionally convulsed and emitting groans.
Hk quoted:

> *He is not here ; but far away*
> *The noise of life begins again,*
> *And ghastly thro' the drizzling rain*
> *On the bald street breaks the blank day.*

Stretched out under the masseur's hands, kneaded, thumped,
    soaped and sluiced MM called out: 'Had he a wife?' and
    HK called back: 'He was engaged to Tennyson's sister.'
MM: 'Why?'

Wrapped in warm towels and laid out for the night, we
    continued our conversation.

HK: Extraordinary, Hallam's fascination. Gladstone was as
    fond of him as Tennyson.

MM: The two great Victorian spellbinders, both spell-
    bound by Hallam. How to explain it?

HK: I suppose it was just because Hallam wasn't a spell-
    binder, and they were two desperate egotists with all the
    weight of their future struggle on them.

MM: You still haven't told me where Tennyson's sister
    comes in.

HK: It rounded it off.

MM: Rounded what off?

It was dark in the streets at six-thirty, but the clouds were
    turning a dull grey. We passed the British Museum, where
    a yellow light shone through tall windows, as though some
    secret trial were in progress. The darkness thinned away in
    Oxford Street, and in Wimpole Street it was already day.

After the carefree variety of architecture in Wigmore Street,
    Wimpole Street was narrow and monotonous and hardly
    changed at all in the hundred years since Tennyson stood
    there at the same hour. Already milk bottles had been left
    at doors. There were the doctors' name plates. Up above,
    a light here and there in a servant's bedroom, but no one
    stirring in No 67.

MM: What a place to see as a deserted shrine! What
    desolation!

HK: *Dark house by which once more I stand*
      Here in the long, unlovely street
      Doors, where my heart was used to beat
      So quickly, waiting for a hand . . .

MM: How he must have loved him, to face the dawn in Wimpole Street! These rich houses, this ghastly mausoleum of affluence!

HK: *And like a guilty thing I creep*
      At earliest morning to the door . . .

We pictured him striding in from Wigmore Street, tall, sallow, and unshaved, not a man, we thought, that anyone would ask the way of, his eye fixed on No 67.

HK: I wonder whether it would have made any difference if Hallam had lived.

MM: I can't see why. If instead of dying in Vienna, he had survived in Downing Street, Tennyson would still have watched by that dark door, and groaned as the blank day broke on bald Wimpole Street.

HK: I suppose so.

MM: A doubly barren love.

If the personality of Kingsmill was to the fore in these literary pieces, Muggeridge was the dominant influence in two little books, *Brave Old World* (1936) and *Next Year's News* (1937), on which they collaborated. Both were parodies of the press, in the style of Beachcomber, consisting of satirical news-items, gossip paragraphs and leading articles. It is likely, as Muggeridge later said, that the authors derived more pleasure from writing the books than the public did from reading them, as neither had a large sale. They were written in Muggeridge's house at Whatlington. Kingsmill lay on the sofa while Muggeridge took notes: 'We would begin our labours,' he remembered, 'often interrupted by irrelevancies, and sometimes by a pleasant walk. At a certain point Kitty would bring in the tea, a meal to which Hughie was deeply devoted; and as we sat in my old study we would watch the evening come down, never failing to find the spectacle delightful, and reluctant to turn on the light and disturb the exquisite dusk which we both loved. At such times Hughie forgot his financial troubles, and radiated a sense of happiness, of serenity, greater than any I have known. If his cares weighed heavily upon him, he had a capacity for shedding them wholly, and then ideas flowed from him effortlessly.'

Running through the books is Muggeridge's conviction that Hitler and Stalin are interchangeable figures, both blood-thirsty power-maniacs, one Teutonic, the other Slav. Such a notion ran quite against the prevailing current. The Left looked to Stalin, the Right to Hitler and Mussolini. Muggeridge in seeing them as equally malevolent forces, was once again the odd man out. In *Brave Old World*, he and Kingsmill devoted much space to the doings of Tamerlane (or Al Rak), a composite of Hitler and Stalin, and parodied the contemporary newspaper reports. A *Times* leader, for example, declared: 'The extreme cordiality that has marked the conversations which have recently taken place between Mr TAMERLANE and his Majesty's Envoy Extraordinary in Dagopolis reflects the satisfactory relations now prevailing between the two countries. Of late years Mr Tamerlane's tendency has been more and more to conform his administrative technique with current practice, and to take for his confederation its rightful place within the comity of European nations. Family institu-tions, once in something like abeyance, have been revived, and their revival personally endorsed by AL RAK in his recent ceremonial visit to his consort. Rank, titles, diplomatic usage, all the décor of civilisation, have been re-established. Question-able ethnological theories, based on the innate superiority of the Dago race, have been, if not discarded, at least relegated to the universities, and unhygienic customs, such as drinking out of skulls, continued, if at all, only ceremonially.'

Kingsmill did not relish the contemplation of either Hitler or Stalin. Like many mystics, he had a horror of any kind of brutality. Once, in their continuing struggle to get some money, he and Muggeridge agreed to contribute to a book called *The Fifty Most Amazing Crimes of the Last 100 Years* which was being published on behalf of the *Daily Herald* as a free gift for new subscribers. Each stood to gain the princely sum of £22 10s. for their contributions, so it was not an offer to refuse. They both went along therefore to see the editor of the book, who in mournful tones outlined the choice of atrocities available – Jack the Ripper, Crippen, the Brides in the Bath – they could take their pick. Muggeridge listened politely, but Kingsmill grew increasingly distressed as the gruesome catalogue continued. Finally, when the man began to describe how a body had been cut up and put in a pram, he cried out in genuine distress: 'Why do they do these things? Why do they do these things?'

Muggeridge embarked without any such qualms on the story of an Alsatian assassin, Jean Baptiste Tropmann – 'His mouth often hung half open, giving him at times, because of his abnormally large lower lip and large teeth, a curious air of ferocity. His hands and especially his thumbs, continued to be prodigiously out of proportion with the rest of his body. They have become legendary. In France people still occasionally say of a big hand, "*C'est la main de Tropmann!*" '

Kingsmill, incapable of writing in this vein, eventually opted for two swindlers, approaching them both with his habitual air of humorous detachment, rather out of keeping with the blood-curdling character of the rest of the volume. Under the heading 'The Gigantic Frauds of Jabez Balfour', he wrote: 'In his autobiography, *My Prison Life*, which was published in 1907, Jabez Spencer Balfour gave a brief account of his parents. "My father occupied a respectable subordinate position in the Ways and Means Office of the House of Commons. . . . My mother was a woman of great intellectual gifts, well known as a lecturer on English literature." His parents were earnest Baptists, and he himself was markedly Nonconformist in temperament and outlook. He ought to have ended life as a millionaire, with an honoured place among the wealthiest lay supporters of his church. But he had inherited, perhaps from his mother, a wayward streak which turned him into a gambler, and so it came about that his autobiography, typically Nonconformist in its anxious concern for the betterment of external conditions and in its guarded personal note, had to appear under the incongruous title already mentioned.'

It was typical of Kingsmill that he should devote as much care and thoroughness to his *Amazing Crimes* as he did to any of his more literary pieces. It was also typical that when the book was at last published, he determined to obtain a copy of it. He went first to the *Daily Herald*, but there were none there. He was directed to a firm in the City which was handling the distribution. They in turn informed him that the books were on their way north by canal and advised him to go to a particular wharf where they were being loaded. Here at last he found several barges stacked with *The Fifty Most Amazing Crimes of the Last 100 Years*, and managed to acquire a copy, with which he returned happily to his home.

In their second collaboration, *Next Year's News*, which originally appeared in *Night and Day*, Kingsmill and Muggeridge, again parodying newspaper reports, set out to predict what would happen in 1938. Particular attention was focused on Russia, where Stalin continued his purges:

> The posthumous trial of Lenin opened in Moscow yesterday, drama being lent to the proceedings by the presence in the dock of the embalmed body of the Bolshevist leader, which had been removed for this purpose from the mausoleum in the Red Square, where it has been on view since his death. At the conclusion of his long indictment, the State Prosecutor, Vyshinsky, shook his fist at the dock and shouted: 'In you, Vladimir Ilyitch, we have at last hunted down the cancer which has been pouring poison through our sweet Soviet State. Out of your vile carcass and none other, has crawled the verminous brood of wreckers, kulaks, Left and Right deviationists, fascists and opportunists, who have sought to pit their wits against our beloved Stalin.'

At the end of the trial Lenin was found guilty, the punishment consisting of 'burial in consecrated ground'. Later in the year Marx was also attacked. *Pravda* stated: 'Our ever loving Leader and Father, Stalin, tirelessly uprooting all enemies of the proletariat now tears the mask from the Jew–bourgeois-emigré face of the arch-Leninist – Trotskyist-Bukharinite Marx.'

Amidst the satire there was one astonishingly accurate prophecy:

HITLER–STALIN MEETING

The meeting between Hitler and Stalin yesterday on King Carol's yacht, *Hannibal*, in the Baltic took place in conditions of great secrecy. The dictators were together for three hours and twenty minutes. On parting they shook hands warmly.

In *Next Year's News* Kingsmill and Muggeridge laboured against the insuperable difficulty confronting anyone who sets out to parody the press – that nothing one invents is likely to prove more ludicrous than the real thing. It was more satisfactory to collect actual news items, which they did in *Night and Day*, under the heading of 'Contentment Column', subtitled 'Reassuring and Inspiring Items from the Press. A corrective to Scare Headlines and Private Worries'.

'We are able to allay apprehension about the intentions of Germany,' the Contentment Column reported, 'on the authority of Viscount Snowden, who says that the Germans like marching and uniforms because "the former satisfies their sense of rhythm, the latter their sense of drama". Meanwhile the *Church Times* had informed its readers, "The Church of England is getting down to its autumn work, and persons of imagination are asking themselves the searching question. 'What exactly are we trying to do, and how are we to set about it?'" '

It was indeed hard to satirise such reports. Unlike Muggeridge, obsessed by politics and journalism, Kingsmill had little interest in what are called current affairs. In the course of his long correspondence with Pearson he hardly ever referred to them, except when a news item combining sexual and ecclesiastical elements took his fancy. Thus, on August 25, 1930 he wrote: 'It seems that the Lambeth conference have unearthed a sermon on the Mount of Venus, from which one gathers Christ sanctions the use of French letters, if donned in an austere and altruistic humour.' His interest was again aroused by the famous case in 1932 of the Reverend Harold Davidson, rector of Stiffkey, who, as a result of years spent seducing young girls in the cafés of London, was charged at Norwich Consistory court with immoral practices: 'I have been somewhat saddened this morning,' Kingsmill wrote to Pearson, 'by the case of the Rev. Davidson of Stiffkey. The poor devil trying again and again to induce Miss Barbara Harris to admit him to her bed, the false theological note in, "He asked me to give myself to him, body and soul just once," the fact that while he was being put through the hoop by stern officials at ABC's his wife was wrapping herself round some well-hung yeoman, all point to the poor man's inability to appraise himself, as Frankie would say, in true relation to the centre of the universe. And then the heavy paraphernalia of a Consistory Court trial, the outraged presence in the middle distance of the Bishop of Norwich, the queue of unraped beauties lining up to expose his miserable attempts to translate dreams into realities, he himself waking at two in the morning with a sickly feeling that, taking himself from any angle or any date, he is, has been, and will continue to be, a complete mis-calculation as a human being – and yet the poor devil, with special trains bearing half the waitresses of the metropolis to Norwich, hoping that a flat denial may restore him to the wife of his and Mr X's bosom, and the amenities inseparable from life as an elderly and undischarged bankrupt in a country vicarage. Depressing.'

Kingsmill's indifference to the contemporary scene extended to literature and he had very little interest in the so-called 'modern movement'. It was therefore with some reluctance that in 1937 he embarked on a biography of D. H. Lawrence. Muggeridge was with him when he went to sign the contract at Methuen's, and noticed that he emerged from the building looking 'slightly mournful about the task before him'. All the same, thanks perhaps to his constant discussions with Mug-geridge during the time he was writing it, the book contains some of his best criticism and recaptures the humorous tone of his *Matthew Arnold*. Lawrence was to Muggeridge in many ways what Harris had been to Pearson – a liberator, seemingly breaking down the puritanical barriers of his upbringing and pointing the way to a finer and freer existence. So strong was the appeal of Lawrence that when Muggeridge heard of his death in 1930, he wept openly at a cocktail party in Cairo. Once again Kingsmill demolished his friend's misplaced enthusiasm, not by pouring scorn but by promoting laughter. *Lady Chatterley's Lover*, like Harris's memoirs, he found neither outrageous nor exciting, but extraordinarily funny. One passage in particular, which he and Muggeridge afterwards never tired of quoting, was the conversation between Mellors, the gamekeeper, and Lady Chatterley's father, the Royal Academician, Sir Malcolm Reid, which takes place after the old man has heard of the couple's intention to marry:

'Well young man and what about my daughter?'

The grin flickered on Mellors's face.

'Well, sir, and what about her?'

'You've got a baby in her all right.'

'I have that honour!' grinned Mellors.

'Honour, by God!' Sir Malcolm gave a squirting laugh and became Scotch and lewd. 'Honour! How was the going, eh? Good my boy, what?'

'Good!'

'I'll bet it was! Ha – ha! My daughter, chip off the old block, what? . . . You warmed her up, I can see that. . . . A gamekeeper, eh, my boy! Bloody good poacher, if you ask me. Ha-ha! . . . That sort of game is worth a man's while, eh, what? I envy you, my boy. . . . Oh, you're a bantam, I can see that. You're a fighter. . . .'

Lawrence was to Kingsmill another man, like Arnold, who had abandoned the world of the imagination for the unproductive regions of the will. Encouraged by his dominating mother, he learned to despise his father, as well as his first love, the Miriam of *Sons and Lovers*, and stifling his poetic instincts embarked on a futile search for happiness through sex and the will. The denial of his better self was manifested partly in Lawrence's snobbishness, 'a form of suffering,' Kingsmill noted, 'usually dismissed as trivial, for there is almost as much dishonesty about what is called snobbishness as about sex. . . .

'Snobbishness,' he added, 'is the assertion of the will in social relations, as lust is in the sexual. It is the desire for what divides men, and the inability to value what unites them.'

Lawrence had expressed his sexual philosophy as follows: *And God the Father, the Inscrutable, the Unknowable, we know in the Flesh, in Woman. She is the door for our in-going and our out-going – In her we go back to the Father: but like the witnesses of the Transfiguration, blind and unconscious.*

Kingsmill commented: 'This passage, which is of great importance to the understanding of Lawrence's reputation as a seer, is a perfect example of pseudo-mysticism. The pseudo-mystic, whether Lawrence with an audience of thousands, or Lenin and Hitler addressing millions, appeals to the will in language borrowed from the spirit. He tells the multitude that the broad way they are treading leads to the straight gate into salvation, and the multitude are relieved and flattered on learning that the appetite for power, money or women is a religious appetite. For an appeal to the will to succeed it must be totally devoid of reason. The sayings of a great thinker, however difficult, as, for example, "Whosoever will save his life shall lose it", are based on experience, and ultimately verifiable by common sense. . . . The passage quoted from Lawrence has the same sweeping imbecility as the programmes of dictators and demagogues. The sexual act has been performed by millions of human beings daily for hundreds of thousands of years. If contact with God could be established in this way, every one would be saved except for a relatively small number of celibates and a rather larger number of perverts and impotents.'

Lawrence, in Kingsmill's view, created his 'phallic cult' as a result of his diffidence with women. 'It is not the phallus,' Kingsmill observed sensibly, 'which focuses the attention of the normal man.' Lawrence, however, was more inspired by his own body than that of a woman: 'Conscious of his own incompleteness, and craving the satisfaction he was unable to attain, he made a deity of the physical desire which stronger men try to transmute. He stood at the starting point of experience and announced that he had reached the goal.'

The explicitly sexual scenes which Lawrence included in *Lady Chatterley* and which have recently been treated by many critics with hushed reverence were to Kingsmill a sign of Lawrence's failure as an artist. 'To be solemn about the organs of generation,' he wrote, 'is only possible to someone who, like Lawrence, has deified the will and denied the spirit. If the sexual act is viewed apart from the other than physical emotions which accompany it, it is either comic or disgusting. Imaginative writers convey passion without using physical details, and are obscene only when they are being humorous about sex, like Rabelais, or are nauseated by it, like Shakespeare in *Troilus and Cressida* and *Timon of Athens*.' 'Physical detail of any kind in fact,' he wrote in *After Puritanism*, 'is most sparingly used in imaginative literature.'

As a biographer Kingsmill was especially taken by the various women who had attached themselves to Lawrence during his lifetime. 'Lawrence was not a conscious charlatan,' he wrote, 'but he had an instinct for exploiting the wide areas of imbecility in the English upper classes.' Such imbecility was evinced by someone even as talented and perceptive as Lady Ottoline Morrell, who befriended Lawrence until he made fun of her in *Women in Love*. Kingsmill was greatly amused by Lawrence's letters to Lady Ottoline; 'I wish I were going to Tibet,' Lawrence wrote, 'or Kamschatka – or Tahiti – to the ultima, ultima, ultima Thule.' Later he advised her: 'Duly drift and let go, let go entirely and become dark, quite dark. . . . Let your will lapse back into your unconscious self, so you move in a sleep, and in darkness, without sight or understanding.'

Kingsmill commented: 'All this must have meant very little to Lady Ottoline Morrell, for whom neither the dark unconscious nor a lean-to on Ultima Thule can have been an alluring substitute for life as a literary-political hostess in an English country house.'

Another of Lawrence's female devotees was Catherine Carswell, who gave an account of her relationship in *Savage Pilgrimage*. In the introduction to this book she wrote, 'I believe that there not only may be, but must be, a new way of life, and that Lawrence was on the track of it. . . . That there can be indeed a new way of life – though possibly only by a recovery of values so remote that they are fecund from long forgetting and as far out of mind as they are near to our blind fingers – is the single admission he seeks from his readers, as it was the belief that governed his actions.'

'One is reminded,' said Kingsmill, 'of the company promoter at the time of the South Sea Bubble, who invited money from the public for "a project to be communicated hereafter", adding that as far as Mrs Carswell was concerned, "her finer qualities are largely in abeyance in her book on Lawrence".'

This view was shared by Muggeridge, who, reviewing the *Savage Pilgrimage* for the *Manchester Guardian* when it was published in 1932, concluded of the characters in the book: 'How sick one gets of Don and John Patrick! How sick one gets of Lawrence himself! How sick, how unutterably sick of Mrs Carswell.' Kingsmill was at the time greatly taken by this passage and paced up and down reciting it over and over again until his wife urged him to desist.

The signs of Muggeridge's pre-war association with Kingsmill are very evident in *The Thirties*, the book he wrote at the end of that decade. The commission came thanks to Hesketh Pearson. Hamish Hamilton had suggested to Pearson that he should write a history of the Thirties. Pearson liked the idea very much, but did not feel that he was the best man to do the book. He mentioned the offer to Muggeridge one day in the Horseshoe and could tell from the way he reacted that he would have liked to do it. Without saying anything to his friend, Pearson told his agent, who was also Muggeridge's, that he thought Muggeridge would do the book much better than himself. Later Hamish Hamilton commissioned Muggeridge.

The Thirties, a brilliant survey of political and social life, brought together many of the topics of the discussions between Kingsmill and Muggeridge, including Lawrence, who was seen by both men as an intellectual equivalent of Hitler – advocating, like him, salvation in a collective Dawnism; thus Lawrence, in his last work *Apocalypse*, had written: 'As a collective being man has his fulfilment in the gratification of his power sense,' while Hitler had declared in *Mein Kampf*: 'Mass demonstrations must burn into the little man's soul the proud conviction that though a little worm, he is nevertheless part of a great dragon.' For Kingsmill the only interest of figures like Hitler lay in their ability to personify the emotions of the mass. 'What is extraordinary about tyrants,' he once said, 'as is evident in Cromwell and Napoleon in not much smaller degree than Hitler, is not their intellectual development but the way in which they embody and act on behalf of some great collective passion. . . . Their power resides less in their faculties as individuals than in their fitness to act as mediums.' Muggeridge in his book echoed this view, applying it in turn to the British prime ministers of the Thirties and in particular Ramsay Macdonald – 'It is impossible for one man, however determined and coercing he may be, to impose his will on other men for long unless they recognise themselves in him.' So too with Baldwin and Chamberlain – each embodied in his way the vacillations of the people as a whole.

Once again, as with *Butler*, the message of the book was a religious one: 'If there is any central theme in Mr Muggeridge's book,' Harold Nicolson wrote in a review, 'it is that during the ten years between 1930 and 1940 the people of Great Britain were seeking to console themselves for loss of faith by the fiction that life upon this earth is a creative and enjoyable thing.' Now however, the nausea and despair which had characterised much of Muggeridge's earlier writings was tempered by a note of humour and detachment – qualities which Kingsmill had helped to bring to the fore. The spirit of Contentment Corner was evinced in quotations – ' "Wider still and Wider shall thy bounds be set" does not indicate any desire for more territory' (Anthony Eden). 'Generally speaking, I am certainly opposed to anything in the nature of third degree or torture' (The Dean of Canterbury). And there was the fruit of many happy hours that Kingsmill and Muggeridge had spent laughing over the leaders in newspapers, like the one in the *Morning Post*, which remarked of Litvinov's lunching at 10 Downing Street that a slug had found its way into 'our fine English Rose'. Muggeridge had not lost his sense of living in a dying civilisation, but now it was no longer with him a cause of despair. He could watch the process without feeling involved, and with an awareness of other permanent values which made his present circumstances irrelevant. That viewpoint was the legacy of Kingsmill.

Chapter 9

One of the most important and beneficial services that Kingsmill performed for Pearson and Muggeridge was to introduce them to Dr Johnson. At the first opportunity in his early correspondence with Pearson, Kingsmill proposed Johnson as a useful corrective of his adulation of Harris and Shaw. Johnson was the great non-Dawnist, the personification of anti-humbug, insisting that charity begins at home and that enthusiasms like that of Boswell for Corsican independence were just silly. 'Johnson,' Muggeridge wrote, 'never fell into what Hughie considered the most reprehensible of all errors – that of seeing mankind as a collectivity rather than as individual souls: of generalising his benevolence into public spiritedness.'

For Kingsmill, Johnson was the best sort of yardstick to measure the sincerity of moralisers and preachers, and in his biographies he was constantly referring back to Johnson to provide a proper comparison. Matthew Arnold, for example, had been an admirer of Marcus Aurelius, who he described as 'perhaps the most beautiful figure in history'. Arnold quoted the great Stoic as an ideal guide to conduct – 'When thou wishest to delight thyself, think of the virtues of those who live with thee: for instance, the activity of one, and the modesty of another, and the liberality of a third, and some other good quality of a fourth.' Kingsmill commented: 'To show this nut-cutlet Caesar in his true proportions it is enough to set a single quotation from Johnson's talk by the side of any of the extracts quoted above.' 'What signifies,' someone said to Johnson, 'giving half pence to common beggars? They only lay it out in gin or tobacco.' 'And why,' said Johnson, 'should they be denied such sweeteners of their existence? It is surely very savage to refuse them every possible avenue to pleasure, reckoned too coarse for our own acceptance. Life is a pill which none of us can bear to swallow without gilding; yet for the poor we delight in stripping it still barer, and are not ashamed to show even visible displeasure, if ever the bitter taste is taken from their mouths.'

To begin with, Pearson, still taking his cue from Shaw, was unwilling to accept Johnson as a guiding spirit: 'Really, I have no patience with the pompous bottom-faced old owl,' he retorted. 'In Bernard Shaw we have something so immensely superior to Johnson – in wit, in humour, in dialectic, in personality, in everything. . . .'

Pearson was to some extent rebelling against his upbringing: 'I loathe with my whole soul the entire tribe of would be virtuous moralisers. A blind spot, you may say, a knot in the intellect. But that won't do. Without that hypocritical twaddle, he would not be Johnson. It pervades him through and through. In fact, the high-falutin' rubbish he used to turn out, and which is now known as Johnsonese, existed for the sole purpose of purveying his sham pretentious morality in a suitable form. To sum up (as Frank would say) – a summary with which any woman in the world would concur – the Doctor is an old bugger! Incidentally I may add that the whole of the civilised world outside Great Britain is on my side. The continent says "I know not the man".'

One cannot say at what precise stage Pearson abandoned Shaw and lined up with Kingsmill, but it is probable that the change was gradual and was accelerated by the transformation which he associated with reaching the age of forty. Certainly by 1933, when Kingsmill was writing his biography of Johnson, he was totally won round and insisted that the book should be dedicated to him, as he did when he first read Kingsmill's anthology, *Johnson without Boswell*. In this insistence one can see the gratitude that Pearson in the end felt to Kingsmill for introducing him to Johnson and the great part which he played in their friendship, equalling Shakespeare as a topic of conversation and even provoking Gladys Pearson on one occasion to complain 'You two can talk about nothing but Dr Johnson's toe-nails!'

In *Samuel Johnson* (1934) and *Johnson without Boswell* (1940), books which are to some extent complementary, Kingsmill was concerned with correcting the Boswellian view of Johnson by putting into proper perspective the evidence of his other biographers, in particular Mrs Thrale, who had long suffered from the hostility of commentators. One side of Johnson was certainly represented by Boswell but, Kingsmill said, 'from his prayers and meditations, from certain passages in his letters and verse, from *Rasselas* and Mrs Thrale's portrait, less amusing but more intimate than Boswell's, I received an impression of an essentially imaginative nature clogged by melancholia, a profound thinker limited by inborn and irrational fears, and an intensely loving and compassionate soul hampered in its expression by lifelong disabilities of mind and body'.

Samuel Johnson was the only biography of Kingsmill's written in a spirit of sympathy with his subject and it is for that reason the most successful of his books and must rank as one of the best short biographies of Johnson. Kingsmill had much in common with Johnson. He expressed himself best in company with others and found writing an arduous task; the circumstances of his life were unfortunate and he had the same habit as Johnson of almost courting discomfort. In his life, too, he reflected something of the spirit of Johnson's *Lives of the Poets*; in which Johnson, when dealing with his lesser known subjects, conveyed the essential absurdity of the literary life – the grand projects conceived and embarked on, the inevitable disappointment and probable oblivion for which the authors and their books were destined. The *Lives of the Poets* remained one of Kingsmill's favourite works and he was reading it on his death-bed. The brilliance of the book was, at least, one matter on which Pearson was always in agreement with him and he could claim to have drawn Kingsmill's attention to a number of favourite passages, including the death of Edmund Smith:

Having formed his plan, and collected materials, he declared that a few months would complete his design; and, that he might pursue his work with less frequent avocations, he was in June 1710, invited by Mr George Ducket to his house in Wiltshire. Here he found such opportunities of indulgence as did not much forward his studies, and particularly some strong ale, too delicious to be resisted. He ate and drank till he found himself plethorick: and then, resolving to ease himself by evacuation, he wrote to an apothecary in the neighbourhood a prescription of a purge so forcible that the apothecary thought it his duty to delay it till he had given notice of its danger. Smith, not pleased with the contradiction of a shopman, and boastful of his own knowledge, treated the notice with rude contempt and swallowed his own medicine, which, in July, 1710, brought him to the grave. He was buried at Gartham.

'Every phrase is masterly,' Pearson wrote, 'even to the mention of the two dates. It is a bare chronicle of happenings – not a syllable too much, not a suggestion of comment – and yet what richness of humour. Look at the phrase "that he might pursue his work with less frequent avocations" and consider it in connection with what follows. Isn't it too gorgeous for words? There is nothing to approach the whole paragraph in biographical literature.'

Kingsmill returned again and again to the book. 'The more I read his *Lives*,' he wrote to Pearson, 'the better I think them. I would rather keep them than any other prose work in the language. Isn't this good on Mallet, to whom one could find a dozen parallels in the contemporary world of letters – "His works are such as a writer, bustling in the world, showing himself in public, and emerging from time to time into notice, might keep alive by his personal influence; but which, conveying little information and giving no great pleasure, must soon give way, as the succession of things produces new topics of conversation, and other modes of amusement".'

Despite these occasional flashes, Johnson was never so good as in the company of Boswell. In June 1936 Pearson stayed at the Green Man in Ashbourne, an inn which Boswell had patronised during his visit, with Johnson, to Dr Taylor in 1777. From here he wrote to Kingsmill asking him to put off dying, 'until I am safely incinerated'. Kingsmill replied: 'I have looked up Bos. on Ashbourne. He is marvellous. His little touches are so good. "While we sat basking in the sun upon a seat here, I introduced a common subject of complaint, the very small salaries which many curates have." Why is this so good? It has, like Frankie, an unanalysable fascination. I suppose, in this instance, the charm comes from the fact that he is so delighted at being at ease in the sun, and forcing

Johnson to give of his best on a subject which called up a pleasing vision of hard-worked nitwits enjoying neither sun, leisure nor the good things of life as found at Taylor's table.'

In October 1936 Pearson visited Kingsmill in Hastings. As they walked back to Laton Road one Sunday through the twilight Pearson suddenly asked: 'Wouldn't it make a very amusing book if you and I followed Johnson and Boswell round Scotland and wrote an account of our own adventures in their wake? We love the lads and every place they visited would interest us?'

A week or so later they visited Hamish Hamilton to try and interest him in the project, and the following dialogue ensued:

PEARSON: Hugh and I have a brilliant idea for a book we want to do together.

HAMILTON: Good. I welcome ideas. The more brilliant the better.

PEARSON: Then you're in luck this morning. As you know, Boswell's original *Journal* of his visit to the Hebrides with Johnson is coming out in a week or so. It's his day-to-day account of the round and there's a lot of stuff in it which he cut out when he published his *Tour* – the only version the public has yet had.

HAMILTON: Yes?

KINGSMILL: Hesketh and I want to follow Johnson and Boswell round Scotland and write an account, not only of our adventures, but of theirs as reconstructed by us on the spot.

PEARSON: Or rather spots. Up to date Scotland to most Englishmen means the country of Burns, Stevenson and Walter Scott, and no one seems aware that Johnson and Boswell covered more ground than they did.

KINGSMILL: The whole of the east coast from Berwick to Inverness, right across Scotland to the west, half a dozen of the Hebrides, and back through the Lowlands.

HAMILTON: Funnily enough –

PEARSON: And it's not only the spots they visited; it's themselves. Wherever they went, humour and incident crowded upon them.

KINGSMILL: And assuming that humour and incident also crowd upon us, the combination ought to make a very amusing book.

HAMILTON: Funnily enough –

KINGSMILL: Part of the humour consisting in the contrast between the glory and discomfort in which Johnson and Boswell travelled –

PEARSON: And the lesser glory and greater comfort in which we shall travel.

HAMILTON: Funnily enough, I discussed this very idea with James Agate and Jock Dent.

KINGSMILL: Oh?

HAMILTON: Jock seemed keen on it, but I've heard nothing further from them. I suppose they're too busy.

PEARSON: Well, as you're bursting to have this book written, I don't see why Hugh and I shouldn't help you. Do you, Hugh?

KINGSMILL: I'm perfectly game. Hamish's idea strikes me as a very sound one.

They discussed details for some time, and as they were about to leave, Hamish Hamilton cleared his throat.

HAMILTON: By the way, you two, you won't tread on *too* many corns, will you?

PEARSON: That's rather an extraordinary suggestion, Hamish. I don't know that either Hugh or I are particularly identified with that kind of thing.

KINGSMILL: Hamish only said it as a matter of form for this sort of book. He knows his men.

PEARSON: Our intention, Hamish, is to write a sunny book. Yes, that's the word – sunny.

KINGSMILL: And serene.

HAMILTON: Of course, of course. I have complete confidence in your discretion.

Kingsmill's enthusiasm grew when the first complete edition of Boswell's *Journal of a Tour to the Hebrides* was published. 'There are some marvellous things in the new Boswell,' he wrote to Pearson, 'which are equal to anything he has put into the *Life* and the published version of the tour. Here is one, about Lady

Macdonald, who is gingerly treated in the usual version, as is her husband, who is amazingly good in the new version: "Mr Johnson called me to his bedside this morning, and to my astonishment he took off Lady Macdonald leaning forward with a hand on each cheek and her mouth open – quite insipidity on a monument grinning at sense and spirit. To see a beauty represented by Mr Johnson was excessively high. I told him it was a masterpiece and that he must have studied it much. 'Ay,' said he." I'll get it off to you tomorrow if I possibly can. There are scores of jewels.'

All that remained was to try and arrange free travel. 'I am writing to the railways,' Kingsmill said. 'The idea of getting away from civilisation grows hourly.' The railways however did not respond too favourably. The name Lunn no longer exercised its old magic. The LNER's Advertising Manager thanked him for his letter but regretted that 'at the moment we are not in need of any articles on the lines suggested'. The LMS were equally unhelpful: 'The scheme as outlined by you is not entertained.' 'I suppose,' said Kingsmill, 'that if the scheme had been outlined by Bernard Shaw instead of us he'd have been sent up to Scotland by a special. . . .'

Pearson added: 'With limousines running on the roads to right and left of the line, in case of momentary desire for that mode of transport should overcome him.'

Kingsmill: 'And every sort and species of vegetable slaughtered in his honour by the railway hotels.'

Only Kingsmill's uncle Holdsworth, in charge of the Lunn hotels in Scotland, was helpful and offered them free accommodation. For a time it looked as if they would have to call the expedition off, but then thanks to the intervention of a friend of Douglas Jerrold, the resistance of the LMS was broken and the company offered free transport on their lines throughout the month of June. It was to prove a generous act of patronage for which the railway received practically nothing in return.

Pearson was taking the project seriously and suggested that they should bring with them Birkbeck Hill's *Footsteps of Dr Johnson*. 'I got Birkbeck Hill's *Footsteps* from the London Library,' Kingsmill reported. 'When I say "I got" I mean the book was lowered by a crane from the attic in which it is housed and transported by Harrods to Hastings, where a shed has been erected for it, in which by an ingenious system of ladders and platforms, I can read it with some comfort.'

'Dear old Birkbeck!' Pearson replied, 'I knew he would be useful. Bring him up in a lorry this week. I would commune with him.' Despite its bulk, Pearson took the book with him to Scotland, but it lay unopened throughout the trip at the bottom of his suitcase.

The next week they finally left for Scotland from Euston. Kingsmill was especially happy. He liked nothing better than a long journey in a first-class compartment paid for by someone else, during which he could be guaranteed a respite from the demands of family and creditors. No one could knock on the door, no postman deliver bills. Pearson began to take notes:

> The train approached the Potteries, and here seemed a theme on which something of significance might be said, but on going into the matter they discovered that neither of them knew anything about the intricacies of manufacture and invention. 'I admit no reason for any modern inventions except gramophones and anaesthetics,' said Pearson, 'let us keep a look-out for Lichfield. It was, as you have so finely said in your book on Johnson, the place where Johnson was born. Ah, there it is!' They stood up and Kingsmill, who now saw it for the first time, looked at it with understandable interest. 'I always think of Lichfield as under a grey sky,' he said, 'and the people there in "a faint struggle with the tediousness of time" – Johnson's wonderful phrase.'

After a brief visit to Stirling, they reached Edinburgh and put up at the Caledonian Hotel, 'on the ground that to put up at any cheaper hotel would involve them in unnecessary expense'. Here they considered whether they should follow the same route northwards which Johnson and Boswell had taken. The snag was how to reconcile their aim, so successfully outlined to Hamish Hamilton, of following in Johnson and Boswell's footsteps, with the fact that they could only travel free to places served by the LMS. They were all right until they got to Aberdeen, and it was there that Kingsmill invented the notion of 'yarrowing' to solve the problem. The word was derived

from a poem of Wordsworth's 'Yarrow Unvisited', composed
during the poet's tour of Scotland:

> Let beeves and home-bred kine partake
> The sweets of Burn-mill meadow;
> The swan on still St Mary's lake,
> Float double, swan and shadow!
> We will not see them; will not go,
> Today, nor yet tomorrow;
> Enough if in our hearts we know
> There's such a place as Yarrow.

'Yes, yes,' said Pearson. 'Now I perceive why I have always
liked that poem. To know which places to "yarrow" and
which not to "yarrow" is the beginning and the end of the art
of travel.' They promptly decided to yarrow Ellon, Banff and
Cullen and set off for Elgin, where they visited the ruined
cathedral, destroyed, so Johnson learned, not 'by the tumultu-
ous violence of Knox, but more shamefully suffered to
dilapidate by deliberate robbery and frigid indifference'. The
ruins and Johnson's remark inspired a brief survey by Kingsmill of the Doctor's religious position:

The real reason why Johnson disliked the reformers was not
because they were intolerant, but because they were unsettling. Johnson would have been a Catholic, as he
admitted, but for 'an obstinate rationality'. He had too
much sense to be a Catholic, but he had also too much
scepticism to be comfortable as a Protestant. That's what
maddened him with Knox and the rest. If he had expressed
himself with complete candour about them, he would have
said: 'Here are these fellows knocking a system which has
grounded itself on the firm basis of sixteen hundred years.
Possession is nine points of religion, as of law. The fact
that the Catholic Church has been in possession of the
mind of mankind for all these centuries means that it has
stupefied the mind of humanity into a pleasing acceptance
of a system which, viewed in the cold light of reason, might
not appear very satisfactory. Now Knox and Calvin come
along, and, being far too stupid to have any doubts themselves, upset the barrier so providentially interposed between
more intelligent persons and the agonies of unbelief.

Leaving the ruins, they set out to the beach and stopped an elderly woman to ask the way:

ELDERLY WOMAN: The sea?
KINGSMILL: The harbour.
ELDERLY WOMAN: The harbour?
PEARSON: The front.
ELDERLY WOMAN: The front?
KINGSMILL: The beach.
ELDERLY WOMAN: The beach?
PEARSON: The promenade.
ELDERLY WOMAN: The promenade?
PEARSON and KINGSMILL: Isn't Elgin on the sea?
ELDERLY WOMAN: No.
KINGSMILL: ⎫
　　　　　　 ⎬Oh!
PEARSON: ⎭

The following day as they sat down to breakfast in their hotel, a fellow guest who had previously passed on 'many interesting facts about Scottish ruins' advised them on the menu: 'I recommend the finnan haddock. The finnan haddock on this coast is very good. You can't do better than have the finnan haddock, because it is always fresh and good here, which is why I always have finnan haddock on this coast.' Pearson and Kingsmill ordered finnan haddock, and their neighbour congratulated them saying: 'I am glad you have ordered finnan haddock. I always recommend the finnan haddock, because the finnan haddock on this coast is very fresh and good, which is why I always order it myself.'

After enjoying their finnan haddock they decided to yarrow Forres, Nairn and Cawdor, and took the train for Inverness where Johnson had given an imitation of a kangaroo. An eye-witness described the scene:

Johnson was in high spirits. In the course of the conversation he mentioned that Mr Banks (afterwards Sir Joseph) had, in his travels, discovered an extraordinary animal called the kangaroo. The appearance, conformation, and habits of this quadruped were of the most singular kind; and in order to render his description more vivid and graphic, Johnson rose from his chair and volunteered an imitation of the animal.

The company stared; and Mr Grant said nothing could be more ludicrous than the appearance of a tall, heavy, grave-looking man, like Dr Johnson, standing up to mimic the shape and motions of a kangaroo. He stood erect, put out his hands like feelers, and, gathering up the tails of his huge brown coat so as to resemble the pouch of the animal, made two or three vigorous bounds across the room!

Kingsmill felt a sudden onrush of pity for Boswell when reading how he and Johnson had attended service at the church and the minister in the course of his sermon had said that 'some connected themselves with men of distinguished talents, and since they could not equal them, tried to deck themselves with merit by being their companions. Boswell remarked ingenuously on "the odd coincidence with what might be said of Johnson and me". "About as odd a coincidence," Pearson said, "as if a minister preaching before Queen Elizabeth, happened to maintain that the Virgin Mary must have been decked with red hair".'

Yarrowing Fort Augustus, they took a coach to Invermoriston, which boasted an excellent hotel 'where Johnson and Boswell would have stayed had it been there in 1773'. The next day they set off by foot on the forty-five mile journey to Glenelg. Pearson was far the better walker of the two and all his life was in the habit of going for long hikes of up to forty miles. He was soon striding ahead of Kingsmill, who found a satisfactory explanation of the widening gap between them 'in the fact that of late years his practical difficulties had been even more exhausting than those of his friend'. By the time Kingsmill reached the Clunie Bridge Inn Pearson was already comfortably ensconced.

A pleasant day of recuperation ensued and they then set out to complete the journey to Glenelg, crossing Mam Rattagan 'or Rattikin, according to Johnson, or Rattachan, according to Boswell, or, again according to Johnson, Ratiken, or, again according to Boswell, Rattakin.' Once again Pearson got ahead, and reached the hotel at Glenelg before Kingsmill. Here, on enquiring if the inn at which Johnson had stayed was still standing, they were introduced to the proprietor of their hotel, a Captain Redmayne, 'who was very much interested in

Dr Johnson and would welcome a talk with them'. Both Kingsmill and Pearson were exhausted after their long walk and looking forward to an early bed, when the Captain joined them over coffee. After some preliminary small talk Redmayne left the room to fetch a volume of press cuttings and during his absence Pearson observed with weary resignation, 'We are clearly in for a lengthy session with one of the world's leading bores.' Captain Redmayne then returned with his press cuttings. He was not, he explained, himself possessed of any great knowledge of Johnson. His own interests were political – 'Shortly after leaving Oxford he had worked at Toynbee Hall. At that time he was a radical – "Measles. We all have it in our youth" – and had been asked by Parnell to sit for a County Clare constituency (he was descended from Strongbow, and his mother was a Fitzgerald). He was, however, persuaded by John Bright's brother-in-law not to stand, as it would alienate his Irish connections. On the English and Scottish side he was related to the Countess of Oxford and the Duchess of Rutland. Later he was asked by the Durham miners, among whom he had done a great deal of work, to stand in the labour interest, but that also fell through. It was curious, he said with a smile, that he should have boxed the compass in this way.'

Kingsmill's face was hidden from Captain Redmayne by a vase of flowers, and the latter was therefore addressing his remarks exclusively to Pearson, who made 'the usual polite interjections'. The contrast between his previous comment about one of the world's leading bores and the courteous 'Ha's', 'Indeed's' and 'Capitals' with which he now greeted the Captain's harangue was too much for Kingsmill, and when Pearson removing his pipe ejaculated 'All three parties! God bless my soul! Capital!' he rose unsteadily and muttering 'Sorry, old man – feeling ill', shuffled across the floor and hurried upstairs.

'I can still see his heaving back,' Pearson later wrote to Muggeridge, 'and his hand pushing a handkerchief into his mouth as he walked unsteadily to the door. Exercising considerable self-control, my belly muscles aching with the contraction necessary to prevent myself from exploding, I remained for two hours with Redmayne. . . . On the way to my room I looked in to see if Hughie was asleep. He was lying on his bed gasping for breath, his body occasionally shaken by convulsions, and a long-drawn sound, something between a groan and a howl, escaping from his lungs at intervals. He was suffering from the after-effects of over two hours' continuous laughter, and as the mere sight of me produced further spasms I deemed it expedient to retire.'

The following day after breakfast they both went into the smoking room of the hotel. As they examined the bookshelves a deep parsonical voice, belonging, as they later learned, to Canon Fowler, the vicar of Rye, intoned: 'You won't find anything good in there.'

Pearson started.

'Do you know this place?' the Canon continued.

'N-no,' Pearson stuttered.

'It's ma -gic.' The combination of the pause between the two syllables and the clergyman's fruity voice brought on another of Kingsmill's laughing attacks and once more he staggered from the room, gasping to the receptionist outside, 'Where on earth d'you get them from?'

Pearson was yet again compelled to keep a straight face as Kingsmill tottered out down the corridor, trying in vain to stifle his laughter.

The following day they crossed over to Skye on the steamer and arrived at Dunvegan, where they were received at the castle by Mrs (later Dame Flora) Macleod. The weather was poor and they spent most of the time bringing their book up to date. Pearson wrote prophetically to his wife: 'We are getting on with the book, which is incredibly good and won't sell a copy.' Meanwhile, they had made friends with the only other guest at the hotel, a Baptist named Sterry. 'I'd like,' he said in the course of their ensuing conversation, 'to ask the Archbishop of Canterbury what Christ would say about his fifteen thousand a year.' 'If that question could stump the Archbishop,' Kingsmill replied, 'he'd still be a curate.'

'I'd like to ask him all the same,' said Sterry.

All in all they spent some five days in Skye and then set off by boat for Mallaig, excusing their diminishing interest in their surroundings by some reflections on Great Men and travel:

PEARSON: It's an undeniable fact that nearly all the greatest men have hardly ever left their native land – Shakespeare, for example.

KINGSMILL: Jesus Christ.

PEARSON: Beethoven.

KINGSMILL: Buddha.

PEARSON: Rembrandt.

KINGSMILL: Wordsworth.

PEARSON: Cromwell.

KINGSMILL: Johnson.

PEARSON: Smith.

Thereafter the scale of the yarrowing increased. On Monday, June 21 they boarded a steamer to sail round the Isle of Mull. They duly disembarked to visit the cathedral at Iona, but stayed comfortably ensconced in deck chairs while their fellow passengers went off to gape at Fingal's Cave. 'We must stand firm,' Pearson said, 'and prove that we are serious yarrowers; men who can make a sacrifice in the cause of yarrowing; men who do not merely yarrow out of indolence or caprice; men who, in short, with Fingal's Cave on one hand and lunch on the other, unswervingly decide for lunch.'

These were the seas, Kingsmill observed as Oban came into sight, in which Johnson and Boswell had been overtaken by a violent storm. 'I was only thinking a moment ago,' Pearson said, 'how funny it would be if we were shipwrecked and drowned while following Johnson and Boswell through these waters. What would your last words be before going under?' 'Rough on Hamish,' Kingsmill replied.

The mention of their publisher prompted the thought that they had now passed by the island of Coll. 'I must have yarrowed it unconsciously,' Kingsmill said, and Pearson felt obliged to remind him that Johnson and Boswell had spent ten whole days there and that to yarrow it unconsciously was therefore 'much the same as doing a Johnsonian pilgrimage in England and absentmindedly overlooking Lichfield'. To make up for the omission, he proceeded to read Kingsmill some passages from Boswell's Journal, including an account of how while on the island he had been compelled one night to share a bed with a young laird. 'I have a mortal aversion,' Boswell noted, 'at sleeping in the same bed with a man.'

'Hardly in the modern spirit,' Kingsmill observed, and a fellow passenger who had been eavesdropping gave a snort and shifted his deck chair in protest. When Pearson finished reading, they both felt that they knew all they wanted to about Coll.

From Oban they made for Boswell's family home at Auchinleck. To their surprise the ticket collector at the station informed them that there was no hotel in the town. However they found a building nearby clearly labelled 'Railway Hotel'. Over supper that night the landlady confided that she knew nothing of Boswell and that they were the first people ever to come to the hotel on his account. If they wanted any information about him they should consult the minister. Foiled here, they mentioned Carlyle, and she smiled sardonically:

LANDLADY: Ay, Tam. A rare turn out! My grandmother was his cousin.

PEARSON: But surely he's a great name in these parts?

LANDLADY: Ay, to visitors. There was an American lady who was very excited about him and said to my grandmother that surely she must have seen Tam's funeral. It passed by my house, said she, but I didn't look out of the window.

KINGSMILL: Well, Burns? *He's* a great name, anyway.

LANDLADY: You can consult my husband about Burns. I've no use for him myself, but he was a great lad with the lassies they say.

After her departure Pearson lamented the indifference on the part of the inhabitants to Auchinleck's greatest son, and Kingsmill said: 'One hears a great deal about the thirst for literature among the Scots. For my part I begin to suspect that a Scot with a passion for books is as rare as a Spaniard capable of killing a bull with a single thrust.' When they went up to their bedroom he acknowledged that at least 'the air breathed by Boswell's contemporaries has been carefully preserved'.

Boswell's only direct descendant, Lord Talbot de Malahide, had recently sold Auchinleck to a distant relative, John Boswell, and it was his sisters who received Kingsmill and Pearson the following day. These ladies, they discovered, were also indifferent and even hostile to Boswell. His father, Lord Auchinleck, was highly esteemed and his son, Sir Alexander, had been 'a very valuable man in the county'. His grandson, Sir James, had been a great gambler . . . even so, they were to understand that he had had many good points besides. Boswell, however, had little to be said in his favour and Sir James's widow had thought so little of him that she had turned his portrait to face the wall.

Leaving the house, they went to Auchinleck church and surveyed the Boswell family vault.

PEARSON: How sad it is that people aren't interested in people who are interested in people.

KINGSMILL: It's not so much lack of interest as active alarm. Society is based on the assumption that everyone is alike and that no one is alive.

PEARSON: And Boswell acted on the assumption that no one was alike and that everyone was alive.

KINGSMILL: And so is regarded by his family as a traitor to society and a disgrace to themselves.

PEARSON: He made the unpardonable mistake of assuming that what people thought about in private they would be eager to talk about in public.

Both men were exceptionally pleased with the book, *Skye High*, which was finished in time for publication later that year. 'I've just been roaring over *Skye High*,' Kingsmill wrote to tell Pearson on October 19, and Pearson replied: 'Talking of *Skye High*, I have been glancing at it again, and I do not think it right to conceal from you the considered judgement that it is one of the major masterpieces of the world, which means of course that it will not sell a copy.' This prediction proved to be unhappily correct. Despite some good reviews, notably by Evelyn Waugh and Harold Nicolson, the book was a total failure. Kingsmill was more than usually disappointed and put the blame on the high price charged by Hamish Hamilton. 'The book would have had a real sale,' he wrote angrily to another publisher, 'not among highbrows but among ordinary intelligent people . . . I have never before passed any criticism on any publisher with regard to the price of a book, but here was a case of a book that demanded to be issued at a moderate figure.'

Only gradually did he get over his disappointment. In later life he constantly re-read the book with pleasure. 'How books gain by distance,' he wrote to Pearson in May 1943. 'It all seems so fresh. . . .' The tour itself remained one of his fondest memories, a few isolated weeks of constant happiness and laughter.

Among Kingsmill's papers in a note dated June 5, 1926 there occurs the following: 'This night I dreamed I was with HP at 88 Abbey Road. We were outside his house, and a mile away, opposite us, was a range of low hills, shining in the early morning sun. The light was more exquisite than in waking life, and an added joy was the feeling that these hills were in Scotland or in some part of England far from London; yet the hills themselves were quite near, thus giving the ecstasy that springs from any transcending of the laws which bind us in life.'

Chapter 10

Throughout the Thirties Hesketh Pearson was subject to the strain caused him by an unhappy love affair. Some time in 1930 he met and fell in love with an actress called 'Dolly'. She was twenty, less than half his age, and Jewish. 'Her hair was dark,' he wrote, 'her expression vivacious, her body lithe. She could be alluringly lovely in one mood, and ruthlessly hard in another.'

'I fell in lust with her,' he told a friend. The resulting conflict of passion and loyalty to his wife at times tormented him. 'I wish to God that you were in England,' he wrote to Kingsmill in December 1931. 'I would rather have you with me just now than anyone on earth. I am passing through a horrible phase, with which you alone could sympathise. I need your advice. I feel frightfully alone. I am between two fires and need a screen to keep the sparks off. However, men must endure, but it's difficult when one's guts are falling out – you know the feeling. The fact that I haven't a pound between myself and the workhouse is hardly noticeable in these emotional cataclysms. Am I writing balls? If so, I can't help it. It's not my fault.'

Kingsmill replied:

> I am so sorry about your present difficulties. They simply must be dealt with, and I wish you would explain the whole situation to Gladys. You can't go on bearing the double strain of acute money worries and two women in a state of misery about you. Personally I think Dolly is wearing you out. The trouble with Dolly is that she is completely selfish. She knew you were married, and she ought to accept things as they are. She can't ask you to break up a marriage with someone who has never given you any provocation of any kind. Dolly reminds me of Eileen,* and I wish you could see

* Eileen Turpin, Kingsmill's first wife.

your way to ending the relationship. I have thought this for a long time, but the wisdom of third parties is out of place in these matters, I know. Only you are so obviously worried beyond endurance that I hope you'll excuse this officiousness. I wish you would clear it all up with Gladys, ask Dolly at any rate for a temporary separation, to think things over, and go off for a rest somewhere. Perhaps your mother would come to the rescue.

All this sounds very unsympathetic to Dolly, but her attitude to Gladys convinces me that you would suffer in the long run as much as I suffered with Eileen, with the additional unhappiness of leaving Gladys on your mind.

I shall go on repeating myself, unless I stop at once, for I have been worrying a lot since I last saw you. Do explain everything to Gladys, old man, and if possible see your mother, who I am sure would help you in every way.

Perhaps the only benefit Pearson derived from his affair was the insight it gave him into the nature of the subject of his third biography, William Hazlitt. Hazlitt, too, had been the victim of a hopeless passion – for Sara Walker, the daughter of his landlady. Hazlitt's emotion was totally misplaced and never returned and yet it was so powerful that it affected him for the rest of his life. Pearson saw clearly that his love for Sara Walker, which previous biographers had played down or ignored, was in fact the most important experience that Hazlitt had and that it explained the melancholy, the looking back to the happy times of youth that are present in much of his best writing. The fellow feeling that Pearson evinced for Hazlitt made *The Fool of Love* the most vivid of his biographies and the favourite of both Kingsmill and Muggeridge. While working on it, Pearson wrote, he seemed to be living Hazlitt's life, 'and I often had the feeling that he was walking just ahead of me in the street, a weird lonely figure whom people turned to stare at.'

Pearson's love affair came to a crisis at the beginning of 1939. Throughout the nine years it lasted Dolly had been trying to get Pearson to leave his wife. Eventually, wearying of his vacillations she became engaged to another man. Pearson then asked his wife for a divorce.

Gladys Pearson had recently been dealt a terrible blow, by

the death of their son Henry. Pearson and Henry had got on quite well together until Henry, who had excelled at school and won a scholarship to Cambridge, became infected by the wave of communism, which at that time swept through the University. Pearson was unable to sympathise with or even understand his son's conversion to Marxism. In the course of a walking tour in Somerset, Henry Pearson suggested to his father that Shakespeare would have been a better writer if he could have read Karl Marx. Pearson exploded with such vehement rage that thereafter the two found it almost impossible to communicate with one another.

When the Spanish Civil War broke out Henry joined the International Brigade and left for Spain without saying anything to his parents. He was killed in the action on the River Ebro. His death, fighting for a cause with which neither of his parents had much sympathy, shattered his mother. When, in addition, her husband asked for a divorce it must have been almost more than she could bear. At any rate, she gave her consent. But it came too late.

Pearson wrote: 'It had taken me several days to brace myself to the ordeal, and when I broke the news to my girl (now a woman of twenty-nine, though I always thought of her as a kid) she told me tearfully that she had lost confidence in my promises and that her marriage had been definitely fixed. Several hours of agitating scenes and mutual recriminations followed and late that night I left her angrily outside the church in Woburn Square, walking many miles of streets to gain some measure of calmness. When I reached home early in the morning Gladys gave me more sympathy than I deserved. My behaviour to her was unforgivable, but she forgave it. . . . My request for a divorce at that particular time was the only action in my life of which I am wholeheartedly ashamed. I have said and done many deplorable things in my life, but I have forgiven myself for everything except this.'

The tension of this period brought Pearson to the point of breakdown. 'I have been terribly unhappy lately,' he wrote to Muggeridge on January 16, 1939, 'that I would welcome Hitler and his bombs; they would at least relieve the void and sickness of my heart. I have got a doctor to drug me into sleep, not having slept properly for eight weeks, but I wake every morning to renewed torture. I suppose it will end, but I would far rather it ended me.'

The crisis in his life is reflected in a biography he wrote during this period of General John Nicholson, one of the heroes of the Indian Mutiny. For the only time in his career as a biographer Pearson tackled a professional soldier and did so with a certain amount of relish, describing the atrocities of the mutiny in gory detail and idolising Nicholson in a way that was quite unlike his normal style. He became uncharacteristically touchy, reacting violently if criticised. 'Alas, I am in bad odour with my family,' he told Kingsmill. 'The other day Gladys and I went to dine with my brother-in-law Dane. . . . While mixing cocktails together he informed me that he had read my Nicholson and asked me in a guarded manner whether I would be offended at something he had to say about it. Now I have had enough of this sort of thing from my family; and in order to prevent an acrimonious discussion and to keep clear of a topic that would be sure to result in friction, I replied firmly, "I should not only be offended but would resent it so much that I should tell you to shut your bloody mouth and confine your remarks to money making." He took offence, stupidly I think, and a row, which I had feared and done my best to prevent, commenced. However, I resolutely refused to quarrel and shut up after telling him he was a shit and a few other things. Throughout the evening he kept bursting forth with animosity – the man has an evil nature – but beyond countering his outbursts with a few emphatic comments on his personal character I maintained an icy reserve.'

For some months after his crisis Pearson was in a prickly, near-hysterical state. It showed itself in behaviour of this kind, which could not be attributed solely to his famous temper.

Walking through the London streets he became a prey to melancholy in which his thoughts reverted to his dead son. 'I again felt the loss of Henry keenly,' he wrote in his diary, 'and I tried to visualise his unknown grave on the banks of the Ebro where he died fighting; a shocking waste of a fine intelligence in a damnable cause. He was such a splendid companion before he went Red and I saw "red". Religion whether it be of church or state is the curse of mankind: it sours the milk of human kindness. He and I got on famously before he went mad and became a communist. Which made him impossible; which made me impossible. I haven't the temperament to endure this sort of thing and we quarrelled. The bare thought of slavery and tyranny makes me scream, and to convert such horrors into ideals for which men will die is more than I can stand. We became utterly incompatible and estranged. The pity of it overwhelmed me once more. I wish I could have died in his place. But there it is. I suppose I should be just as unsympathetic, be just as pig-headed, if it were to happen all over again.'

Like Brian Lunn, when he was depressed, Pearson sought out Kingsmill. He asked him to come for a week's holiday in the Cotswolds. They had already conceived the idea of a successor to *Skye High* which was to be rather loosely based on Shakespeare, but had so far failed to find a publisher. Hamish Hamilton had been disappointed by *Skye High*. The 'yarrowing' did not go down well. The poor sales seemed to suggest that the public shared his low opinion of the book. He listened without enthusiasm as Kingsmill outlined his ideas for a sequel: 'Hesketh has never been to Marlborough, so that is to be our starting place. We are just going to wander about that part of the world, drifting gradually towards Stratford, and piecing Shakespeare together as we go.' 'Piecing . . . Shakespeare . . ? Together?' Hamilton muttered dubiously.

'Well, Hamish,' said Kingsmill, after a brief silence, 'we mustn't take up your time. You've been very good to us in the past.'

They rose, and Pearson, shaking Hamish's hand cordially, said he must lunch with them some day. Hamish said he would be delighted, and Pearson must give him a ring.

Having failed to secure an advance and being by now almost completely broke, Kingsmill in desperation, conceived the idea of getting some money off Shaw, on whose biography Pearson was about to embark. 'After much reflection,' he told Pearson later, 'it occurred to me that as you were taking this trip to tone yourself up for your Shaw biography, a kind of connection, however frail, had established itself between Shaw and me.' He set off from Hastings to London and having obtained Shaw's telephone number from William Gerhardi, rang him up. Shaw answered in person, and Kingsmill said he wanted to speak to him about a matter connected with Hesketh Pearson. Shaw asked him to come round. Kingsmill found Shaw 'sitting upright at his writing table silhouetted against the window', and was despite his pressing financial worries moved by 'the mixture of tenacity and solitude in the old man's erect bearing'. The following conversation, recorded by Kingsmill, then ensued:

GBS: Well, and how is Hesketh? Is it about him that you wished to see me?

KINGSMILL: He's not very fit at present, and wants to go into the country. He's asked me to go with him, and I thought that as you're interested in Hesketh –

GBS: I'm not interested in Hesketh. Hesketh's interested in me.

KINGSMILL: I really can't go on with my preposterous errand unless you're willing to listen to me.

GBS: Quite so, quite so.

KINGSMILL: Hesketh's my host, and I can't ask him to support my family when I'm away. I've just published a book on D. H. Lawrence which has fizzled out, and I have no cash at the moment.

GBS: T.E. finished D. H. Lawrence off. There's no interest in D.H. any more.

KINGSMILL: So I have found. I wondered therefore if you would come to my assistance.

GBS: But what about Sir Henry? He's still alive, isn't he?

KINGSMILL: He's on a cruise, and in any case, apart from other complications, the travel business isn't what it was.

GBS: That's a fine hotel your firm has up in Scotland. And there's one at Hastings. I have stayed there myself.

KINGSMILL: So have I. Nonetheless . . .

GBS: I'm a poor man too. I've just had to borrow two thousand from my wife.

KINGSMILL: I'm so sorry. (Rising): In that case. . . .

GBS: Would a tenner be any use?

KINGSMILL (sinking back): Certainly. It's extremely good of you.

Shaw wrote out a cheque. Kingsmill rose, took the cheque, and they shook hands. 'I was really touched, and was conscious of a very warm feeling towards the old man, but was unable to find words in which to express it,' he told Pearson, who, after listening to the story, said: 'Why didn't you touch him for a hundred while you were about it?'

His financial situation ameliorated, Kingsmill joined Pearson at Paddington on January 23 and they boarded the train for Marlborough. They passed by Reading and its famous gaol, which Pearson described as 'Oscar's last country house'.

'Whenever I am on this line,' Pearson said, 'I remember that remark made by Sherlock Holmes to Watson on one of their crime jaunts to the West – something to the effect that those creeper-clad cottages, the praises of which, my dear Watson, you have just been singing, conceal crimes compared with which the agonies of women hammered by gin-sodden brutes in hideous alleys are an absolute picnic. Holmes was right. Leave little clumps of people to fester together and everything they do and think is poisoned.'

Kingsmill agreed: 'The permutations and combinations in a nice old English village are matter for a higher mathematician. Everyman his own mother, is the only way I can put it.'

From the King's Head Hotel in Cirencester on January 27 Kingsmill wrote to Muggeridge:

My dear Mugg,
We have been having a very interesting time. Marlborough was really wonderful. Both the Savernake Forest and the town. The sun was so bright as almost to be inconvenient, and the forest had the most beautiful avenue I have ever seen. We went through Bristol to Marshfield, an old Cotswold Village, and by the time we got there on Wed. evening there was a howling snowstorm. The Davenports* live there, and we put up with them, and they put up with us. Of this visit I would write at great length. 'It bred new thought in me', as Frankie says somewhere. They are an extraordinary couple. Clement is a really amazing black and

---

* John Davenport, writer and sometime literary editor of *Vogue* magazine married Clement Hale, who after leaving Davenport, married the musician Sir William Glock.

white artist who whiles away the time with drawings which would make Poe, etc, begin all over again, or take up knitting. It is genuine horror. She is at the same time very sincere and longs for an escape from the inferno in which her imagination is imprisoned. John Davenport is as strange a phenomenon as I have ever seen. He already weighs 18½ stone. Their child, aged fourteen months, neither inspires nor feels enthusiasm for any person or thing. Sitting on her mother's knee, with Hesketh and self to right and left of her, she turned her eyes first towards one of us and then towards the other, about twenty times, with a cold scrutiny, as though trying to decide which of us was the more valueless. Hesketh seemed to me to be enduring this ordeal calmly enough, but Davenport suddenly said to the nurse 'Take her out.' And added, 'Hesketh doesn't like her.' The snow kept us there two nights in all, and we were somewhat relieved to continue our journey, leaving Giant Despair and his wife Diffidence (not to mention the child Distemper).

At Bibury, two days later, Pearson flew into a rage on finding the village invaded by a hunt and strode red-faced along the street shouting angrily about the vileness of bloodsports.

Later, over tea in a hotel, Kingsmill 'taxed Pearson with having covered a nostalgia for his fox-hunting youth with an outburst of exaggerated spleen'. This inspired one of Pearson's finer tirades in what Kingsmill called his 'sunstroke style': 'There are two types of men who get my goat: those who damn the sins they have a mind to, and those who damn the sins they have no mind to. The first is the Puritan who suppresses his natural instincts, and whose sex goes rancid within him. Of such was W. T. Stead. The second is the ex-rake and debauchee who, after a life-time of guzzling like a hog, drinking like a fish, and copulating like a stoat, turns over a new leaf when he can no longer gorge, soak and womanise, and preaches temperance, sobriety and chastity. Of such was Tolstoy. Compared with these two, the idiot of a fox-hunter strikes me as a relatively harmless cad.'

'A powerful speech,' said Kingsmill. 'But haven't you confused the issue?'

'I hope so,' Pearson replied.

Pearson now started work in earnest on his biography of Bernard Shaw. He had had the idea of such a biography as early as August 1938 and discussed it then with Kingsmill, who gave his opinion in a letter dated August 16: 'I think a life of the old boy would be really lucrative, especially with his blessing.' Pearson then wrote to Shaw outlining his plans in detail and received the answer on a postcard. 'Don't.' Shaw added: 'I shall dissuade you personally any time you like to see me.' Pearson called on him on October 21, and during a long talk succeeded in getting Shaw to change his mind. Shaw was charmed by Pearson's outspokenness and liked his lack of scholarly pretensions. Pearson always spoke his mind to Shaw. 'It is far better to know nothing like me,' he told him once, 'than to know everything and get it all wrong like you.' Shaw for his part admitted that he found Pearson's company both 'restful and invigorating'. At any rate, he gave the book his blessing. Pearson was thrilled. 'I floated on air down Whitehall Court,' he wrote, 'hugging an inscribed copy of his Corno di Bassetto essays on music.' On the strength of Shaw's approval he was able to secure an advance of £1,500. A month later he told Kingsmill: 'My book on him may be good in every other way but it will be wholly uncritical because he is being so extraordinarily nice to me. I just couldn't say a nasty word about him. He is the sweetest old dear that I have ever come across.' Kingsmill admitted rather begrudgingly that Shaw was 'a good old boy from certain angles'.

It must have been difficult for Kingsmill not to feel a little envious of his friend's new-found wealth, particularly as it was he who had done so much to promote it. In the financial year 1939–40 Kingsmill earned only £400. It was not enough to provide the bare support for his family and he was forced to look for other work. He wrote to a number of schools offering his services as a master, but had no reply. To add to his difficulties there now came the war. In May 1940 Hastings was declared a Danger Zone. 'Suddenly,' he wrote, 'on the French shore across the water from Hastings there were German troops and at the Memorial end of Queen's Road a flurry of anxious faces. Two or three nights later, when I was looking from my window towards the sea, a mile distant, I felt a great weight of foreboding, almost of horror, resting on the town. It seemed like a place in a dream: the old landmarks there but everything unfamiliar and menacing.' Kingsmill and his family were forced to leave the Laton Road house. 'Dorothy and the kids are going into Somerset,' he wrote to Pearson, 'and I suppose I shall never live at Hastings again, which saddens me, as it is the place that I have cared for most, and I love 24 Laton Road and hoped to linger out my last years there.' At last he received an offer from the headmaster of Marlborough to replace a German-born teacher who had been interned. He left Hastings on May 30, 1940 to take up his post: 'The first news from Dunkirk was coming in, with a steadying reassuring effect. Here was an evacuation that put the retreat from Mons in the shade; the final issue was by no means certain yet, but we had made a good start.' He soon adapted himself to the public school life, but quite naturally missed his family and friends: 'There are some nice chaps among the masters,' he told Pearson, 'but no one with whom I can take off my tie and throw my boots under the sofa.'

In the meantime he was grappling with a book commissioned by Douglas Jerrold in which he was supposed to trace the historical process that resulted in the emergence of Hitler. In its final form it consisted of four long essays, preceded by an introduction, on Elizabeth I, Cromwell, Napoleon and Abraham Lincoln. Jerrold was keen for Kingsmill to tackle Lenin as well, but this proved too much for him. 'Why does Lenin always talk of Dialectical Materialism instead of the Lord God,' he complained to Pearson, 'it's so much longer.' The book, which was eventually published in 1943 under the title *The Poisoned Crown*, gave Kingsmill a great deal of trouble. He was bored by men of action and of his subjects only Lincoln was in any way sympathetic. 'He is a marvellous chap,' he wrote to Pearson, 'the only politician in whom one can take the kind of interest, though more blurred, that one takes in Johnson, say.'

He found the job of untangling Cromwell's career an arduous one: 'It has taken me longer than I thought, the chaos of his doings being so extreme. I have frequently had to resist the temptation to say – "Out of the welter of the next few years one fact emerges", and then give one fact, for want of knowing two or more. My affection for the old rascal has returned, but

I haven't found any evidence, however slight to warrant the view that he ever did a disinterested action in the whole course of his life.'

Napoleon was even less congenial: 'I simply couldn't find any sense in anything he aimed at, apart from the ability he showed in organisation, etc. The epitaph of the nineteenth century should be – "It admired Napoleon".' Hitler was worse: 'Am toiling on Hitler,' he reported. 'I'm trying not to mention his name at all but suppose it will have to appear occasionally.' Hitler, like the *50 Most Amazing Crimes*, was actively distressing to contemplate and could give rise only to the despairing cry: Why does he do these things?

In the introductory chapter to *The Poisoned Crown* Kingsmill returned to the themes he had first outlined in *Matthew Arnold*, relating the Romantic movement to the emergence of Hitler. 'Most of the avoidable suffering in life,' he began, 'springs from our attempts to escape the unavoidable suffering inherent in the fragmentary nature of our present existence. We expect immortal satisfactions from mortal conditions, and lasting and perfect happiness in the midst of universal change. To encourage this expectation, to persuade mankind that the ideal is realisable in this world after a few preliminary changes in external conditions, is the distinguishing mark of all charlatans, whether in thought or action. In the middle of the eighteenth century Johnson wrote: "We will not endeavour to fix the destiny of kingdoms: it is our business to consider what beings like us may perform." A little later Rousseau wrote: "Man is born free and is everywhere in chains." Johnson's sober truth kindled no one. Rousseau's seductive lie founded the secular religions which in various forms have dominated Europe since Rousseau's death.'

The French Revolution was the first example of Rousseau's philosophy in action and this established a pattern which was to be followed subsequently – 'Wild rejoicing among the masses at the destruction of old abuses and the ruin of their oppressors, the improvisation of a new order, the necessity in the general confusion for ruthless methods of imposing it, the increasingly rapid elimination of those Utopians in whom humanity was stronger than practical sense, the welcome threat of foreign intervention and ensuing diversion of revolu-

tionary passion, now a menace to the Utopians at the top, into
patriotic fervour, and finally a military dictatorship and a
series of crusades against reactionary neighbours.' The worship
of Napoleon was paralleled in the literary world by that of
Byron who in the best Dawnist manner prophesied, 'There will
be blood shed like water and tears like mist, but the peoples
will conquer in the end'.

Kingsmill's detachment from the Spirit of the Age was once
again evinced in his rejection of communal solutions at a time,
during the war, when they were at a premium. 'Many remedies
for a shattered world,' he concluded, 'are now being offered to
mankind, but they are all collective remedies, and collective
remedies do not heal the ills produced by collective action. . . .
What is divine in man is elusive and impalpable, and he is
easily tempted to embody it in a concrete form – a church, a
country, a social system, a leader – so that he may realise it
with less effort and serve it with more profit. Yet, as even
Lincoln proved, the attempt to externalise the kingdom of
heaven must end in disaster. It cannot be created by charters
and constitutions, nor established by arms. Those who set out
for it alone will reach it together and those who seek it in
company will perish by themselves.'

While working on *The Poisoned Crown* Kingsmill suggested to
Muggeridge that they should embark on an exchange of
letters which would eventually, he hoped, be published. He
managed, with his usual dedication, to secure an advance, but
the book failed to materialise, partly because Muggeridge, like
many people during 1940, had other things on his mind.

At the outbreak of the war he had immediately joined up,
not for any patriotic reason, but more from a feeling of restlessness and a desire for change. Leaving Kitty and the children
at Whatlington, he was taken on the staff of the Ministry of
Information in London, but was after a month or two drafted
into the Intelligence Corps. As an acting unpaid lance-
corporal in an army hut at Ash Vale he finished *The Thirties*,
learning shortly afterwards that it was a Book Society choice.
It was his first real success.

Pearson wrote to him to say how entertaining he had found
the book, adding, 'It's not my view of the '30s, but how could
it be? History, like every other art, is a form of autobiography,

and the picture one gives of a period or a person is a sort of self-portrait.' A few days later, on March 16, 1940 Kitty Muggeridge came up to London to take the children to the Zoo. In the evening they all had dinner with the Pearsons at their flat in Hampstead. Malcolm said that both British and French troops were demoralised because nothing was happening. He thought there would be a move by President Roosevelt and the Pope to organise a peace conference. If it happened, he said, he and his family would clear out to Canada. The next day, after seeing his children off at Victoria, he returned for a three-hour talk with Pearson.

'I agree with him,' Pearson wrote, 'that we ought to assassinate our politicians and the French theirs. We long to go for a walk together, twenty-odd miles a day, from here to the Scottish border via the Severn Valley and Cumberland. No political talk, no equipment, drinking every evening in a pub.' As the year wore on and still nothing happened Muggeridge's gloom increased. In June, over dinner at Richmond, he predicted to Pearson that the war would be over in four weeks and that Lloyd George would be 'trotted out' to do a deal with Hitler. As always, Pearson found Muggeridge's doom-laden forecasts somehow exhilarating. 'We all had a grand evening and laughed ourselves sick,' he noted. A few weeks later the two friends visited the House of Commons. 'Malcolm wanted to see the revolting swine in session for the last time,' Pearson told Kingsmill. They sat in the Distinguished Strangers' Gallery, trying hard to pick out a face 'that hadn't crook or fool written all over it'. 'Their time is nearly up,' Muggeridge observed with glee. 'We shall not see them again.' He was very nearly right. On May 12, 1941 Pearson noted in his diary: 'News in the paper that the House of Commons has been bombed: unfortunately the M.P.s were not in it.'

By contrast with Muggeridge, Kingsmill always remained optimistic about the war. He met the Pearsons just after it began, in September 1939 and, when Gladys Pearson expressed apprehension, Kingsmill assured her that there was no reason for despondency and that the war would be over in two years. 'The German of today,' he said, 'after all he has gone through in the last twenty-five years, wants nothing but a quiet life.

Hitler doesn't symbolise pugnacity, but resentment and despair. He may have whipped up the youth of the country, but you can't fight a long war with nothing behind you but the bloodlust of perverted boy scouts.'

Even in July 1940, when you did not have to be Malcolm Muggeridge to expect the worst, Kingsmill's optimism remained unshaken. 'Muggeridge is entirely subjective in his view of Hitler,' he told Pearson; 'I don't think that there is anything to worry about, as far as Hitler is concerned. What cleaning up the world will be like afterwards is another matter. Everything Hitler has attempted against us has failed – U-boats, air attacks, pocket-battleships, French battleships, and when owing to Leopold,* he had our army completely in the air, he foozled it again. He may blow a lot of people to bits, but his number is up. I say this with the detachment of a completely useless member of the beleaguered fort.

'I know the Germans fairly well,' he added in a postscript, 'and while liking the simpler ones, do not think much of the rest. Nor do they think much of themselves. One of the stupidest things about them is their over-estimate of the English.'

It was in this same confident state of mind that, shortly after becoming a schoolmaster, he embarked on the projected correspondence with Muggeridge:

I meant to open my correspondence a fortnight ago [he wrote], but this has been a hopeless time in which to reflect on things in general, with so many things in particular on the move. One evening I turned on the wireless at nine, and the news seemed quite good until the announcer ended with 'The situation is one of increasing gravity'. Hoping for something better at midnight, I turned the wireless on again, and having been cheered by the news, which seemed distinctly better than at nine, was about to turn it off when the announcer added – 'The situation is one of increasing gravity'. I think it was on the next day that we heard of Leopold's capitulation. Although the battle for Paris is in full blast as I write, I believe Leopold's surrender will turn out to be the lowest point in our fortunes, coming as it did on top of that uncanny rush to Boulogne, with the Maginot

* King of the Belgians.

line far away in the distance, 'untouched' as the papers kept on saying, stressing a virginal quality which few people look for or desire in a system of fortifications.

Leopold's collapse was immediately followed by two more examples of the extraordinary by-products of Hitler's career. Churchill delivered a speech with no rhetoric in it, and I was offered a job. . . . The offer was very opportune financially, and I left Hastings on May 31. By this time the town was full of rumours about the imminent descent of parachutists, the ticket collector (to whom I tried to explain that my departure had no connection with the happenings across the Channel) telling me that half the town was already gone.

At fifty one does not want to enlarge one's experience, but to live at ease, one's family about one. I was not going very far from my home, and I was going to a place which would be a paradise to any of the millions of refugees in Belgium and France, but this kind of abstract comparison never seems of much use at the moment, and I got no more comfort from it than a man falling into a bed of nettles would from visualising a rack and thumbscrews. Also I was doubtful about my job, recalling Johnson's 'Every man that has ever undertaken to instruct others can tell what slow advances he has been able to make, and how much patience it requires to recall vagrant attention, to stimulate sluggish indifference, and to rectify absurd misapprehension.'

Things turned out better than I expected, chiefly because the boys are so extraordinarily pleasant. I have never met such good manners, not in the least sophisticated and perfectly natural. Had anyone told me that there was a school in England where there was a tradition of courtesy among the boys, I should have advised him to become a leader writer on *The Times*. Yet it is so here, but several masters tell me that it is peculiar to this place, though I think it must in some degree be connected with the general change from the vulgar opulence and security of England thirty years ago to the dangers and uncertainty of the present.

This change may not be felt much at Eton and Harrow, but it is probably felt here, at least by the older boys, one of whom, in an essay I have just been reading on Galsworthy, writes: 'One passage, though perhaps not meant to be humorous, appears to be worthy of notice: "He could take nothing for dinner but a partridge, with an imperial pint of champagne".'

A few weeks later Kingsmill wrote again:

Shortly after reaching Marlborough I saw the new moon through glass. This always depresses me more than not seeing it through glass cheers me, and, sure enough, a few days later France gave out, thereby compelling me to advance the lowest point in our fortunes from Leopold's surrender to Laval's re-emergence in the affairs of his unhappy country. To make certain that England would not follow France, I went out one evening round about the time of the next new moon, and saw it from the downs. On my way back I met one of my pupils, who on hearing what I had been doing gave an approving nod, and said 'National Service, sir'. I like the boys as much as ever. They have just enough corporate life and none of the spirit which gives a few persons the illusion that they are different in kind from the rest, because their greater force has made them different in degree. Public schools thirty years ago had a great deal in common with Nazi Germany.

At the end of term concert the hundred and twenty boys who were leaving went on to the stage and sang school songs and *Auld Lang Syne*. There was none of the emotionalism I have been accustomed to on these occasions. They all sang very cheerfully, no wallowing, no self-love in a melting mood such as Goering might feel at a reunion of any old army comrades still at large.

When his term ended Kingsmill went up to London to do some work at the British Museum Reading Room. Pearson, who had moved to Chipperfield at the beginning of the war, lent him his flat in Goldhurst Terrace, off the Finchley Road, where his sister-in-law Beatrice was living. 'When he arrived at our flat,' Pearson recalled, 'he had no ration book, and used to wash his underwear in the bathroom. When Beatrice took his old ration book to the shop to see if anything could be bought with it, the woman said, "You can put that in the British Museum".'

Kingsmill was meanwhile enjoying his stay. He told Muggeridge: 'London is very peaceful after Marlborough, where aeroplanes are constantly roaring overhead. I have not enjoyed it so much for years. Hampstead Heath is quite near, and I go up there sometimes and look over the great city which has always seemed to me different from other cities, as though it were something co-extensive with life, confused and aimless and corrupt at close quarters, but with a secret meaning which shines through at a distance. A day or two ago I was up there with Gerhardi and on our way down we passed through Church Row with its delightful houses, and descending came to a secluded little place on a woody slope. There were two houses by it, one in the simple lines of contemporary architecture, the other, which was called "Blue Tiles" like a house in an opera. "What a wonderful place London is," I exclaimed to my calmer companion. "Look at it – probably some fantastic eighteenth-century retreat for the mistress of a nobleman who had been touring the Continent and seen something like it in Lower Austria. There is nothing you cannot find in London." "Very nice, very pretty," said William, a wary glint in his eye. At this moment two grizzled men came out of the other house, and addressing the more communicative-looking of the two, a shrewd humorous man by his appearance, I said we had been admiring "Blue Tiles", and how like a house in an opera it was.

' "You are right," he said. "It is very like a house in an opera. It was built by Gracie Fields and Archie Pitt. They used to live there. There was a cocktail bar on the ground floor. If you look over the wall, you will see the ground floor. The house has three storeys, not two, as you might suppose. The cocktail bar was on the ground floor."

' "Thanks so much."

' "Not at all."

' "I must be more careful in future before expressing enthusiasm."

'He smiled tolerantly, and we parted, I a little dashed. But on reflection it occurred to me that though the departure of England's darling to the States, with Italian husband and some thousands of pounds, has dimmed her glamour, time will brighten it again, and "Blue Tiles" in a hundred years will be clothed with the charm I prematurely gave it.'

The peace of Hampstead was rudely shattered a few days later when the first instalment of the Blitz began. Kingsmill however remained calm and when three large bombs fell only a few hundred yards from Pearson's flat, he remarked nonchalantly to Beatrice, 'What a racket!' During the ensuing ten days, while the neighbours sheltered from the German bombardment on the cellar steps, he sat contentedly listening to the gramophone. (When Pearson eventually returned to his flat at the end of the war he found that certain records – Nimrod from the Enigma Variations, the slow movements of Beethoven's Violin, Triple and Emperor concertos, the cavatina of the B flat quartet – were almost worn out.)

Muggeridge had by now been posted to the GHQ Home forces at Kneller Hall. There, as the excitement provoked by the prospect of an imminent German invasion faded, he at last felt able to write to Kingsmill, who had returned to Marlborough:

My dear Hughie,

Please forgive me for having been so long in answering your letters. There's no excuse except inertia. I've had heaps of time, and not a hair on my head has been endangered. The forces are the sheltered life in this war; women and children last its slogan. I've just been going on from day to day waiting for the sirens, as residents in the Albany Hotel used to wait for the post; not expecting a letter, yet anxiously awaiting the postman's appearance because it was something to wait for.

London is very strange now; Barcelona in England's green and pleasant land. It conforms to what I've always felt it should have been. Who could have cared for Carlton House terrace when Curzon lived there; even less when the Savage Club and Herr von Ribbentrop succeeded him? But now, a ruin, with gaping glassless windows and shattered walls, it's rather lovable. I always half expect to find Bee* and the Pitchers living there, with a notice – 'Unexploded bomb', affixed by Bee to where the front door was, to protect them from intruders. It's the kind of idea that might well occur to him – carrying Rowton House one stage further, with not even a shilling a night to pay.

* Brian Lunn, Kingsmill's brother.

From this you will gather that I'm not what Churchill always says the Army is, 'in good heart'. At the same time, I shouldn't say I was unhappy. I've known unhappier times. This war has, in comparison with previous ones, many advantages. Since the attack has been directed exclusively at the civilian population we are spared Sassoonery. No one can say 'What you need is a bit of France', when all, or almost all, have had a bit of London. The non-combatant is as foolish as the combatant; and in the underground are many mansions of darkness and hate. Nor do I anticipate much post-war romanticism. Ex-officers in British Warms are unlikely to look for Pixies. Hitler, the great Pixie, does not need any looking for; and residual British Warms will probably be impounded to protect other than ex-officers' backs from wind and rain. The Rupert Brookes *de nos jours* have all, thank God, become American citizens; and no *Journey's End* will be apparent, rather a beginning. Sad was it at that time to be alive, but to be young was very Hell. There are two states after drunkenness – the Carry Over and the Hangover; similarly after fornication, war or any other indulgence of the Will. In the present case, I gratefully expect hangover, rather than, as after the last war, carry over – hand, somewhat shaky, reaching for Aspirin; step somewhat uncertain, homewards turning; gaze, somewhat confused, resting uneasily on an abhorrent but inevitable scene.

I've just spent a week's leave in Whatlington. There, too, they have their crater, a proud possession. Any faint expectation I had that coming from the metropolis, I might be received as a tired warrior needing rest was soon disappointed. As there are now no schools in the vicinity Pan and John go each morning to the Battle curate. John told me proudly that he was learning divinity. I asked him what divinity was, and he said 'Well, I drew a sloping line and underneath I writ: "The Upward Struggle".' For such an answer he deserves to be made a bishop in the Anglican Church at once. He's fallen deeply in love with Elizabeth Hallinan, and until the H's went away, he spent all his time with her. It was interesting as bearing on the point you've so often made about there being no necessary connection between love and passion. Once Kitty was singing an atrocious sentimental song of the usual type, and he said, as though he'd made a great discovery, 'Why, that's Elizabeth and me!' A more adult lover would have hesitated to admit that such sentiments were his own: but J, unaware of the basenesses (as well as ecstasy) of passion saw in the song only whatever it had of imaginative truth and failed to notice the rest. In the same way, a vegetarian might go into a lavishly stocked butcher's shop and see in the way of nutriment only a banana which the girl in the desk had brought in for lunch. John's love affair is the most serene that has ever come to my notice. There are no quarrels, no caresses, no money given or spent. It made me think of the Garden of Eden.

I still carry on the practice we've often shared of reading *Times* leaders, and the other day read a leader pointing out that Hitler was not the only person in the world with ideas about a new order. There was, for instance, Printing House Square, where something pretty hot in the way of a New Order was being hatched. This New Order, the leader contended, would, among many other benefits in accordance with the *old motto*, give to each according to his needs and take from each according to his capacity. May I not include among Hitler's achievements (conquering France in three weeks, installing you at Marlborough) this transforming of the Communist Manifesto in the eyes of *The Times* into a collection of old mottoes, suitable perhaps for Christmas crackers. Are you coming to London for the holidays? If so I shall look forward to seeing you.

At the end of 1940 the German-born Mr Hone whom Kingsmill had replaced at Marlborough was released from internment and Kingsmill was politely informed that he would no longer be needed. 'So far as headmasters are concerned,' he noted, 'I am an acquired taste, and though the Headmaster of Marlborough expressed great regret at losing my services and attributed our parting only to the return of a master who, as an enemy alien, had been interned after the fall of France, I felt that the Marlborough landscape probably seemed a little more normal to him with a Berlin lawyer than with myself in the middle distance.'

He now took up another teaching post at Merchant Taylors

in Northwood, Middlesex. Though he regretted leaving the pleasant atmosphere of Marlborough, he felt more relaxed at Merchant Taylors which, being a day school, did not share the rather exclusive monastic atmosphere of Marlborough. He was required to teach boys of all ages from thirteen to eighteen. 'With the kids of the lower fourth,' he wrote, 'whom I was supposed to instruct in the elements of English history, I found it difficult to preserve the gravity proper to my position. If I was in a good humour, they would sit looking preternaturally solemn, as though co-operating with me in a task fraught with immensely significant issues. The faintest suspicion of a smile on my part, and there was a shout of "Ooh-good! You're nice now, Sir!" after which it took some time to renew their interest in domestic implements of the Bronze Age or the secular functions of the Mediaeval Church.'

Kingsmill was better equipped to cope with the older boys. 'Life,' he wrote, 'is intensely interesting to boys as their minds begin to awaken. If it were equally interesting to older men, teaching would become the greatest of all professions.' He himself was interested in life and for that reason was a great teacher. Like Pearson and Muggeridge, many of the boys acquired from Kingsmill a lasting love of literature. He read Shakespeare and Wordsworth to them, as well as passages from *Skye High*, and though many remained unmoved, others were so inspired that thereafter they never forgot the experience.

Fellow masters were more suspicious, resenting his boisterous ways and his obvious enthusiasm for his subject matter. But here again there were those on whom he left an indelible impression.

Another member of the staff, Arnold Pilkington, writes:

He was such a delightful friend that I find my recollection of him becomes more vivid as time passes. He always seemed so glad to see you and was always full of amazing stories and observations. He was quite the least boring person I have ever met and every time you saw him brought a new joy. . . . He was a marvellous talker. I remember once taking him to lunch at the King's Head in Harrow to meet two friends of mine. He was on top form – as nearly always – and talked, as usual, in somewhat loud tones, with no pretence of privacy

and confidence. Very soon all the other guests stopped talking
and were listening to his ludicrous account of the time when,
in the company of certain celebrities, he was given a degree
at Dublin. The staff could not contain themselves either and
I can remember the helpless laughter of one of the waiters
who was serving. Of course he talked in exactly the same way
to everybody, including pupils of all ages. There was no
modification in his language when he stopped in the corridor
to chat to some boy. The boys soon got to accept this and
ceased to be surprised. I remember once there was a phone call
for him when he was teaching. I went along to his form room
to tell him – 'You're wanted on the phone.' 'Woman?' –
'Yes, I think so' – 'Christ!' None of the boys reacted at all
to this. It seemed quite natural to them that he should talk
in this way.

He loathed pompous or over-serious people who thought
themselves important. The result of this was that he made
himself unpopular with one or two of the senior members of
the staff who regarded him as scruffy and unconventional
and for whom he had no respect at all. I remember how
horrified they were one day when he started talking in the
coffee room in his usual loud voice about the Masons and
saying how absurd he thought they were. This, as you can
imagine, put a number of important backs up straight away.

As a teacher I think he was only fully appreciated by some
of the elder boys – many of them found themselves irritated
by his refusal to stick to the syllabus or to produce the sort of
things they could churn out in an examination answer. He
always enlivened his talk about books with sidelights on the
private lives of authors. Schiller, he said, suffered terribly
from indigestion and Goethe could hear him howling with
pain from the other side of the square in Weimar. This
delighted some but struck others as irrelevant.

I remember that there was one prodigiously 'clever' and
irritatingly precocious boy in the VIth form at the time.
While they were doing Chaucer and the others in the class
were busy taking notes and writing little explanations, he
would sit with his head on one side and holding the book in
front of him with one hand, memorise quietly any scraps
of information that seemed to him worth remembering. One

day – as I was told by a boy in the class – when this boy had asked some academic question which was particularly irritating, Kingsmill, instead of replying, looked out of the window in that rather distant way he could put on and said, 'I say, there's an awfully pretty girl coming up the drive'. This pleased the class enormously – and those of us who heard about it afterwards.

Meanwhile, Kingsmill was trying to find somewhere to live which would be near to Merchant Taylors, but this was proving difficult. 'The circumference of London,' he reported to Pearson, 'appears to be packed with people who don't want to be blown to bits in the centre. Natural enough from their standpoint, but it has put prices up, and I am paying more than I ought to for something far different from what I would like – a commercial hotel at Harrow, a gloomy place tenanted, so far as I could gather from a cursory glance, by homeless people who have given up all hope of a home from home, and ask for nothing better than a grave from the grave.' Kingsmill was now fifty-one, and did not find living in the hotel congenial: 'My curiosity about other people is dwindling. I am conscious of a less ardent desire to hear the stories of their lives from chance met strangers. I still believe that everyone is capable of being interested about himself for half an hour, but nowadays, when I am on a train journey of an hour or upwards, I am no longer willing to be bored during the last part of the journey in consideration of having been entertained during the first part.'

After a few weeks of silent suffering at the boarding house he found rooms in Northwood. There he was visited by his brother Brian and wrote an account of the meeting to Muggeridge:

My dear Mugg,

I take up my typewriter to prolong the experience of a day with B with someone so capable of enjoying it. I had not seen Bee since last August. We agreed to meet at Harrow station, in order to visit the scenes of our early years together. The roar he let out on seeing me was blurred, and sure enough he was at least half-seas over. This I could bear, but I became rather impatient of the extraordinarily involved reasons he gave for his state. He is always reasonable at bottom, and on my saying that I thought it unfair that I should have to grasp the intricate causes of his state as well as suffering from it, he at once desisted. As it was now nearly three I looked forward to his becoming progressively more companionable. He of course had foreseen the dead hours, and as we walked along produced a bottle of whiskey from his hip pocket, and implored me to have a nip. It was a critical moment, but I was firm and the rest of the afternoon passed without any further hipward movement. On reaching Orley Farm, which I love and have mentioned in *The Fall*, we paused. The name of the drive is Julian Hill, and Brian suddenly burst out 'I am glad it is called Julian Hill. I am GLAD. Julian the Apostate *deserves* not to have been forgotten.' We then retraced our steps to the Kings's Head, where we had tea, Brian's plea to the waitress for some beer on the grounds that he was an old Harrow resident falling flat. Brian confirmed my memory that our parents regarded the King's Head with horror. It is the chief pub in Harrow, and nowadays has a large comfortable lounge. I dimly remembered, I think at the age of seven, Father and Mother taking us in for a meal, presumably because we had just come out from London, and there was nothing at home, and even after more than forty years the gloom they diffused lingers – the feeling that in the interests of their already unpromising offspring they were ready to touch pitch, prepared as it were, to be blotted from the Book of Life so as to preserve their thankless brood from starvation. In those days to a Nonconformist teetotaller, a pub was almost as bad as a brothel – and without that redeeming interest which a brothel, could it have been legitimately entered, would no doubt have had at least for my father.

On coming out of the King's Head, we noticed that the sign was a head of Henry VIII, which we agreed would still further exaggerate my father's ill-humour, Brian holding that what would chiefly have moved my father's envy would have been the facility with which Henry murdered his wives, I stressing the six wives, all married with the Church's blessing. 'By Jove, yes' Bee agreed, 'Henry knew how to use his theology. *He* knew what to do with Bishops.'

Following the route Father took to the station each day, we felt a nostalgia for him, and would have been glad to see

him hurrying in front of us. There was a withered Wyke-
hamist fellow, Sir Frederick Kenyon, head of the British
Museum, who went the same route, and whose main
preoccupation was to go it alone, or at least without Father.
Brian recollected that Kenyon had an enormous stride with
which Father used to complain it was impossible to keep up,
though whether this stride distinguished Kenyon before my
father went to Harrow neither Brian nor I can say. We
thought of the millions of ideas which had buzzed in my
father's head on all these mornings, the bishops he would
invite to join committees, the politicians he would send to
Switzerland for nothing, the companies he would try to
float, the other companies he would allow to sink – and then,
on the side, as you would say, a little manipulation of the
office staff, and a pretty secretary to take over some new
enterprise, which would require all one person's time – 'and
I won't have Miss Jones raising any objections' – Miss Jones
being the old lady who was his chief secretary and had
constituted herself the guardian of his morals.

Alas, poor Yorick – I feel that my father is a much more
fruitful subject for a Yorick Speech than a deliberate jester.
. . . What was annoying in him has all passed with him,
which shows it was not deep-seated. With Beaverbrook, to
say nothing of Simon,* I do not believe death would notably
soften one's feeling, but Father really was affectionate and
lovable, and no doubt for that reason unsuccessful.

Muggeridge was now an intelligence officer at the Head-
quarters of V Corps at Longford Castle outside Salisbury. 'I
wish you could come up to London some weekend or on a
Sunday,' Kingsmill wrote on May 15. 'I could meet you any-
where and we could have a good six or seven hours talk. . . .
In my account of my afternoon with B, I forgot to tell you that
he informed me of an arrangement he has with one of his
pupils, a boy of seventeen or so, whose verse he has been pressing on Gollancz. Arnold [Lunn] and Iris [Pitcher] having in
succession failed to respond to B's suggestion that he should keep
them advised of how much he drank, in fortnightly or monthly

* Lord Simon, formerly Sir John Simon, Chancellor of the Exchequer in
the National Government.

statements, he has now arranged for a weekly interchange with
this boy, the boy informing Brian whether he has slept with any
of the other boys during the preceding week, and Brian detailing
his drinks. In answer to an enquiry from me, Bee said the
system was working well, but in view of his condition I assumed
that it was working well only from the documentary statistical
standpoint. . . .'

Four days previously the Deputy Fuhrer of the Third Reich,
Rudolf Hess, had parachuted into Scotland: 'The day before
yesterday I prophesied that Hess would soon be compared with
Francis of Assisi, and in yesterday's *Daily Mail*, Ward Price
compared him not only with Francis of A, but also with
Buddha, thus bearing out what we have often said about the
impossibility of keeping up with the press. Yesterday evening a
headline in the *Star* was RUDY – BY HIS NURSE.'

Muggeridge speculated whether Hess's descent would set a
precedent to be followed by other political leaders and
Kingsmill replied (May 27):

> In form, while the
> children are studying
> the career of Hannibal.

My dear Malcolm,
   I like your extension of the Hess idea. Could Laval
descend in Madame Mussolini's garden? Musso, I think,
might make for Arundel. He won't want to take any more
chances, but should feel pretty safe in a battle of wits with
the Duke of Norfolk. . . .

   Let us meet soon for a good long talk. One hears a good
thing at rare intervals these days. This, by one master of
another is first rate – 'He is like a long drink of barley water
on a cold evening'. There is a nice young master here, quiet
and melancholy, who, when I complained the other day
that the tea in the Common Room was always either hot and
weak or strong and cold, sighed, 'Isn't that rather like life?'
. . . This morning I had a chat with him about *The Times*,
and we agreed that on the morning after the Day of Judgment it would have a leader entitled 'A Situation Clarified',
and beginning 'It is now possible to take a comprehensive
view of. . . .'

   Have you read Proust? I was lent two volumes of him, and

go to bed early and read him. In a vague way it seems a reasonable thing for an ageing schoolmaster to do in bed.

On Sunday I went to see a friend, Rupert Thompson, son-in-law of de la Mare. Rupert was out, so I spent the afternoon with de la Mare. He is sixty-nine, and his wife is eighty-one, and a permanent invalid, who is always upstairs in his very large and delightfully comfortable house. A man and wife called for tea, and happened to mention a youth and girl who had just got engaged, whereupon de la Mare turned to me and said – 'And if that boy and girl came in now, you and I would be *tolerant* in their love. *Tolerant* of life's best thing!' I need not point out to you the various elements in it that combined to make me dissatisfied with this remark.

Muggeridge meanwhile, thanks to Graham Greene's help, had been recruited by the Secret Service. He left Longford, much to the relief of his fellow officers. His gloomy prophecies about the war and constant disparagement of Winston Churchill had not gone down well in the mess. In April 1942, trained in the ways of espionage, he sailed for neutral Lisbon on his way to become the MI 6 man in Laurenço Marques, Mozambique. Kicking his heels in Portugal, he wrote again to Kingsmill: 'You are not more tired of the empirical world than I am, I can assure you. Some days ago I climbed up a hill near Cintra (you will remember Wordsworth on the Convention of; Byron, also, dealt with the same subject but, I understand, characteristically described the wrong building as the scene of it being signed, and probably the wrong convention) to a little deserted hermitage where five monks lived for several centuries. There were their little cells and a stone slab they used for a table, and a chapel, and one of the most wonderful views I have ever seen; all so quiet, so remote. At first I thought: How fortunate they were! Then it occurred to me that probably one of the cells was rather less draughty than the others, one place at the stone slab to be preferred to another, and that as much passion would have been expended on these conquests as by, say, Hitler on his. It was a place which Lawrence would undoubtedly have used if he had happened to find his way there with Frieda and the deaf Hon. Bret, and I thought of the pleasant afternoon we might have spent together imagining what he would have made of it. Alas! yet (as Johnson said) why Alas, since life is such? I've been here quite a time but am now pushing on. . . . I very much enjoy the rival propaganda shows, ours and the G's. They're in adjacent shops. The Portuguese look at both, having plenty of time. One likes other countries' propaganda as one likes other men's wives. It's as a Sergt. in the Military Police put it to me once, "a bit of strange". How interesting that Hitler should have fixed on Mrs Roosevelt rather than on R as the target of his venom. She is, indeed, his most formidable adversary; and it shows great perspicacity in him that he should recognise this. . . . Now I'm struggling through *Don Quixote* in Portuguese. Not that it's any more enjoyable in that language; but of all books it seems to me at this time most sympathetic. If only you would suddenly appear, striding along, with five books from the Hastings Public Library under your arm. . . .'

A few weeks later Muggeridge sailed for Laurenço Marques. His assignment was to frustrate the German sabotage of allied ships round the South African coast. Here in the Mozambique capital, isolated from his family, cut off from the excitement and drama of the war, he once more became the prey of a despair which grew so intense that in the end it drove him to a suicide attempt. He swam out one night into the sea, intending to drown himself. At the last moment he turned back.

It was during the preceding period of unhappiness that there occurred an incident that shows the close telepathic relationship between Muggeridge and Kingsmill. Throughout October 1942 Kingsmill wrote repeatedly to Pearson asking for news of Muggeridge, which Pearson could be expected to hear as he was now living almost next door to Kitty. 'Have you any news of Mug?' he asked on October 5. 'I have a feeling – very definite – that he is not flourishing.' He asked again on October 26: 'Any news of Mug? I continue to wonder how he is.' Pearson was no doubt puzzled by the sudden spate of enquiries. Eventually, in a letter dated October 30, 1942 Kingsmill explained: 'What happened was that on September 20th when I was approaching my bedroom I heard a voice saying "Hughie" – apparently in some distress. I went into the bedroom and mentioned this to Dorothy, asking if it was her.

She said it wasn't, and added that she had also heard it. I said that the voice sounded like Mug, and she agreed. A curious experience, but if Kitty has heard since September 20th, it can't mean he is dead, though it might mean he was ill at the time. . . . I didn't like to mention this until it was practically certain she would have heard of his death.'*

---

* 'He mentioned a thing as not unfrequent, of which I had never heard before – being *called*, that is, hearing one's name pronounced by the voice of a known person at a great distance, far beyond the possibility of being reached by any sound uttered by human organs.' (Boswell: *Life of Johnson*.)

Chapter 11

Towards the end of April 1941 the Pearsons moved to Whatlington. Some neighbours of Muggeridge, called Hallinan (it was with their daughter that John Muggeridge had fallen in love), vacated their house, Woods Place, when the German bombing began. It was an old red-brick farmhouse, part early nineteenth century, part Tudor, reached by half a mile of cart track which turned off the main road opposite the Old Mill. The house itself was high up, looking out, Pearson said, over 'ridges of low wooded hills undulating towards the hidden sea'. All through his Hebridean journey he had been looking for 'the perfect harbour for a storm-tossed life'. Woods Place, even though it was in the danger zone, was the nearest he ever came to this ideal. He grew vegetables, shot game in the woods, kept chickens and went for long walks with Gladys. 'I should like to stay here for the rest of my life,' he wrote. 'There are all sorts of disadvantages (having to fetch our post, our milk, our drinking water, etc) but I love the place, the country round about, the isolation, the peace and quiet.'

Pearson took the war in his stride. His main worry was not Hitler but the Archbishop of Canterbury. On June 17, 1940 he noted: 'The Archbishop of Canterbury called the nation to pray yesterday for the French people. The prayer was answered at midnight, when the French army laid down its arms.' Talking to an old lady in the village of Whatlington he shocked and surprised her by referring to the Archbishop as 'Public Enemy No 1': 'I quickly ran over his malign exploits. His national Day of Prayer for Poland was followed by the collapse of Poland. His ditto for France resulted in ditto. And last Sunday's prayers for England have been speedily followed by the signing of a pact between Hitler and Jugoslavia. The man is a menace, and if he proposes another Day of Prayer I hope he'll be put in a padded cell. God obviously dislikes him very much. But my unanswerable case against him failed to placate the old girl.'

In June, having completed his *Shaw*, as well as a short life of Shakespeare, Pearson was amenable when Kingsmill proposed that they might resume work on their book. They arranged to meet in London to discuss it. Having spent the day at Harrow revisiting the scenes of Kingsmill's youth, they had dinner at the King's Head and afterwards sat out on the terrace smoking and drinking coffee:

PEARSON: I can't have been more than twenty-one when I last saw that view. Life stretched before me, and seemed as wonderful as the scene then was, fresh, unspoilt, varied and enticing. All the houses that have since sprung up in that landscape remind me of the obstacles and dis-illusionments of my pilgrimage.

KINGSMILL: Disillusionment is the result of discovering that other people are as egotistical as oneself.

PEARSON: True, if inharmonious at the moment.

Pearson suggested that a better theme for their book than Shakespeare would be England. Kingsmill agreed. 'We can start with the Cotswold journey, and then proceed with no settled plan. It would be un-English to deal with our subject systematically. As we are both English, it is reasonable to assume that England will emerge from the book. I do not say the whole of England, but much more than if we were both French. It will be a book from which the sensitive reader will be able to infer England. That gets it. *Infer* England.'

Publishers were by now thoroughly wary of Kingsmill. Following the failure of *Skye High*, Rupert Hart-Davis, then working for Jonathan Cape, wrote to him: 'The truth is there is some sort of voodoo on the whole of your relations with the publishing trade. No matter how good your books are, some publisher always seems to lose money on them.' Douglas Jerrold, at Eyre and Spottiswoode, remained loyal, and so did Alan White, of Methuen's, who published both *D. H. Lawrence* and his novel *The Fall*. But White, too, had his difficulties, as he told Muggeridge after Kingsmill's death: 'There were a number of agreements on the strength of which Hughie had advances, but for which he had produced no manuscripts. Annually, when our auditors checked our books, I was asked by my boss to account for these sums. Piqued by his tone, I said tartly that works of the imagination could not be written with mechanical regularity. He stared for a full minute at his papers, and then remarked, without the trace of a smile (though he was not without humour on subjects unconnected with business): "Works of the imagination is right".'

Alan White, over lunch at Pearson's club, agreed to sponsor the inferring of England and a title for the book was fixed – *This Blessed Plot*. 'It expresses our feeling,' said Kingsmill, 'it will ensnare readers of thrillers and it will give you, Hesketh, an opportunity to recur to your recent exploits with fork and spade.' 'Not that I have ever called any of the plots I've been digging "blessed",' said Pearson. 'Have you been digging for victory too?' asked White. 'No, for gluttony,' Pearson replied.

On July 28 Kingsmill, his term over, came down to Sussex to work on the book. Pearson met him at Battle Station and they took the bus out to Whatlington and then walked up the track to Woods Place. 'Over everything a sense of freshness from the not far distant sea,' Kingsmill noted. After dinner they discussed the affair of P. G. Wodehouse, whose broadcasts from Germany on an American network had excited a storm of anger among fellow writers. 'Most of these people,' said Pearson, 'seem to think that Wodehouse is under an obligation to the public, but, as the critics always used to reiterate, the public is under an unrepayable obligation to him – unrepayable till they got the chance of repaying it with bad eggs and dead cats.'

KINGSMILL: Did you see *Janus** in *The Spectator*? I have been carrying it about with me for some days, and it runs as follows: 'I have never till today been rather thankful that Lord Oxford – Mr Asquith – is dead. But I am glad he did not live to see a writer he so unreservedly admired as he did Mr P. G. Wodehouse broadcasting from a German station!' Asquith died in 1928. Since then there has been the biggest slump in history, beginning with twelve millions unemployed and starving in the States.

* Wilson Harris.

PEARSON: The inhabitants of China have been bombed in hundreds of thousands and drowned in millions.

KINGSMILL: The natives of Abyssinia have been exterminated by the Italians, which I need hardly say implies a disparity in armament unparalleled in war.

PEARSON: Spain has been decimated by fratricidal strife.

KINGSMILL: The Russian peasantry has been immolated to further the millennium.

PEARSON: And there has also been Hitler.

KINGSMILL: But Mr Asquith, according to *Janus*, would have felt no desire to turn his face to the wall until he unexpectedly heard the once loved voice of P. G. Wodehouse speaking from Berlin.

As usual, the conversations between Kingsmill and Pearson were concerned with literature, and many of them were recorded for their book. Pearson was, on the whole, content to play Watson to Kingsmill's Holmes, and Kingsmill usually had the last word. A discussion on St George led to Gibbon's famous description of him as a bacon contractor and to Kingsmill's view of Gibbon: 'I like the detachment with which in his autobiography he sums up the varying merits of his six volumes; his serene melancholy over the autumn of his life is moving; and I love the account of the evening when he completed his history, and took a turn or two up and down an avenue of acacias, Lake Leman below him in the calm moonlight. But he bought his irony too cheap, and is, with Jane Austen, the favourite reading of a certain kind of academic prig, who likes to find persons of undoubted genius as preoccupied with cash and comfort as himself.'

On Sunday, August 3 they spent a lazy afternoon, Pearson lying on one sofa reading *Great Expectations* and Kingsmill on another reading *The Newcomes*:

KINGSMILL: I used to love *The Newcomes*, and looking at it now brings back the emotions of those days. It is full of Thackeray's nostalgia for his youth, and when I read it at the age of thirteen his retrospective regret seemed to be mine too, and I shared his longing for a sunny time now gone for ever, vaguely thought of as a period when barouches bowled by, with demure young damsels and severe matrons inside, and young men roamed a leisurely Europe, making innocent love to flaxen-haired girls along the Rhine, and revelling in the gay open-air life of France, with its funny little soldiers marching along in their red breeches.

PEARSON: Dickens was the creator of London to me, and when I arrived there I spent a lot of time in searching round corners for his characters. But there is nothing of my own early years in Dickens, and in re-reading *David Copperfield* lately, although I think the first quarter of it the best bit of writing in English fiction, I never felt I was out of fairyland.

KINGSMILL: I still, at odd moments, when I'm walking in London, see corners of houses, or name-boards over shops, or a leaning lamp-post, as though they belonged to the London of Dickens and Phiz.

A momentary impression, but leaving behind a sense of regret utterly different from that left by Thackeray. The world of Thackeray is one which you have lost, Dickens' one which you have never found.

One afternoon Kitty Muggeridge took Pearson and Kingsmill to call on her parents, Mr and Mrs Dobbs, who now lived in a cottage in Whatlington. Kitty's family, like that of Kingsmill, contained its fair share of eccentrics, and her mother, the sister of Beatrice Webb, was one of them. After the death of her first husband she wandered through Europe as a wealthy widow in the company of her little son and his governess. Somewhere in the course of her travels she encountered Mr George Dobbs, who later became an employee of Sir Henry Lunn, and they were married, living afterwards in a state of what Kitty called 'not unreasonable strife'. Mrs Dobbs was a woman of strong views and liked whenever possible to give them an airing. Muggeridge described how she would desert her cooking at a crucial moment in order to join in a discussion: 'Over the explosive sound of a brew boiling over, in the lurid light of a roast catching fire one would hear her affirming her views. . . .' She was especially interested in the question of immortality and at her husband's burial, as the coffin was lowered into the ground she grasped the undertaker by the arm, he presumably being an expert on the matter, and asked him earnestly, 'Is there life after death?' In 1939 she and her husband settled at Whatlington, where she became a familiar figure. Dressed in long flowing clothes, she was often mistaken for a gypsy. She had a disconcerting habit of lying down and taking a nap whenever and wherever she felt like it and Muggeridge once spotted her stretched out on a tombstone in Battle churchyard.

Kingsmill was not at his best in the company of Mrs Dobbs and on one occasion, when she was expounding her belief that all life would ultimately be one, he became appalled by the thought of his merging in eternity with Mrs Dobbs and let out a strangled cry of, 'Yes – but not for a very long time!' He preferred her son Leonard, an equally eccentric figure, whom he described pointfully as 'more loveable than likeable'. After taking a first in science at Cambridge, Dobbs failed to find his vocation. He had been both a schoolmaster and a sculptor, without success, and his marriage to a French girl, Mlle Cantaloupe, was short-lived. At Whatlington, where he came to live early in 1936, he indulged his taste for improvising gadgets of all kinds – constructing a new type of loudspeaker, as well as a pressure cooker for his sister Kitty. Like his mother, he was a person with theories into which he would launch at every opportunity. 'Leonard's favourite position,' Kingsmill recalled, 'was on the hearthrug in Malcolm's study, a long room which, when the Old Mill was an inn, could have accommodated three score or so of diners, and which now seemed to stimulate a latent gift for oratory in Leonard. Once off, he was very hard to stop, and gazing past us into the shadows at the far end of the room, he would boom on with the air of one who held his audience in the hollow of his hand. There was no subject, or at least it never fell to my lot to discover a subject, which did not afford Leonard matter for a speech. On one occasion, I recall, I dropped a remark about Dungeness, something to the effect that its coastline looked very beautiful from Fairlight. Neither Malcolm nor I had much energy to spare that evening and drooped in silence while Leonard developed a theory of coast erosion, with special reference to Dungeness.'

The first time Hesketh Pearson saw Dobbs he was lying in bed, having cracked his head open while doing physical jerks in a room 'the ceiling of which made it unsuitable for high jumping'. Pearson noted that 'although bloody and supine, he was quite capable of developing an argument and spent some minutes in explaining why, other things being equal, his head should not have come into contact with a beam six feet from the ground.' Pearson subsequently discovered that Dobbs was a man of wide interests, including the poetry of Goethe, communism, surrealism, relativity, psycho-analysis, engineering, chemistry, loudspeakers and a number of other, to Pearson, uncongenial matters. It was hardly surprising that the two men failed to see eye to eye and the Pearson temper was frequently in evidence during their meetings. Later, however, Dobbs, prompted by Pearson, developed an interest in Shakespeare and during his last months wrote a book on the subject, which was published after his death thanks to the efforts of Kingsmill.

Kitty's aunt, Beatrice Webb, did not approve of Muggeridge's views and was equally dubious about his friends. 'What does Malcolm's friend Pearson *do*?' she once asked Kitty. When informed that he wrote books, she said firmly: 'I see. Not an Active Citizen!' While Pearson was working on his biography of Shaw, Muggeridge took him to see the Webbs, but the conversation, which should have been about Shaw, turned instead to Frank Harris. Sidney Webb had just suffered a stroke and found it difficult to articulate. All that Pearson and Muggeridge could make out was the curious expression 'bulldog round the neck'. This they decided afterwards was Webb's assessment of what it was like to have a rich wife, and applied as much to himself as to Harris.

Some time later Kingsmill and Pearson were greatly amused to hear of a conversation which had passed between Kitty and her uncle.

'How do you occupy your time, Uncle Sidney?'

'I read one novel a day.'

'What are you reading now?'

'I am reading the novels of Sir Walter Scott.'

'Do you like them?'

'No.'

Much of Kingsmill's stay with Pearson at Whatlington was spent walking, in and around the neighbouring villages – Burwash, Etchingham, Hawkhurst. Pearson had a great love of pubs and usually they would call in at one for refreshment, though the presence of the two voluble, loudly laughing men was not always welcomed by the clientele of the more respectable establishments. At the Bell Inn, Burwash, they stopped for lunch one day, and afterwards, as they sat in the lounge – 'discussing Mahomet and Hitler', an old lady in an armchair rose with a frown and having ferreted around in the interstices of the chair, to make sure that she had left no belonging of any value, went out of the room. In his 'local', the Royal Oak at Whatlington, Pearson was more at home and had many happy sessions there. 'Country people,' he told Kingsmill, 'have a lot of time on their hands for solitary brooding, with the result that, once they get going, they easily become the world's leading non-stop talkers; and they are liable to record episodes the comedy in which may not appeal to outsiders. For example, I heard the following account of a dialogue the other day, which stuck in my mind because of the gusto with which it was told and the hilarity with which it was received:

' " 'Ow's your turnips?" ses ee. " 'Ow's my turnips?" ses I. "Yes," ses ee, " 'ow's your turnips?" "Well," ses I, "come to that, 'ow's yourn?" " 'Ow's mine?" ses ee. "Yes," ses I, " 'ow's yourn?" "Oh," ses ee, "they beant too bad." "No more," ses I, "ain't mine." (Laughter) "No more ain't mine," ses I. (More laughter).'

On August 13 the two friends went to stay the night with their publisher Alan White at Hildenborough. After dinner the talk turned inevitably to the war and Kingsmill again expressed optimism. 'The Russians are nearing their eighth week, and no one expected them to last more than three.' 'With the single exception of Bernard Shaw,' Pearson added. 'I'm always glad,' said White, 'to meet anyone who is optimistic. Up in London no one seems very cheerful, though of course we are glad the bombing is over for the time being.' 'What sickens me about the English,' said Pearson, 'is that though the most conceited nation in the world, they always jump at the first opportunity to disparage their own amazing feats. Here we are, who two years ago would have had to be polite to Portugal, and in the last twelve months have with one hand shattered the mightiest armada ever launched against us and with the other cleaned up our blasted cities. We have beaten every transport record in history by removing the Italian armies in North Africa from behind their front lines to behind our rear ones; we have cleared the oceans for our goods and armies; we have blocked all the efforts of the French to pull us into the mire in which they are wallowing; and in short we have knocked hell out of allies and enemies alike – and yet now – when Russia, who has been dithering behind her steel ramparts all through this and performing feats of appeasement which would have made Neville Chamberlain blush – is at last attacked, the cry goes up from us: What are we doing for this gallant people? Are we to stand idly by while these architects of a new world are fighting hammer and sickle to make a Better Britain possible?'

'I like to hear you talk like that,' said Alan White. 'He likes it himself,' Kingsmill added.

And yet, White went on, there was no sign to date that Germany was on the downgrade. 'The Germans,' Kingsmill replied, 'are so romantic about war that they are bound to lose, unless they win very quickly. In the first heat of a war they can still believe that they are in the middle of a Wagner opera, but after a year or so it begins to dawn on them that blood and lice and bits of scrap iron raining on them, and synthetic bread and genuine dead horse, aren't the right stage properties for a satisfactory performance of *Siegfried*.'

Two days before Kingsmill was due to leave Woods Place the two friends took a bus into Hastings. Previously, on visiting the town and seeing his old house at Laton Road, Kingsmill had been overcome by melancholy. The sight of his untenanted home, he wrote, gave him 'a disconnected sensation as though the magnet that had held Hastings together had disappeared and the whole which he had loved been scattered into unrelated fragments.' By now he had overcome his nostalgia and rather liked the town's deserted air and the barbed wire along the front. They went first to St Helen's cemetery, which had always been one of Kingsmill's favourite spots and where he used to walk with Muggeridge before the war. The epitaphs, Kingsmill observed, were not inspiring. '*At Rest* predominates. Non-committal and inexpensive. I have sometimes tried to think out something with less than six letters. *Dead* is too obvious, and if the Latinist among the survivors suggested *Vale*, the others would say that it didn't make any sense without

Of Tears, and not much with it.' Pearson said the best epitaph he knew had been spoken by a farmer he overheard in a train at Leominster in October 1939: 'There was an old lady who died here three weeks ago, an' she was an hundred, an' she had eleven children, an' her name was Mrs Firkin.'

They walked to the north wall of the cemetery and admired the view over the Weald, then to the east end from which they could see Romney Marsh, Rye and Winchelsea, and the coast from Beachy Head to Dungeness. Then they went down through St Helen's Wood to Old Roar, a ravine through which a little stream flowed, and Pearson remembered it was at this spot, five years before, that they had conceived the idea of *Skye High*. 'How fantastic it seems,' he said. 'This isn't the way to make money.' 'Or to grow younger,' Kingsmill added. They walked on down to Alexandra Park, where they found the railings removed and onions instead of dahlias in the flower beds. 'How preposterous,' Pearson exclaimed, 'that the small place given to the common man should be made repulsive by onions.' Kingsmill opined that 'the Town Council, having been compelled to beautify the upper portion of the park by removing the railings, needed a litter of leeks to calm their jangled nerves.' After two double whiskies in a pub near the memorial they took the bus back to Whatlington.

In September Kingsmill returned to Woods Place to complete *This Blessed Plot*. The book had so far wandered from its subject, England, and both felt the need at least to round it off with an appropriate summary. Looking out over the Sussex landscape, Pearson began by observing that in his youth he had always run down England as being symbolic of all he hated – 'school discipline, parental authority, the established religion, and everything else against which I was in healthy revolt.' But now, in his fifties, he found himself convinced 'that ours is the only delectable country and its inhabitants the only decent people on earth.' How did one explain it?

Kingsmill replied: 'In youth one expects other countries to be better than one's own, just as one expects new acquaintances to be of quite a different and superior stamp to old ones. Later, one is drawn back to the people and the language through which one has felt life most deeply, unless of course one has come to hate life so much that one's own country focuses this hatred most strongly just because it is the country one knows best. That is why treachery in war time is so horrifying. Not because it is equivalent to a vote of no confidence in the government, or an expression of dissatisfaction with the prevailing social system, but because of the abyss of self-loathing it reveals. To work for the enemy, or even to hope for his victory, is to confess complete spiritual bankruptcy. Treachery may disguise itself as a reasonable wish for power, refused by one's countrymen and now bestowed by a more far-sighted government. But essentially it is a denial that life has anything to offer beyond the gratification of egotism, that neither the earthly affections nor the spiritual intuitions which are woven with one's own land have any value.'

Kingsmill having failed to answer his question, Pearson proceeded to do so himself: 'The explanation seems to be that, lacking any fanatical element in myself, I love a nation that does not go off the deep end on the slightest provocation. We are a balanced race. Our main virtue is that we never feel enthusiasm for abstract ideals. Humour is our greatest gift, our divinely rational merit. Kings may come and kings may go, but we scarcely trouble to notice whether a Plantaganet is followed by a Tudor, a Tudor by a Stuart, a Stuart by a Dutchman, a Dutchman by a Hanoverian, or even (as we have seen recently) a Hanoverian by a Hanoverian. We change our religions with equal indifference. Neither the agitation of a dispossessed Pope nor the fury of a falling monarch can create enough interest among us to bring a crowd into the streets. We are in fact a nation of individualists.'

'Potentially,' Kingsmill said, 'we are more individual than other peoples. Actually, we produce one Johnson for ten million more or less indistinguishable persons. Why is the Englishman so tongue-tied? Because he ought to be a poet, but has enough sense to know he isn't one.'

Chapter 12

In early 1942, while he was still teaching at Merchant Taylors, Kingsmill was offered the literary editorship of *Punch*. He at once accepted. The pay was good – £15 a week – and it meant that he could now be re-united with his family. Dorothy and the children came up to London from Somerset and they rented a flat in Holland Park. Kingsmill reported for work at the *Punch* offices in Bouverie Street on April 7.

'It is a palatial place,' he informed Pearson, 'tenanted by rather silent folk and visited at all hours by somnambulistic octogenarians. I miss the kids of fourteen to sixteen, but I suppose the charm of the place will seep in gradually.' Muggeridge wrote from abroad to congratulate him – 'Sir Henry should have lived to see the day!' – and Kingsmill replied on the back of a writ, to indicate that any rejoicing should be muted.

'No one,' Kingsmill said, 'can form an opinion on the transcendent brilliance of *Punch* who has not read the stuff that doesn't get in.' His own contributions were book reviews, though for a time during the war he was also the film critic, remarking to Pearson that having to sit through the films was worse than the Blitz. As always, he was immensely painstaking about his work and his reviews contained some of his best writing. 'Whenever I see an old copy of *Punch* lying about,' Muggeridge wrote, 'I always pick it up now and look for your initials. I understand so well your mind, how it works, that your reviews are like the muffled sound of your voice; like speaking to you on a long-distance telephone, though of course I can't reply: only listen.' His pieces were short (about five hundred words for the main book article, and one hundred to one hundred and fifty words for the short notices) and the books chosen more for what they would fetch second-hand from

Gaston than for their literary value. Kingsmill tended to be more interested in the works of amateurs, like the writers of memoirs, than those of professional men of letters, though even then he could never lose sight of the high peaks. A typical Kingsmill review began: 'Autobiographies vary, and the autobiography of Sir Stephen Tallents (*Man and Boy*. Faber 21s.) has little in common with the self-revelations of St Augustine, Bunyan and Rousseau.' Reviewing a biography of Frank Woolworth, founder of the chain store, by one John K. Winkler, he observed that the book was written 'by an unqualified admirer. This is just as well, for anyone who was not an unqualified admirer of Frank Woolworth might have suppressed much of which Mr Winkler records, and thus given the world an emasculated portrait of a very interesting figure in the modern business world.'

Both in *Punch* and in the *English Review* Kingsmill was least sympathetic towards dons and scholars, partly because, like many other writers, he was subconsciously envious of the greater leisure and comfort that they enjoy. Goldsworthy Lowes Dickinson was thus dismissed as 'a fellow of King's and a congenital bachelor', who could 'observe the perils of life at a comfortable distance, as one observes through a telescope on a hotel terrace a party climbing Mont Blanc'; 'Lord David Cecil,' he said, was 'essentially an academic type. One suspects him of a distaste for life until it has been removed to a considerable distance,' adding, 'to argue that one can find everything in Jane Austen is to suggest a desire to ignore what is arduous or painful in life.' The Shakespearean scholar G. Wilson Knight was dismissed as follows: 'There is really nothing to say about Mr Knight except what Wordsworth said about Ruth – "An innocent life, yet far astray!"' Successful men of letters, too, got short shrift. A review of Arthur Koestler's *The Yogi and the Commissar* concluded: 'On the whole, the impression left by this book is that the author would be happier about the future of the world if it contained more people with his combination of insight and experience;' while of the novelist Charles Morgan, Kingsmill wrote, 'It would be easier to express appreciation of Mr Charles Morgan's merits if there were any reason to infer from his writings that he was blind to them himself.' He remained alert to the air of insincerity which infects the bulk of criticism. Reviewing a book of essays by his *bête noire*, Desmond MacCarthy, he noted, 'Mr MacCarthy is indeed too indulgent to the men he portrays. Even when he writes of those long dead, Goethe, Renan, Rossetti, his pen seems stayed by an apprehension that he may meet them at dinner on the day his essay appears.'

Hardly ever did a note of malice or cruelty obtrude. Kingsmill's observations were always good-humoured and perhaps for this reason tended to give offence, as they could not be dismissed by the victims as the opinions of an envious or embittered man. The theatre critic James Agate, author of a series of autobiographical diaries under the title *Ego 1, 2*, etc., was outraged when Kingsmill, reviewing *Ego 5*, in *Punch* wrote: 'Everyone, it is said, has one good book inside him and, if this be so, it would be unkind to suggest that Mr James Agate is the exception that proves the rule. All one can in fairness say is that his good book is not among the thirty-six he has so far produced.'

It was shortly after Kingsmill's move to *Punch* that there occurred the only major quarrel that he and Pearson ever had. The occasion was the publication of a short book about Shakespeare that Pearson had written in 1940, while he was waiting for Shaw to finish correcting his manuscript. Pearson took offence when Kingsmill decided not to review the book in *Punch* himself, on the grounds that it was dedicated to him, and passed it on to another reviewer. In the past neither of them had felt any compunction about reviewing the other's books, usually in flattering and often extravagant terms. Kingsmill's decision on this occasion was therefore untypical, but was probably due to the fact that he had only been in his job for a few weeks and did not wish to lay himself open to criticism. Whatever the reason, Pearson flew into a rage and in a series of three letters accused Kingsmill of letting him down in his own interests and engaging in dirty tricks.

Dorothy Kingsmill then wrote to Pearson: 'Hugh has barely settled in his *Punch* job and yet you have already succeeded in thoroughly upsetting him. He came home last night white and shaken with his weekly article, already overdue, still unfinished. How can you behave like this to a man who, whatever his faults, has given you twenty years of devoted friendship. . . . I have known for some years now that with increasing confidence in your literary ability would come increasing criticism of Hugh and irritation with him, and knowing too all the love and confidence he had for you and in you, I have watched this development with increasing distress.'

Pearson counterattacked: 'Dorothy, you have thrown a boomerang which, if I did not knock it down, would return and flatten you. Be grateful for my Christ-like forbearance. Your letter displays a mind so distorted by rage, hatred, and spite, that I cannot even believe your statement that Hughie is upset. Your hysterical animosity, which must be due to my having quite unwittingly wounded your vanity, carries you beyond all bounds, and you hold Hughie up to ridicule in a manner that his worst enemy would envy. . . . Now be a good girl; attend to your clothes and your cooking: and in future do not meddle with things you cannot understand. I have already forgiven you, and shall have forgotten the nonsense you wrote before you read this.'

But the row was not over yet. Pearson was clearly under the impression that he was fighting Dorothy alone. Kingsmill now made it plain that this was not the case. 'I saw a copy of Dorothy's letter,' he told Pearson, 'on the evening of the day she wrote to you. It is of course true I was upset. You had accused me of letting you down in my own interests, and you had repeated this in a second letter. And in a third you were talking of dirty tricks. You cannot insult a friend of twenty years who has never in any way let you down, and then having relieved your own feelings, expect him to behave as if he had none himself. Dorothy was naturally angry at seeing how much you had upset me . . . I don't want to break our friendship, but as this trouble was started by you it is for you to end it, not to bluster and bluff and pretend nothing has happened, but by admitting for once that you have gone too far. If anything solid remains in your affection for me, you will do this, but if I have become indistinguishable from the publishers and other people you fly out at whenever you want to relieve your feelings, you won't.'

Pearson was not going to give in. 'I have wounded Dorothy's feelings,' he replied, 'how or why I of course cannot say, as I have never given her a thought except when you have borrowed money from me for the necessity of your establishment, when I have occasionally wondered whether she was being as economical with my money as Gladys was forced to be without it. . . . You must not complain if I add that, quite apart from the sums of money you have borrowed from me when I could ill afford them, but which your rich friends could not spare you, I have never asked you to pay your whack at any bar or restaurant whenever we have met in the last fourteen years or so. I have never worried you to pay back a penny you owe me: in fact, when you offered to repay one loan, I told you to keep it until you could return it without hardship to yourself . . . I have merely to add that I bear you no malice; that if ever I have an opportunity of doing you a good turn I shall do it with the utmost pleasure; but that if you imagine I am going to apologise for expressing irritation over your shabby treatment of my Shakespeare book, you have learnt very little about me in twenty years of companionship. But for your shocking approval of Dorothy's crazy letter, I would never have written in this strain, or indeed pursued the subject at all. You have your wife and yourself to thank for it; and you ought to be ashamed of yourself for treating with such ingratitude and dishonesty a friend who has never done you anything but good, never written of you but with admiration, and never spoken of you but with affection.'

'It is not true,' Kingsmill replied, 'that you have been the host at our meetings for fourteen years. When we were both hard up, our meals were simple, there were no drinks, and each paid for himself. When, relatively to myself, you became rather better off, your meals became less simple, and you started to pay for me. I ought never to have drifted into this, but of course I had no premonition of the day when you would use your hospitality against me. . . . I did not expect you to apologise for your abusive letters. I only hoped you might. You ought to have learnt by now that the truth always comes out in the end, and if you had expressed your regret the story of our friendship would have had a very different conclusion.'

The row ended as suddenly as it had begun. Pearson, in his own words, 'proffered the olive branch', which was immediately accepted. Dorothy wrote to Pearson regretting what had occurred and Pearson replied: 'I agree with you that mothers should defend their children by every means, you will also agree with me that an artist is justified in losing his temper when a pal to whom he has entrusted his newly-born literary babe allows an unsympathetic stranger to knock it about. All this however belongs to a dim past which will soon be blotted out completely.'

A row is never about what it's about, Muggeridge says. There was nothing unusual in Pearson flying off the handle, but he had never done it before with Kingsmill and it was unlike Kingsmill to respond with such vehemence. Perhaps beneath his anger there were traces of envy. 'Worst sellers,' he had written in *The Sentimental Journey*, 'are easily jarred by best-sellers,' and though Pearson's biography of Shaw had yet to appear, all the signs were that the book would be a best seller. At the same time, Kingsmill must have resigned himself by this stage to the fact that he would never achieve the recognition he knew he deserved, although his friends might do so, to some degree at his expense. Authors are seldom keen to acknowledge their debt to other authors, and a reader of Pearson's books would not have gathered from the one or two acknowledge-ments to Kingsmill the extent to which his philosophy as a whole had been shaped by his friend. He himself was not really aware of it, or if he was, did his best to evade the issue. When Dorothy Kingsmill told Pearson, 'I have known for some years that with your increasing confidence in your ability would come increasing criticism of Hugh and irritation with him,' she touched an exposed nerve and in the ensuing argument Pearson never attempted to reply to the point. But, whatever the causes of the row, it was soon forgotten and the tensions which surfaced temporarily were quickly submerged by the greater power of friendship.

Pearson's life of Shaw was eventually published in 1942. It was an immediate success and sold 30,000 copies in the original English edition and 100,000 in a cheap reprint. In its final form the book had been considerably revised and rewritten by Shaw himself. This dual authorship caused Pearson some misgivings and he suggested at one point to Shaw that his passages in the text should be distinguished by the use of square brackets or indentations. 'Not on your life, Hesketh,' Shaw replied. 'What

I have written I have written in your character, not my own. . . .
If you are not prepared to father my stuff, you can rewrite it;
but you must not publish it as mine. . . . Don't run away with
the idea that your readers – least of all the critics – will spot
any difference between your stuff and mine. They won't.'

In fact it is quite easy to detect Shaw's hand at work,
particularly in the chapters dealing with his political life.
Pearson had little interest in Shaw's politics, regarding them in
rather the same way as Wilde's sexual habits, signs of a regrettable but unimportant aberration on the part of his hero. He
had no urge to grapple with this aspect of Shaw. 'As one who
has not read Karl Marx,' he admitted, 'who has no intention
of reading Karl Marx, and who would rather die than read
Karl Marx, it is a little difficult for me to trace the precise
nature of his influence on Shaw.' The result was that Shaw was
able to impose his own view of himself and others on the
political sections of the book. Elsewhere, it is not difficult to
spot Shaw's interpolations, as in the musical description of
Frank Harris – '. . . an artistically metrical voice that would
have made his reputation as the statue in *Don Giovanni* . . . he
tromboned his way through the world . . .' phrases that are
typical Shaw. One can see the nature of Shaw's little additions
by comparing Pearson's account of Shaw rehearsing the
original production of *Androcles and the Lion*, given in his first
book of memoirs, *Thinking It Over*, and the same story as it
appears in *Bernard Shaw*:

> . . . he danced about the stage, spouting bits from all the
> parts with folded arms, turned our serious remarks into
> amusing quips . . .
>
> *Thinking It Over*

> . . . he danced about the stage, spouting bits from all the
> parts with folded arms, turned our serious remarks into
> amusing quips and our funniments into tragedies.
>
> *Bernard Shaw*

That 'and our funniments into tragedies' is an obvious Shavian
embellishment, and, it might be added, one that does nothing
to improve the original text.

Kingsmill could not approve of the way in which Shaw, as it
seemed to him, had foisted his own views on Pearson:

I enjoyed the early part of the book enormously, it gave me for the first time a picture of Shaw as he really is, with all the reasons why he developed as he did. But I did not care at all for the self-dramatisation which Shaw has pushed in. In fact, it thoroughly depressed me. The value of the book is what you have dug out of him, and that will in time cancel his own picture of himself. As an example of what struck me as completely out of key with your presentation of him, there is a long paragraph at the beginning of a chapter in which he talks of himself as being in the forefront of the revolution in morals heralded by Nietzsche, Wilde, etc. and ending in the dictators. As you point out, his totalitarianism directly contradicts some of his own sayings. Yet he still clings to it in his pig-headed way. Obviously from your account of his early years, he was driven to this attitude by his desire to make up for his early misery, and to forget the individual in the mass, with himself as one of the greater robots running the lesser robots. It is essentially the same evolution as a dictator's, but Shaw has inherited his father's kindliness, and a real strain of humour and fancy – hence his plays, and hence his absence of any cruelty. I wish he hadn't this insane desire to impose himself as a Superman. It spoils for me the total effect of his character. If it had been a phase and he had emerged into reality, all would have been well. However, he is an amazing chap, and you have got him on the stage as he really is, even if he has done his best to tog himself up in fancy dress.

Pearson's next book was a life of Conan Doyle. Though he by no means conformed to the pattern of the typical Pearson subject, Doyle had always been a favourite author of Pearson and Kingsmill. Pearson's overall view of him owed much to Kingsmill, and his book, which might have been simply a readable account of Doyle's life, gained in depth by being based on Kingsmill's conception of him as the ordinary man 'who acted as a medium for all the subconscious fears and desires of his age'. 'The ordinary man,' he wrote in a review of Pearson's book, 'is not so exclusively homely and endearing in his desires as his panegyrists make out. Folk lore, which is a mirror of the common man throughout the ages, reflects his fears, his morbidity and his flashes of cruelty, as well as his kindliness, his fortitude, his love of wife and children. The stories of Conan Doyle were the folk lore of the late nineteenth century and Conan Doyle the medium through which an over-civilised age poured its nostalgia for adventure, mystery and horror.'

Left to himself, Pearson could well have misinterpreted the investigations into spiritualism which preoccupied Doyle during the last years of his life. Doyle himself was convinced that in his maturity he had put aside worldly things to study the affairs of the spirit. A biographer might easily accept this view, for it is a common misconception that an interest in the supernatural – ghosts, seances and the occult – is the sign of a spiritual or religious temperament. Kingsmill was able to steer Pearson away from any such errors. Doyle's dabblings in the spirit world marked no new departure for 'the ordinary man' and were quite in keeping with his character. 'Spiritualism,' Kingsmill had written in his essay on W. T. Stead, 'is the mysticism of the materialist' and Doyle's interest in the super-natural was a sign of his ordinariness, as was his liking for the horrific. Developing Kingsmill's theme Pearson wrote: 'All unimaginative folk love the fanciful, the horrible, and the uncanny which for them add a relish for life, just as people without sensitive palates love curry. The imaginative ones do not require such stimulants, finding the common round enough to stir their creative or engage their contemplative faculties.'

Doyle was a relatively short book, quickly researched and completed. Pearson next embarked on a project that he had toyed with for many years, a life of Oscar Wilde. He had been a Wilde enthusiast ever since he was eighteen when he read *The Soul Of Man Under Socialism*, attributing to the book's influence his emancipation from his conservative upbringing. At once he tried to obtain other works by Wilde, but this proved difficult at a time when going into a bookshop and asking for anything by Wilde produced an H. M. Bateman scene: 'The shopmen used to blush, glance round fearfully and make signs of anxious protestation; while the customers used to disappear hurriedly behind the bookshelves.'

Later, when the boycott of Wilde began to collapse and the complete works, collected by his friend Robert Ross, were published, Wilde became the object of a cult, particularly among the young, and his biographers did their best to replace him on the pedestal he had occupied before his downfall. But the men responsible, Robert Sherard, Frank Harris and Lord Alfred Douglas, had all been friends of Wilde and each was determined to put himself forward in the best possible light and do whatever he could to discredit his rivals. At the same time, their interest and that of their readers centred inevitably on the melodramatic last five years of Wilde's life. The result was a series of bitter wrangles about who was to blame for Wilde's downfall and who had done most to help him in his hour of need.

From his first acquaintance with Wilde's books Pearson decided that one day he would write something about him. He began to collect material from everyone who had known him – theatrical men like Beerbohm Tree and George Alexander, Robert Sherard, and of course Harris. In 1916, when he was in the army he managed to get an evening's leave to have dinner with Wilde's closest friend Robert Ross from whom, in the course of a conversation that lasted all night, he obtained a great deal of information, including one of the best Harris stories: 'In the spring of 1896 Ross received a wire from Frank Harris, then editing the *Saturday Review*: "Will you lunch with me at the Cafe Royal at 1 o'clock today – only a few friends, to meet the Duc de Richelieu." On arriving, Ross found that Harris had forgotten to engage a room, so about fifty guests, including many notable writers, had to wait while a large table was placed in the centre of the principal dining-room, to the inconvenience of the other visitors, who were crowded at small tables against the walls. The lunch began, and their host was soon chatting away amicably with the Duke on his right hand. Suddenly the deep booming voice of Harris, which could be heard above the roar of the loudest traffic, silenced the din of conversation: "Homosexuality! No, my dear Duke, I know nothing of the joys of homosexuality. You must ask my friend Oscar about that!" Wilde was then in prison, his name never breathed in public, and the combination of his Christian name with the unmentionable crime that had caused his downfall stunned the roomful of people. Not even the clatter of a fork broke the deathly silence, while every luncher held his breath and wondered what would happen next. "And yet," continued

Harris reflectively, in a lower but still resonant voice, "If Shakespeare had asked me, I would have had to submit!" '

Pearson continued to collect material and in 1926 he first mentioned to Kingsmill the idea of writing Wilde's life: 'Don't you think there is room for a good biography of Wilde?' he asked. 'Wilde has always interested me enormously. He really did stand for a readjustment of moral values. At its best his life was a revolt against the cheap, ready-made standard of current Christianity. . . . Yes, I think I shall. Shall I? advise me. . . . I know you don't like ow as much as I do; but lay aside your dirty masculine prejudices for a moment and give me a piece of sensible advice.'

Kingsmill agreed that a biography of Wilde was a good idea, but Pearson must first jettison any thoughts on the subject which were derived from Harris. Harris's book on Wilde was not 'the master portrait, the poignant soul study' which he, Pearson, had dubbed it. Harris, defending Wilde on the charge of obscenity, had praised the delicacy of his speech, but, Kingsmill insisted, 'the hallmark of the homosexualist is his delicacy of speech. . . . FH has no eye for the distinguishing qualities of the homosexualist – he keeps on saying that Wilde's talk was pure, vowed to all beauty, etc., as if that had any bearing on the question of Wilde's morals. He doesn't see that the homosexualist, with his exaggerated femininity, shrinks from Rabelaisianism, not for moral but for aesthetic reasons. Also, to be delicate and fine in speech is an unconscious protest against the conventional view of the homosexualist as a depraved sensualist. Secondly, FH doesn't realise that Wilde's theatricality is the very essence of the man. FH was attracted to Wilde because FH, as a full-blown snob, admired the skill, so superior to his own, with which Wilde captured the upper classes. The secret of Wilde's success was that he flattered the upper classes by identifying social and intellectual aristocracy. His dupes had just enough intelligence to be tickled in their vanity by this amazing feat, and naturally were far too unintelligent to see its absurdity.'

In 1930 Pearson got his first opportunity to write on Wilde when he was invited to edit and introduce a collection for the Everyman Library. He informed Kingsmill, who was at the time in the Birmingham Nursing Home having his boil lanced, and asked what he thought of Wilde's poetry. '. . . I think Wilde's poetry completely contemptible,' Kingsmill replied. 'I think it is worse than Drinkwater. It is an entirely insincere imitation of Keats' imitators, with a pinch of pseudo-Baudelaire sifted in by way of variety. There is one poem, something about the dawn with silver sandals, which you might conceivably put in your Wilde anthology, with profuse apologies. Of course I except the *Ballad* – not that I like it as a whole but it has some good lines.

'Sorry I am not more helpful, and discount my vitriol if you like, on the ground that at this particular moment I'm not exactly in the humour to see virtue in a bum fan.' Pearson's anthology did not, in the event, contain any of Wilde's poetry apart from the *Ballad of Reading Gaol*.

A week later, on May 29, 1930, Kingsmill returned to the subject of Wilde's snobbery: 'I don't know if you would agree, but I'm convinced that Wilde's early death was due to his social ostracism. I have just read *Lady Windermere's Fan* again, and have been more struck than ever by his absolute mania for society. I am convinced his passion for society far outweighed his passion for boys, to say nothing of his interest in his writing gifts.

'I attribute this social mania chiefly to his morbid feminine strain, with which he was born and which his mother intensified by her bloody imbecile treatment of him as a child – the posing bitch! However, I suppose she was born daft, too. So pardon is the word to all.

'In addition to this feminine craze for society, Wilde was an Irish protestant. The Irish protestant, belonging to the conquering race (I speak of the pre-1923 era), is, whatever his social position, under the curious delusion that he is an aristocrat. Not being entirely secure in this delusion, he has to feed it. Hence the incredible Irish snobbery – the most clotted and offensive in the world.

'Wilde, thus doubly doomed, was utterly incapable of supporting life away from London. Of course, he was absolutely first rate for the dining-out job. The whole of his nature and all of his faculties were shaped from youth on to the end of social success. Unfortunately, the strain of Irish caddishness ruined him. The hatred he incited was chiefly due to his ridiculous snobbishness in regard to journalists, etc. He not only did nothing to abate the edge of envy, but did everything he could to sharpen it.

'The return to his wife would not have helped him. She does not seem to have been of any use to him socially, except for her £800 a year, which meant nothing after his theatrical successes. The only thing that could have saved him would have been to be received back by society. This seemed hopeless to him, so he took to the next best things, boys and drink.

'Personally, I think that if he had settled down to work he would have won back a good deal of his old position in ten years, and of course the war would have put him absolutely straight again. He would have been sixty then, and would have lectured, subscribed enormously to hospitals, coined endless anti-German epigrams, and by 1924 would have been the most popular of our dramatists, and, with ten edifying prose works, written between 1900 and 1914, the best read of our *belle lettristes*.

'However, he hadn't the guts for a long struggle in untitled society, and so broke up very soon. If there is anything outside oneself which is more important to one than what one carries inside oneself, one should live much more cannily than Wilde did; otherwise one would find oneself separated from it in due course.'

Despite his general lack of sympathy for Wilde, Kingsmill was prepared to take up the cudgels on his behalf if by doing so he could have a crack at Bernard Shaw. Shaw had given his seal of approval to Harris's *Oscar Wilde: His Life and Confessions*, when it was brought to him by Pearson in 1916. 'Wilde's memory will have to stand or fall by it,' he wrote. Immediately Harris's rivals were up in arms, in particular Wilde's first biographer, Robert Harborough Sherard, who put on his armour and prepared to do battle with Shaw and Harris.

It is self-evident that much of Harris's book is imaginary, in particular the long conversations between himself and Wilde. Nevertheless, Sherard spent a great deal of time and energy going through them line by line to prove that they could not have occurred at the time or in the manner described. One charge, in particular, stuck in Sherard's gullet. Shaw had described Wilde, during his last years in Paris, as an 'unproductive drunkard and swindler', while Harris suggested that he had reverted to type in such a way as to attract the attentions of the gendarmerie. In order to set the record straight Sherard visited the police authorities in Paris and with the help of the Prefect established that there was no evidence in the files of any official interest in Wilde. All this ammunition he assembled in book form and it was eventually published under the title *Bernard Shaw, Frank Harris and Oscar Wilde* (1937). When the book was still in manuscript Sherard sent it to Kingsmill, whose *Frank Harris* he had read with appreciation. 'I suggested that when I had finished the manuscript,' said Kingsmill, 'that I should pass it on to Shaw, who could not fail to be convinced by it of his mistake in recommending Harris's book as the work by which Wilde's memory must stand or fall. I did not think Shaw would much mind withdrawing his endorsement of Harris's *Wilde*.' (In fact, Kingsmill knew perfectly well that Shaw hated to admit that he had made a mistake about anything. He also knew, as his previous letter to Pearson confirms – 'he took to boys and drink' – that the charge of 'unproductive drunkard and swindler' was not wholly without foundation. He was prepared, however, to overlook this for the sake of a good scrap with Shaw.)

Shaw invited Kingsmill to come and talk the matter over, but it was clear from the start of the interview he was not going to budge an inch, or as Kingsmill put it, 'the effect of a knock-down blow is entirely neutralised if its recipient chooses to overlook the fact that it has been delivered'. Shaw put paid to any hope of a serious discussion on the subject by remarking at the outset: 'You know, Harris's *Wilde* is far more interesting than the real Wilde.'

'But Mr Shaw,' said Kingsmill, 'the point isn't whether Harris's *Wilde* is more interesting than Wilde was. The point is whether his biography deserves to be endorsed by you as the authoritative life by which Wilde must stand or fall. You call Wilde, on the strength of Harris's picture of his last days, "an unproductive drunkard and swindler". If you would look through Sherard's manuscript, I am sure you would not send down this phrase uncorrected to posterity.' Kingsmill outlined the evidence which Sherard had collected, with special reference to that of the Prefect of police, M. Chiappe.

'Mr Shaw looked thoughtful over M. Chiappe,' Kingsmill

wrote; 'I felt that I was getting him in a corner, but a moment later he was back in the middle of the ring, listening with courteous attention to my attack on the disgusting and ridiculous scene in which Harris saddles Wilde with his own dislike of women during pregnancy.

'Ah, yes, yes. Ah, to be sure. Yes. Yes.'

No wonder, Kingsmill thought, the Irish problem is insoluble.

'It's not a question of whitewashing Wilde,' he persisted, 'or even of taking Sherard's view of him. It's simply a question of making it clear that no confidence at all is to be placed in Harris's *Wilde*, which on the strength of your endorsement is everywhere accepted as the true account of Wilde.'

'Oscar could be really charming at times . . .'

At the end of an hour Kingsmill gave it up. When Pearson raised the question subsequently with Shaw he remained adamant, declaring that 'if a biography showed what manner of man its subject was it did not matter a straw if every line in it was inaccurate.'

Including this observation in his life of Shaw, Pearson added a telling footnote: 'I have not noticed that his attitude is quite the same to a biography of himself.'

Pearson's book on Wilde is his most original and successful biography. Shedding, with Kingsmill's help, his earlier view of Wilde as a revolutionary moralist – a view derived from Bernard Shaw – and putting in their proper perspective the trial, imprisonment and collapse, which all his predecessors had concentrated on, Pearson set out to establish Wilde not as a martyr, nor even a great writer, but as an inspired and brilliant wit in the tradition of Sydney Smith.

'There is nothing,' he wrote, 'in Wilde's conversation to show that he had ever read or admired the letters and sayings of Sydney Smith: yet the parson is his closest affinity as man and wit in the world of letters. They were both good natured, self-indulgent, fond of the table and society: their humour was by turns affected, rich and nonsensical; they were eccentric in outlook, behaviour and appearance; they were as high-spirited as they were kind-hearted; and one may add that each of them became decidedly fat.'

With the exception, however, of *The Importance of Being*

Earnest, Wilde's writings did not convey his inspired humour. Pearson therefore performed the same service for him that he performed for Smith, which was to accumulate from all their various sources, from the reminiscences of the living and the dead, his jokes, stories and aphorisms, and so build up a portrait of Wilde, not as the decadent or the aesthete, but the great humorist who 'raises common sense to poetry, lifts the burden of life, releases the spirit, imparts happiness, creates brotherhood, and cleanses the mind of cant, pretentiousness and conceit'.

Taken simply as an account of Wilde's life, the book is not so satisfactory. Because of his great sympathy with his subject Pearson could not give a full or dispassionate account of Wilde's collapse, and his description of the trials is so perfunctory that it is by no means clear exactly what the offences were of which Wilde was found guilty. (Kingsmill had foreseen this, and in a letter sent to Pearson while he was working on the book, gave a ludicrous parody of how Pearson might deal with the last period: 'In 1897, after serving a sentence for bigamy, or some such trivial offence, Oscar Wilde made for France, a despicable country except for its wine, which Oscar had always enjoyed. He was accompanied by two or three women, an old soldier, who acted as his valet, and the old soldier's wife, who acted as lady's maid and *accoucheuse* to the women.')

To be fair to Pearson, it must be said that in telling the story of Wilde's last years he was, like his predecessors, hampered by the continued presence on earth of Lord Alfred Douglas. Douglas inherited a good deal of his father's lunacy and this manifested itself, in one form, in a love of litigation. (It was partly Alfred Douglas's longing for a court action against his father, in which he hoped to appear as the star witness, that had set in motion the downfall of Wilde.) After Wilde's death Douglas took to suing almost anyone who wrote anything about Wilde. When the young critic Arthur Ransome, later to become famous as a writer of children's books, published a short work on Wilde in 1913, Douglas immediately issued a writ. Ransome produced as evidence to support his case the hitherto unpublished part of *De Profundis*, in which Wilde launched a ferocious assault on Douglas. The book took the form of a long letter written to Douglas from Reading Gaol, which Wilde originally sent to Robert Ross with instructions to forward it to Douglas. Ross never did so, but when Douglas sued Ransome, he allowed the unpublished parts to be read out in court. Written when Wilde, for the only time in his life, glimpsed the true nature of Alfred Douglas and the destructive effect of his relationship with him, the letter, though containing some hysterical and self-pitying passages, comprised a damning indictment of his lover. This body blow, posthumously delivered, sent Douglas into further rages, and having lost his legal battle with Ransome, he now turned on his old rival Robert Ross.

The nature of the antagonism between Ross and Douglas was described, some time after Douglas's death, by Pearson: 'Ross had been intimate with Wilde for five years before Douglas appeared on the scene and elbowed Ross into the wings. Throughout the period of Wilde's splendour Douglas was undoubtedly the favourite. But during his two years in prison Wilde managed to convince himself that Douglas had been solely responsible for his downfall, and Ross resumed his sway. Freed from gaol, Wilde retained Ross as his chief friend and adviser for three or four months; but the attraction of Douglas proved too much for him, and again Ross found himself deserted. Poverty proving too much for Douglas, he left Wilde, and was once more cast as the villain of the piece, while Ross was reinstated in the part of hero. It was as if, in a more normal establishment, the wife had been discarded for a younger and more attractive mistress: the man had then ruined himself by his infatuation, was restored to favour by the wife, could not resist the renewed blandishments of the mistress, and was again pardoned by the wife. This is only a rough and ready comparison, as there appear to be complications in the homosexual system which an outsider cannot unravel.'

After the Ransome libel action Douglas began to harry Ross, subjecting him to a barrage of public insults and libels of such ferocity that in the end Ross was obliged to sue. Finding himself on weak ground, however, he withdrew, and died a few years later of a heart attack.

Douglas continued to sue and be sued. (He was sent to prison for six months in 1923 for publishing a criminal libel of Winston Churchill.) Anyone who embarked on a life of Wilde with the intention of describing the true nature of his relationship with Douglas was asking for trouble. Frank Harris's book could only be published in America and A. J. A. Symons, who started a life of Wilde, was deterred, in part, by the threat of legal proceedings from Douglas.

Pearson was well aware of the nature of the beast. His very first book *Modern Men and Mummers*, which contained a sympathetic portrait of Ross, had elicited a violent and menacing letter from Douglas. The result was that in his quest for material about Wilde, Pearson did not think it would serve any purpose to approach the eccentric nobleman. Kingsmill, however, felt no such qualms and, deciding to beard the lion in his den, called on Douglas at his flat in Hove. He found him unattractive, reporting to Pearson: 'The first thing that struck me about Douglas was his looks. He is decidedly plain. I cannot imagine that even in his prime his nose can have meant much to connoisseurs. . . . He lives with a sister, Lady Something or Other, a dear old lady, stout and with a rather non-committal smile. She gave me the impression of having long since found a formula by which she was enabled to account to her own satisfaction for the strange and admittedly rather unexpected things that would keep on happening to her nearest and dearest. . . . The thing that appealed most to my imagination during the afternoon was our walk along the front. A bitter east wind; Douglas wizened and bowed; his nose jutting out from beneath his soft hair. If anyone had been told by God (he would not have accepted it from lesser authority) that one of these two men had been the handsomest man in England in his youth, he must have picked me out.'

Some time in the late Thirties Kingsmill took Pearson and Muggeridge to tea with Douglas, but the visit, the purpose of which doubtless had puzzled Alfred, was not a success. Douglas had prepared a schoolboy spread of buttered toast, scones, cream cakes and tarts. Kingsmill, Pearson and Muggeridge were put at one end of a long table while Douglas sat, like a housemaster, at the other. 'We could only guess,' Pearson reflected, 'that the usual gatherings at Douglas's flat were juvenile.' Kingsmill and Pearson listened politely to their host's egotistical reminiscences, while Muggeridge felt overcome with nausea, enhanced by the disparity between the 'horrible little, bulbous nosed man' seated before them and the handsome youth displayed in huge portraits all round the walls: 'He only wanted to talk about himself,' Muggeridge recalled. 'I tried to draw him out on the subject of Wilde's visit to North Africa with Gide, but it was no use. The subject was always dragged back to Douglas, to his nobility of character, to his constancy in defending and standing up for his friend, to the base manner in which he had been misunderstood.'

When they left the flat and waved farewell to Douglas, both Kingsmill and Pearson experienced the feeling that they had, as far as Douglas was concerned, ceased to exist. 'So strong was the impression,' Pearson said, 'that each of us took several seconds to recover the consciousness of his own identity.'

Pearson was reminded of the dangers and difficulties of writing about Douglas while working, a few years later, on his life of Conan Doyle. Amongst Doyle's papers he found a letter from Douglas, written when Doyle was going through his last spiritualistic phase:

Sir,

What a disgusting beast you are with your filthy caricature of 'Christ'.

The proper way to deal with such a man as you would be to give you a thrashing with a horse whip. You are running the spiritualistic business simply to get money and notoriety and in short for the same purposes and with the same flat-footed low persistence as you worked your idiot 'Sherlock Holmes' business which you imprudently stole from Gaboriau. You are an apostate Catholic and there is nothing worse than that. I give you warning that your blasphemous ravings if continued will soon draw on you a dreadful judgment.

Yours with the utmost contempt,
Alfred Douglas.

To which Conan Doyle replied:

Sir,

I was relieved to get your letter. It is only your approval which could in any way annoy me.

Yours faithfully,
A. C. Doyle.

(In the published life Pearson was unable to refer to Douglas by name, describing the letter as coming from 'one Roman Catholic convert' and then quoting only snippets of it.)

When he at last began working on his life of Wilde, Pearson wrote to Douglas informing him of the fact, and a meeting was arranged. Douglas was by now an old man of seventy-four and had recently come out of a nursing home, where he had been treated for heart trouble. The interview got off to a bad start. Pearson had a particular blind spot about literary homosexuals who were in the habit of adducing Shakespeare as one of their number, on the evidence supposedly contained in the Sonnets. The slightest suggestion that Shakespeare, whom he most loved, was a homosexual, a type of person he most disliked, was enough to make him fly off the handle. Douglas opened the conversation by referring to Wilde's theory that the WH to whom Shakespeare dedicated the sonnets was a boy actor called Will Hewes. The next hour was spent in spirited argument, at the end of which Douglas complained that he was in pain. Pearson then left, cursing himself for having allowed his passion for Shakespeare to get the better of his interest in Wilde.

A week later he returned to Douglas's flat, bringing a dozen eggs and a bottle of brandy as a peace offering. Douglas seemed pleased and for some time the two men talked of Wilde, until Douglas became bored with the subject and began to complain of his own poor health. Pearson advised him to think of other things: 'Brooding on one's ailments,' he said, 'is the surest way of intensifying them. Why not – why not re-read Shakespeare's plays and study the sonnets with a clearer idea of the man who wrote them?' 'Oh, damn Shakespeare!' Douglas exploded. Pearson tried to restore harmony, but the damage was done and they parted in an atmosphere of 'muted discord'.

When Pearson had nearly finished his book he sent Douglas the two chapters dealing with Wilde's trials and imprisonment. (This precaution was presumably taken at the instigation of his publisher.) Douglas at any rate was pleased, which he had every reason to be, as Pearson had dealt with him lightly. 'I have read the chapters you sent this morning,' he wrote. 'They are admirable and moving, in fact I found it exceedingly painful to read once more the dreadful story of cruelty and hypocrisy and humbug. Your book will be by far the best written on the subject.'

Although Douglas within a week or two of writing this letter was dead, Pearson did not revise the relevant chapters, but when a second edition was published in 1954 he added an appendix, the opening paragraph of which would undoubtedly have caused Lord Alfred to withdraw his seal of approval: 'The explanation,' he wrote, 'of how a man of genius was sacrificed to a family squabble lies partly in the close resemblance between Lord Alfred Douglas and his father, the Marquis of Queensberry. Both were arrogant, insolent, egotistical, quarrelsome, self-righteous, self-pitying: both were convinced that they were right and all who disagreed with them were wrong; each believed himself the victim of a conspiracy and suffered from persecution-mania: each went his own headstrong way regardless of other people's feelings: opposition to their wills aroused a frenzied violence in both of them; and hatred was the main driving force of their natures. To complete the resemblance, if either of them were to read the foregoing, he would assault the writer, institute legal proceedings for defamation of character and spend the rest of his life illustrating the accuracy of the comparison.'

_____

At the end of the war the owners of Woods Place returned. In July 1945 the Pearsons left Sussex and, returning to London, set up house at 14 Priory Road, NW6. This was to be Pearson's home for the rest of his life. He experienced, he said, a spasm of self-pity on leaving the country, which he attributed to an ancestral feeling that he should have been a country squire. But the emotion quickly passed. As usual when feeling gloomy, Pearson sought out Kingsmill and they set to work on another collaboration, this time for Eyre and Spottiswoode, whose managing editor Douglas Jerrold remained a keen supporter. Also at Eyre and Spottiswoode was Jerrold's fellow Catholic Graham Greene, who greatly admired Pearson's work. Kingsmill and Pearson went round to fix up the contract and Greene was curious to know about their technique. 'How do you two do your books?' he asked. 'Does one take the pen at one sentence, one at another.' 'We take notes as we go around,' Pearson replied, 'from time to time putting down anything that has struck us as interesting or amusing, and recording the details of chance encounters as soon after as possible. So far as our own conversations are concerned, they are sufficiently faithful reports of our own conversations. Then when enough material has been accumulated, we put it together, Kingsmill holding the pen, I striding up and down, or seated, as the case may be.'

The new book involved more jaunts round London, expeditions to Winchester, Constable's country and Rochester, and visits to Stanley Baldwin, Bernard Shaw and Hilaire Belloc. It was difficult, however, in the post-war period to conjure up the same air of jollity, and though Pearson, in the wake of his successful Shaw and Wilde books, was now more assured and even quite well off, Kingsmill was showing the effects of years of failure and poverty. His health was beginning to suffer and when one day Pearson quoted to him Brutus' lines from Julius Caesar:

> Night hangs upon mine eyes, my bones would rest
> That have but laboured to attain this hour

Kingsmill said gravely, 'Others have felt like that.'

Good spirits returned when, in the company of friends, he could forget domestic and financial worries and talk about books. A favourite meeting place after the war was the Authors' Club in Whitehall Court. The club was small and quiet, with a room looking out over the embankment, where they had a favourite window seat. The members were writers and journalists, a few civil servants and clergymen, not all of whom welcomed the loud talk and laughter of Kingsmill, Pearson and Muggeridge. Kingsmill, who once described clubs as 'places where elderly gentlemen promote arteriosclerosis by extended slumbers after lunch', could be relied on to play the fool. 'I remember clearly,' Louis Wilkinson wrote to Muggeridge. 'It was Hugh who came unexpectedly behind me when I was before a looking glass in the lavatory of the Authors' Club and said "Fine face, isn't it?" '

Pearson recalled another incident: 'During a session in the Authors' Club we were criticising clichés, deploring their prevalence in the press, the pulpit, literature, conversation and politics, and wondering whether anything could be done to suppress the vice, say a fine of one shilling every time writers, speakers and talkers displayed their intellectual bankruptcy in this way. The question of how the money thus collected should be disposed presented no problem: it should be handed over to the founders of the Anti-Cliché Guild – ourselves. Meanwhile, we determined to commence operations single-handed, or more exactly double-handed, and protest strongly and even volubly whenever anyone was so ill-advised as to use clichés in our presence. Having ratified our decision, we got up to leave the Club. As we reached the entrance-door, a clergyman who had just come in held it open for us, and intoned "Speed the parting guest". We went out with bowed heads and cowed hearts, but when we reached the street we could hardly proceed for laughter.'

Pearson, as always, was liable to be provoked into explosions.

One day Kingsmill arrived to find him flushed after interchanging opinions with a fellow member: 'He asked me whether I had considered that I had made a success of life. I gave an unqualified "Yes", which led him to suppose that I had made a mint of money. I was then compelled to inform him that in relation to success there are four types of cad. The highest type thinks that success depends on the number of women a man can pop into bed with; highest because, after all, there is some reciprocity and humanity in the business. The next-best type identifies success with titles, public honours and so forth; and that is bearable because it implies a more or less harmless form of vanity. Next comes the cad who judges success by the amount of power a man can exercise over his fellow-creatures, which at least implies that he is aware of other people's existence. But, and at this point I favoured him with a truly baleful glare, the really well-spawned cad is he who estimates success in terms of money. It was my intention to conclude with a few words on true success, but I found that he had gone.'

Muggeridge had quietly discharged himself from the secret service at the end of the war and was now working on the *Daily Telegraph*. He sold his house at Whatlington and moved to a flat in Buckingham Street overlooking the Embankment Gardens, with Kingsley Martin resident above. On August 18, 1946 Kingsmill, Pearson and Muggeridge all three met for lunch at the Café Royal as guests of Pearson's old friend and patron, Colin Hurry. In the austere post-war period a lunch with Hurry was greatly welcomed, especially by Kingsmill: 'I love being a guest of yours, Colin,' he said, as they sat down, 'because I know I shall have all the amenities which Somerset Maugham describes so accurately and which, when I read him, I despair of ever encompassing by my own efforts – no doubt the effect he wants his readers to get. Here, for example is a bottle of – let me see – Balaton Traminer. To me, at least, that has a Somerset Maugham ring.' 'You read Maugham with pleasure,' said Pearson, 'yet I've never heard you say anything amiable about him.'

'I sometimes *feel* amiable about him,' Kingsmill replied, 'but the words refuse to come.'

Emptying his glass, Kingsmill expressed the view that the

world was on the road to recovery, but Muggeridge was as usual less sanguine, and described how he had recently been motoring from Paris to Brittany with petrol and cigarettes to pay his hotel bills. 'It's coming here too. And probably in a year or so. . . . You agree, Colin?' Hurry agreed, and he and Muggeridge discussed the economic situation at some length before Kingsmill interrupted: 'This isn't conversation. Economics isn't conversation. I don't know what they are, but I do know what they aren't.'

It was at the Café Royal a few weeks later that following a long improvisation on the theme of Macaulay's love life, Muggeridge remarked: 'Why do politicians bother to finish their sentences? Everyone present knows exactly what's coming after the opening words. For instance, Attlee's speech at the first meeting of UNO would be just as intelligible and just as stirring if abbreviated as follows:

On this historic occasion when . . .
There can be no-one here present who . . .
We have just passed through an ordeal that . . .
No thinking man will underestimate the . . .
While there are many circumstances which . . .
There are solid grounds for hoping that . . .
The Nations of the World here gathered together for . . .
It is surely incumbent on all of us to . . .
While recognising the reality of . . .
No mere conflict of interest should . . .
The immeasurable strides that Science has . . .
Such is the choice that at present confronts . . .
It is idle to think that the politicians can . . .
It rests with the common people to . . .
With head erect and clear purpose, we . . .
That goal towards which the Nations of the World are . . .

Kingsmill never gave up trying to lure Muggeridge away from journalism and politics, but without success. In 1946 Muggeridge went to Washington for a stint as the *Daily Telegraph*'s correspondent and while he was there wrote to Kingsmill: 'I agree . . . with what you say about disentangling myself from politics. Isn't there a sexual aberration called being a voyeur? Graham [Greene] I fancy, refers to it rolling the vowels savagely. Well, I'm a voyeur as far as politics are concerned, peeping with fascinated disgust at the obscenities of power. However, I have a conviction that this time really is the last, and that when I escape from this entanglement it will be for ever. (Every sexual aberration, carrying on our old analogy, has its political equivalent. There are even power-homosexuals, like, for instance, Stephen Hobhouse; and eunuchs like Sir John Anderson, who are allowed into the harem because it is thought they can do no damage, and hardened old fornicators like Winston, and uxorious husbands like Herbert Morrison, and other husbands like Attlee who continue faithfully, regularly but not excessively to perform their marital functions)'.

Muggeridge was once again feeling out on a limb: 'There is something very wonderful about this country, but not for me. In no country that I've been in have I felt so completely an outsider as here. It makes me very lonely even when you see a lot of people. Though they speak English, and go to church, and wear pyjamas, they make me feel much more alien than even the Russians did. In fact, I'm hopeful that being here will, for some reason I can't explain, cure me of my Russian obsession. Already I find myself slightly less heated in my denunciations of Russia, and though I won't say that it would not give me the most exquisite pleasure to hear that Molotov was dying by slow torture, a very delicate instrument would I fancy detect an appreciable modification of my attitude towards him after one of Truman's press conferences. Did you know, by the way, that his "S" initial stands for no name at all, is just an initial? An American columnist with another poetic flash always calls him "Harry S. (For nothing) Truman", which I think gets him remarkably well. Presumably his parents exhausted their inventive powers when they thought of Harry, and just threw in "S" in case at a future date he or someone else might be able to put a name to it. He hasn't bothered.'

Kingsmill's attitude to politics sprang partly from his invincible optimism. Being by nature as optimistic as Muggeridge was pessimistic – he once jokingly referred to Muggeridge as a 'Dawnist turned Eveist' – his feeling that everything was going to be all right made him genuinely unconcerned about what was going on in the political world. This indifference made him suspect in some quarters. In an essay, 'Notes on Nationalism' written in 1945, George Orwell described both Kingsmill and Muggeridge as exponents of a species of Nationalism which he called 'Neo-Toryism'. 'The real motive of neo-Toryism,' he wrote, 'giving it its national-istic character and differentiating it from ordinary con-servatism, is the desire not to recognise that British powers and influence have declined. . . . The anglophobe who suddenly becomes violently pro-British is a fairly common figure.' Like much of Orwell's criticism, it was ridiculously wide of the mark, Kingsmill never having been either an anglophobe or expressed any views which could possibly be described as 'violently pro-British'.

In an article answering Orwell in the *New English Review*, Kingsmill asked, 'What are politics, and why only too often do they cause men to gibber? In theory they are the methods by which the administration of the community is directed and supervised; and here and there, for example in Switzerland, whose size and position make it unsuitable for the purposes of a Napoleon, politics do really confine themselves within these salutary limits. Hence the obscurity in which Swiss politicians pass their lives, and the contempt for Switzerland felt by Lenin and Trotsky and Mussolini and the other revolutionaries who used that stable republic as a base from which to launch an ordered life upon their fellow countrymen. In less stable countries politics are proportionally less rational, and in extreme cases (the Puritan Revolution, the Napoleonic Empire, the totalitarian states of today) all the hopes and dreams of men are absorbed into politics, which become for the few the technique of self-aggrandisement, for the many the key to paradise, and to all a collective hallucination which at last collapses into despair. Such is my view of what Orwell calls nationalism . . .'

For his part, Kingsmill never really warmed to Orwell, whom he once described as 'a gate swinging on a rusty hinge'. They had been introduced by Muggeridge some time in 1945. 'The meeting was not a success,' Muggeridge recorded, 'though a good deal of mutual regard survived it.' While disagreeing with Orwell's view of his own political position, Kingsmill recognised his sincerity and his gifts. 'Mr George Orwell,' he wrote in a review of *Animal Farm*, 'a social critic of uncompromising sincerity, has never fitted into any party and belongs to the left because he wants better conditions for others, not because he wants power for himself. Had he lived in the Commonwealth, he would have judged Cromwell by his failure to realise the dreams of the Levellers. Under the First Empire he would have condemned Napoleon for betraying the expectations of 1789.'

Kingsmill admired *Animal Farm* noting that it 'revealed the poetry, humour and tenderness in Orwell; but it seems to be only when he thinks of men as animals that he can see them as human beings and feel at one with them.' Kingsmill saw in Benjamin the donkey, the only animal on the farm not to accept the official explanation when Boxer is sent to the Knackers' yard, 'a modest embodiment of the author, with whom he also shares a sardonic contempt for the consolation derived from religion: "He would say that God had given him a tail to keep off flies, but that he would sooner have had no tail and no flies".'

Orwell's nearest equivalent as a critic, Kingsmill thought, was G. K. Chesterton: 'Like Chesterton, he is not interested in literature either for aesthetic reasons or as a revelation of human nature, but as a clue to the social, political and religious opinions of the age. It was Chesterton's most stimulating quality that he could write with the same gusto about an ode by Milton or a penny dreadful. Everything was significant to him because everything was interrelated.' Orwell for his part came to have a high opinion of Kingsmill's work and described *The Poisoned Crown* as a brilliant and outstanding book. He was especially enthusiastic about *The Sentimental Journey*. In a review for the *New York Times*, written shortly before he died, Orwell said that it was, despite its hostile tone, 'perhaps the most brilliant book ever written on Dickens'. It was typical of Kingsmill's bad luck that this compliment, the highest ever paid him by an eminent critic, should have appeared in a foreign newspaper on the day after his death (May 16, 1949). Nor was it reprinted in the massive four-volume *Collected Essays, etc.* of George Orwell.

To Muggeridge, his friend Orwell was another Quixote: 'I said to Hughie once,' he told Pearson, 'that Orwell reminded me tremendously of Don Quixote, whom he even seemed to resemble physically. Hughie agreed, but added that he doubted if he would have liked Don Quixote much, in the sense of enjoying his company; whereas Sancho, though, like Boswell, an unedifying character in many respects, would have been a pleasant companion.'

Still, it was rare for Kingsmill to find anything good to say of his contemporaries. He admired the work of friends like William Gerhardi and Edwin Muir, but found the bulk of modern literature lacking in clearness and vitality, two necessary ingredients, in his view, of good writing. He read Graham Greene's *The Heart of the Matter* and was very contemptuous of it, observing to Muggeridge that the best elements in the book were the vultures who represented 'authentic life beating down on Graham's strange and diseased creations'.

Greene's fellow Catholic, Evelyn Waugh, suffered acutely from boredom and Kingsmill, who was never bored, found his work for this reason unsympathetic. T. S. Eliot, he said, had only enough vitality to see that he hadn't got any. Too much modern poetry was written in an embittered spirit. 'Aggrieved poets,' Kingsmill said, 'do not write great poetry, and a feeling of grievance permeates nearly all contemporary verse.' Obscurity, he always insisted, was incompatible with good writing. 'In defence of the obscurity of many modern poets,' he wrote, 'we are told that Donne was equally obscure to his contemporaries. But what we remember of Donne are not his conceits but such lines as

> All day the same our postures were
> And we said nothing all the day

And

> Or as I'd watched one drop in the vast stream
> And I left wealthy only in a dream

The fact that there is a great deal of false simplicity in Tennyson and other Victorian poets is not a valid reason why there should be a great deal of genuine obscurity in modern verse. Great poetry always consists of ordinary words transfigured by extraordinary emotion – "I cannot but remember such things were, which were most precious to me." "Thou the golden fruit dost bear, I am clad in flowers fair." "Or flocks, or herds or human face divine." The greatest thought, too, however far it may be from the understanding of most men, is always expressed in familiar language – "Except a man be born again, he cannot see the Kingdom of God." '

Although he knew his favourite authors almost by heart, Kingsmill was always returning to them and making fresh discoveries. One writer for whom he acquired a liking in middle age was Thomas Carlyle. As a young man he hated him, along with all the Victorians. 'What a loathsome fellow Carlyle is,' he wrote to Pearson in 1928, after re-reading *The Life of Cromwell,* 'a snarling bum sucker, glaring out at me from behind Cromwell's buttocks with an air of sole proprietorship which I for one resent. Not through envy, but through a natural annoyance at his supposing I wish to displace him from that malodorous position.' But as he grew older Kingsmill's attitude softened and he came to see that Carlyle, for all his unattractive qualities, was one of the few Victorians to possess a sense of humour, though this was not always apparent in his books. 'His genius,' Kingsmill wrote at a later stage, 'comes out less in his writings than in his spoken comments on men and life, all clothed in his quaint idiom, which has a half-poetic, half-humorous fascination as soon as one realises that it was natural to him to talk in that way. Here is an incident which show Carlyle as vividly as any of Boswell's little vignettes show Johnson. Carlyle and two friends passed some street urchins who were turning somersaults in a private enclosure. One of the boys, perhaps alarmed by Carlyle's appearance, piped – 'I say, mister, may we roll on this here grass?' Turning slowly towards the boy, Carlyle replied – 'Yes, my little fellow, roll at discretion.' Carlyle walked on, and one of his companions heard a little girl repeating meditatively – 'He says we may roll at discretion'.

In June 1945, in the course of writing *Dick Whittington,* Kingsmill and Pearson paid a visit to Carlyle's house in Cheyne Row, Chelsea and were shown over the premises by the caretaker Mrs Strong: 'Kingsmill, moved by the tortured expression in a portrait of Jane Carlyle, expressed himself emphatically to Pearson about the horror of being cooped up with Tam, but was sternly taken to task by Mrs Strong, who quoted many favourable verdicts on Carlyle passed on by people who did not have to live with him.' On their way down from the top floor they recalled a story which Kingsmill had recently heard from E. S. P. Haynes: 'Joseph Chamberlain, at the height of his fame as a Radical politician, visited Carlyle one day with W. H. Mallock, who had just come down from Oxford with the reputation of a brilliant youth with a great career before him. Mallock, apparently, had been too brilliant during the visit, for, as he and Chamberlain were putting their coats on, Carlyle, who had gone up the first flight of stairs, leant over the balustrade and called out, "Can ye hear me, Mr Mallock?" Mallock having expectantly signified that he could and no doubt thrown himself into a cordially receptive posture, Carlyle continued: "I didna enjoy your veesit, and I dinna want to see ye again." '

Muggeridge, too, often discussed Carlyle with Kingsmill in the Hastings days. 'An anecdote about Carlyle which Hughie always considered highly symbolic,' he wrote, 'was recorded in one of my mother-in-law's interminable journals about her father, Richard Potter, an enormously rich Victorian industrialist. It appears that Carlyle used to take a walk in Battersea Park every Sunday afternoon, and that Potter and a number of other millionaires used to follow him, keeping a good distance behind. They were not allowed actually to walk with Carlyle, but he was pleased enough to be trailed respectfully by them. Hughie and I often imagined Carlyle, with his plaid wrapped round him, striding along and muttering to himself, well aware that five or six top hats, all with substantial deposit accounts, were padding along behind him.'

To Pearson and Kingsmill, both brought up in the period before the First World War, the great literary figures of that time – Shaw, Kipling, Wells, Belloc and Chesterton – inevitably loomed larger than any writers who came after. Kingsmill however regarded all of them as examples of men whose creative instincts had been in some measure stifled by the urge towards Dawnism of one kind or another. He liked the early novels of Wells – *Mr Polly*, *Kipps*, and *Tono Bungay* – while regarding his later works of political prophecy and propaganda as the products of a near-lunatic.

Belloc was another writer who, like Arnold and Lawrence, had forsaken his muse and taken to propaganda, in his case for the Catholic Church. As a young man he had, like Words-worth, 'a sense of the visible world being an image of divine reality' and his early writings were full of poetry.

'This is a really wonderful passage,' Kingsmill said one day in Pearson's flat, taking down *The Path to Rome*, ' "thoughts at evening in an Italian village", the best and deepest thing he ever wrote: "In very early youth the soul can still remember its immortal habitation, and clouds and the edges of hills are of another kind from ours, and every scent and colour has a savour of Paradise. What that quality may be no language can tell, nor have men any words, no, nor any music, to recall it – only in a transient way and elusive the recollection of what youth was, and purity, flashes on us in the phrases of the poets and is gone before we can fix it in our minds. Whatever those sounds may be that are beyond our sounds, whatever is Youth – youth came up that valley at evening, borne upon a southern air. If we desire or attain beatitude, such things shall at last be our settled state; and their now sudden influence upon the soul in short ecstasies is the proof that they stand outside time, are not subject to decay." '

'Yes,' said Pearson, 'that's the top note of the book. But there's another passage that moves me equally, because it's a picture of the solitude from which he was sometimes able to escape in his youth but which even then was always closing round him again. Here it is: "They drank my wine, I ate their bread, and we parted; they to go to their accustomed place, and I to cross this unknown valley. But when I had left these grave and kindly men, the echo of their voices remained with me; the deep valley of the Enza seemed lonely, and as I went lower and lower down towards the noise of the river I lost the sun." '

In 1946 Belloc was seventy-six. A stroke four years before had weakened his powers and he had long since given up writing. Nevertheless, Kingsmill and Pearson decided to visit him at his old house, King's Land, near Horsham. An appoint-ment was duly arranged, by Kingsmill's Catholic brother Arnold and Belloc's daughter Eleanor, who with her husband, Reginald Jebb, lived with Belloc during the last years of his life. The fact that Belloc was past his prime was delicately suggested by the account which Kingsmill and Pearson sub-sequently wrote of their meeting: 'Kingsmill having been

introduced to Hilaire Belloc as Arnold Lunn's brother, Belloc
shook Pearson's hand and asked after Arnold Lunn.' But once
they sat down and began to talk, the old man, bearded and
patriarchal in appearance, perked up and, prompted by his
visitors, gave his opinion of his contemporaries and others –
F. E. Smith: 'Superficial. No brains. A politician'; Winston
Churchill: 'A genial fellow. A yankee'; Lloyd George: 'A
little country solicitor who got on. Made a lot of money, but
didn't know how.' Gladstone: 'Talked nonsense in a magnificent way'; Kipling: 'He wrote trash'. Inevitably the
question of the Jews cropped up: 'It was the Dreyfus case that
opened my eyes to the Jew question,' Belloc said, 'I'm not an
anti-Semite. I love 'em, poor dears. My best secretary was a
Jewess. Poor darlings. It must be terrible to be born with the
knowledge that you belong to the enemies of the human race.'

KINGSMILL: Why do you say the Jews are the enemies of
the human race?

BELLOC: The Crucifixion.

KINGSMILL: I see.

PEARSON: You must have influenced GKC a lot?

BELLOC: People said Chesterton took all his ideas from
my talk. It's not true, not true at all. It was from my books
he took them, whole passages, perhaps without knowing it.
He popularised my ideas on property – for the middle
classes. He was a poor speaker. His brother Cecil was a
better speaker and a better writer. A very able man.

Pearson asked him if he was going to write his autobiography:

BELLOC: No. No gentleman writes about his private life.
Anyway, I hate writing. I wouldn't have written a word
if I could have helped it. I only wrote for money. *The Path
to Rome* is the only book I wrote for love.

PEARSON: Didn't you write *The Four Men* for love?

BELLOC: No. Money.

PEARSON: *The Cruise of the Nona*?

BELLOC: Money.

KINGSMILL: That's a wonderful passage in *The Path to
Rome* about youth borne up the valley on the evening air.

BELLOC: Oh – yes.

KINGSMILL: I love the poetry in your essays, especially
the volume *On Nothing*.
BELLOC: Quite amusing. Written for money.

As they left the house shortly afterwards they looked back at the
South Downs outlined against the evening sky and recalled
'the verse of Belloc which follows his praise of their bare and
noble line':

> A lost thing could I never find
> Nor a broken thing mend
> And I fear I shall be all alone
> When I get towards the end.
> Who will there be to comfort me
> Or who will be my friend?

An element of quiet sadness and nostalgia was more and
more infecting Kingsmill's thoughts. Visiting Winchester
Cathedral with Pearson a few weeks later, he stopped before
the memorial window to Izaak Walton: 'Walton looks very
peaceful up there,' he said, 'fishing by that stream with the
pleasant hill beyond. I remember Hugh Thomson's illustrations to him in the Cranford series, and his name always brings
back Hugh Thomson's day-dream England, the old coaching
times seen from the steam age – people and houses just far
enough away, diminished but distinct, a little Eden of jollity
and content, far more appealing in certain moods than any
heaven one must work to get into.'

Later, strolling after dinner in the walled garden of the
Royal Hotel, they listened to the sound of church bells. 'One of
the reasons they move me so much,' Pearson said, 'is that their
sound is unchanging from age to age, and Chaucer and Lady
Jane Grey and Shakespeare and dear old Anna Seward all
heard those chimes just as we hear them, and they accompany
one's own journey in the same unchanging way. One's tastes
take different forms from year to year, but church bells are
always the same.' 'And so,' added Kingsmill, 'they both recall
the past, and being unchanging themselves, promise something
that does not pass away.'

Chapter 14

Early in 1948 Kingsmill moved with his family from their London flat to a cottage at Partridge Green, between Horsham and Steyning. Almost immediately he began to be subject to attacks of vomiting which left him exhausted. He was trying to write a novel, *Miserrimus*, but found it hard to summon up the energy. 'I would like ever more to be comfortable, sheltered, warm, mildly and delicately fed,' he wrote to Pearson. 'Mozart in the distance; no work, no worries, no absence of vitality.'

Though he did not know it, Kingsmill was suffering from a duodenal ulcer, brought on by years of stress. But, such was his natural cheerfulness, that his friends and family found it difficult to take his illness seriously, 'Everything's otsy-totsy' was his catch-phrase with his children and they found it hard to believe otherwise. On March 30, he had a haemorrhage and was admitted to the Royal Sussex Hospital in Brighton. 'On the journey here after my haemorrhage,' he wrote to Pearson from hospital, 'the ambulance stopped at the doctor's, who gave me a blood transfusion to keep me going, with the help of the local vicar, who wrapped a muffler round his neck so that I wouldn't see he was a parson and suspect extreme unction in the offing. Twelve hours after my arrival here, a chap blew along, told me I was in a mess, and asked me what I had been up to. I explained briefly, 'Well you can wait a week if you like to find out if you've got an ulcer,' he said.

'What'll happen by the end of the week?'

'You'll probably die.'

'Any alternative suggestion?'

'You can be operated on at once to find out if you've got an ulcer.'

'What'll happen in that case?'

'You'll probably die at once.'

'A bit difficult to make up my mind, especially in its present state. I'd like to discuss it with my wife.'

'It's your decision not hers.'

'Well, as there seems nothing in it, and I prefer drastic measures, I'll be operated on at once.'

'Thereupon a replica of the first gravedigger in *Hamlet*, about four feet high, tough and reddish-hued, came along with a safety razor, bowl, etc. I asked him his purpose, and he said, "I'm the prepper", meaning the preparer. Whereupon he nonchalantly sheared me. Hamlet would have resented the incident: there was certainly not much of the "daintier sense" about the knave. But enough of these details. Incidentally, I needn't have been cut up at all, as they not only discovered no ulcer, but nothing wrong with any organ at all. However, surgeons, like Falstaff, no doubt feel it is no sin to labour in their vocation.'

This failure to diagnose the ulcer was to prove fatal. But meanwhile Kingsmill remained sanguine. He had always been totally without fear and during the war, for example, had never given the doodle-bugs a moment's thought, refusing to join his family as they crouched under the table. Muggeridge visited him on April 17, afterwards recording in his diary: 'I went to see Hughie in hospital and was relieved to find him in quite good shape, though of course somewhat haggard and old-looking. He was asleep when I got there, but when he woke up and saw me sitting by the bed, such a smile of happiness came on his face that I was deeply moved. We talked for about two hours, and he was quite up to his old form. He is in a public ward, and is quite a centre of interest to the other patients. He said that, as always happens, as they came and went, all the standard human characters appeared – a Dickens, a Hitler, etc. He had been re-reading the Sherlock Holmes stories and said that, with all their inherent absurdity, they never quite lose their charm, especially when one is ill or fatigued. He quoted a line from Browning's *Andrea del Sarto*: "I am often tireder than you think," and said it was one of those ever-lasting remarks which can be described as "husbandly".'

On May 5 Kingsmill was released from hospital, and on the 7th went to stay with the Muggeridges for two days in the flat they had moved into in Cambridge Gate, Regent's Park. The weather was fine and the two men spent many hours in the park, of which Kingsmill was particularly fond. During the ensuing months Muggeridge was to see much of his friend, and for once he kept notes of their meetings:

June 9th. Returned home late, and found Hughie sitting in the sitting-room in his night-shirt, reading Keats – a comical but delightful figure.

August 12th. Hughie and I discussed the Godwin-Shelley relationship. I said that Godwin had shown the most remarkable practical ability in that by writing a book against property and against marriage, he had managed to get his unattractive daughter married off to Shelley, a near baronet, whom he was able to touch thereafter for regular financial help. Hughie pointed out that he had not only touched him, but that he refused to accept financial help in the form of a cheque drawn by Shelley because he didn't want his bank to know that he was receiving it. Hughie read me a sentence Godwin had written to Mary Wollstonecraft, one at which we laughed much as an outstanding example of the truth that dishonesty of purpose inevitably makes language involved to the point of incomprehensibility. 'Ideas which I am now willing to denominate prejudices, made me by no means eager to conform to a ceremony as an individual, which, coupled with the conditions our laws annex to it, I should undoubtedly, as a citizen, be desirous to abolish. Fuller examination, however, has since taught me to rank this among those cases, where an accurate morality will direct us to comply with customs and institutions which, if we had a voice in their introduction, it would have been incumbent on us to negative.'

October 28th. Hughie came to lunch. We discussed Arnold Bennett and agreed that he was an exceedingly pitiable figure. Hughie said his last words, addressed to Dorothy Cheston, were very sad and touching: 'Everything is going wrong, my girl.'

November 11th. Hughie looked in early, and we spent the morning pleasantly talking. He was very amusing on the subject of St Thomas Aquinas, who, he said, had been taken up by neo-Catholics as a substitute for belief.

I read him a passage from Lincoln's speech when he was elected President in which he said: 'I have been selected to fill an important office for a brief period, and am now, in your eyes, invested with an influence which will soon pass away; but should my administration prove to be a very wicked one, or what is more probable, a very foolish one, if you, the people, are true to yourselves and the constitution, there is but little harm I can do, thank God.'

We agreed that Lincoln was incomparably the most sympathetic man of action of modern times, and Hughie said that his fearful melancholia was due to the fact that he really was an embodiment of all the vain hopes which people had felt in going to America. I agreed, and said that he represented whatever was great in the American people. He was, as it were, their Shakespeare, only it took the form of this curious life of action instead of literature.

Jan 20th. Hughie came to lunch, and we were much amused by an extract from Archbishop Lang's memoirs in the *Sunday Times*, particularly the statement that on a stalking expedition, in order to protect the King from a heavy shower 'the Archbishop, claiming the privilege of a subject to cover the person of his Sovereign, lay down on top of him'. On this awesome picture Hughie dwelt at great length, imagining what would have been the reaction of some Highland gillie who had come upon the monarch and the archbishop thus disposed under an overhanging rock.

Pearson, too, saw a great deal of Kingsmill during these last months of his life. Kingsmill frequently called at his Priory Road flat, either for dinner or an after-dinner talk. On these occasions he liked to play the gramophone, preferring to listen to slow movements, in particular those of Mozart's Clarinet Quintet, Elgar's Violin Concerto, and Beethoven's A Minor Quartet, as well as the Benedictus from Beethoven's Mass in D Major. On October 7 Pearson and Gladys went to stay in Sussex near the Kingsmills. During the evenings Pearson and Kingsmill sat in the White Horse at Steyning choosing their favourite extracts of Shakespeare for a new hardback edition of Pearson's *Life*. The extracts were called 'pringles', a word which was intended to convey 'the peculiar physical symptoms evoked by a perfect passage of poetry, which gives me a pricking in the scalp or a tingling in the spine, or it produces a flooding sensation about the heart, or its effect is lachrymal.'

'It was quite remarkable,' Pearson told Muggeridge, 'how thoroughly we agreed: I don't suppose there are more than half a dozen passages in my anthology that had only pringled one of us.'

A few days after his return to London Pearson received from Kingsmill the proofs of *Progress of a Biographer*, a collection of his literary criticism taken mainly from the *New English Review*. Though the essays were written over a long period and on subjects ranging from Karl Marx to P. G. Wodehouse, they have an underlying unity. Kingsmill continued to stress the necessary connection between the artist's life and work: 'If criticism is to be more than an academic diversion, a critic should not be content to play about inside a man's work as though it were a glass bowl suspended in a vacuum. A man's work expresses his character and each should be used to illuminate the other.'

In his life of Wagner, Ernest Newman had said, in answer to those who raised the question of Wagner's political and racialist beliefs, 'It is only with Wagner the artist, not Wagner the muddle-headed political phantast, that the civilised world has any concern today.' But, Kingsmill maintained, when reviewing the book, 'Wagner the artist and Wagner the political phantast were not separate persons. A man's artistic faculty is merely the means by which he communicates his vision of life, and however brilliant, however complex, cannot purify a corrupted vision or deepen a shallow one: for how a man sees life is determined by how he lives it.' It was therefore no accident that Wagner's music made a particular appeal to the Nazi leaders. 'It is not by chance,' he wrote, 'that a man of action is drawn to a poet, a musician or a thinker. Voltaire, shrewd, worldly and disillusioned, suited Frederick the Great, the cloudy visions of Ossian and the self-pity of Werther nourished Bonaparte with the mixture of hope and despair he desired in the years of his obscurity, and there is hardly a moment in this volume when Wagner says or does anything which would have jarred on Hitler.'

Throughout *Progress of a Biographer* Kingsmill emphasised

the unhappiness which he detected in so many writers and which, to him, could not be reconciled to great work. Dissatisfaction, self-pity or despair were to Kingsmill the signs of failure. He noted Aldous Huxley's 'innate disgust with life', the 'limping bitterness of Kipling's last years'. Dickens, he wrote, was 'wretched at the close', while the death mask of Sir Walter Scott looked 'inexpressibly forlorn and forsaken'.

In each case Kingsmill would have said that the unhappiness was due to a failure to achieve a transcendental view of reality, a mystical or religious insight which he could see pre-eminently in the lives and writings of Shakespeare, Cervantes, Johnson and Wordsworth. Without it there could be no true happiness in this world, as Shakespeare had recognised when in his last play, *The Tempest*, he spoke through Prospero:

> And my ending is despair
> Unless I be relieved by prayer.

– one of Kingsmill's favourite quotations.

On February 23 Kingsmill and Pearson met in London. Kingsmill wanted to see Hitchcock's film *The Lady Vanishes*, which was being revived at the Baker Street Classic. Afterwards they dined at the Authors' Club for the last time. On April 10 Kingsmill was re-admitted to the Royal Sussex County Hospital in Brighton. He was too ill to be operated on and was kept alive by blood transfusions until his death on May 15.

The realisation that Kingsmill might not have long to live brought Muggeridge and Pearson closer to each other than ever before. They were drawn together by a realisation of what they would lose by his death. On April 13 they lunched at the Authors', talking of their friend, and afterwards walked in Regent's Park. It was perhaps on this occasion that Muggeridge said to Pearson that if Kingsmill died, half the pleasure of living would at one stroke be gone. Pearson agreed. Meanwhile, they were prevented from going to see him, as he was not well enough to have visitors, apart from his family. 'I hope to be seeing you very soon,' Kingsmill wrote to Pearson. 'To see you in this belching groaning cave of wind and waters will be wonderful. . . .' He knew that he was dying, but was not afraid: 'Balmy spring breezes blowing in from the sea outside, but I hope that this decaying old husk will release me at not too long a date to recover all the beauty of those old days, in some other form. . . . About three years since Winchester, I think. How well I remember the old walled Garden and the Chimes.'

'My dear old man,' Pearson replied. 'It was a great pleasure to hear from you, but I would much rather you didn't write if it takes anything out of you. The only good news you can give me is that you are better and better, and the way to get better is to expend no nervous energy . . . I wish I could see you coming up the road, preparatory to a stroll on Hampstead Heath. I miss you very much. Do please get well. . . . Ever yours, old lad, Hesk.'

He wrote again two days later.

Malcolm and I lunched at the club yesterday and there were many enquiries after you, among others from John Trevor and a bloke named Haynes, who I didn't know, but who came up and asked after you. Your dear old pal Ernest Short was also most solicitous, and informed us that everybody loved you. Now, you can't say fairer than that. . . .

Then Malcolm and I took the tube to Hampstead and I, in my best proprietorial manner, showed him the Heath . . . I took him straight to North End, so that he could see the house where Dickens had spent a week or two after the death of Mary Hogarth, stopping Pickwick and Oliver in order to weep in peace. Malcolm wanted to know if his wife had been with him. 'Naturally,' I said. He let it go with a sigh. But he bucked up amazingly when I said that William Blake used to sit at the door of that same house and watch for his friends coming from London to see him, appearing over the very hillock which he and I had just descended. After that he referred at intervals to the little house where Blake had watched for his friends, and I replied 'Yes, the little house where Dickens retired to mourn.'

Bois de Caen was incredibly beautiful in the spring sunshine, and we sat on the terrace talking of you for some time. . . . He was anxious to see Leigh Hunt's cottage; so we crashed across the Heath, and I drew his attention to the pond whereon Shelley sailed paper boats for the little Hunts, which did not appear to thrill him, and spoke of Hazlitt's objections to footpads, and told him of Hunt's other visitors, including William Wordsworth, who, we agreed, would have been avoided by footpads, unless with their intention of handing over to him the sums they had collected from Hazlitt, Coleridge, and other callers. . . . Coming to the main road, I told him that Dickens, Thackeray, Carlyle, and other notables, but especially Dickens, had dined or supped on innumerable occasions at Jack Straw's Castle, but he did not seem unbearably excited.

We called at the Holly Bush Inn and had a couple of whiskies, and then dropped in on Alan and Marjorie White, both of whom send their love. We parted at Chalk Farm round about 8 o'clock. Since then he has rung up and found that you are better, which we feel must be due to the fact that we have done a five mile walk and talk devoted almost exclusively to you: the exercise, as it was being done for you, did you good, and the conversation, as you did not have to contribute to it, had a bracing effect on you.

Bee [Pearson's sister-in-law, who shared the flat with Kingsmill during the Blitz] was in tears about you yesterday, and shuffled off into her room murmuring, 'My Romeo.' Now we really can't have this sort of thing going on in a house where sobs can be heard from floor to floor; so pull yourself together and come and dry her eyes . . .

Pearson wrote again on April 26 to thank Kingsmill for the inscribed copy of *Progress of a Biographer*. 'There is nothing to touch it in critical literature,' he wrote in his habitual vein of hyperbole, and then, thinking undoubtedly, if perhaps subconsciously, of his friend, added: 'Do you know Gorki's reminiscences of Tolstoy? There is a wonderful passage in them which moved me as much as anything in Shakespeare moves me. Gorki sees Tolstoy sitting by the seashore, motionless like the stones about him, his head on his hands looking out to sea. "I cannot express in words what I felt rather than thought at that moment," writes Gorki; "in my soul there was joy and fear, and then everything blended into one happy thought: 'I am not an orphan on the earth so long as this man lives on it'." ' It somehow recalls Bardolph on Falstaff, a tribute brought forth by another great man, though of a different sort: 'Would

I were with him, wheresome 'er he is, either in Heaven or Hell!'

'We think and talk of you a great deal here. Nothing could give us greater joy than to hear that you are really on the mend; nothing could give us half the joy.'

On April 30 Pearson heard from Dorothy Kingsmill that her husband was feeling much better and a visit was accordingly arranged for May 4. Pearson called at the hospital at three o'clock, but had to wait an hour while Kingsmill was given a blood transfusion. 'It was four o'clock,' he recalled, 'when the other visitors left, before I could sit by his bed. He seized my hand and held it as long as I was there; and every time I attempted to leave because I thought the talk was exciting him too much, he would not let me go. "You're a good colour," was one of the first things I said. "Not mine, old boy," he laughed. "It belongs of right to others, who have kindly contributed to my present appearance." ' They then talked – of Shakespeare, and books and life in the hospital. After an hour, the sister said it was time for Pearson to go and, as he got up, Kingsmill again recalled the day they spent at Winchester three years before and the sound of the church bells in the old walled garden. He was crying as Pearson left.

Three days later Muggeridge saw him for the last time. They talked of Johnson, and Kingsmill said he would like to have the *Lives of the Poets* more than any other book. In spite of his illness Kingsmill was still able to joke and quoted with amusement one of the nurses who had said that he was holding onto life 'like grim death'. 'He was very weak,' Muggeridge wrote, 'and held my hand – an unusual thing for him, who was, by temperament, undemonstrative. He had, he said, some good news to impart: something wonderful which had come to him about our human situation. He never did manage to get it out, but, nonetheless, unspoken, it has often comforted me.'

On May 14, the night before he died, Kingsmill had a vision. His wife later described what had happened in a letter to Gladys Pearson: 'He was in great pain when the vision came to him. The ward filled with blazing light and in the middle of it there was an enormous cross. In telling me this Hugh at this point buried his face in his hands and between his tears said, "The horror of the vision was that I was the Cross and all the pain of Christ was passing from him to me like a great devouring flame. . . ." He became unconscious about midday and only recovered consciousness for two brief flashes, but was too ill to speak. Edmée and I were with him at the end. About ten minutes to nine I noticed that the breathing had become so soft as to be hardly perceptible and as the tower clock nearby began to strike his expression became that of one who has passed beyond either consciousness or unconsciousness and was seeing something far away, beyond, awe-inspiring, majestic. The death rattle, his head sank on the pillow, a last deep sigh, and it was over. The last impression we got as the nurse pulled the sheet over him was of tremendous power.'

Chapter 15

Two months after Kingsmill's death, Pearson and Muggeridge, reviving his wartime idea of a book consisting of an exchange of letters, began to write to one another 'About Kingsmill' – the title of the book, published in 1951. Both felt a strong urge to put down their memories, while they were still fresh, of a man who they thought would otherwise be forgotten.

Pearson's contributions were typical of his biographical writing. Using the correspondence which he had carefully preserved, he built up an anecdotal portrait in his usual straightforward style – recalling their first meeting in 1921, their endless talks about Shakespeare and Harris, the expedition to the Hebrides and their collaborations.

In writing of his friend Pearson's first thought was of the laughter which he had always enjoyed in his company. 'Hughie's laughter,' he said, 'was the thing that at once attracted me to him. It was the laugh of a man who enjoyed life. It was a laugh without reserve.'

Muggeridge agreed. More so than Pearson, who was by nature high-spirited and genial, he had experienced the uplift that Kingsmill's laughter could bring. He remembered a favourite quotation of Kingsmill's from *King John*, when the tyrant speaks of 'that idiot laughter, a passion hateful to my purposes'. Humour, like poetry, was a sign of the imagination at work. Laughter dissolved the absurd solemnities of the will, of power, of the world of action; Harris, Lawrence, Shaw, the *Manchester Guardian* – all their pomposities had been for Kingsmill not a cause of anger or indignation – 'To be angry is to be wrong', he once said – but of mirth. So in his company, Samuel Butler, trudging earnestly to Handel Street, became a comic figure, Harris a clown, Sir Henry a Quixote, and the leaders in *The Times* extraordinarily funny.

But the humour of Kingsmill's company, his capacity to reduce people to helpless hysterics could never be recaptured, nor could the hours and hours of talk. Looking through the diary he kept during the war, Pearson was appalled by how little he had preserved: 'Monstrous, when one remembers that he said something either funny or profound almost every time he opened his mouth. Oh, dear! why on earth didn't I Boswellise him? I suppose because I was enjoying his company so much. And now the best of him is lost for ever, because of my laziness. I always thought I would die first.'

Kingsmill's greatest achievement was as a teacher, and it was in this capacity that Muggeridge had a clearer picture of him than Pearson. There was a sense in which Kingsmill and Pearson could only go so far. Equally, in writing about Kingsmill, Pearson tended unconsciously to play down his debt to his friend and promote himself as his equal.

Muggeridge's biographical approach could not have been more different than Pearson's. He has always had a strong aversion to records, old letters and cuttings – the 'material' from which a 'Life' is shaped. He even dislikes looking back on anything which he himself has written in the past. His work therefore has a freshness which makes up for any minor historical inaccuracies, and it is just this spontaneity, combined with a real and radiant affection, which makes his contribution to *About Kingsmill* some of the best writing he has ever done.

The difference in outlook between Pearson and Muggeridge came out most clearly when they considered Kingsmill's religious position. In their early days Pearson and Kingsmill had crossed swords about Christianity. Pearson lashed out in his 'sunstroke style' when Kingsmill quoted with approval a favourite passage in Bunyan – 'Some also have wished that the next way to their father's house were here, and that they might be troubled no more with either hills or mountains to go over, but the way is the way and there is an end.'

Pressed by Pearson to explain himself, he said that though he didn't subscribe to Christianity, there were a good many symbols of truth in it, like Original Sin and the Fall of Man. But he never could bring himself to belong to a church, deriving consolation from the rather presumptuous thought that

'Mystics never have any use for priests. They (the mystics) know. The priests don't.'

Pearson would not admit to any interest in such matters, but his hostility died down as he grew older and he was able afterwards to joke about religion. 'May the Lord bless you and keep you,' he wrote to Kingsmill, 'and not bugger you about too much.' As for mysticism, following an evening spent in Kingsmill's company with another writer, John Hargrave, Pearson wrote to him: 'After you left us the other evening, Hargrave wondered whether you were as breezy a bloke as you appear to be. I informed him that you were of the most happy disposition, and that if it weren't for something a trifle bullshitty about you which you call mysticism, you would be the first living example of the healthy normal man. He seemed to sense a sinister something in you, which I instantly ascribed to the foresaid:

' "What is mysticism anyway?" he wanted to know.

' "It explains what is inexplicable in terms that are incomprehensible" was my reply: which seems to me, on reflection, to settle the whole question of mysticism.'

Aware of a residue of prickliness on Pearson's part, Kingsmill did not bring up religion when he could help it. But the signs are that in middle age he was drawn back towards Christianity. There was a strong religious streak in the Lunns. His sister Eileen had been a saintlike figure, who wore herself out helping the East End poor and died aged twenty-four. Kingsmill's son Brooke became a priest, and his daughter Edmée a nun, though neither had any formal Christian upbringing. When Kingsmill was dying, he wrote to his wife: 'A verse from an old hymn, by Richard Baxter, which used to move me greatly as a boy, has been in my mind all day –

> Christ leads me through no darker rooms
> Than he went through before
> He who into God's Kingdom comes
> Must enter through this door.'

Kingsmill would never have written to Pearson in the same vein and when at about this time a Catholic nurse pressed a cross into his hand and he repeated some prayers after her, he felt obliged, like St Peter, to discount his behaviour when writing to Pearson: 'I feel I owe you an apology, old man, but when one's nearly dead one does anything to oblige.'

With Muggeridge it was a different matter. Pearson saw the secular side of Kingsmill, Muggeridge the spiritual: 'It might surprise those who knew Hughie only slightly that he was by temperament deeply religious,' he wrote in *About Kingsmill*. 'His reaction against his father's Nonconformity in no wise predisposed him against religion as such. On the contrary, especially as he grew older, he became more and more convinced that what he always called the "empirical" was no more than an image of some larger reality, and this earthly life was only a preparation for another in terms of eternity. . . . As far as I personally was concerned it was a view which I came increasingly to share. To a certain extent, Hughie doubtless influenced my feelings in the matter, but only, I think, to the extent of making conscious what had been formerly unconscious, of giving a shape and coherence to convictions which had formerly been only vaguely and imprecisely held. It was taken for granted between us that the reality of life transcended its phenomena, and that earthly desire in all its aspects was at best no more than a clumsy reaching after spiritual perfection, and at worst, quite ludicrous . . .

'Because I was so completely in tune with Hughie in his essentially religious attitude of mind I never felt constrained to formulate then what it signified. Thinking about him since his death, I have tried to do this. . . . Hughie was a mystic, and whatever appealed to him in life and literature had in it a mystical strain. He never could say over quite unmoved those marvellous lines in *Lear*:

'. . . come let's away to prison:
We two alone will sing like birds i' the cage.
When thou dost ask me blessing, I'll kneel down,
And ask of thee forgiveness. So we'll live,
And pray, and sing, and tell old tales, and laugh
At gilded butterflies; and hear poor rogues
Talk of court news, and we'll talk with them too,
Who loses, and who wins, who's in, who's out;
And take upon's the mystery of things,
As if we were God's spies; And we'll wear out

> In a wall'd prison pacts and sects of great ones,
> That ebb and flow by th' moon.*

'Hughie was a unique person whose greatness lay, as all true greatness must, in his faculty to see into the mystery of things. In the light of this, all considerations of success and failure, of recognition and neglect became utterly irrelevant . . . what remains is the only thing that ever does or can remain – his deep and undeviating purpose to seek out the significance of life, as distinct from its phenomena, his unsparing and inexhaustible interest in his fellows, with all the bright hours it brought to those privileged to be his friends: the memory of him which they will always cherish.'

In the years that followed Kingsmill's death Pearson continued to write his biographies with unabated energy. *Dickens*, written at the suggestion of Bernard Shaw, had been published in 1949 and it was followed in regular succession by *Disraeli* – a subject who he admitted would not have appealed to Kingsmill – *Whistler*, *Walter Scott*, *Beerbohm Tree*, *Charles II* and others. None of these books were remarkable for any new insights, but all were written with his habitual vigour and vitality.

In 1951 Gladys Pearson died after a long crippling illness which she endured with great courage. Some months later Pearson married Joyce Ryder, who with her sister Jean had occupied the ground floor flat at 14 Priory Road and who had helped nurse Gladys during the final phase of her illness.

His high spirits and zest for life never left him. 'Personally I would rather be dead than half-alive,' he wrote in his memoirs, 'and I have enjoyed the experience of living so much that I now ask nothing of life but a quick death.' His wish was granted. On March 3, 1964 he was admitted to hospital, inoperable cancer was diagnosed, and he died on Thursday, April 9 aged seventy-seven. His passion for Shakespeare stayed with him till the end.

> When he lay dying [Muggeridge wrote in *The Times*] and I visited him, he still talked about Shakespeare as though

---

* 'The lines . . . which bring Shakespeare nearer to me than anything else he ever wrote, so that I can see him writing them, and am sure he was shaking like a leaf'. (Kingsmill to Pearson, October 1, 1940.)

he were present in the room with us. Apropos Essex's down-fall, he said he thought that Shakespeare ever afterwards had a feeling that he had been disloyal, and so became obsessed with the idea of Loyalty. He might have been referring to some friend, whose behaviour, humanly and forgivably, had fallen short of what was to be expected of him.

Pearson loved the English countryside, and English bells sounding across it; the English language, and all who have tried in however humble a capacity to use it worthily . . . with him and the late Hugh Kingsmill I spent some of the happiest hours of my life. . . . He never could manage to finish reciting Wordsworth's verses upon the death of James Hogg. The closing lines –

> 'How fast has brother followed brother
> From sunshine to the sunless land' –

were too much for him. I shall always think of him stumbling over the poignancy of those exquisite verses, and hope that the land will, after all, turn out not to be sunless.

Muggeridge, the only survivor of 'the Horseshoe Group', has, in his old age, achieved a kind of contentment. His restlessness, his desire to kick over the traces, have finally left him. He has re-discovered his faith and in his small way fulfilled the wish expressed so many years ago to Kingsmill and Pearson to become a saint in his old age. Kingsmill is continually in his thoughts and conversation. 'It is a mistake,' he says, 'to think that the memory of those who die fades: in many ways it grows brighter.' Almost any book he opens recalls Kingsmill to his mind. Any article he writes contains some echo of his friend. Once more he is living in Sussex, at Robertsbridge, not far from Whatlington, where he spent those happy years before the war; when he would see Kingsmill nearly every day, feeling an intense happiness as the familiar figure came rolling into sight along the narrow lane, hearing again his cry of welcome – 'Hullo, old man, hullo!'

Sayings of Hugh Kingsmill

The Rich
The well-to-do do not want the poor to suffer. They wish them to be as happy as is consistent with the continued prosperity of the well-to-do.

Listening
People who can repeat what you are saying are not listening.

Vision
Where there is vision the people perish. I admit they also perish where there is no vision. Either way, in fact, their situation appears to be damnably awkward.

Systems
Systems, whatever the philosophy out of which they have grown, necessarily value truth less than victory over rival systems.

Writers and Money
In their financial aspect the lives of writers, painters and musicians suggest a man leaping from ice floe to ice floe across a wide and rapid river. A strenuous, not a dignified spectacle.

Language
The greatest thought, however far it may be from the understanding of most men, is always expressed in familiar language – 'Except a man be born again, he cannot see the Kingdom of God.'

Humour
Most humour derives from the contrast between what a man expects from life and what he gets.

Life and Work
No man can put more virtue into his words than he practises in his life.

Suicide
The coward's way in.

Unpopularity
Men are disliked not for what they do, but for what they are.

Spiritualism
Spiritualism is the mysticism of the materialist.

Disillusionment
Disillusionment is the result of discovering that other people are as egotistical as oneself.

Peace
A nation is only at peace when it's at war.

Sex
If the sexual act is viewed apart from the other than physical emotions which accompany it, it is either comic or disgusting.

Snobbishness
Snobbishness is the assertion of the will in social relations, as lust is in the sexual. It is the desire for what divides men and the inability to value what unites them.

Liars and Bores
Liars are forgivable if they are amusing, bores are bearable if they are accurate.

Homosexuality
Homosexuality, which aims at duplicating the self instead of complementing it, is the natural outlet of exaggerated self-love.

Oliver Cromwell
It is hard to decide whether a man gravitates towards sacking towns because he is somewhat of a tough, or becomes somewhat tough after having disembowelled a certain percentage of his fellow citizens.

Tyrants
What is extraordinary about tyrants, as is evident in Cromwell and Napoleon, in not much smaller degree than in Hitler, is not their intellectual development but the way in which they embody and act on behalf of some great collective passion. Their power resides less in their faculties than in their fitness to act as mediums.

Anger
To be angry is to be wrong.

Friends and Disciples
The last word in wisdom is not to desire disciples, but to keep friends.

Debunking
'Debunking' is a modern vulgarism meaning the substitution of the truth for pleasant fictions.

The Desire for Power
The desire for power over other men is common to all energetic and imaginatively undeveloped natures in every age, and is behind all the wars, revolutions, and persecutions in history.

Dialectical Materialism
Why does Lenin always talk of Dialectical Materialism instead of the Lord God? It's so much longer.

War
There is everything in a war, even fighting.

Mysticism

Mysticism is the intuition of a harmony which envelopes but does not penetrate this life, and which can be apprehended but not completely possessed.

The Common Man

No one admires a single common man, or wants to be one, or would be anything but chagrined if hailed as a satisfactory specimen of one.

Talent and Genius

A man of talent thinks more highly of himself when he has a success, a man of genius thinks more highly of the world.

Reason

One only talks of reason when one's unreasonable, *ie*, 'It stands to reason that. . . . Anyone with an ounce of reason would admit that . . .'

Charlatans and Thinkers

A charlatan makes obscure what is clear, a thinker makes clear what is obscure.

Shyness

Shyness is egotism out of its depth.

Weakness

Weakness alone is punished in life and is certain to be punished.

Loving Mankind

It is difficult to love mankind unless one has a reasonable private income, and when one has a reasonable private income one has better things to do than loving mankind.

Bibliography

BOOKS BY HUGH KINGSMILL
The Will to Love (1919) · The Dawn's Delay (1924) · Blondel (1927).
Matthew Arnold (1928) · After Puritanism (1929) · The Return of William
Shakespeare (1929) · Invective and Abuse (anthology) 1929 · Behind Both
Lines (1930) · More Invective (anthology) 1930 · The Worst of Love
(anthology) 1931 · Frank Harris (1932) · The Table of Truth (1933) ·
Samuel Johnson (1933) · The Sentimental Journey (1934) · What They
Said at the Time (anthology) 1935 · Parents and Children (anthology)
1936 · Made on Earth (anthology) 1937 · D. H. Lawrence (1938) · Courage
(anthology) 1939 · The Fall (1940) · Johnson without Boswell (anthology)
1940 · The Poisoned Crown (1944) · The Progress of a Biographer (1949).
The High Hill of the Muses (anthology) 1955 · The Best of Hugh Kingsmill
(ed. Michael Holroyd) 1970

BY HUGH KINGSMILL AND HESKETH PEARSON
Skye High (1937) · This Blessed Plot (1942) · Talking of Dick Whittington
(1947)

BY HUGH KINGSMILL AND WILLIAM GERHARDI
The Casanova Fable (1934)

BOOKS BY HESKETH PEARSON
Modern Men and Mummers (1921) · A Persian Critic (1923) · The
Whispering Gallery (1926) · Iron Rations (1928) · Doctor Darwin (1930).
Ventilations (pub. in U.S. only) 1930 · The Smith of Smiths (1934) · The
Fool of Love (1934) · Gilbert and Sullivan (1935) · Labby (1936) · The
Swan of Lichfield (1936) · Tom Paine (1937) · Common Misquotations
(1937) · Thinking It Over (1938) · The Hero of Delhi (1939) · Life of
Shakespeare (1942) · Bernard Shaw (1942) · Conan Doyle (1943) · Oscar
Wilde (1946) · Charles Dickens (1949) · The Last Actor Managers (1950).
Dizzy (1951) · G. B. S. (a postscript) 1951 · The Man Whistler (1952).
Walter Scott (1954) · Gilbert: His Life and Strife (1957) · Johnson and
Boswell (1958) · Charles II (1960) · The Pilgrim Daughters (1961) · The
Lives of the Wits (1962) · Henry of Navarre (1963) · Extraordinary People
(1965) · Hesketh Pearson by Himself (1965)

BY HESKETH PEARSON AND MALCOLM MUGGERIDGE
About Kingsmill (1951)

BOOKS BY MALCOLM MUGGERIDGE
Winter in Moscow (1934) · The Earnest Atheist (1936) · In a Valley of
This Restless Mind (1938) · The Thirties (1940) · Affairs of the Heart
(1949) · Tread Softly for You Tread on My Jokes (1966) · Chronicles of
Wasted Time 1: The Green Stick (1972) · Chronicles of Wasted Time 2:
The Infernal Grove (1973)

BOOKS BY MALCOLM MUGGERIDGE AND HUGH KINGSMILL
Brave Old World (1936) · Next Year's News (1938)

Index

Agate, James, 148, 202
Alexander, George, 209
Anderson, Sir John, 225
Aquinas, St Thomas, 236
Arnold, Matthew, 39, 72–81, 124, 143
Asquith, 57, 60, 67, 191
Attlee, Clement, 224
Augustine, St, 104

Bagnold, Enid, 40, 43
Baldwin, 141, 221
Balfour, Jabez, 134
Balfour, Lord, 60
Baxter, Richard, 246
'Beachcomber', 132
Beaverbrook, 93, 94, 113, 184
Beerbohm, Sir Max, 28, 35, 36, 89
Beerbohm-Tree, Sir H., 27–31, 209
Belloc, Hilaire, 7, 221, 230–3
Bennett, Arnold, 37, 42, 236
Betjeman, John, 129
Birkenhead, Lord, 62, 232
Blake, William, 116, 124, 240
Boswell, James, 53, 106, 114, 144–8,
    153, 156–8, 188
Bottomley, Horatio, 39
Bronte, Emily, 72
Browning, Robert, 72, 235
Bruce-Lockhart, R. H., 100, 113
Buddha, 116
Bunyan, John, 245
Butler, Samuel, 81, 100–3, 244
Byron, Lord, 171, 186

Carlyle, Thomas, 72–3, 75, 157, 229–30
Carswell, Catherine, 140
Cathie, Albert, 108
Cecil, Lord David, 201
Cecil, Lord Robert, 60
Cervantes, 53, 239
Chamberlain, Sir J., 58, 61, 230
Chamberlain, Neville, 141, 197
Chesterton, Cecil, 232
Chesterton, G. K., 9, 56, 73, 92, 104,
    121–3, 227, 232
Churchill, Winston, 57, 174, 178, 186,
    216, 225, 232
Clough, A. H., 76
Cockburn, Claud, 7
Cole, G. D. H., 103
Coleridge, Samuel, 35, 73

Connolly, Cyril, 125
Corrigan, General, 67
Cromwell, Oliver, 94, 141, 169, 227,
    232
Cudlipp, Percy, 100
Curtis-Bennett, Sir H., 66

Darwin, Erasmus, 88
Davenport, John and Clement, 166–7
Davidson, Rev. H., 136–7
Dickens, Charles, 72, 75, 76, 121–3,
    193, 239, 240
Dickinson, Goldsworthy Lowes, 201
Dobbs, George, 96, 193
Dobbs, Leonard, 97
Dobbs, Mrs, 193–4
Donne, John, 228
Don Quixote, 73, 98, 116, 228
Douglas, Lord Alfred, 209, 215–20
Doyle, Sir A. Conan, 207–8, 218

Eden, Anthony, 142
Edward VII, 57
Eliot, T. S., 218

Farrar, Dean, 81
Fields, Gracie, 176
Fisher, H. A. L., 19
Fitzgerald, Edward, 72
Fraser, Lovat, 38
Frederick the Great, 238
Frost, David, 35
Fowler, Canon, 155
Fowler, Sir R., 47

Garray, Lt., 22
Garvin, J. L., 61
Gaston, Thomas, 127
Gerhardi, William, 11, 67, 71, 121, 164,
    176, 228
Gibbon, Edward, 192
Gilbert, W. S., 88
Gladstone, W. E., 131, 232
Godwin, William, 236
Goldring, Douglas, 118
Gorki, Maxim, 241
Gosse, Edmund, 48
Greene, Graham, 89, 129, 186, 224, 228
Gue dalla, Philip, 89

Haldane, J. B. S., 63
Hallam, Arthur, 130–2

Hamilton, Hamish, 92, 141, 147–8, 156, 158, 164

Hamlett, Col. 'Dane', 63, 163

Hardy, Thomas, 35, 57

Hargrave, John, 246

Harris, Frank, 34–51, 52, 54, 124, 209, 210, 212, 217, 244

Harris, Nellie, 37, 40

Hart-Davis, Rupert, 190

Harvey, Basil, 9, 32

Hastings, Sir Patrick, 64–6

Haynes, E. S. P., 230

Hazlitt, William, 88, 93, 105–6, 161

Hess, Rudolf, 185

Hill, G. Birkbeck, 150

Hitchcock, Alfred, 239

Hitler, Adolf, 133, 141, 170, 179, 187, 189, 251

Hobhouse, Stephen, 225

Hogg, James, 249

Hoggart, Richard, 103

Holms, John, 20, 64, 67, 71, 81

Holroyd, Michael, 8, 119

Housman, A. E., 19, 85

Hunt, Leigh, 240

Hurry, Colin, 90–1, 223–4

James, Henry, 57

Jebb, Reginald & Eleanor, 231

Jerrold, Douglas, 110, 149, 169, 190, 221

Johnson, Samuel, Dr, 35, 88, 89, 116, 143–56, 170, 174, 188, 199, 239, 242

Jones, H. Festing, 108–10

Keats, John, 236

Kenyon, Sir Frederick, 184

Kingsmill, Hugh; *passim*; family and father, 11–16; school and Oxford, 16–19; 1914–18 war, 19–22; works with Frank Harris, 35–41; on Harris, 44–9; novels, 68; first marriage, 68–71; *Matthew Arnold*, 72–81; *After Puritanism*, 81–2; *The Return of William Shakespeare*, 82–4; *The Table of Truth*, 85; at Hastings, 114; *The Sentimental Journey*, 121–3; attacks Desmond MacCarthy, 124–6; anthologies, 126; *Literary Pilgrimages*, 129–32; *D. H. Lawrence*, 137–40; *Samuel Johnson*, 144–5; *The Poisoned Crown*, 169–71; schoolmaster, 179–82; *This Blessed Plot*, 164–7, 191–9; *Punch* 200–2; quarrel with Pearson, 202–5; political views, 225–7; last illness and death, 234–43; religious views, 245–8; sayings, 250–3

Kipling, Rudyard, 35, 42, 230, 232, 239

Knight, G. Wilson, 201

Knox, Ronald, 16

Koestler, Arthur, 201

Labouchere, Henry, 88, 93

Lane, Allen, 57, 61, 62, 65, 66

Lane, John, 60

Laval, Pierre, 175

Lawrence, D. H., 101, 137–41, 165, 186, 244

Lawrence, Frieda, 76

Lawson, J. M., 93

Lenin, 57, 59, 74, 169

Leopold, King, 173–4

Lincoln, Abraham, 104, 169, 237

Lloyd-George, D., 57, 232, 246

Ludwig, Emil, 89

Lunn, Arnold, 16, 71, 231–2

Lunn, Brian, 12, 14, 96, 117–21, 182–5

Lunn, Brooke, 9, 246

Lunn, Dorothy, 84–5, 114, 187, 200, 202–5, 242–3

Lunn, Edmee, 85, 243

Lunn, Eileen, 16, 246

Lunn, Mrs Eileen F., 68–71, 96

Lunn, Sir Henry, 11–17, 38, 63, 71, 82, 96, 99, 118–19, 126, 183–4, 193, 244

Lunn, Holdsworth, 149

MacCarthy, Desmond, 111, 123–5, 202

Macdonald, Ramsay, 99, 141

Mackail, Professor, 48

Macleod, Dame F., 155

Maiden, Joe, 107

Mallet, David, 146

Mallock, W. H., 230

Mare, W. de la, 186

Marriott, Sir W., 47

Martin, Kingsley, 223

Marx, Karl, 206, 238

Maugham, W. Somerset, 53–4, 223

Maupassant, Guy de, 47

Moore, Thomas, 11

Morrison, Herbert, 225

Muggeridge, H. T., 96

Muggeridge, John, 178, 189

Muggeridge, Kitty, 37, 97, 132, 172, 178, 187, 193

Muggeridge, Malcolm; *passim*; family and early career, 96–100; first meets Kingsmill, 96; *The Earnest Atheist* and Samuel Butler, 100–3, 108–12; meets Pearson, 104; at Whatlington, 113; collaborations with Kingsmill, 128–36; *The Thirties*, 141–2; wartime, 171–9; in Laurenço Marques, 186–8; Washington and politics, 224–6; last meetings with Kingsmill, 235–7; *About Kingsmill*, 244–8

Muir, Edwin, 228

Murry, John Middleton, 37, 39, 76

Mussolini, 57

Napoleon, 51, 52, 141, 170, 226, 227, 238, 251
Newman, Ernest, 238
Nicholson, General J., 163
Nicolson, Harold, 141, 158
Nietzsche, 73, 74, 207
Northcliffe, Lord, 59, 61

Orwell, George, 89, 121, 226-8

Paine, Tom, 88, 94, 106
Pearson, Gladys, 31, 144, 161-3, 172, 204, 242, 248
Pearson, Henry, 162-3
Pearson, Hesketh; *passim*; early years, 23-8; on the stage, 28-31; marriage, 31-2; 1914-18 war, 32-3; with Frank Harris, 40-2; first writings, 55-6; *Whispering Gallery* affair, 56-66; character and early biographies, 86-94; *Skye High*, 147-59; family crisis, 160-4; *This Blessed Plot*, 164-7, 191-9; *Bernard Shaw*, 168, 205-7; at Woods Place, 189; quarrel with Kingsmill, 202-5; *Conan Doyle*, 207-208; *Oscar Wilde*, 208-20; later biographies, 248; death, 248-9
Pearson, Joyce, 248
Pilkington, Arnold, 180
Pitcher, Mrs, 120
Potter, Richard, 230
Price, R. G. G., 89
Proust, Marcel, 185

Queensberry, Marquess of, 220

Rabelais, 139
Ranicar, Gladys, 71
Ransome, Arthur, 97, 215
Redmayne, Capt., 153-4
Rhodes, Cecil, 55, 57, 61
Riddell, Lord, 60
Rider, Dan, 37
Robespierre, 74
Roche, Raphael, 34
Rodd, Sir Rennell, 57, 61, 62, 66, 92
Roosevelt, Mrs, 187
Ross, Robert, 208-9, 216-17
Rossetti, D. G., 73
Rothermere, Lord, 59, 91
Rousseau, Jean Jacques, 74, 170
Ruskin, John, 72, 73
Ryder, Jean, 248

Scott, C. P., 97

Scott, Sir W., 239
Shakespeare, William, 35, 82-3, 239, 248-9
Shaw, Bernard, 35, 36, 42, 51, 52, 54, 57, 63, 73, 74, 97, 102, 44, 149, 164-6, 168, 196, 205-7, 212-14, 221, 230, 248
Shelley, P. B., 236, 240
Sherard, R. H., 209, 212-14
Simon, Sir John, 184
Smith, Edmund, 145
Smith, Florence, 49-50
Smith, Sydney, 88, 92, 214
Snowden, Viscount, 136
Stalin, Joseph, 133, 135
Stead, W. T., 15, 81-2, 167, 208
Strachey, Lytton, 53, 56, 88-9
Sutro, Alfred, 31
Swift, Dean, 51, 111
Swinburne, 73
Symons, A. J. A., 217

Tallents, Sir Stephen, 201
Tawney, R. H., 97
Tennyson, 72, 130-2
Ternan, Ellen, 76, 122-3
Thackeray, W. M., 73, 75, 192-3
Thompson, Rupert, 186
Thomson, Hugh, 233
Tolstoy, Count, 73-4, 167, 241
Trevelyan, G. M., 92
Trevor, John, 240
Trotsky, Leon, 226
Truman, Harry S., 225

Voltaire, 238

Wagner, 238
Walton, Izaak, 233
Waugh, Alec, 9, 11, 20, 21, 68, 84, 118
Waugh, Evelyn, 129, 158, 228
Webb, Beatrice and Sidney, 195
Wellington, Duke of, 51
Wells, H. G., 42, 57, 73, 74, 230
White, Alan, 190-1, 196-7, 241
Wilde, Oscar, 42, 50, 55, 57, 86, 103, 208-19
Wilkinson, Louis, 222
Willet, B. W., 65
Wilson, Edmund, 89, 123
Winkler, John K., 201
Wodehouse, P. G., 69, 191-2, 238
Wollstonecraft, Mary, 236
Woolworth, Frank, 201
Wordsworth, William, 74-5, 104-6, 116-17, 130, 151, 186, 241

HAMISH HAMILTON PAPERBACKS

'Among the most collectable of paperback imprints . . .'
Christopher Hudson, *The Standard*

All books in the Hamish Hamilton Paperback Series are available at your local bookshop or can be ordered by post. A full list of titles and an order form can be found at the end of this book.

A LATE BEGINNER

Priscilla Napier

In 1921, Priscilla Napier, aged twelve, left Egypt where her father worked in the colonial administration. In this funny and perceptive memoir she brilliantly recreates a child's view of the exotic surroundings of those early years. It was a world of comfort and security, of calm routine and Cadbury's Tropical Chocolates, with the excitements of scorpions in the nursery cupboard and black beetles in the garden, and long sea voyages to England, a country of endless green lawns inhabited by endless relations. But the impact of war was far-reaching and the world changed.

'She is a born writer. Mrs Napier displays the most professional skill in modulation between her childhood feelings and adult commentary.' Raymond Mortimer, *Sunday Times*

AUTOBIOGRAPHY

Neville Cardus

Against all odds, Neville Cardus achieved an outstanding reputation as a writer on both cricket and music. Born in the slums of Manchester in 1889, he worked as an office boy from an early age and educated himself by dashing out at every opportunity to the local library to read voraciously everything he could find. In his early twenties he became assistant cricket 'pro' at Shrewsbury School. He was twenty-seven when he finally realized his ambition of joining the *Manchester Guardian* where he eventually became famous as a music critic and for his 'Cricketer' articles.

'He is a writer who has learnt how to write, and the result is glorious. He writes so exquisitely that often he leaves me more profoundly moved than I have been by any other book I have read.' J. B. Priestley

MARY BERENSON:
A Self Portrait from Her Letters and Diaries

eds. Barbara Strachey & Jayne Samuels

This superbly edited book of extracts from Mary Berenson's letters and diaries provides an absorbing picture of her extraordinarily complex relationship with Bernard Berenson, and of their life and work together in Italy.

'Mary . . . writes with a startling, unsettling, often hilarious candour which makes it hard to put the book down.' – Hilary Spurling, *Observer*

THE DRAGON EMPRESS

Marina Warner

From 1861 to 1908, the Empress Dowager Tz'u-hsi dominated China. In this immensely readable biography, Marina Warner lays bare Tz'u-hsi's complex personality, and portrays a China in rapid decline as poverty, civil war and foreign exploitation and invasion brought about the fall of the Ch'ing dynasty.

'A fresh and fascinating account that reveals China's last imperial reign as surely the most absurd government ever to have had charge of a major nation. I read every word.' – Barbara W. Tuchman

HUGH WALPOLE

Rupert Hart-Davis

'Rupert Hart-Davis's book is a remarkable feat of understanding and restraint. . . . He shows us the man himself, and the spectacle is delightful.' Edwin Muir

'Fully to appreciate how remarkable an achievement is Mr Hart-Davis's biography of Hugh Walpole, it is necessary to read the book. No summarised comment can convey the complexity of the task accomplished or the narrative skill, restraint and self-effacement with which it has been carried through.' Michael Sadleir.

THE LIFE OF ARTHUR RANSOME

Hugh Brogan

For a man who longed for a quiet existence, Arthur Ransome had an extraordinarily adventurous life comprising two stormy marriages, a melodramatic libel suit, and a ringside view of the Russian Revolution. In this absorbing book, Hugh Brogan writes with sympathy and affection of the author of some of the best loved books for children.

'The wonder is, from Mr Brogan's enthralling account, that Ransome ever got down to writing *Swallows and Amazons* at all.' A. N. Wilson, *Sunday Telegraph*

ANOTHER PART OF THE WOOD
A Self Portrait

Kenneth Clark

Kenneth Clark's sharp, witty account of his eccentric Edwardian upbringing and his swift success in the world of art after leaving Oxford is a classic of its kind and a pleasure to read.

'An immensely entertaining memoir . . . rich in deliciously dry tales . . . all told with perfect brevity and wit.' Michael Ratcliffe, *The Times*

'A stylish, dazzling work flecked with touches of learning and imagination, wit and malice.' Kenneth Rose, *Sunday Telegraph*

VOLTAIRE IN LOVE

Nancy Mitford

In this very funny book Nancy Mitford writes of the famous love affair between Voltaire and the beautiful blue-stocking Marquise du Châtelet. It is rightly regarded as her most successful essay in history.

'There is not a dull page . . . witty, vivacious, accurate, informative and a delight to read.' – Harold Nicolson, *Observer*

'A witty and absorbing account of one of the great love stories of the world.' – Cyril Connolly, *Sunday Times*

PETER HALL'S DIARIES

ed. John Goodwin

Peter Hall's diaries, a top bestseller in hardback, cover the hectic eight years from 1972 to 1980 during which he fought to create the three-auditorium 'palace', the National Theatre, on London's South Bank. He reveals what it is like to be head of a great artistic enterprise under burning public scrutiny. He illuminates how he develops his own productions. And he tells the story of the personality clashes, the constant delays to the opening of the building, the press attacks, strikes, and resignations which had repercussions throughout the entire theatre world.

'This is a stupendous book. It is the most absorbing book on the theatre I have ever read.' Harold Hobson

MRS. PAT
The Life of Mrs. Patrick Campbell

Margot Peters

Beautiful, witty, talented, Mrs. Patrick Campbell became a legend in her own lifetime. Her theatrical career encompassed tremendous triumphs and unmitigated failures. Her private life was controversial and tragic. In this superb biography Margot Peters captures the magnetism of an outstanding actress and extraordinary woman, who remains today as intriguing as ever.

'The book has been researched with exemplary care and accuracy. The famous bons mots – nearly always witty, sometimes cruel and personal, but usually devastatingly apt – are quoted with appropriate relish. There is a wealth of material, never before made public, to enthrall the reader.' John Gielgud, *Observer*

Available in Hamish Hamilton Paperbacks

NANCY MITFORD	Harold Acton	£4.95 ☐
MEMOIRS OF AN AESTHETE	Harold Acton	£5.95 ☐
JOHN MASEFIELD	Constance Babington Smith	£4.95 ☐
MISSION WITH MOUNTBATTEN	Alan Campbell-Johnson	£5.95 ☐
A CACK-HANDED WAR*	Edward Blishen	£3.95 ☐
UNCOMMON ENTRANCE*	Edward Blishen	£3.95 ☐
THE DREAM KING	Wilfrid Blunt	£4.95 ☐
THE LIFE OF ARTHUR RANSOME	Hugh Brogan	£4.95 ☐
DIAGHILEV	Richard Buckle	£6.95 ☐
AUTOBIOGRAPHY	Neville Cardus	£4.95 ☐
ANOTHER PART OF THE WOOD	Kenneth Clark	£4.95 ☐
A DURABLE FIRE	ed. Artemis Cooper	£4.95 ☐
TWO FLAMBOYANT FATHERS	Nicolette Devas	£4.95 ☐
PETER HALL'S DIARIES	ed. John Goodwin	£5.95 ☐
HUGH WALPOLE	Rupert Hart-Davis	£6.95 ☐
GOD'S APOLOGY*	Richard Ingrams	£4.95 ☐
ASQUITH	Stephen Koss	£4.95 ☐
VOLTAIRE IN LOVE	Nancy Mitford	£4.95 ☐
A LIFE OF CONTRASTS	Diana Mosley	£4.95 ☐
A LATE BEGINNER	Priscilla Napier	£4.95 ☐
BEYOND FRONTIERS Jasper Parrott with Vladimir Ashkenazy		£4.95 ☐
MRS PAT		
The Life of Mrs. Patrick Campbell	Margot Peters	£5.95 ☐
THE SECRET ORCHARD OF ROGER ACKERLEY	Diana Petre	£4.95 ☐
ALBERT, PRINCE CONSORT	Robert Rhodes James	£4.95 ☐
MARY BERENSON eds. Barbara Strachey and Jayne Samuels		£4.95 ☐
BISMARCK	A. J. P. Taylor	£5.95 ☐
THE YEARS WITH ROSS*	James Thurber	£4.95 ☐
THE DRAGON EMPRESS	Marina Warner	£4.95 ☐
QUEEN VICTORIA	Cecil Woodham-Smith	£5.95 ☐

All titles 198 × 126mm, and all contain 8 pages of black and white
illustrations except for those marked*.

All books in the Hamish Hamilton Paperback Series are available at your local bookshop, or can be ordered direct from Media Services. Just tick the titles you want on the previous page and fill in the form below.

Name_____

Address_____

_____

Write to Media Services, PO Box 151, Camberley, Surrey GU15 3BE.

Please enclose cheque or postal order made out to Media Services for the cover price plus postage:

UK: 55p for the first book, 24p for each additional book to a maximum of £1.75.

OVERSEAS: £1.05 for the first book, 35p for each additional book to a maximum of £2.80.

Hamish Hamilton Ltd reserve the right to show new retail prices on covers which may differ from those previously advertised in the text or elsewhere, and to increase postal rates in accordance with the PO.